THE SONG OF THE GLADIATOR

Also by Paul Doherty and available from Headline

The Rose Demon
The Soul Slayer
The Haunting
Domina
The Plague Lord
Murder Imperial
An Evil Spirit Out of the West

Ancient Egyptian mysteries
The Mask of Ra
The Horus Killings
The Anubis Slayings
The Slayers of Seth
The Assassins of Isis

The Sorrowful Mysteries of Brother Athelstan
The Nightingale Gallery
The House of the Red Slayer
Murder Most Holy
The Anger of God
By Murder's Bright Light
The House of Crows
The Assassin's Riddle
The Devil's Domain
The Field of Blood
The House of Shadows

Hugh Corbett medieval mysteries
Satan in St Mary's
Crown in Darkness
Spy in Chancery
The Angel of Death
The Prince of Darkness
Murder Wears a Cowl
The Assassin in the Greenwood
The Song of a Dark Angel
Satan's Fire
The Devil's Hunt
The Demon Archer
The Treason of the Ghosts
Corpse Candle
The Magician's Death

The Canterbury Tales of murder and mystery
An Ancient Evil *(Being the Knight's Tale)*
A Tapestry of Murders *(Being the Man of Law's Tale)*
A Tournament of Murders *(Being the Franklin's Tale)*
Ghostly Murders *(Being the Priest's Tale)*
The Hangman's Hymn *(Being the Carpenter's Tale)*
A Haunt of Murder *(Being the Clerk of Oxford's Tale)*

The Journals of Sir Roger Shallot
The White Rose Murders
Poisoned Chalice
The Grail Murders
Brood of Vipers
The Gallows Murders
The Relic Murders

THE SONG OF
THE GLADIATOR

Paul Doherty

headline

First published in Great Britain in 2004 by
HEADLINE BOOK PUBLISHING

10 9 8 7 6 5 4 3 2 1

Cataloguing in Publication Data is available from the British Library

ISBN 0 7553 0778 X (hardback)
ISBN 0 7553 2407 2 (trade paperback)

Typeset in Trump Mediaeval by
Palimpsest Book Production Limited, Polmont, Stirlingshire

Printed and bound in Great Britain by
Clays Ltd St Ives plc

Headline's policy is to use papers that are natural, renewable
and recyclable products and made from wood grown in sustainable
forests. The logging and manufacturing processes are expected to
conform to the environmental regulations of the country of origin.

HEADLINE BOOK PUBLISHING
A division of Hodder Headline
338 Euston Road
London NW1 3BH

www.headline.co.uk
www.hodderheadline.com

To Angela Francescotti, with grateful thanks.

PRINCIPAL CHARACTERS

THE EMPERORS

Diocletian: the old Emperor, now in retirement

Maxentius: formerly Emperor of the West, defeated and killed by Constantine at the Milvian Bridge

Constantine: new Emperor of the West

Helena: Constantine's mother, Empress and Augusta

Licinius: Emperor in the East

IMPERIAL OFFICIALS

Anastasius: Christian priest and scribe, secretary to Helena

Burrus: Helena's bodyguard

Chrysis: head of Constantine's agents

THE VILLA PULCHRA

Gaius Tullius: Captain of the Guard

Athanasius

Justin   orators

Septimus

Dionysius:

Narcissus: a slave

Timothaeus: a steward

Meleager: a gladiator

Rufinus: a merchant banker, friend of Constantine

THE CHRISTIAN CHURCH

Militiades: Pope, Bishop of Rome

Sylvester: Militiades's assistant, principal priest in the Christian community in Rome

AT THE SHE-ASSES

Polybius: the owner

Poppaoe: his common-law wife

Oceanus: former gladiator

Januaria: a serving maid

Claudia: Polybius's niece

Murranus: a gladiator

Simon: the Stoic

Petronius: the Pimp

Sallust: the Searcher

Spicerius: a gladiator

Valens: former army physician

Agrippina: Spicerius's girlfriend

Dacius: a gang leader

Introduction

During the trial of Christ, Pilate, according to the Gospels, wanted to free the prisoner. He was stopped by a cry that if he did so, he would be no friend of Caesar's. According to commentators, Pilate recognised the threat. Every Roman governor and official was closely scrutinised by secret agents of the Emperor, 'the Agentes in Rebus', literally 'the Doers of Things'! The Roman Empire had a police force, both military and civil, though these differed from region to region, but it would be inaccurate to claim the Empire had anything akin to detectives or our own CID. Instead, the Emperor and his leading politicians paid vast sums to informers and spies. These were often difficult to control; as Walsingham, Elizabeth I's master spy, once wryly remarked, 'He wasn't too sure for whom his own men were working, himself or the opposition.'

The Agentes in Rebus were a class apart amongst this horde of gossip-collectors, tale-bearers and sometimes, very dangerous informers. The Emperors used them, and their testimony could mean the end of a promising career. This certainly applied to the bloody and byzantine period at the beginning of the fourth century AD.

The Emperor Diocletian had divided the Empire into East and West. Each division had its own Emperor, and a lieutenant, who took the title of Caesar. The Empire was facing economic problems and barbarian incursions. Its state religion was threatened by the thriving Christian Church, which was making its presence felt in all provinces at every level of society.

In AD 312, a young general, Constantine, supported by his mother, Helena, a British-born woman who was already flirting with the Christian Church, decided to make his bid for the Empire of the West. He marched down Italy and met his rival Maxentius at the Milvian Bridge. According to Eusebius, Constantine's biographer, the would-be Emperor saw a vision of the cross, underneath the words '*In hoc signo vinces*' ('In this sign you will conquer'). Constantine, the story goes, told his troops to adopt the Christian symbol and won an outstanding victory. He defeated and killed Maxentius and marched into Rome. Constantine was now Emperor of the West, his only rival Licinius, who ruled the Eastern Empire. Constantine, heavily influenced by his mother, grasped the reins of government and began to negotiate with the Christian Church to end centuries of persecution. Nevertheless, intrigue and murder were still masters of the day. There was unfinished business in Rome and the Agentes in Rebus had their hands full. Helena favoured the Christian Church, but soon realised that intrigue and murder were as rife there as they were at court . . .

Chapter 1

'Pallida Mors, aequo pulsat pede pauperum
tabernas Regumque turres.'
('Pallid Death strikes impartially at the cottages of
the poor and the towers of Kings.')

Horace, Odes, I.4

'Iugula! Kill him!' The roar from the mob in the crowded, dusty, flea-infested amphitheatre thundered up to the sky. The day was turning very hot. The summer sun, a veritable demon in the blue sky, beat down on the spectators, who had whetted their appetite for blood and now bayed for more. In the amphitheatre two men fought for their lives, slipping and slithering on the sand, bodies drenched in sweat, limbs screaming with pain, throats as dry as the very sand they kicked up.

The Editor, or Promoter, of the Games, the banker Rufinus, had done his best to keep the tens of thousands of his invited guests as cool as possible. A great woollen awning, drenched in water, had been pulled across the top of the amphitheatre by a complicated system of pulleys and ropes to provide meagre shade, whilst perfumed water, drawn up by special pumps, had sprayed some coolness on the crowd. However, Rufinus need not have worried. Heat, thirst, dust and the merciless sun were no obstacle to the mob's hunger for blood. Many of them had been there since before dawn, filing into the yellow-ochre and black vomitoria, the cavernous tunnels which divided into a series of smaller ones and took the spectators up to their ticketed places. Each arrival carried the prized piece of bone bearing the number allocated to him. Many of these had been distributed free by the Promoter. Rufinus was doing his best to please Rome's mob, not for himself, but for the new Emperor Constantine, who had seized the imperial purple some eighteen months previously and was now settling down to enjoy the fruits of his victory.

Across the amphitheatre, above the podium, rose the brilliantly decorated imperial box, its front, sides and balustrade draped in costly purple cloths over which gold-painted ivy had been carefully twisted. The crowd was so busy watching the two gladiators fight, they were hardly aware of Rufinus, who sat next to his Emperor, or the person on the other side of Constantine, 'Helena Augusta atque Pia Mater', the Emperor's 'Noble and Holy Mother'.

The Emperor himself was ignoring the games, his heavy-jowled faced all screwed up in concentration: tongue jutting out from the corner of his mouth, he balanced a writing tray in his lap and read the various documents his Imperial Chamberlain, the fat-faced Chrysis, passed for perusal. Helena was similarly occupied, studying reports handed to her by her personal secretary, Anastasius, the Christian priest. Helena employed Anastasius not only because of his links with the new faith, but also because he was a man of learning, skilled in the Greek and Hebrew tongues. Above all, he was most discreet; he could not speak, as his tongue had been plucked out by the imperial torturers during the recent persecutions.

Helena stared down at the piece of parchment resting on her lap, the report of a spy on the city council in Corinth about certain naval manoeuvres. She kneaded her thigh with her fingers, a common enough gesture when her teeming mind was considering some problem. Her beloved son was now Emperor, at least of the Western Empire, but at Nicomedia lurked the upstart Licinius, self-proclaimed Emperor of the East. Helena narrowed her eyes and stared down at the gladiators in the amphitheatre.

'One of them is in trouble,' she whispered to herself. She leaned against the balustrade. Yes, the Retiarius, the golden-haired net man, had suffered a bloody wound to his right shoulder and was slowing down.

Helena stared at the gladiators but her mind was distracted. If the truth be known, her son, Constantine, and Licinius were themselves gladiators, fighting for the greatest prize in the world, an empire which stretched from the Great Western Ocean to the Black Sea, from the searingly hot sands of north Africa to the icy forests which fringed the Rhine. At the moment, the pair were circling each other, looking for a weakness. Sooner or later – and sooner rather than later – Constantine would have to close with his opponent. Would his armies march east, or would Licinius invade the West? Could Licinius's troops be bought, the officials of his court seduced from their allegiance?

Helena gnawed at her lip. Would it be easier to poison Licinius, a few grains of powder mixed with his wine? But what would happen then? Some other upstart? She studied the report again. Licinius was definitely up to something with this increased activity at his court, and what was his fleet doing, massing in the Bay of Corinth? Manoeuvres? Or preparing for battle? Beside her, Constantine hastily slurped his wine, and Helena nudged him with her elbow. Her son, as he always did, turned and pretended to scowl, but that did not concern Helena. She prided herself on her icy demeanour and calm nerve; that was the way she'd dealt with Constantine's father, not to mention upstart priests and mutinous army officers. She would act as she always did, as mistress of the Empire.

Helena's grey hair was coiffed in the traditional fashion, and a purple gold-fringed shawl was draped around her shoulders, contrasting sharply with her simple snow-white linen gown. She deliberately wore no jewellery except for an amethyst ring on the little finger of her left hand. She had kicked off her costly Spanish sandals and now savoured the cool perfumed foot bath a slave had brought. As a veteran of her husband's and son's military campaigns, she never forgot the old soldier's advice: 'If you want to stay cool, slap water on the back of your neck and stick your feet in a cold bath.' She wore no make-up, no paint on her long face with its high cheekbones, deep-set dark eyes and snub nose over a full mouth and firm chin. She saw no point in such decoration; she wanted to be severe and appear as such. Some whispered she had no taste; after all, wasn't she the daughter of an innkeeper? Helena paid no heed to such gossip, and her only concession to fashion was to shave her eyebrows and put a little carmine on her lips. She was keen to imitate the warrior matrons of ancient Rome. More importantly, as she confessed to her son, in public the heat made even the costliest cosmetics run.

Helena peered around at the ladies behind her and smiled dazzlingly. Silly bitches, their faces now looked like German warriors! Ah well. She turned back, flexed her toes and gave her son another nudge. She had told him a thousand times never to pick his nose in public! Another document was brought. She clutched the arm of Anastasius, speaking slowly so that he could read her lips. He replied quickly with hand signs which Helena hoped only she could understand. She glanced around the amphitheatre. Good, the mob was still screaming at the poor bastard stretched out on the red-gold sand of the arena. Helena preferred the crowd to stare at the fighters rather than at the imperial box. She nudged her son to pay more attention. The crowd didn't like it if they thought the great ones, the Lords of the Purple, were not revelling in the carnage and bloodshed of the show.

'Constantine?'

The Emperor, in deep conversation with Rufinus, ignored her.

'Beloved son?' The Emperor still kept his back to her. 'Constantine!' Helena bellowed. 'Don't turn your back on me! Stop whispering to Rufinus and keep an eye on the crowd.'

'Mother.' Constantine turned, his heavy face showing an unacceptable unshaven stubble, his forehead, beneath the fringe of dark cropped hair, laced with sweat, his dark blue eyes tired and red-rimmed.

'Constantine, you have been drinking, too many late nights with your officers.'

He glanced up sharply as the roar of the crowd subsided. He saw the reason why: the fallen gladiator had made the most of the respite and was now rolling away from his opponent, who had been caught off guard. He'd thought the net

5

man was finished and had been staring at the imperial box. Now the net man was back on his feet and the mob became absorbed as the fierce struggle was renewed.

'Priests,' Constantine whispered hoarsely.

'What about them?' Helena was now all attention. She didn't care any more if Constantine ignored the crowd.

'Christian priests,' Constantine grated. 'They are at it again, Mother. The Christians are fighting over matters of obscure doctrine.'

'Mere words!' Helena scoffed.

'There was a riot at Ostia,' Constantine declared, 'between the adherents of two sects. Apparently they are fighting over the substance of God. Is Jesus Christ, who became man, of the same substance as, and equal to, God the Father?' Constantine's stubby fingers scratched at the sweat on his face. 'They want me to resolve the matter, yet I don't understand a bloody word of it. Perhaps we should get the silly bastards to fight it out in the arena.'

'Constantine!'

'My apologies, Mother.'

'Don't drink too much.'

'Of course not, Mother.'

Constantine sighed, turned away and stretched out his cup for a page to fill with purple wine.

Helena shook her head and gazed out across the arena. The awning, caught by a breeze, flapped and ruffled. Helena stared at the crowd. This was the Empire. In the lower tiers of the amphitheatre, separated by walls from the rest, sat the white-garbed aristocracy, and above them the dark tunics of the lower sort, with the poor of the slums at the very top. They're the problem, Helena reflected, picking up her fan and shaking it vigorously, the tens upon tens of thousands of poor in

Rome and all the great cities of the Empire. How were they to be united, bound together? Worship of the Emperor? Yet there'd been civil war for decades. Christianity? Helena smiled.

The new faith was now emerging from the catacombs of Rome with its revolutionary radical teaching that God had become man, been crucified and risen from the dead. Christ brought a new message that all men were equal. Eternal life was promised to everyone, even a slave, if he or she followed the teaching of the Crucified One. What other faith promised that? Former Emperors had viewed Christianity as a threat and persecuted it vigorously. Constantine had changed all that. An ambitious general, he had brought his legions from Britain to challenge the old Emperor, Maxentius, and had defeated him at the battle of the Milvian Bridge. That was where it had all begun!

Helena fanned herself vigorously. She had always wondered at the truth behind the story. She'd pestered her son to tell her, time and again, what had truly happened. Constantine was a sun worshipper, if he believed in anything. Nevertheless, before that fateful battle, he had dreamed that Christ had appeared to him and ordered him to have his soldiers wear the *Chi* and *Rho* symbols on their shields, the first two letters in Greek of 'Christos', the Anointed One, Jesus of Nazareth. The next day Constantine had had another vision, of a cross, black against a fiery sun, underneath it the words 'In this sign you will conquer'. Had he really seen a vision, or was it just his fanciful imagination? Constantine could act the rough soldier, be as coarse as a mule, yet he was also a dreamer. As a boy he would have fits, become withdrawn, as if staring at something Helena couldn't see.

Helena snapped the fan shut. The vision had been true!

Her son had been proclaimed Emperor of the West, Master of Rome. He had exterminated his opponents. One day he would march east, bring that drunken ninny Licinius to battle, utterly destroy him and proclaim himself '*Imperator totius mundi*', Emperor of the entire world.

For all his visions, Constantine had not ostensibly changed: he still acted the foul-mouthed, sweaty soldier, who gulped his wine, ate too much and liked to slap the bottoms of courtesans. Nevertheless, in his own way he *had* changed, become more dependent on Helena. Once his legions had swept into Rome, she and Anastasius had been given charge of the 'Agentes in Rebus', that horde of spies and secret agents which the Empire controlled both within and beyond its borders. Helena had seized the reins of power, determined to strengthen her son's rule, eager to reach an understanding with the powerful Christian faith. If she could control that, she could control the mob. She had opened secret talks with Militiades, the Christian leader in Rome, and with his lieutenant, the silver-haired, golden-tongued priest Sylvester. Perhaps, in time, the Empire could reach accommodation with this radical faith.

'Mother, Mother.' Constantine leaned across, shaking her arm. 'Mother, you mustn't go to sleep.'

'I'm not sleeping,' she snapped. 'I'm looking forward to leaving this flea-ridden heat. I want to get out of Rome.' She glared at her son. 'We should move soon . . .'

'Ah, the Villa Pulchra,' Constantine teased. 'The beautiful villa, cooled by the hill breezes. Don't worry, Mother, we'll be there soon.' He winked. 'And you can bring all your friends with you.'

Helena knew to whom he was referring. Constantine had granted toleration to the Christians, but now the new faith had produced problems of its own. Helena ground her teeth. Problems, there were always problems.

'Mother, look.' Constantine was determined to tease Helena. 'The fighting is coming to an end.'

The blond Retiarius in his red and silver-fringed kilt had not been fortunate. Dressed in his white padded leg armour, similar padding protecting his left arm, the shoulder above covered by a gleaming bronze plate, he was trying to bring the fight to an abrupt end. He had taken his net, fastened to his left arm, and flung it in a widening arc. Equipped with weights on the rim, the two-yard net should have trapped his opponent, a Thracian, who was garbed in heavy armour, on his head a visored helmet with a red and yellow horse-hair plume. But the Thracian had been faster. Wary of the net and the speed of his lighter-armed opponent, he had kept shuffling back so that when the net came stretching out he caught it on his rounded shield and tried to pull his opponent on to his pointed sword. The Retiarius quickly dropped his trident, drew the knife from his embroidered belt and cut himself free. Then he picked up the trident in both hands, retreating up against the podium wall. The Thracian followed, feet kicking up the golden sand. The net man was finished; he was now trapped. The crowd roared for the fight to be brought to an end but the Thracian remained cautious. The heat was intense. Neither man had drunk for hours, and the net man was bleeding profusely, losing his strength. The Retiarius panicked. He could feel himself weakening and lunged, aiming his weapon at the Thracian's chest. The Thracian knocked it aside with such force the trident was sent spinning, then thrust his sword deep into the net man's neck. The fight was over. The net man slumped to the sand, blood pumping from his wounds. This time the Thracian wanted to make sure. He stood over his opponent whilst the mob roared.

'*Hoc habet! Hoc habet!*' Let him have it!

The Thracian knew the rules; he was a gladiator not a butcher. He watched the life-light fade from his opponent's eyes, his body jerk in the final death throes, before lifting his sword and shield to receive the plaudits of the crowd. Elated, the Thracian did a lap of honour, every so often stopping to raise his weapons, revelling in the coins and flowers being showered upon him.

The iron-barred gates to the tunnels beneath the podium were opened and a ghastly figure emerged wearing the terra-cotta mask of Lord Charon, the Ferryman of the Dead. He was escorted by another attendant dressed as Mercury, the Shepherd of Souls. While the Thracian received the acclamation of the mob, these two ghoulish figures approached the dead gladiator. Mercury carried a red-hot iron bar, with which he prodded the fallen man to ensure he was dead, whilst Charon struck the prostrate figure on the head with his mallet to proclaim ownership and confirm death. A group of stretcher-bearers hastened on, and while the victor surrendered his weapons to the Lanista, his manager, his dead opponent was dragged off. His body would be stripped, whatever blood was wiped off would be drained into containers and sold as a cure for epilepsy, and the rest of his mangled remains would either be tossed into some obscure grave or hacked up as food for the wild animals.

In the imperial box Helena sat back in her throne chair. The crowd, its blood lust now satisfied, was being diverted to other things as they waited for the great game of the day: the contest between Spicerius, the most famous net man in Italy, and Murranus, the Secutor, the darling of the Roman mob. Both gladiators were skilled, with a string of victories to their names. Both had received the *rudis*, the wooden sword of freedom, and both hoped, by the time the period of these games had finished, to receive the Corona, the crown, as Victor Ludorum, champion of the games.

In the amphitheatre the sand was being raked, turned over and dusted with sparkling grit. Attendants armed with buckets of water washed the blood stains from the marble-walled podium. In the various tiers above, the crowd moved like murmuring surf. Some hurried away to buy a drink or something to eat. Others, eager not to lose their place, shouted and bawled at the traders selling cheap wine and bitter ale, spiced sausages, honey cakes, smoked fish, sesame biscuits and even sugared figs coated in vine leaves. Musicians with trumpets tried to create music but no one really listened.

Helena sipped at a goblet of chilled white wine and leaned over in her chair, eavesdropping on her son, who'd drunk so much he was now virtually shouting, sharing his business with all in the imperial box.

'See how these Christians love each other, eh, Rufinus?' Constantine joked. 'They are at each other's throats over whether their Christ is equal to God the Father.'

Helena, however, did not regard this as funny. She needed the Christians and strove to understand their triune god. She had tried to grasp the basics. Apparently their God was three in one, Father, Son and Holy Spirit. The Son had become man, Jesus of Nazareth, yet he still remained equal to the Father, of the same substance as Him. However, a group of Christians led by a scholar called Arius believed Jesus was not equal, not of the same substance as the Father. Militiades, Bishop of Rome, had decreed this was heresy, and appealed to Helena for her son to intervene.

Helena mopped her face with a perfumed cloth. She'd had her way. Despite his mockery, Constantine owed a debt to the new religion. He had decided to celebrate his birthday by spending a week at the Villa Pulchra to the south of Rome, and had invited representatives of both Christian factions to debate the matter before him. A group of rhetoricians, public speakers, from the school in Capua had been cited by the Bishop of Rome as an example of this vexatious problem. The school was riven by the heresy, some following the teaching of Arius, others the orthodox line that Father, Son and Holy Spirit were of the same substance. Helena was astonished at how intense the theological rivalries at Capua had become. The violence over the issues was such that scholars came to their debating hall armed with swords and shields; they even had bodyguards to protect them. Outside, a mob would gather, some shouting that Son was equal to Father, others that he was not. Houses had been attacked, mud and filth brought into the debating hall so opponents could be pelted. There had even been attacks at night and savage knife fights in the taverns and eating houses.

Constantine, totally mystified, had ordered three rhetoricians from either side to attend him at the Villa Pulchra. Helena closed her eyes and sighed. Constantine loved practical jokes, and liked nothing better than watching people engage in heated debate. That was fine as long as he kept his mouth shut and didn't start roaring with laughter. Helena had done her very best to sweeten the occasion by offering lavish hospitality and the opportunity for these visiting scholars to inspect and venerate a great Christian relic, the Holy Sword, a Roman *gladius* miraculously preserved over the centuries, the very sword used in the execution of the Christian apostle Paul by the Emperor Nero. Now that was

12

one thing which fascinated Helena! She had a passion for such finds and was busy collecting Christian relics. She was still searching for the Crown of Thorns thrust on to the head of the tortured Christ during his passion, the spear which had pierced his side, and the nails which had fastened the Christian Saviour to his Cross. The Holy Sword had been Helena's greatest find so far. It would be displayed at the villa; it might even remind the Christian scholars of the need for unity.

'Now! Now! Now!' the crowd howled. It had slaked its thirst, satisfied its hunger and wanted the fight between Murranus and Spicerius to begin.

Helena put her cup down and turned. Behind her sat officials, notables, priests and Vestal Virgins. The latter were distinguishable by their Greek gowns with heavy over-folds, their hair hidden by white and red woollen ribbons wrapped closely round their heads and tied at the back with the ends hanging over their shoulders. But Helena wasn't interested in them. She peered across at the far corner of the box, where a young woman sat on a stool placed advantageously on a raised tier so as to obtain a good view of the arena below. Helena winked at Claudia, her little mouse, her scurrier, her most proficient of spies. She wagered that hardly anyone in the box would have noticed Claudia, with her boyish figure and close-cropped black hair. Her skin was ivory pale, her features regular; if she possessed any beauty it was those large, lustrous eyes with their calm, unblinking gaze. She wore no paint or jewellery; just a round-necked tunic which fell beneath her knees, and on her feet stout boot sandals like those of a soldier.

Helena mouthed the words 'little mouse', which was acknowledged by a quick twisted smile and a bob of the head.

Helena returned to her reflections. Claudia would be helpful in the problems the Emperor faced; that shrewd little mouse, that most perfect of agents, with her nose for mischief! She was a child of the slums, a former actress; she could act the lady if she wanted to but she rarely did. She did not like to be noticed, and that made her both valuable and dangerous. People chattered as if she wasn't there, and she had a sharp eye for observing little incongruities and idiosyncrasies. Was Claudia a Christian? Helena wondered. There was certainly some link between her and the priest Sylvester, as there was with Rufinus. Perhaps the banker had promised to help Claudia find the man with the purple chalice tattooed on his wrist who had raped her two years ago after murdering her simple-minded brother Felix. Strange, Helena reflected, that Claudia had accepted her invitation to the games; the girl had declared she did not like such occasions, but wasn't she sweet on one of the gladiators?

'Augusta, may I join you?' Fulvia Julia, Rufinus's wife, was standing next to her; beside her hovered a household slave carrying a stool.

'Of course.' Helena's smile was as false as Fulvia Julia's.

'Very good.' Fulvia Julia sat down. 'Augusta,' she cooed, tapping the arm of Helena's chair, 'you're so brave, refusing to wear jewellery or paint. It's so . . .' the bitch shrilled with laughter, 'so basic!'

'Haven't you read Ovid's *Remedies of Love*?' Helena smiled. 'He says all is concealed by gems, gold and paint.' She leaned closer. 'A false woman is the least part of herself.'

'Oh! Augusta, you're so knowledgeable. Now,' Fulvia Julia clapped her hands and pointed at the arena, 'who do you think is going to be killed?'

*　　*　　*

Murranus the Gladiator, standing in the darkness of the tunnel entrance beneath the amphitheatre, was asking himself the same question. He'd prayed before a statue of Mars, and sprinkled some incense over the flame, mixing in a tuft of red hair from his close-cropped head. He had bathed his eyes against the dust and dabbed on a little black kohl, which emphasised their blueness. He was ready for the contest. He and his opponent were free men, so they could carry their own weapons; they would not have to wait until they entered the arena. They were here by choice. Murranus shook his head. He was here because he had to be; this was the only thing he could do – fight.

Murranus squinted out at the sunlight. He was Frisian by stock, but really nothing more than another fighting man from the slums with no kith or kin. Fortunata, his sister, was dead, and his only friends were his companions at the She-Asses tavern. He had bounced the tavern wench, Januaria, but as for his heart ... Well, he grimaced, little Claudia would know all about that.

He gazed round the tunnel. Its walls, painted a macabre yellow and black, were covered by graffiti, the last words and signs of other gladiators who'd waited here before the Gate of Life, the blinding light of the arena beckoning them on. Would this be the day he died? Murranus was the victor of at least a dozen fights. He had lost only two, being judged 'Amissus', defeated but allowed to live.

'Are you ready, Murranus?' Polybius, Claudia's uncle, and keeper of the She-Asses tavern, gestured at the table where his armour was piled. Polybius was full-faced, with mischievous eyes. He now tried to look sad, rubbing the end of his fat nose and pulling down his laughing mouth as if Murranus had already lost the contest.

15

'I'm the one who's fighting,' Murranus joked.

Polybius patted the sweat-soaked hair on his own balding head, then rubbed his grubby hands on his dark blue tunic.

'I wish you weren't!' Oceanus came out of the shadows. He was a former gladiator, barrel-chested and pot-bellied, with arms and legs as stout as pillars. Claiming it was better to have an empty garden than a few straggling flowers, he shaved his pate every day and rubbed in cheap oil so that, as Polybius said, it gleamed like a fresh pigeon's egg. He had only one ear, which sported a huge brass ring; the other had been bitten off in a contest. Oceanus had dried it out, pickled it in brine and now it hung on a cord slung round his neck.

Others from the tavern gathered around. Simon the Stoic, the self-proclaimed philosopher, was garbed in his usual shabby cloak. Today his mournful face was even more lugubrious, his bitter lips ready to recite some tragic line. Murranus wanted to be alone, but they were only trying to help; at least they distracted him from the blood stains on the floor, as well as those two ghouls, Charon and Mercury, standing with their backs to the wall, staring at him as if he was a bullock primed for the slaughter. Outside, the chanting of the crowd thundered ominously, but when it subsided the strident music ruffled Murranus's nerves and made the sweat break out on the back of his neck. He wished the waiting was over.

'I'm ready,' he declared. He moved across to the table and stripped. Oceanus washed his body with a sponge soaked in cold water, dried him off and began to rub in oil. Once he had finished, Murranus wrapped a triangular loincloth about his waist, pulling the end up between his legs and pushing it through a knot at the front. Next came the thick belt with its golden stitching. Murranus jogged up and down, bulging out his stomach muscles. Once he had pronounced himself satisfied, he put on a leather guard over his left arm, followed by the embossed bronzed leg guards over their thick linen padding. Oceanus made sure all the straps were tied securely and rubbed more oil on Murranus's bare feet, thighs, chest and right arm. The gladiator picked up his stout stabbing sword and oblong legionnaire's shield, weighing them carefully, checking all was well. Finally the visored helmet, with a panther carved on top sporting a blue-black horse-hair crest, was handed to him. Its straps and buckles were sound, and Murranus slipped it over his head, making sure it sat comfortably, peering through the eye holes at his friends standing in a semi-circle around him.

'Pray for me, my friends.' His voice sounded muffled. 'Let fortune be with me.'

He took the helmet off and grinned, although his stomach churned and a muscle in his right thigh trembled. Murranus had made his farewells the night before at the Cena Libera, the Free Supper, where gladiators due to appear in the arena the next day celebrated what might be their last night alive. He turned at the sound of voices, and saw a gang of young men, their faces painted, hair dyed, eyelids fluttering, come tripping down the tunnel. Oceanus drove them back.

'Perverts!' Oceanus jibed. 'The only way they can get a hard-on is by watching a man getting ready to die.'

Murranus laughed, eager to lessen the tension. He told them about how such perverts, both male and female, clustered round the Gate of Life to pester and taunt the Noxii, criminals condemned to be thrown to the beasts; how these degenerates would often push their bodies up against the manacled prisoners. On one occasion a former Emperor had issued secret orders that when the Noxii were driven out, these perverts should also be pushed out to face the wild beasts. Murranus's story provoked merriment, abruptly cut short by loud laughter echoing along the tunnel.

'Spicerius,' Polybius declared, 'and all his entourage.'

The net man came swaggering out of the darkness, tall and lithe, quick on his feet, his bushy black hair kept in place by a red headband. He was already armed, resplendent in his silver loincloth with his gold-embroidered belt, a wickedly pointed dagger pushed through a ring just near the buckle. Gold-coloured padding protected his legs and left arm; an ornamented arm guard on his right displayed a snarling lion on the front with bulls' heads around the rim. He wore a silver cord about his neck from which hung a lion's tooth. Spicerius claimed to have killed its owner with his bare hands. As soon as he deigned to notice Murranus, he lifted the pointed trident and dangled the net tied to his left hand.

'Come on, Murranus, come and get it.'

Murranus put his helmet down and walked over. He scrutinised the net man carefully, those quickly darting close-set eyes, that smirking mouth. He noticed how Spicerius, as was his custom, had painted his face and drawn deep-green kohl rings around his eyes. His lips were carmined and he stank of some expensive perfume. Spicerius thrust his face closer, eyes fluttering.

'Kiss, kiss, Murranus?'

The young woman on Spicerius's left shrieked with laughter, so loud Murranus suspected she was drunk.

'This is Agrippina.' Spicerius introduced her. 'A noble daughter of a noble family.'

Agrippina was tall and willowy, her black hair tied up in a net, a gesture of comradeship with her boyfriend. The snow-white linen wrap around her shoulders did little to hide the plunging neckline of her gown. She wore mullet-red shoes, and earrings, bracelets and bangles of the same colour, as if proclaiming her love for the colour of blood.

'I've come to kiss Spicerius goodbye,' she announced pertly. 'No,' she shook her head, 'on second thoughts, just to wish him well. I'll proudly kiss him on his return!'

'Kiss my arse!' Oceanus bellowed from where he stood behind Murranus. Spicerius moved to confront him but Murranus blocked his way.

'There'll be time soon enough,' he murmured.

'Aye,' the net man replied, lowering his trident to rest under his arm, 'there'll soon be time for everything.'

The Director of the Games, all flustered and sweaty, came forward, gesturing at a tray bearing a flagon of wine and two cups on the shabby table against the wall. He beckoned the gladiators forward and filled the earthenware cups. Each took one and toasted his opponent.

'*Usque ad mortem,*' Murranus declared.

'*Usque ad mortem,*' Spicerius replied. 'To the death.'

They drained their cups and returned to their entourages for the final preparations. The Director was standing at the Gate of Life, gesturing with his hands. A strident blast of trumpets silenced the crowd, and both gladiators returned for one more drink. Spicerius checked the net tied to his wrist whilst Murranus lowered his helmet on his head.

'Now,' a voice bellowed.

They walked out of the darkness into the blazing light. Trumpets shrilled, cymbals clashed, the crowd thundered its applause whilst the heat caught them like a blast from a fiery oven. The musicians, sand-rakers and cleaners had disappeared. Murranus walked carefully across the sand, Spicerius keeping pace. They stopped before the imperial box and gave the salute, and a figure high above them lifted his hand in languid reply. Both gladiators turned, saluted each other and quickly drew apart. The clamour of the crowd subsided into a whispering chatter as so-called experts delivered their judgements on the combatants.

Murranus tried not to be distracted. Claudia was in the imperial box; he wished she wasn't. He did not feel good and tried to shake off his fears. He had visited a magician, who had sacrificed a dove in a pool of water and prayed that all the gods would assist Murranus. Murranus did not want to die. He had to be Victor Ludorum and receive the gladiator's crown. Spicerius was still moving away, drawing free of the wall, which could impede his net. Murranus followed slowly. Spicerius began that strange dance all net men did, moving swiftly to the right then the left, trying to detect whether his opponent's view was blocked or hampered. Murranus brought up sword and shield. He ignored the net and trident, but watched Spicerius's face, those eyes: which way would he go?

Murranus's bare feet caught something in the sand. He stepped back and looked down: a severed arm overlooked by the rakers, a grisly reminder of the beast hunt earlier that day. Spicerius hadn't noticed it. Murranus moved forward quickly and pretended to stumble. Spicerius darted back, net whirling above his head. Murranus quickly retreated, and the net fell short. Murranus rushed in. Spicerius was faster, thrusting his trident towards Murranus's face. He quickly drew away. The crowd roared their approval. Spicerius was dancing again, showing off. He came in too close and paid the price, a cut to his right thigh which warned him off. Murranus ignored the applause and followed Spicerius, but something was wrong: the wound he had inflicted was superficial, yet the net man was blinking, shaking his head. Was this a trap? Murranus cautiously paced forward, then stopped. Spicerius no longer crouched. He was standing up straight, staring at his opponent, eyes puzzled, mouth moving. The trident dropped from his hands. He took a step forward, tangling his feet in the net, his legs buckled and he fell to the ground.

For the briefest moment there was silence, shattered by a roar of disapproval. The crowd had come for blood, not to see someone collapse in the sand. The Gate of Life opened, and Mercury hurried across with his red-hot iron. He jabbed Spicerius's leg, but the net man only groaned, tried to move, then lay still. Charon turned the body over. Spicerius's face was pale, his eyelids fluttering, and he was coughing and spluttering. Charon turned him back and Spicerius began to vomit.

'Poison!' The word seemed to carry like a bird whirring round the amphitheatre.

Murranus walked away just as the booing began. He strode towards the Gate of Life. The Director of the Games had already picked up one of the wine goblets and was waving it around.

Gaius, principal centurion in the Imperial Comitatus, the cavalry escort which always guarded the Emperor, bit into a soft golden apple. He closed his eyes and savoured the sweet juices. Gaius was sitting in the cool colonnade which over-looked the peristyle garden of the Villa Pulchra. He was deep in thought; he had so much to reflect on, so much to do, so little time to do it. Nevertheless, he opened his eyes. This was a very pleasant change from the musty barracks and hot stable yards of the imperial palaces. He was relieved not to have to wear the imperial dress uniform; instead he could relax in a cool embroidered tunic and short toga, although beneath the folds of that robe he wore a narrow leather belt with a long stabbing dagger in an embroidered sheath.

Gaius had been born not far from this very villa. He claimed he was Roman, though some said his ancestors were Spaniards, which accounted for his dark good looks and fiery temper. He had not yet reached thirty and was already one of Constantine's most trusted officers. He had received the crown of bravery for his courage at the battle of the Milvian Bridge and his ruthless pursuit of the enemy when it retreated. However, he still couldn't believe his luck at being brought here for such a meeting. Of course, he hadn't objected and good-naturedly received the envious congratulations of his fellow officers. He had left Rome a few days ago, escorting the carts and pack ponies, the long lines of slaves and servants, bringing goods from the Palatine palace to this imperial villa. It had been so refreshing to leave the city, travelling along the Via Latina before taking the country roads to Tibur and Constantine's summer residence.

This great villa, with a large farm attached, stretched across the brow of the Alban Hills, a place of dark green woods, pastures and meadows, all fertilised by the cool, sparkling Anio River. The villa was protected by its own curtain wall with guard towers and a wide fortified gate. Inside stretched a veritable paradise of gardens, sparkling fountains, man-made channels and rivulets, garlanded porticoes and shaded colonnades. The villa boasted avenues of cypresses, olives and pine trees which, the garrulous old gardener had assured Gaius, were watered with wine. Elm and holm-oak flourished, as well as shrubs such as myrtle, box, oleander, laurel and bay. Around the villa were sweet-smelling orchards of apple, pear, peach and cherry, and beds of roses, lilies and violets, whilst exotic lotus blossom floated on pools and fish ponds.

Once the carts were unpacked and the sumpter ponies unburdened, Gaius had spent the last two days wandering the villa. Its entrance hall or atrium was breathtaking in its beauty, with its long pool beneath an open sunlight, gorgeously carved pillars and vividly painted wall frescoes. The triclinium, or dining room, was just as luxurious, as were the various chambers and rest rooms for the imperial family and their court. Every luxury and need was catered for. The villa had its own kitchen, bake houses, vineyards and wine cellars. There was even a latrine with twenty marble seats at the far side of the villa, near the wall which divided it from the farm, which was a small estate in itself with its stables, pig pens, chicken coops, dovecotes and vegetable gardens.

Gaius had his own chamber beyond the peristyle, rather narrow but it did possess a large window, a carved chest, a stool, a small table and a comfortable cot bed. There was even a wall tapestry depicting Aeneas fleeing Troy, whilst the floor mosaic was of a dolphin's head thrusting up through sky-blue waves. Gaius had little to do but plan and plot while ensuring his guards were vigilant. The preparations for the arrival of the Purple Lords were not for him; those were left to the chamberlains and stewards. Gaius was in charge of security, and he had scrupulously memorised the plan of the villa. Only one distraction concerned him: the other soldiers. These were not from the imperial regiments; merely German mercenaries in their baggy trousers and tunics, their ruddy faces almost hidden beneath straggling hair and moustaches. The Germans were friendly enough, under the command of Burrus, Emperor Helena's personal bodyguard. They'd arrived two weeks ago in order to guard what they called in their broken Latin the

'Sanctus Gladius', the Holy Sword, apparently a great Christian relic which the Empress had found near the grave of Paul, one of the first leaders of the Christian Church. Paul had been decapitated by the Emperor Nero some two hundred and fifty years earlier; the faithful had obtained the sword which severed his neck and kept it in a secret place. Gaius regarded it all as childish trickery but the Germans were overcome by awe and took their task seriously.

Gaius scratched at a cut on his arm and gazed down at the golden carp nosing lazily amongst the reeds. He couldn't believe a sword had been preserved for over two hundred years, but there again, everything was changing. Gaius narrowed his eyes in disdain. The Christians . . . well, they swarmed like rats spilling out of their sewers and underground caverns. When they were not nosing where they shouldn't, they were busy fighting each other. Gaius tapped his foot impatiently. He and the other officers did not like how this coward's faith was replacing the glories of Mithras. Was this what they had fought for? Their allegiance was to Rome, yet the Augusta was insistent that that bloody sword had become more precious than an imperial standard. Burrus had told him all about the so-called relic; the German was garrulous, especially after he had drunk a few cups of the heavy wine of Lesbos, and had confessed to Gaius how he took his task most seriously, out of awe, as well as love for his Empress.

'She feeds me so well,' Burrus had slurred. 'Dormice,' he continued. 'I never thought I'd like them, but, soaked in honey, with a sprinkling of sesame seeds . . .' He stroked his stomach appreciatively. He was not so polite about the arrival of the philosophers, however. 'Christians,' he jeered, 'with nothing better to do than chatter like jays. The sword has been brought here to impress them.'

'Where's it kept?' Gaius had asked.

'Just behind the atrium,' Burrus confided, 'stands a door with steps leading down to a cellar. Apparently the builder of this villa had hoped to create an ice house by plastering the walls and laying a cement floor with a great circle of earth in the centre where the ice tub would stand. It was a dismal failure, so the cavernous chamber was turned into a strong room where the owner could keep his treasure. Now,' Burrus leaned closer in a heavy gust of wine, 'there,' he stumbled over the words, 'is the Locus Sacer, the Sacred Place.'

Timothaeus, Chief Steward of the villa, a self-confessed Christian who wore the fish symbol around his neck, had nodded in agreement. The steward, with his jovial red face and infectious laugh, always joined their little suppers. He never took offence at Burrus's contempt for Christians, but always warned that the mercenary should be careful, for surely one day the Empress Helena would be baptised and received in the only true faith? The German had grunted his disapproval and started asking questions about this great Paul, before offering to show Gaius the renowned relic. The steward had accompanied them down the steps to the iron-studded cellar door. At each side of this squatted two of Burrus's men, looking rather fearsome in the dancing light of the pitch torches pushed into wall brackets above them. They rose, swaying drunkenly.

'Is your leg better?' one of them asked Timothaeus.

'Oh yes,' the steward replied hurriedly. 'Now, Burrus, your key . . .'

Apparently there were two locks to the door, each served by a different key. Burrus held one, Timothaeus the other. The mercenary inserted his and turned it; the steward followed suit and swung open the door to the sacred place.

The inside of the cellar was dark, reeking of incense and beeswax. Gaius stepped over the threshold and stared around.

The chamber was long and cavernous, a place of shifting shadows due to the candles in their translucent alabaster jars fixed in niches along the walls. The ceiling was high, ribbed by stout beams supporting the floor above. In the centre stretched a huge circle of sand sprinkled with gold dust and edged with polished bricks arranged in a dog's-tooth fashion. Pots of incense displaying the *Chi* and *Rho* of the Christian faith were placed around the circle, the crackling charcoal sending up fragrant gusts of incense. The object of all this veneration hung on a stout chain from a rafter beam: the Holy Sword of the legionary who had executed St Paul. Around the stone-rimmed circle were prayer stools for the faithful to sit or kneel whenever they came to venerate the sacred relic.

'Where's Burrus?' Gaius asked. Timothaeus had followed him in, but the German had stayed chattering to his companions outside.

'He's frightened,' the steward whispered. 'This is a sacred place. Burrus is frightened of the Christian angels.' Gaius grunted and walked to the edge of the circle.

The sword was an old legionary weapon, now replaced as standard issue by the long curved sword Gaius had used during his military career. He studied the relic with great interest. The hilt was of pure ivory, a sparkling ruby on the pommel; its blade, designed for stabbing, was two-edged, with a ridge down the centre, and had been polished so it shone like a mirror. Gaius could understand why the room had been chosen. The sword was on full display and you could walk right round it, but the smooth sand would betray any footprint, whilst the sword hung more than an arm's length from where he stood. At the bottom of the chain was a sharp ugly hook to which the ring on the end of the hilt had been attached.

Gaius studied the sword, more out of curiosity than anything else. He found it difficult to accept that it was as old as Timothaeus claimed.

'The hilt has probably been replaced,' the steward hastily assured him, 'but its blade certainly bestowed on our blessed Paul the glorious palm of martyrdom . . .'

Now Gaius stared down at the carp amongst the reeds. He had soon lost interest in the sword and couldn't understand the growing interest of the Emperor in such matters. He'd heard the Emperor joke how his August mother was busy ransacking the Empire in her hunger for relics. The philosophers, the rhetoricians invited from Capua were deeply interested in the sword. Gaius had studied what he secretly called 'those loathsome creatures' ever since their arrival the day before yesterday. He had taken a personal dislike to all of them; they had no redeeming virtues, and their appearance and manner confirmed all he'd learned about them. A true nest of vipers! Of course, they had visited the sword as soon as they had arrived. According to Timothaeus, their fingers had positively itched, although the steward didn't know if it was the sacredness of the relic or the gleaming ruby in its ivory hilt which attracted them. All veneration had soon disappeared though, as the rhetoricians started to squabble about St Paul's teaching on Christ. Timothaeus had been truly scandalised, grumbling that if they were not prudent the good Lord would send a plague or pestilence to unite them against the common danger.

Voices echoed along the peristyle. Gaius closed his eyes. It was the rhetoricians, braying like asses! Justin, leader of the Arian delegation, came into the garden, bony finger waggling as he lectured his two companions on some obscure point of theology.

'What we have got to decide,' he declared, 'is whether Jesus Christ is of the same substance as the Father, or can he only be likened to the Father?'

His two companions nodded wisely. Gaius glared at them, but of course, he was a mere soldier; in their eyes he didn't exist. Justin was fat, with bulbous eyes and a mouth like a fish. Gaius stared down at the carp. No, he reasoned, that was an insult to the fish. Justin was a bloated frog. He liked to describe himself as ascetic, so he insisted on wearing a shabby tunic which reeked of the stables and sandals which would look scruffy on a beggar. His two companions, Dionysius and Malachus, were plain young men, both balding. They tried to imitate the Greeks with their sparse moustache and beards, eyes screwed up in concentration, lips half open as if ready to declare some great truth hidden from the rest of mankind.

They drifted away and Gaius lay down in the shade of a laurel bush and wondered what would happen. Memories came and went. When they were boys he and Spicerius used to visit a rich old man with a garden like this. He wondered idly what his former comrade would make of it all. Before long he had drifted off to sleep.

He was woken some time later, the shadows lenghtening, by the clash of cymbals, loud cries and shouts. At first, in his half-sleep, Gaius thought the villa was being attacked. Burrus came running into the garden, throwing his hands up in the air, then fell to his knees and began to howl like a dog.

'By all that is light,' Gaius muttered. He jumped to his feet and ordered the German to shut up.

'The sword,' Burrus wailed, 'the Holy Sword is gone! And Timothaeus is dead!'

28

Chapter 2

'Vita summa brevis spem nos vetat incohare
longam.'

('The brevity of life stops us from far-reaching
hope.')

Horace, *Odes*, I.4

The She-Asses tavern, on the edge of Rome's not so salu-
brious quarter, near the Flavian Gate, was ablaze with light.
The tavern occupied the ground floor of an *insula* or apartment block near the decaying temple of the Crown of Venus.
It was a spacious hostelry with a fine main door, nailed to
which was a placard listing what was on the menu, which
wines and beers were served, as well as a stark warning to
gamblers, fighters, sorcerers and travelling tinkers that they
were banned from trading under pain of a broken nose. Above
the door perched a carved statue of Minerva which Polybius
had 'borrowed' from the nearby temple, whilst on the top of
each doorpost squatted a grinning Hermes. Oceanus had

29

appropriated these on a long-term loan from a bath house the police had closed down for acting as a brothel without paying them their dues. Inside the main folding door, Polybius had transformed what used to be the atrium into a spacious high-ceilinged eating room. The counter stood at one end and at the other what Polybius grandiloquently termed 'the garden door'. The room was lit by oil lamps, rush lights and lanterns hanging from wall and ceiling hooks.

This particular evening, after the games had finished, the small carved tables had been pushed together and ringed with makeshift couches and stools. Pride of place was taken by a stern-faced Murranus, lounging on Polybius's one and only proper couch. Claudia sprawled on cushioned stools to Murranus's right. Polybius, his few hairs greased to circle his balding head like an athlete's wreath, shared a broad, throne-like chair with his plump, pretty wife, Poppaoe, whom Polybius always called his 'little ripe plum'. Simon the Stoic, sitting opposite, could only silently agree as he stared lust-fully at Poppaoe's full ripe breasts straining against her low blue-edged gown.

All the regulars had been invited, even Saturninus, the bleary-eyed commander of the local Vigiles, who acted as watchmen, firefighters, police and, as Polybius grumbled, unofficial tax collectors. The wine had circulated, both red and white. Polybius claimed they were Falernian, from northern Campania; Claudia suspected the jars were from the local market and the wine from the vines Poppaoe tended in the large garden behind the She-Asses. Polybius had certainly savoured every cup. Now, flush-faced, he lurched to his feet and, in an attempt to make Murranus smile, bellowed out the doggerel words:

*　　*　　*

'Look man is just a bag of bones,
Here today and gone tomorrow
Soon we'll all be dead as stones
So let's drink up and drown our sorrow.'

He glanced sharply at the sober-faced Murranus, then picked up a pair of small cymbals and clashed for silence. 'I'll tell you a story,' he declared and before anyone could object, he had walked into the centre of the dining circle and, ignoring Poppaoe's warning glance, launched into his tale.

'Once there was a poor carpenter who had a wife who loved bed sport. Day and night, whatever the weather, she was ripe for it.' Polybius raised his hands at the jeers this provoked. 'She had a lover whom she would most royally entertain when her husband was gone. One day she and lover boy were at their pleasures when husband unexpectedly arrived home. Her lover had no choice but to hide in a large, empty but very dirty wine vat standing in the bedroom corner. He was safely hidden away when the husband came into the room. The wife immediately started stripping the bed. "What are you doing here?" she shouted. "You lazy good-for-nothing! I'm working my fingers to the bone and you arrive home without a penny for a crust."

'"There's no work," her husband replied, pointing to the corner, "but I've just sold that wine vat for seven denarii, so you can help me clean and remove it."

'"You idiot," the quick-witted wife retorted. "Seven denarii? I've just sold it for twelve. The buyer's inside it, checking to see if it's all right." On cue, lover boy pops his head up. "I'll take it!" he shouts. "On one condition. You," he pointed to the husband, "get in here and clean it."

'So husband climbs in and starts to clean the wine vat

whilst lover boy and the lady of the house return to their pleasures, with the poor husband being encouraged by his wife's shouts, which he thinks are directions to clean the vat as thoroughly as possible . . .'

Polybius's audience collapsed in laughter.

'Is this a true story?' Festus the Fornicator shouted.

'Yes,' Polybius retorted.

'Which means,' Petronius the Pimp bellowed, 'you must have been either the man on the bed or the husband in the wine vat!'

Petronius ducked as Poppaoe threw a piece of meat at him. Polybius lurched back to his seat, and the guests turned to chatter with their neighbours as well as enjoy the fresh crates of wine Polybius sent round, followed by dishes of fried liver and coriander, pork in a piquant sauce and bowls of herb purée with walnuts.

'It'll never happen,' Polybius bawled at Murranus in one final attempt to draw the gladiator from his sombre mood.

'It *has* happened,' Murranus whispered to Claudia. She sipped at her watered wine and, stretching out, cupped Murranus's cheek in her small hand.

'Tell me again.'

'We were in the arena, I was fighting well, you saw that.'

'No I didn't,' Claudia retorted. 'I'd closed my eyes.'

'Spicerius began to sway, then he collapsed. I thought he was dead till he began to vomit. By the tits of a pig, I've never seen a man vomit like that. By the time they had got him back through the Gate of Life, whatever he had taken he'd spat most. of it out. May the gods be thanked for that old soldier doctor; he made Spicerius take salt water and he continued to vomit. He kept slapping Spicerius's face, telling him not to go to sleep. I have never seen so much water poured down a throat.'

'Poisoned?' Claudia asked.

'Perhaps,' Murranus replied. 'The doctor inspected the vomit, said it stank like a sewer pit. It may have been belladonna, foxglove, or just something to make Spicerius sleep. The doctor said he was very lucky; because he has a constitution like an ox, he survived. But now they are blaming me. Spicerius's wine cup was tainted – they found grains of a powder at the bottom of it – but mine was free, as was the wine left in the jug.'

Murranus indicated with his thumb. 'But of course things are not helped by the fact that Polybius is my supporter and he brought the wine down. To cut a long story short, I am being blamed for drugging Spicerius. They say I could be guilty of attempted murder.'

'But that's untrue,' Claudius replied heatedly. 'The cup was on the table, all sorts of people were milling about, Polybius told me that. Anyway, what will happen now?'

'Next week Rufinus is to stage special games in honour of the Emperor's birthday. I will fight again. This time there will be no wine, and it will be a fight to the finish!'

'Why don't you give it up?' Claudia pleaded.

'I will one day, when I'm Victor Ludorum and receive the crown.'

'But there's one more fight after Spicerius?'

'Ah yes, one more. Spicerius, or I, must face Meleager, the Marvel of a Million Cities.'

'And is he?'

'No, that's just what he calls himself, but he's a cunning-eyed bastard. He'll laugh his head off when he hears the news.'

'There's no real damage done.' Claudia touched Murranus on the tip of his nose. 'They have no proof you poisoned the wine and you'll both fight again. By the way, how is Spicerius?'

'He's much better this evening; rather quiet when I visited, but said he didn't hold me responsible. He clasped my hand and claimed he was still the better man.'

'He could have taken it himself,' Claudia declared. 'He wouldn't be the first gladiator to try some magical powder. But come, smile, Uncle is really trying to do his best.'

'And what are you doing?' Murranus leaned closer and, ignoring Januaria's jealous hiss, removed a smudge of grease from the corner of Claudia's mouth with his napkin. She smiled dazzlingly and silently wished that the handsome green-eyed, red-haired fighter would be satisfied, retire and always stay with her.

'What are you thinking, little one?' Murranus whispered. 'Are you still looking for the man with the purple chalice tattooed on his wrist? You told me he was probably a soldier serving in an Illyrian regiment. Didn't you say Rufinus the banker knew something about him? Is that why you are working in the palace?'

'I'm a scurrier.' Claudia smiled. 'The Empress's messenger maid.'

'I'm sure you are.' Murranus lowered his voice so the hubbub of their companions swept over them. 'Are you a spy, Claudia? One of the Agentes?'

'Why, Murranus.' Claudia fluttered her eyelids.

'Are you?'

She paused as the door opened and a pedlar entered, a tray slung round his neck full of trinkets, Egyptian scarabs, medals of Isis and packets of sulphur matches. He stretched out his claw-like hand full of denarii and bellowed for a drink, any drink. He caught Claudia's gaze. 'And some fish,' he added cheekily. 'I've walked the Via Appia, up and down, set up shop just near the tombstones on the third mile.' He gave a cracked-toothed smile. 'You know the place, where the Christians say Sebastian was shot to death with arrows. I'll be back there tomorrow, about the sixth hour, so I need food and a good night's sleep.' He bawled on and on until a servant brought him a small jug of wine and a dish of diced fish. The pedlar glanced quickly at Claudia again before retreating into a corner.

Claudia looked away. Sylvester had sent his message. She had to be in the catacombs the following morning, amongst the gravestones of the cemetery near the third milestone along the Appian Way . . .

Claudia woke long before dawn. She always slept well in her small chamber above the tavern. Poppaoe had done her best to make the room comfortable and pleasing, with the tapestry of leaping ibex on the wall, a bronze tripod table, an acacia-wood stool and a carved Egyptian chest where she could store her belongings. Claudia rose and went to the spring in the garden which lay at the centre of the *insula*. The breeze was cool, the sun had yet to rise, so the garden was still fresh before the humidity and heat set in. She washed herself carefully, then returned to her chamber to put on clean undergarments, a green tunic with an embroidered hem, and a dark brown cloak which she used to hide the dagger in the belt around her waist. She grabbed her staff and broad-brimmed hat and went down to the kitchen, where a sleepy-eyed pot boy served her some of yesterday's meal in the small bread room which lay off the kitchen. She drank some watered wine then, telling the pot boy to go back to bed, opened one of the shutters, climbed up and lowered herself down.

She looked to the right and left. There was no one there. No beggar pretending to doze or a drunk urinating against the wall. The street was deserted. She hurried along towards the main thoroughfare. The water carriers and street sweepers were out; schoolchildren were being forced down to the local school room, where a travelling teacher would teach them the rudiments of mathematics and the alphabet. Men going to the baths walked briskly or were carried in their sedan chairs, their slaves hastening behind with baskets of strigils, combs, towels, jars of perfume and flasks of oil. The hucksters were preparing for a day's trading. Barbers had set up their stools, hot water and brushes at the ready. Cooks, their saucepans full of sausages, fired their mobile stoves, hoping the smell of spiced meat would whet the appetite of passersby. In the workshops, craftsmen started to hammer. The usual din of the day was beginning.

The street was being cleared of carts, according to Caesar's law, except for those of builders bringing in masonry and timber. The crowds were out. Here and there the fairground people, with their strange tricks, tales and lurid appearances, were preparing to entertain; already a viper trainer had attracted a small audience. Windows were open, shutters being pulled back, chamber pots emptied, flower baskets hung, and barrows of refuse thrust out of doors to be taken down to the local midden heap. A squad of soldiers swung by, weapons clattering, the red-eyed auxiliaries, with their blue shields and leather helmets, eager to return to their barracks after a long night's duty. Claudia recalled Murranus, fast asleep in the guest room overlooking the garden, and felt a pang of sorrow at the misfortune facing her friend.

Claudia had fallen asleep trying to picture in her mind that dark, macabre tunnel where Murranus had been standing waiting with Spicerius to enter the arena. She had questioned the gladiator most carefully before turning on Polybius and Oceanus. She believed that someone had tried to weaken

Murranus's opponent, hoping Murranus would kill him before the effect of the potion made itself felt. She knew a great deal about gladiators. Spicerius, a true professional, had probably not eaten since the *cena libera* the previous evening. On the morning of the fight he would empty his bowels and probably chew nothing more than a dry husk. He would be excited and tense; the wine and the potion must have curdled his stomach so that he vomited them out before any real damage was done. So who was responsible? She had been most forceful with her uncle. Polybius could be as cunning as a serpent and had a finger in every pie, yet he had protested his innocence. Was it Murranus himself? Claudia drove away a mongrel yapping at her and shook her head. Murranus was a killer, a fighter, but he was honourable, not perverse or corrupt; a man who fought because he could not find anything else to do, except dream of owning a tavern like the She-Asses.

Claudia reached the main thoroughfare leading down to the gates. She'd kept to the edge, dodging people coming in and out. At the city gate one of the guards whistled at her and asked to see more of her legs. She made an obscene gesture and, with the guard's laughter ringing in her ears, hurried through the gates and on to the Via Appia. The crowds thronged busily, merchants, traders, pedlars, travelling musicians. Only once did she stop, to watch a troupe of actors, their faces hidden behind grotesque masks, bodies garbed in gaudy robes, perform and sing as they went up to the city. Two little boys, satyr masks pushed back on their heads, tried to coax coins for their begging baskets. Claudia walked purposefully on. She remembered being part of such a troupe travelling up and down Italy, from its southern tip to the approaches to the cold mountains in the north. She had enjoyed herself, but the manager had drunk the profits so she had returned home. Nevertheless, she had received an education of sorts. She could read and write, speak the lingua franca of the cities and had a nose for mischief. She could act and mime and knew, line for line, the poetry and plays of Ovid, Terence and Seneca.

Occasionally Claudia paused as if to adjust the strap on her sandal or take her hat off so the breeze might cool the sweat on her brow. As she did so, she glanced around, looking for anyone who might be following her. On one occasion she retraced her footsteps, and when she reached a line of tombs and graves which spread out on both sides of the road, she wandered into them as if to inspect some monument or read an inscription. She was satisfied no one was following her. She passed the third mile station and found the trackway leading into what Sylvester now called the Cemetery of St Sebastian. Claudia knew nothing of Christian saints except that here, during the great persecution, the Christians had dug and developed underground passageways and tunnels, hacking out the porous rock which stretched beneath the outskirts of Rome. She found the usual tomb chest and entered, fumbling in the agreed place for the oil lamp and packet of sulphur matches. After a great deal of scraping, the lamp was lit. She put it in the lantern horn, took off her hat, placed this at the top of the steps and carefully climbed down into the silent musty darkness.

Every time she visited the catacombs, she thought how much she hated the place. She wasn't afraid of demons or ghosts; it was just the oppressive silence, the walls closing in. She reached the bottom; the tunnel here was about two yards wide, the ceiling well above her head, the floor of beaten earth sure under her feet. She walked carefully, holding the lantern out, her walking cane tapping the ground, echoing like a drum-beat. She turned a corner and entered the

Christian burial place. Here, on ledges in the wall, protected by a thin coating of makeshift plaster, lay the Christian dead. Most had died naturally; others were the victims of persecution: strangled, decapitated, or in some cases just the pathetic remains of what had been left after they had been thrown to the wild beasts in the amphitheatre. Roughly carved inscriptions as well as Christian graffiti covered the walls, some with the usual *Chi* and *Rho*, a cross, or prayers to St Peter and St Paul. Claudia knew these signs by heart; they were her guide to which tunnel to follow, which passageway to enter. At last she reached the tomb of Philomena, 'Virgin and Martyr', so the graffiti proclaimed, and sat down on a marble bench stolen from the cemetery above. This was a junction of three tunnels, a safe place, where Claudia and Sylvester could hear anyone who approached and so take another way out.

Claudia put her stick carefully against the marble seat and waited. She checked the lantern; there was plenty of oil in the container and the wick was strong. She leaned against the cold stone, dabbing the sweat from her face, and wondered what Sylvester wanted. He had told her about some meeting out at the Villa Pulchra that she would have to go to; the Empress Helena would need her. Claudia was more worried about Murranus. She wondered if Rufinus the banker could throw any light on the attempt on Spicerius.

At last she heard a sound, a clatter, the usual sign whenever Sylvester approached. She cupped her hand to her mouth, whistled sharply and then waited for the three whistles in reply. She breathed a sigh of relief: Sylvester was here. A shadow moved down one of the tunnels, and the silver-haired priest, his lean, tired face wreathed in a smile, emerged from the darkness. They exchanged the kiss of peace. Sylvester sat down next to Claudia and, opening a napkin, shared the bread and figs he had brought, as well as the small flask of wine.

'Why do we meet here?' Claudia asked between mouthfuls. 'The danger has passed.'

'The danger is never past, Claudia, there is always danger. We Christians are tolerated, not approved; we have only begun the journey.' Sylvester took a piece of cheese and broke it in his hands. 'There's also danger for you, Claudia. You spy for the Bishop of Rome, but you also spy for the Empress.'

'I never have, never would, betray either.'

'One day you might. Choices have to be made, crossroads reached. Your father would have approved of what you are doing.'

'My father is dead.'

'He was one of us.'

'Whether he was one of you or not, he would still have hunted down and killed the man who raped his daughter and murdered his son.' Claudia turned on the marble bench, still half listening for any sound from the tunnels. 'I don't come to you, Sylvester, because I love you or your faith. If you remember, I came to you for help, and you promised you would find that man.' Claudia tried to keep the pleading out of her voice. 'The assassin with the purple chalice tattooed on his wrist.'

'Claudia, we *are* helping you. Your assailant had a purple chalice tattoo, the mark of those who follow the rites of Dionysius, the drinkers of the grape, who worship the demons Bacchus and Pan. They include officials, priests and soldiers, a powerful sect.'

'Magister, with all due respect, I couldn't care if the man worshipped the Emperor's arse.'

Sylvester laughed drily and patted her on the hand. 'I have

40

news for you, Claudia, though perhaps it's not very good. Rufinus, the banker, claimed such a man was serving with the Illyrian regiment. Well, I'll tell you this, half the regiment wear such a mark.' He pressed a finger against his lips. 'I have done careful research on your behalf. You were not the only one to be attacked and raped; you were lucky to escape with your life.'

'My brother didn't.'

'Hush now. The man who attacked you may have wanted you to see that tattoo, to distract you. It might have been a cover for other criminal activities, a symbol which could be washed off later. No, no, Claudia, listen, you know about tattoos, I could have one inscribed on my arm which I can never remove. I can also ask an artist to copy such a one, as easy to remove as a linen cloth from your neck.'

Claudia moaned softly. Darkness hung all around her; only the lamp flickered. She'd never thought of that, she had been so convinced that one day she would find a man with a tattoo which couldn't be hidden. Sylvester's intelligence was always good, yet she remembered her assailant. She always would: his smell, his touch, his voice. She took a deep breath and tried to suppress a shiver.

'I'm sorry, Claudia, but you must consider the possibility of what I've said. There are other alleyways and streets we can search. Close your eyes. I know it's hard, but that evening on the banks of the Tiber, your brother was collecting shells, wasn't he?'

Claudia closed her eyes and nodded.

'And the man approached you.' Sylvester continued. 'He killed Felix because he wanted no witnesses, nobody to protect you. Imagine him fighting, his body, the muscles of his arms, back and stomach.' Claudia did so, and felt sick. She was back beside the river again, the sun setting, that man lurching over. She could recall his legs, the muscles of his calves, the strong arms like a vice of steel, the hot, wine-laden breath.

'Soldier or priest?' Sylvester asked abruptly, squeezing her wrist tightly.

'Soldier,' Claudia retorted. 'Yes, he must have been a soldier. There wasn't an ounce of fat on him; it was like fighting an armoured man.'

'Good,' Sylvester murmured. 'Here's a man drunk, wandering the riverside, he doesn't care whether he's caught, he wants his pleasure. What he did was hideous, but he also ran a great risk. Tell me, Claudia, why should a soldier do that? Think of the soldiers in Rome. Most of them are flabby; even those called back from the frontier soon put on weight, let the muscles run to fat.'

Claudia felt a thrill of excitement. Sylvester had been a lawyer; she always respected the sharpness of his thought, the logic of his argument. She opened her eyes and smiled at him.

'We're talking about an athlete, aren't we? Someone who is in constant training?'

'No, Claudia, we are talking about a fighter. You described to me in great detail what happened; I told you to do that, to clear your mind, purge your soul.' Sylvester made a circular movement with his fingers. 'Could your attacker, the murderer of your brother, be a gladiator?'

He half smiled at the hiss of disapproval from Claudia. 'No, no,' he added gently, pushing a lock of hair away from her forehead. 'Claudia, reflect! Gladiators are killers, often lonely men. Oh, they are hero-worshipped, but only because they have killed someone. They are in constant training. The women who worship them are either whores or degenerates from court. No,' his smile widened, 'I'm not talking about you and Murranus; he is very fortunate! I'm talking about those who hang about the gladiator schools and want nothing more than to give their bodies. Next time you mix with Murranus's friends look at them carefully, consider what I've said. Was your attacker looking for fresh prey? An innocent maid? Some respectable young woman, a change from the usual? It's common enough.' Sylvester sighed. 'As the Lord of Light knows!'

Claudia stared at the far wall as if fascinated by the graffiti there: figures of men and women joining hands around a table and, underneath, Christian symbols about eternal life. She noticed the Alpha and Omega, the first and last letters of the Greek alphabet, the symbols of the Christian God. She was distracted by what Sylvester had said. Sometime soon, when she was in a darkened room by herself, she would meditate, reflect on what he had said. She felt a spark of excitement, a secret thrill, as if she realised she was on the verge of the truth.

Sylvester broke off another piece of cheese, popped it in his mouth and walked over to examine the graffiti. Claudia sighed noisily.

'Why am I here this morning? Why now?'

'The Villa Pulchra, at Tibur,' Sylvester replied, eager to change the subject. 'Two matters of importance. The Empress Helena, as you may know, is collecting Christian relics. She seems to have a passion for them; her agents are scouring the countryside around Jerusalem searching for the True Cross. The Empress Helena believes she has found the sword used in the execution of the apostle St Paul. She has put it on show in a special room in the Villa Pulchra, a sort of exhibition when certain philosophers, the rhetoricians from Capua, debate matters of doctrine.'

'And?'

'To cut a long story short, yesterday afternoon, or so our agents tell us, the sword disappeared. The chamber or cellar has no secret entrances, and it was guarded by mercenaries. The door could only be opened by two keys. Timothaeus the steward held one of these, Burrus, the scruffy German who adores Helena, the other. Anyway,' Sylvester bit into a fig, 'yesterday afternoon Timothaeus, as usual, decided to check on the sword. The door was opened. Burrus, because he is frightened of the place, stayed outside. Timothaeus went in. Burrus heard a thump and a cry but dismissed this. A short while later he peered in. Timothaeus was lying by the circle of sand.'

'Circle of sand?'

'Yes, you will see, it stretches beneath where the sword hung from a chain. Only yesterday afternoon, the chain was empty. The sword was gone.'

'And Timothaeus?'

'Burrus thought he was dead, but the man had simply fallen in a faint. The alarm was raised, the guards called, Timothaeus was removed and the chamber searched. But no sword was found. A true miracle.' Sylvester grinned. 'Timothaeus believes that because of the squabbling between Christians, the Angel of the Lord came and removed the sword.'

'Of course, it was stolen?'

'So it seems, but by whom, why and how are truly a mystery. The Augusta will not be pleased. She will send for you. In fact, I'm sure that a message or messenger will have already arrived at the She-Asses ordering you to the Villa Pulchra.'

'But there's something else, isn't there?'

'Oh yes, there's always something else. The Emperor has invited six rhetoricians, self-proclaimed philosophers, from the

44

School of Oratory at Capua, a prestigious academy where many scholars study theology and philosophy and perfect their public speaking skills. It's now become a thorn in the side for us, as the Arian heresy flourishes there. One of its most skilled advocates is a scholar called Justin.'

'What is the bone of contention?'

'The bone, Claudia? Why, the truth of our faith. Who is God? How does God act?'

'I'm not a philosopher, I'm certainly not a Christian.'

'No, you're better,' Sylvester retorted. 'You are a woman of integrity with a keen mind and sharp wits. This is what we believe, Claudia. Our God is a triune God, three persons in one. The Father, pure spirit, sees an image of himself; that image is the Son, eternal and real, like the Father but not the Father. For all eternity the Father has always co-existed with His image. He loves that image and the love which exists between them is another person, the Spirit. Three persons but one God. Our faith teaches that the Son became incarnate, Jesus Christ, God yet man, confined yet infinite. The Arians, however, preach a different faith which would destroy the Trinity and reduce Christ to some glorified angel.'

'And?'

'The Arians must not win the debate. I will be joining you at the Villa Pulchra, Claudia, to persuade the Empress to give us her support. I want the Arian heresy to be destroyed and our unity maintained.'

'What happens if they resist?'

Sylvester rubbed his cheeks with his hands. 'More stringent methods might be necessary; a diseased limb must be cut off.'

'You mean, you'll have them killed? You Christians who love each other?'

'Heresy in our Church is like treason in the State.'

'But what about the love of Christ?' Claudia teased.

'Let Christ love them,' Sylvester replied tartly. 'The Church must survive, but that is only one half of the problem.' He paused to collect his thoughts. 'On the one hand we have men like Timothaeus the steward; he is orthodox to the point of fanaticism. He doesn't like the debate, he thinks the Arians should shut up or be silenced. On the other side are the likes of Chrysis, Constantine's agent and chamberlain, a pagan born and bred. He rejoices at these divisions amongst the Christians; he will ridicule the debate, try and cast us all as agitators.'

'But there'll be your Bishop's representative, the one who will defend orthodox teaching?'

'Oh yes,' Sylvester laughed sharply, 'and he might do more harm than good. Athanasius is hot-tempered, a true firebrand.'

'Do you think any of these philosophers could have stolen the sword? They were present when the relic disappeared?'

'It's possible. They could have seen it as something sacred to Christianity, not to be put on show by pagans. Others could have stolen it, soldiers, officials. Chrysis was coming and going to the villa; he would like nothing better than to upset the Christians. Or,' Sylvester took a deep breath, 'it could have been an ordinary thief, attracted by the ivory hilt or the sparkling ruby. But that's not important, Claudia.' Sylvester gestured around. 'What do we care about graves, relics, philosophical debate? The Church is leaving the catacombs, it must remain strong. At this moment in time we are tolerated, not accepted. One day we shall be. We shall be the Empire. Can you imagine it, Claudia?' he whispered. 'Church and State, working as one, the City of God?' His voice trailed away and he sat dreaming his own dreams of Empire before recollecting where he was. 'I understand your friend Murranus is in difficulties?'

'Murranus is always in difficulties.' Claudia got to her feet, picked up her cloak and staff. 'So we meet again at the Villa Pulchra?'

'I'm leaving for there now.' Sylvester smiled up at her. 'I'll arrive within the hour and see what mischief is planned.'

'Mischief?'

'Just a feeling . . .' Sylvester rose to his feet and gestured to one of the tunnels. 'I'll leave by another route. Safe journey.'

'Oh, Claudia?' She turned.

'Yes, Magister?'

'When you met Murranus for the first time,' Sylvester walked over, measuring his footsteps carefully, 'was it by accident or design? Did he seek you out or did you him?' He raised a hand in a gesture of peace. 'Think about that.'

Claudia did so as she raced hot-faced through the tunnel, holding the lantern up, aware of the pool of light moving around her. Sylvester's words had unsettled her. She was in the Kingdom of the Dead; behind these plastered walls lay the remains of those who had died violent deaths. Almost unbidden, her nightmares returned, of racing along tunnels like this, chased by her assailant with a purple chalice tattooed on his wrist. She could hear his breathing, and somewhere in the distance Felix was also fleeing, little legs moving fast. She wanted to reach him, but hands and arms came through the wall to grab at her. Claudia stopped at a corner.

'Don't be a stupid hussy!' she whispered. 'Be more frightened of the living than the dead.'

She strained her ears; there was no sound, and she walked purposefully on. When she reached the steps, she replaced the lantern and found her hat had not been moved. She put it on and climbed up into the sunlight. Gripping her staff, she walked amongst the tombs. An old beggar woman, cloaked in black, hiding in the shadows, stood up abruptly, claw-like hands begging for alms. Claudia recalled the witches and warlocks who frequented this place to sacrifice a black cock at midnight. She would have screamed abuse, but the old woman's face was seamed by time and her eyes were a milky white.

'Just a denarii,' the beggar lisped, 'some money for some wine.'

Claudia handed across two coins and hurried on. She joined the crowds thronging along the Via Appia, losing herself amongst them, relaxing at the usual smell of dirt, freshly baked bread, spiced meat and the ever-pervasive stench of oil. The travellers to the city were breaking their fast, so the cooks and food sellers, water carriers and wine pedlars were doing a roaring trade. Claudia slaked her thirst whilst gossiping to a farmer laden with two crates full of squabbling ducks. She asked him about his small farm and the prospect of a good harvest. The farmer, flattered by such attention, chatted like a magpie whilst Claudia stared back, narrow-eyed, along the way she had come.

Once inside the city, Claudia left the broad thoroughfare into a warren of side streets. She was in a quarter she knew; the dyers and the tanners, the merchants behind their stalls, all those who frequented the She-Asses shouted out their greetings. Claudia hastily replied but her mind was still full of what Sylvester had told her, particularly about Murranus.

She found the She-Asses quiet. Oceanus informed her that Polybius was still sleeping off the effects of the night before, whilst Poppaoe had gone down to the marketplace.

'You know who I want?'

'He's out in the garden, little one.' Oceanus said, leaning down. 'He's got very special visitors.'

Claudia's heart almost skipped a beat. However, Murranus

wasn't entertaining a lady of the city but a young athlete with a sharp sardonic face and black bushy hair. Next to him squatted a grizzled old man who was allowing a tamed snake to wind itself around his arm. From the staff on the table, with its emblem of Aesculapius, Claudia reckoned he must be a physician. Murranus had his back to her; his visitor leaned over, tapping him on the arm, and pointed. The gladiator sprang to his feet. Instinctively Claudia looked at his wrist and felt guilty: there was no tattoo there. Murranus wasn't a rapist, a child-killer! She was not so convinced about her admirer's visitor. He was of medium height, with mocking eyes and cynical lips. A man who had a beautiful body, and revelled in his glorious physique.

'You know who this is?' Murranus rubbed his hands. 'Spicerius, you remember Spicerius? No one forgets Spicerius.'

Claudia nodded, mouth open but nothing to say. Spicerius was staring at her coolly, carefully examining her from head to toe as if she was a slave in the market. The insult was quite studied, then he hastily apologised, rose, grasped Claudia's hand and lifted it to his lips.

'A beautiful name, Claudia.' His light blue eyes were full of mockery. 'A beautiful name for a beautiful woman.'

He let her hand drop.

'Murranus, you didn't tell me about her, at least not in detail.' For a short while there was laughter, then Spicerius introduced his old friend Valens, formerly physician in the Tenth Pannonian legion. Oceanus brought out some drinks and strips of honeyed bread, and they all sat down on the grass in the shade of a tree. But behind the laughter and jokes, Spicerius was studying Murranus carefully, as if trying to memorise every detail. Now and again, his darting eyes shifted to Claudia. The gladiator had not yet returned to full health.

On whispered instructions from his physician, Spicerius ate and drank very frugally. He noticed Claudia watching him.

'I came to make my peace with Murranus.' He smiled.

'Why so quickly?' Claudia asked. 'Some people claim he tried to poison you.'

'I don't think so,' Spicerius laughed, 'and there's one good way of finding out . . .' He paused, clutching his stomach. Claudia noticed how his face was painted, delicately, like that of a woman. Nevertheless, this couldn't hide the shadows around his eyes or the drawn look to his cheeks, or the way his eyelids kept fluttering as if he was still in some discomfort.

'He's talking about the betting.' Murranus spoke up. 'Polybius and I have proved that neither of us laid wagers on who would win. If we had, Spicerius here might think we were trying to help the odds.'

'And I saw nothing.' Spicerius shook his head. 'I was in the tunnel, waiting. The wine cups were filled. I never saw Murranus's hand go near my cup. In fact I saw nobody's. I'm always very careful. It's not the first time a drink has been spiked or food tainted; all sorts of nasty games are played.' He turned his wrist to show Claudia a scar; and she stared in horror at the purple chalice tattoo which his leather brace couldn't conceal. She drew back; Murranus followed her gaze.

'What's the matter?' Valens, the doctor, spoke up. 'What's the matter with you, woman? You look as if you have seen a ghost.'

Claudia half rose to her feet, knocking over the bowl of bread and honey, kicking aside the jug of beer. Murranus grasped her wrist.

'Claudia, it's not what you think . . .' But she broke free and, spinning on her heel, ran back into the tavern.

Chapter 3

'*Omnia Romae cum pretis.*'
('Everything in Rome comes with a price-tag.')

Juvenal, *Satires*, III

Dionysius, follower of Justin and not-so-ardent supporter of the teaching of Arius, was thinking about death: not his own, but death in general. The self-proclaimed philosopher was preparing a speech on that chilling phrase of the sophists: 'I was not; I am; I am not; I don't care'.

The Villa Pulchra lay quiet after all the excitement caused by the arrival of the Lords of the Purple in their palanquins and sedan chairs. The Emperor, of course, had arrived on horseback, clattering into the broad cobbled yard bawling for wine and a warm bath to cool the imperial arse. Carts and sumpter ponies had crowded in. Servants and slaves bowed down with burdens hurried around the villa with the furniture and furnishings and personal belongings of Constantine and his court. The kitchens had already been prepared, the oven fires lit, the baking house opened; now the smoke boiled from the kitchens like mist over the river. The air turned savoury with the dishes planned for that evening's banquet: eggs poached in wine, beef casserole, hare in a sweet sauce, ham in a red wine and fennel gravy, baked plaice and oysters in vine leaves.

Dionysius's mouth watered, his empty stomach grumbling at the prospect of such delicacies. He and the rest had been invited to the supper party and Dionysius wanted to impress everyone with something witty or thoughtful. He planned to recite his short speech on death, followed by some verses from Ovid, or Virgil's *Aeneid*, perhaps a comparison between Homer and Herodotus? He walked deeper into the garden, entering the shade of the orchard. He hunched his shoulders and rolled his head, trying to release the tension in his neck. He was glad to be out of the sunlight. The villa had settled down for the afternoon rest, except for the Empress, who was prowling the corridors and passageways like a panther seeking its prey. The Holy Sword had gone, the blessed relic had disappeared.

Dionysius closed his eyes and shook his head. That stupid German had cried like a child whilst the Captain of the Guard, Gaius Tullius, trying to keep his face straight, had searched the villa and garden to no avail. Timothaeus the steward, white as a ghost, had quickly recovered, and at supper had told them all what had happened. How he had walked down to the Sacred Place to see the Holy Sword; how Burrus and he had unlocked the door and, as usual, the German had stayed outside to talk to his companions. Timothaeus remembered looking at the sand – it wasn't disturbed – and only then, to his horror, did he notice that the sword was gone.

'It was the chain,' he whispered. 'Just hanging down so straight and still. I fainted.'

Poor Timothaeus had collapsed half in, half out of the circle of sand. Burrus had looked in, seen what had happened and immediately fallen into a fit of hysterics. Gaius Tullius, roused from his nap in the peristyle garden, had taken charge. He and Dionysius had entered the cellar, but could find nothing disturbed except the edge of the sand where Timothaeus had fallen. They had removed the steward with the help of a slave from the House of Mourning. Gaius had checked he was breathing before returning to search the cellar, only to find nothing. Timothaeus was carried to his room and Gaius had set up his own enquiry. A number of facts emerged. First, Burrus and Timothaeus swore that no one could get into that room without both keys. Secondly, there was no sign of forced entry or secret tunnel. Thirdly, the chain hung empty but undamaged. Fourthly, the sand betrayed no sign of anyone standing on it. The disappearance of the relic was truly a mystery.

The Empress, of course, was outraged. According to reports, she'd slapped Burrus roundly for his hysterics and openly wondered if the two guards outside had been involved in the theft. They had been summoned, beaten and harangued by their imperial mistress, but they swore the most sacred oaths that they had done their duty and noticed nothing wrong. Empress Helena screamed that she would see them all crucified before flouncing off to her own bedchamber. In the end her anger cooled: the Holy Sword was gone and there was not a shred of information about how it had mysteriously disappeared. Justin, of course, wondered if their opponents had stolen it, spitefully pointing out that Athanasius, Aurelian, Septimus and other members of the orthodox party were all poor and would have envied the ivory and ruby.

Dionysius, muttering to himself, crouched down at the base of an apple tree, using it as a back rest. He stretched out his legs, savouring the shade, the cool grass and the soothing coos of the birds. 'Justin should keep his mouth shut!' he mumbled to himself. 'Everyone admired the sword, anyone could be a suspect – and that includes that great hulk Burrus and his hairy Germans.' Dionysius wanted Justin to shut up and not make a bad situation worse.

The philosopher wetted his lips and gazed at the circle of wild flowers arranged in vivid colours which caught the sun as it poured through gaps in the trees. Disagreements, he reflected, always led to worse. Dionysius had experienced enough horror in his life and tried not to frighten himself. He had been converted to Christianity in his teens. He'd debated the existence of angels and demons, yet his pagan upbringing also evoked the Manes, spirits of the dead, some of whom, because of the way they had died, came back to haunt the living and blight their lives. Dionysius returned to his reflections on death, only to be distracted by the prospect of the impending debate. He was no fool. He realised that Bishop Militiades and his assistant, the presbyter Sylvester, had the ear of the Empress. He had secretly reviewed his own position, concluding that it might be best to renounce the teaching of Arius and embrace orthodoxy. That was the way to proceed, to get noticed and so win approval, and what better way than in public, declaring, ever so humbly, how he had been convinced by the arguments of his opponents?

'Are we enjoying the garden?'

Dionysius started and glanced up at the figure towering over him. Because of the position of the sun, the philosopher couldn't recognise who it was who had addressed him. He lifted his hands to shade his eyes, but he had hardly stirred when the rock smacked against his head. He felt a searing flash of pain and the tang of blood at the back of his throat, then slumped over. His assailant hastily bound his hands and feet and laced a coarse rope round his middle. Dionysius tried to move but couldn't. He was pulled across the ground like a sack, his body jarring against hidden stumps and stones. The pain drove him in and out of consciousness. He was choking. He tried to scream, only to realise that the pain in his mouth was caused by the stout gag forced between his lips.

Now they were going deeper into the trees, and the rope pulling him went slack. A blindfold was put across his eyes and his hands were freed. Dionysius tried to struggle, but it was fruitless. His opponent hummed quietly as he pegged the philosopher out against the ground and proceeded to slice his captive's arms, legs and chest. Dionysius really believed the Manes had come. He was in a sea of pain, tossed here and there, his feverish mind drifting in and out of consciousness. He was back in Capua, in the schoolroom or walking out in the fields, until another cut brought him back to the tortured present. His body bucked against the ropes. His assailant was slicing his flesh as he would a piece of beef.

Eventually Dionysius lost consciousness and his assailant left him there, pegged on the ground, blood running out like rivulets across the lush green grass. It took him an hour to die.

His corpse was discovered by Gaius Tullius as he was doing his usual rounds with four of his men. They all gazed in horror at the blood-soaked body, the ground around saturated with a dark stain.

'Fetch the Empress,' Gaius ordered.

'And his Excellency?'

'I said the Empress,' Gaius insisted. 'The Augusta will know what to do.' He smiled thinly. 'Our Noble Emperor has taken a few cups of wine; he is with some of the maids and would not like to be disturbed.'

A short while later, the Empress, accompanied by her woebegone bodyguard, came striding through the trees. She gave an exclamation of horror, then walked round the corpse, noticing how the legs and arms were held taut, the rope tied to pegs driven into the ground.

'How long, Captain?' she asked.

Gaius, his sandals squelching on the grass, gathered up his gown, leaned down and pressed his hand against the dead man's face.

'At least two hours, possibly less.' He ran his hand across the stomach. 'This is hardly bloated with gas.' He got to his feet. 'Whoever killed him truly hated him. Augusta, shall I arrest the others?'

'Nonsense!'

'There is a physician in the villa,' Burrus murmured.

'Unless he can resurrect the dead, he is of no use here,' Helena retorted. 'I wonder—'

She broke off as Timothaeus the steward came hurrying up. He took one look at the corpse and turned away to retch. Helena walked over and patted him gently on the back.

'I'm afraid,' she murmured, 'it is not your week, is it, Timothaeus? Now, be a good chap, take this hulking piece of meat,' she gestured at Burrus, 'and, when you have settled your stomach, go back to Rome, to the She-Asses near the Flavian Gate, and bring Claudia. I want her here tonight.'

Helena walked into the trees, breathing heavily. Yes, she

thought, it's time my little mouse was here, with her twitching nose and scurrying feet. She will help resolve these mysteries . . .

Murranus brought Claudia back to the garden. He grasped her hand and whispered to her not to be foolish. Claudia already felt embarrassed; after all, there were many men in Rome who wore that tattoo on their wrist. She had already met a few, so why such a violent reaction to Spicerius?

'It's because of Sylvester,' she whispered.

'Who?' Murranus asked.

'Nothing.' Claudia remembered herself quickly. 'Just a friend I talk to about my problems.'

'I thought you had no friends except me.'

Claudia, in an attempt to distract him, smiled up at him. 'Well, you learn something new every day.'

Spicerius and Valens were still sitting in the shade. The gladiator rose as Claudia came back.

'I'm sorry,' he apologised. 'Murranus did tell me what happened. I tried to hide my tattoo beneath the wrist guard.' He squatted down as she did. 'I know something of your background,' he continued, 'but this tattoo,' he undid the wrist guard and displayed the design, 'has only been done in the last six months.'

'Do many gladiators wear it?'

'Ask Murranus.' Spicerius shrugged. 'It's common enough. It's linked to the worship of Dionysius, the God of Wine.' Claudia noticed how his eye teeth were sharpened like those of a wolf. 'Dionysius and Eros,' he continued. 'What more can a gladiator expect from life?'

'You're not the only one!' Valens, who had been studying her closely, spoke up. 'I know of at least three girls from the slums, one as young as twelve, who were attacked and raped

57

by a man with that tattoo. One of them claimed it was a gladiator, but there again,' he patted Spicerius on the shoulder, 'these men get blamed for everything. If a woman is raped or a man killed . . .' He paused. 'Yet I have found more honour amongst them than I have a group of priests.'

'Is there a temple devoted to Dionysius?' Claudia asked. 'I mean, one where the sign is the purple chalice?'

Spicerius shook his head.

'Many temples are dedicated to Dionysius or Bacchus, they are as common as fleas on a dog. No, it's more of a sign that you are a wine worshipper, which can earn you comradeship at a drinking club.' Spicerius paused and clutched his stomach. 'Just a cramp.' He winked. 'I'll be well enough to fight your man. This time, let the mob spare him.'

'Last time,' Claudia, embarrassed, was eager to change the subject, 'when you drank the poisoned wine, you saw nothing untoward, nothing out of the ordinary?'

'I was in the tunnel,' Spicerius replied, 'near the Gate of Life. I wanted the contest to begin. I drank the wine.' He tapped the tattoo on his wrist. 'I know my wine, it cleanses my mouth and wets the back of my throat.'

'Did you feel strange?' Claudia asked.

Spicerius screwed his eyes up. 'Ask your boyfriend here. Of course you feel strange before a fight. Your stomach pitches like a boat in a storm. Strange sounds echo in your ears. A drumming begins in your head. You want to run and shout and scream, but at the same time there is this icy coldness. You become aware of the smallest thing.'

'And in the arena?' Claudia asked.

'I went out,' Spicerius's face grew smooth; he had lost that mask of cynical arrogance, 'I really believed I had a chance. Suddenly I saw double, like you do when you have a knock on the head.' He patted his stomach. 'A fire was lit in my belly, I thought it would pass, but then my legs lost their strength. One thing I realised was that I had to vomit; if I didn't, I would die.' He turned and embraced Valens, drawing the old man close and kissing him on his head. 'If it wasn't for my good friend here, the great Spicerius would have died like some slave fainting with fear before a lion or panther.'

'Somebody drugged you,' Claudia insisted. 'Why?'

'Three reasons,' Murranus intervened, ticking the points off on his fingers. 'Somebody loves Murranus, or somebody hates Spicerius.'

'And thirdly?' Claudia asked.

'Somebody wagered heavily that I would win. It certainly wasn't me or anyone at this tavern.'

'But you should have died.' Claudia turned to Spicerius. 'You weren't meant to faint. Your secret attacker intended to kill you.' She glanced at the old physician, who was chomping on his lips, face turned to the sun, though he had been studying her carefully out of the corner of his eye.

'By the cock!' Valens whispered. 'You have a sharp one here, Murranus! Keen as a surgeon's knife. You're right, Spicerius should have died. Three things saved him. He has the constitution of an ox, he vomited the poison, and I was there to administer treatment. There's one further . . .' His voice trailed off.

'Yes?' Claudia asked. She was aware of how silent the garden had fallen. A butterfly flew between them, fluttering white in the light breeze.

'He should have died,' Valens murmured, 'but the assassin made a mistake. He, or she, didn't give him enough poison. It was sufficient to make him vomit, to cause the pain, but not enough to finish him off.'

'Spicerius!'

Claudia turned. A young woman, black hair floating around her face like a veil, came tripping across the grass, the folds of her costly gown flapping around her, a shawl protecting her back and shoulders from the sun. Behind her an old slave carried a parasol and two fat cushions. The woman paused and turned on him.

'Can't you keep up, you old fool!' she screamed. 'And this parasol is supposed to shade me from the sun!'

'Agrippina,' Spicerius murmured.

The young woman ran up in a gust of perfume and, without being invited, crouched down, flinging her arms around Spicerius's neck, kissing him hungrily on the side of his mouth and face before shrieking to the old slave to put the cushions down. Then she drew apart, made herself comfortable and gazed around, an impudent smile on her cheeky face.

As Agrippina blew a kiss at Murranus, Claudia tried to hide her stab of envy. The woman was truly beautiful. She had lovely expressive eyes in her ivory-skinned face, and her jewellery and earrings, all a blood red, glittered every time she moved, in a clatter of bangles and bracelets. She wore a wild flower in her hair and carried a perfumed napkin to cool the sweat on her neck and arms. She waggled her fingers at Valens but dismissed Claudia with a half-smile and a flick of her eyes.

'I've been searching for you everywhere,' she cooed, turning to Spicerius. 'What on earth are you doing in a place like this?'

'It's my place,' Claudia spoke up, 'and I'm wondering what a person like you is doing here.'

The smile disappeared from Agrippina's face. The old slave

hastily retreated. Agrippina took a fan from a pocket in her robe, snapped it open, stared hard at Claudia and then burst out laughing. She took a bracelet from her wrist and thrust it into Claudia's hand.

'I'm such a bitch,' she confessed, 'and such a snob! I meant no offence.'

'None taken,' Claudia answered, slipping the bracelet on to her wrist. 'Would you like some wine?'

Agrippina shook her head. 'I've been drinking all morning. What have you been discussing?'

'Who tried to kill Spicerius.'

'Well, it wasn't me,' Agrippina retorted. She leaned against her lover. 'We observed the rules, didn't we; we neither drank nor ate that morning. What Spicerius does, I always follow.' Her eyes turned soft. 'No offence, Murranus, but I truly thought Spicerius would win. My father is furious. I bet a fortune and lost.'

'I thought all money was to be returned?' Spicerius said.

Agrippina kissed him on his shoulder. 'No, that's what everyone is haggling about now. They will probably agree to hold the money until the next fight. Now listen, Spicerius, you must stay in the shade. Claudia – it is Claudia, isn't it? Do you mind if I stay here? I will help you.' She chattered on, talking so fast she hardly stopped to breathe.

Claudia excused herself, went across to the tavern and sent Oceanus out to see if all was well, she then returned to her own chamber. She drew the bolt across the door and lay down on the narrow cot bed. Polybius was now up, bellowing in the kitchens at whoever got in his way. Claudia's mind drifted back to the catacombs earlier that day, and the tattoo on Spicerius's wrist.

'One day,' she whispered, as her eyes grew heavy and she drifted into sleep.

She slept long and deep, and it was mid-afternoon before she woke. She splashed some water over her face and went down into the garden. Murranus and the rest were still there. They had decided to make a day of it playing dice and knuckle bones whilst ordering the best wine and food. Polybius of course, much the worse for drink, had been surly until he realised how wealthy Agrippina was. Now the cooks were busy roasting beef and goose, while in the cellars the tap boys were broaching the best casks. Claudia decided to join the company. Murranus was already deep in his cups and insisted on giving her the biggest hug and wine-drenched kisses. Claudia teased him back, and they were discussing the merits of Meleager the Magnificent when Polybius came hurrying out across the grass.

'There's a messenger from Tibur,' he declared. 'Claudia, you are to join the court at the Villa Pulchra.'

'My, my, my,' Murranus declared, 'you do have powerful friends.'

Claudia pulled a face and shook her head. 'I'm only a maid.' She kissed Murranus full on the mouth before he could add anything else.

'The imperial court?' Spicerius lifted his cup. 'When you get there, Claudia, give my love to the Captain of the Imperial Guard, Gaius Tullius. Tell him not to wear his airs and graces. I remember how, bare-arsed, we used to chase each other through the fields of Sisium. You won't forget, will you?'

Claudia promised, and hurriedly followed her uncle back into the tavern. There she recognised the pop-eyed steward, Timothaeus, face all red, laughing at a doleful Burrus, dressed in his shabby armour, who was being teased by one of the pot boys. The huge German mercenary seemed to fill the room. He had ignored his taunter but was glaring at Simon the Stoic, who knew some German and hadn't hesitated in using it to insult the visitor. Januaria, however, was suitably impressed. She had sidled over, plucking at the great bearskin which, despite the heat, Burrus had draped over his shoulders. Poppaoe came out of the kitchen, screaming abuse, and Januaria disappeared. Claudia greeted both the guests and clattered up the stairs to collect her cloak and hat and push a few possessions into a set of leather panniers.

When she came back downstairs, she kissed Poppaoe and Polybius goodbye, waved to the regular customers and went out to where a small crowd had gathered to gape at Burrus's entourage. The mercenaries recognised Claudia and grunted at her. Anyone else would have regarded this as an insult, but Claudia knew that it was the warmest greeting these dour men would give. They had brought a gentle cob for her to ride. Burrus helped her mount, and they left for the city gates and the Via Latina.

The day's business was finishing and people were streaming out of the city. The streets were packed, people shoving and pushing, the air riven with the chatter of different tongues, hordes of screaming children, and the hustle and bustle of the markets as stalls were cleared and put away for the night. Craftsmen in their workshops used the last hours of the summer day to finish their tasks. Outside the entrances to these shops and eating houses, pedlars and hustlers bawled, desperate to make a sale before sunset. The dusty air reeked of grease, tallow candle, burnt oil, incense, cooked meat, dried fish and, above all, the sweat of the hot, tired crowd. Soldiers from the garrisons mingled with customers at the wine booths and beer shops, reluctantly moving aside for the sedan chair or litter of a wealthy nobleman. Claudia loved such sights. People of various nationalities thronged around, Ethiopians and Nubians in their panther and leopard skins, Egyptian priests garbed in ostentatious white robes, shaven heads gleaming with oil, Syrians in their striped cloaks, dark bearded faces glistening with sweat. Of course, as the day faded, Rome's underworld also came to life: the sorcerers and conjurors, the footpads and pickpockets, all brushed shoulders with dancers, whores and pimps as they came into the streets eager for mischief.

Claudia's party skirted the main thoroughfare and crossed the square, where the Vigiles were fighting a gang of youths who'd flung a pig from the top floor of an apartment block. A mad old man now danced round the gory mess, chanting a garbled hymn. A group of gladiators were gathering on the steps of the temple to pay votive thanks to a god. Claudia wondered what Murranus would be doing that evening. Once across the square, Burrus and his escort moved to the front and forced their way on to a broad avenue lined by statues. They had to move slowly. They'd left the slums and were now on the main approach to the city gates. Here the crowds were even thicker, the wealthy carried by their slaves, the poor pushing some ancient relative wrapped in a blanket and placed in a wheelbarrow. They passed colonnaded walks and arrived at the city gates; these were guarded by Samaritan mercenaries who lounged against the walls or wooden posts wolf-whistling at any attractive woman. The noise, the dust, the heat and flies made any conversation impossible. Burrus was in a deep sulk, although Claudia could see Timothaeus was desperate to talk to her.

As they moved along the Via Latina, the buildings grew fewer, the smell of the countryside more fragrant. They passed the city cemeteries; the tombs rearing up, dark against the light blue sky, grim reminders of the brevity of life.

Somewhere in the crowd a boy began to sing a lovely lilting tune, with sweet verses about a house with a welcoming table set out in the shade of an olive grove. Claudia listened intently but Timothaeus was now eager to make speed and produced his imperial pass to move more briskly through the crowds. At last they reached the crossroads, marked by soaring wooden poles with skulls placed at the base: a place of execution. Criminals would carry their cross bar here, against which they would be crucified. Someone had lit an oil lamp near the posts and placed beside it a bouquet of wild flowers. Claudia wondered about their significance as she reflected on what a topsy-turvy world she lived in, where the Empire now did business with a religious sect whose God they had crucified. She recalled what Sylvester had said to her, and, studying Timothaeus's anxious face, wondered what was awaiting at the Villa Pulchra. She quietly prayed, to any god who bothered to listen, that Murranus would take care of himself during her absence and keep out of mischief.

They paused to drink at a water fountain. Claudia revelled in the dark coolness of the laurel, cypress and olive trees, and the greenery, albeit scorched by the sun, of the bushes and grass stretching out either side of her. Birds swooped above them, whilst in the grass along the track crickets continued their busy song. Burrus grated an order and they remounted. They crossed brooks and streams, their horses' hoofs clattering nervously. Now and again they would be greeted by servants and children running down a lane from a villa or farmstead.

After a while, Timothaeus pulled his horse back, drawing alongside Claudia's. They had met before, at court, but Timothaeus, ignoring all protocol and etiquette, now chattered to her like some long-lost sister. Not pausing for a breath, he described in rushed sentences how the Holy Sword had been stolen, the uproar this had caused, followed by the brutal murder of Dionysius.

'No one knows who did it!' Timothaeus shook his head as if talking to himself. 'No one at all, but I have a theory. I mean, if you are going to murder someone, why not just bang them on the back of the head and leave them. Not like that poor bugger. He was bound and dragged through the garden, pegged out like some criminal in the amphitheatre.' He leaned across, eyes round with amazement. 'He must have bled to death.'

'And no one heard his screams?'

'Gagged, he was, a piece of hard leather pushed into his mouth.'

'You were talking about the murder. You have a theory?'

'Oh, yes.' Timothaeus gathered the reins with one hand, lowering his voice as if Burrus was an eavesdropper, but the German seemed more intent on finishing the wine skin he'd unhooked from his saddle horn. 'I believe,' the steward continued breathlessly, 'that Dionysius was killed by those other philosophers. You know what a group of bitches they are, jealous about this, jealous about that! I expect they got into an argument and decided to kill him.'

'In which case,' Claudia smiled, 'why didn't they do as you describe, just hit him on the head and leave it at that?'

'Ah, yes,' Timothaeus screwed his face up in concentration, as he tried to reflect on that great mystery. Of course, he had his answer: how the philosophers were a cruel group of bitches. Claudia half listened, realising with a sinking heart that she was about to enter a snake pit. From what Timothaeus had told her, she had already concluded that Dionysius's murder was not an act of passion but a cold, calculated, cruel act where the victim was made to suffer for as long as possible.

Burrus, who had finished the wine skin, and was desperate for more, now urged them into a gallop. The air was growing cooler, shadows laced the path and the red-gold sky was darkening. Eventually they reached the winding track leading up to the Villa Pulchra. Claudia had visited it many years ago, but she was still surprised by the grandeur and opulence of the buildings clustered on the brow of the hill. They passed guard posts, soldiers on picket duty crouching round their camp fires, a glowing avenue of flame stretching up to the main gate set in the soaring curtain wall. Timothaeus demanded entrance; an officer came out, passes were inspected and the gate swung open. They entered the courtyard, which reeked of the stables. Soldiers and servants lounged on benches, drinking and chattering as they played with knuckle bones and dice.

Claudia dismounted. Ostlers came to take her horse, and any aches or pains she felt were soon forgotten as Timothaeus led her on a hasty tour of the villa. First they visited the peristyle garden, exquisitely perfumed and lit by hundreds of oil lamps in their translucent alabaster jars, glowing like fireflies against the dusk. Claudia was aware of lush lawns, irrigated by narrow canals and overlooked by countless carved statues of gods and goddesses, nymphs and fauns. As she walked, she glimpsed fountains and pools of purity, reed-ringed carp ponds, colonnaded walks, marble walls and floors, gorgeous paintings, beautiful ornaments, brilliant-hued tapestries and delicate furniture. They went down corridors and galleries, guarded by soldiers from the imperial regiments as well as mercenaries from the personal comitatus of the Emperor and his mother. The kitchens, carving rooms, bakeries and pantries were busy with sweat-soaked servants hurrying around. The imperial banquet had already begun, the doors closed, so they kept well away from the triclinium where the Emperor and his guests ate and drank to the soft music of the imperial orchestra.

'Dionysius's death,' Timothaeus commented sharply, 'was certainly no excuse to spoil a good supper party.'

He took Claudia to the kitchens for a light meal of spiced sausages, damsons and a cup of chilled white wine. Afterwards he showed her to her chamber, a narrow closet containing a bed, a stool, a carved chest and a peg on the door to hang her clothes. She was allowed to wash and change before being taken to the Empress's antechamber, a white-walled, marble-floored room, the brilliance of its colours deliberately emphasising the dark blue and red medallion paintings in the centre of each wall. Claudia sat on a couch and stared up at one of these paintings depicting some Emperor entering Rome in triumph. She was fascinated by the detail, the way the horses on the chariot turned their heads, so life-like she expected the animals to move and to hear the clatter of their hoofs or the crack of reins.

'Well, little mouse!'

Claudia started. The Empress had opened the door and was leaning gracefully against it. Claudia jumped to her feet, and would have knelt, but the Empress, face rather flushed, grasped her by the hand and sat down beside her on the couch, staring up at the painting.

'That's supposed to be the great Caesar, Claudia, after he had conquered Egypt and brought Cleopatra back to Rome. I always look for her but can't find her. The painting is fascinating, isn't it? If you stare at it long enough you feel as if you are becoming part of the great triumph. Well, little one, you are now part of my world again and I want you to watch, study and listen. You had a pleasant journey? Good.' Helena didn't wait for a reply. 'And how's your Murranus? You should thank the gods that he didn't kill Spicerius.' She smiled at Claudia's astonishment and kissed her gently on the brow. 'Sometimes, little mouse, you can be as cunning as a serpent, at other times as innocent as a dove. You hadn't thought of that, had you?'

'No, no, your Excellency.'

'Augusta will do.' Helena smiled, 'Oh, forgive my friend-liness. I drank one cup too many of Falernian. But yes,' she caressed Claudia's hand, 'that's where Murranus could have made a terrible mistake. It was obvious Spicerius was in diffi-culties. You saw me watching? I was fascinated. I even forgot the letter I was reading. Any other gladiator would have closed in, seized the moment, and that's where the real trouble would have begun.'

'And what would have happened?' Claudia asked. She had forgotten her tiredness and the fact that she was in the pres-ence of the Empress.

'I don't really know.' Helena chewed the corner of her mouth. 'That's an interesting question. My son will know, I must ask him. But come.' She got to her feet, dragging Claudia with her. 'I've drunk too much and it's hot in here.' She gestured at the oil lamps on the table. 'And if I keep staring at them, I'll fall asleep.'

The Empress took her out into the small garden, one of those private paradises especially set aside for the imperial family, with a lawn, flowerbeds and marble seats around a fountain carved in the shape of Cupid carrying a fish. The garden was bounded by a high red-bricked wall with no gate, the only entrance being from inside the palace.

'You see,' Helena declared, sitting down on the marble bench with her back to the fountain, 'you can sit here, chatter away and watch the entrance. Not like those other gardens, eh, where a spy can crouch under a bush or even up a tree? Oh yes,' she laughed, 'I've heard of that happening. Now, Claudia, forget about your gladiator and listen to what I have to say.'

The Empress's description of the theft of the Holy Sword and the murder of Dionysius was similar to Timothaeus's except that, as usual, Helena saw darker, more sinister motives.

'The sword could have been stolen,' she concluded, 'to embarrass me or, perhaps, so that suspicion would fall on the Christians gathered here. After all, I do know they resent a pagan like myself collecting their sacred relics.'

'But you are not a pagan, Augusta. You support the Christian faith.'

'I haven't been baptised,' Helena whispered, 'and neither has my son. One day, perhaps, but until then, in the eyes of many Christians I am just another pagan.'

'And Dionysius's murder?'

'Again,' Helena dabbed water from the fountain pool on to her face, 'it might be the work of a troublemaker trying to provoke the resentment which separates the two groups of Christians.'

'Or?' Claudia asked.

'May the Lord of Light prevent it, but Dionysius's murder may truly be the work of the Christians themselves. That's why you are here, Claudia.' Helena stood up and patted her gently on the cheek. 'Tomorrow morning begin your scurrying, ask your questions.' She began to stroll away, but then stopped and glanced over her shoulder. 'Go to bed, little mouse, and never forget, where there's mice there's always a cat!'

'It's strange, isn't it, how the white lotus flowers only at night and the blue only in daytime?'

Claudia whirled round. The man in the shadows behind her was dressed in a long tunic, the folds of his toga hiding one arm, but in his free hand Claudia caught the glitter of a wicked-looking curved sword. Its owner brought it up in a swift arc, slicing the air between them. Claudia remained still; again the sword cut, swishing through air, then the stranger brought it back so the flat of the blade was against his face, the tip pointing upwards.

'Claudia, I salute you.'

'Some people would say you are trying to frighten me.'

'And some people would say that's impossible. I know all about you, Claudia. The Augusta calls you her "little mouse", though one, I suspect, with very sharp teeth and claws.'

Gaius Tullius came into the pool of light. Claudia had seen him before, though only from afar; she recognised the sharp, narrow face and rather soulful eyes. Gaius was a professional soldier, one of the Emperor's drinking partners, a man he trusted implicitly. Now he sketched a bow, placed the sword on the ground and sat down next to her on the edge of the pool. Claudia never moved, watching the soldier stare into the water, rippling it with his fingers, sending the carp darting away.

'I've drunk too much,' he sighed, flicking the water from his fingers. 'Imperial supper or not, there's still duties to be done and guards to be checked. I know you arrived a short while ago; I met Timothaeus. That man runs around like a frightened duck, but he's good-hearted enough.'

'I bring you greetings,' Claudia replied. 'Spicerius the gladiator said you are to have no airs and graces, for he remembers you when you were a bare-arsed boy . . .'

'So long ago,' Gaius declared wistfully. 'So much has happened.' He pointed to the lotus blossom. 'I served in Egypt. I visited the temples of Memphis, Karnak and Luxor. The lotus always fascinated me. It is carved everywhere, a symbol of so much.' He leaned a little closer, his eyes smiling. 'It is also the source,' he whispered, 'of the most fragrant perfume, Kiphye. They say Cleopatra bathed in it.'

'I thought she used asses' milk?'

Gaius pulled a face. 'Not so sweet,' he conceded. 'Anyway,' he shrugged, 'in ten years there will be Christian symbols everywhere. All is changing.'

'Are you opposed to them?'

'I don't care, Claudia. I'm a soldier. I pay my dues to the Sun God Mithras and fight the enemies of the Empire.'

'Timothaeus told me you found Dionysius's corpse?'

'Yes, pegged out like a tanner's skin. Sometimes it's hard to realise how much blood the human body contains.'

'Do you suspect anyone?'

'Perhaps his colleagues.' Gaius stared up at the sky. 'Or one of his friends. I'm telling you a lie,' he murmured. 'I'm not really here just because of guard duty. In fact, I've been searching for you. I've brought you this.'

He dug into the folds of his robe, took out a small scroll and handed it to Claudia.

'I had Dionysius's corpse brought to the House of Mourning,' he explained. 'It's nothing more than a brick-built shed with a tiled roof. It's the villa's mortuary. Then I went to Dionysius's chamber. I thought the motive for the killing might be robbery, but the room was undisturbed, though not very clean – after all, Dionysius was a philosopher. There were a few books, some manuscripts. I searched amongst them and found that.' Gaius half smiled. 'I know that you work for the Empress!' He patted Claudia on the shoulder and got up. 'Read it. I'm not sure if it is a draft or the original.' He picked up his sword and walked away.

'Gaius! I can call you Gaius?'

'Of course,' he smiled, coming back.

'Did you see anything about that corpse, any evidence pointing to a possible killer?'

He shook his head.

'And the Holy Sword?'

Gaius snorted with laughter. 'I was fast asleep when it was stolen, but how, why and by whom?' He was about to continue when the air was rent by a high-pitched scream, followed by the bray of trumpets and the clash of cymbals as the alarm was raised.

Chapter 4

'O tempora! O Mores!'
('What times! What Manners!')

Cicero, *In Catilinam*, I

By the time they had hurried along passageways and colonnades, across gardens and through gates, the House of Mourning at the far side of the villa was almost consumed by fire. The flames were so strong, the heat so intense, the roof had already fallen in and the facing wall was buckling. Servants, officials, soldiers and members of the imperial family came hurrying through the trees, yet there was nothing to be done. Timothaeus was trying to organise a chain of water carriers but this was fruitless. Burrus ran up with a bucket but he was so drunk he threw both water and bucket into the fire then nearly careered into the burning house and had to be pulled back by a member of his own retinue. The Germans then began to sing and dance, intoning one of their wild hymns, until the Empress's voice cut like a lash telling them to shut up. Claudia turned and glanced across, the smell of wood smoke making her cough. The imperial party was sheltering under an outstretched sycamore. She walked towards them. Sylvester was standing serenely behind the Empress; Constantine sat on a camp stool, face all flushed, hands on his knees, thoroughly enjoying the spectacle.

'Was anyone in there alive?' he bawled.

'Just two corpses, Excellency,' Timothaeus shouted back. 'Dionysius and a wanderer in the woods, a beggar man found dead on the track outside.'

'Well, they are truly dead now, grilled and cooked to a cinder!' the Emperor joked.

Helena gestured at Claudia to draw closer. Constantine blew her a kiss. Sylvester, still standing behind the Emperor, sketched a bow whilst Chrysis, his fat, oiled face beaming with pleasure, poked his tongue out at her.

'Lovely fire,' the Emperor sighed. 'Marvellous to watch the flames.'

'Arson,' Helena snapped back. 'An imperial building has been destroyed.'

'Arson?' Constantine glanced up at his mother. 'By all that's holy, who would want to burn corpses?'

'Perhaps the Imperial Treasurer?' Chrysis sniggered. 'It's saved the cost of a burial.'

'Was it arson?' Constantine repeated, all humour draining from his face.

'Look at the fire,' Helena answered exasperatedly. 'What would cause flames to burn so fiercely? Timothaeus,' she shouted, 'was there anything combustible in there?'

'Nothing, Augusta.' Timothaeus came over, face covered in ash. 'Nothing at all.' Without being invited, he sat down on the grass, mopping his face with a rag.

'Why arson?' Rufinus the banker repeated the Emperor's question.

Helena nudged Claudia.

'Dionysius was murdered.'

'Speak up, girl!' Constantine barked.

'Dionysius was murdered,' Claudia repeated loudly. 'His body was placed in the House of Mourning. I suspect the corpse bore some clue as to the identity of his killer.'

'But what?' Helena asked. 'He was sliced like a roll of ham and bled to death. I scrutinised his corpse.'

'Augusta,' Claudia smiled, 'you asked me a question and I replied. I'm not too sure what the arsonist wished to hide.'

'It could have been someone else.' Chrysis's voice was rich with spite. 'Oh, how these Christians love each other! Don't they say that those who attack the teaching of their faith will be consumed, body and soul, in Hell's fire?'

'Not at my expense they won't,' Constantine grumbled. 'Chrysis,' the Emperor got to his feet, 'find the bastard who started that blaze, and if he hasn't got a good explanation, crucify him outside the gates. Mother, I've seen enough of this. We need to talk.'

The imperial party swept back into the palace. Claudia stayed under the sycamore tree, and in the light from the fire she read the scroll Gaius had given her. The letter was short and to the point. Signed by Dionysius, it was directed to Athanasius, leader of the orthodox party. In it, Dionysius confessed how he had prayed, fasted and reflected, and now saw the error of his ways. Accordingly, at the appropriate time, when the Holy Spirit directed him, he would renounce his errors publicly and accept the forgiveness of his Bishop.

'Doomed in life! Doomed in death!' The voice was rich and

carrying. Claudia looked up. Three men stood like shadows before her, their backs to the fire.

'I'm sorry,' she smiled, quickly hiding the letter, 'are you talking about me or the late departed?'

The figure in the centre walked forward. He was short and thick-set, narrow-faced with fierce eyes and hungry mouth, he was dressed in a simple dark tunic over thick baggy leggings.

'My name is Athanasius.' He gestured to his two companions. 'This is Aurelian and Septimus. We wondered who was speaking to the Empress and someone told us you are Claudia, Augusta's messenger. Others say you are her spy.' Athanasius leaned down, lips parted to show fine, strong teeth. 'Presbyter Sylvester speaks highly of you.'

Claudia moved so she could get a better look at these three members of the orthodox party. Athanasius exuded strength, with his harsh mouth and square jaw. He reminded her of a soldier, his auburn hair cropped close to his head, while his clothes were those of a mercenary rather than an orator. His two companions were more disciples than colleagues, young and smooth-faced with shaven heads. They too were dressed rather coarsely, in long gowns with cords round the middle and sandals on their feet.

'They're my disciples,' Athanasius explained, 'who have been baptised and accept the one true faith. Do you accept the true faith, Claudia?'

'I accept the truth,' she replied, gesturing at the fire, 'and I do wonder, as your God will, why Dionysius should die in such a horrid fashion and his corpse be so dishonoured. Don't you Christians have burial rites?'

'It is the spirit which counts; the flesh doesn't matter.'

'Does that include yours, Magister? If Dionysius was

murdered, why not another orator? Has murder replaced philosophy in the debate?'

'We don't know why Dionysius died,' Athanasius replied.

'And we don't really care,' Septimus shouted, like a spiteful child. 'He got his just deserts.'

Even from where she stood, despite the poor light, Claudia could see the prim set of Septimus's mouth, and the quivering disapproval in his face.

'People will ask,' she gestured at the fire, 'are you responsible?'

'We are not responsible,' Athanasius declared.

'Why are you so certain?' Claudia took a step forward. 'Is it because Dionysius was planning to change sides, acknowledge your arguments?'

Athanasius looked shocked; his two companions hissed their disapproval.

'He was planning to change sides,' Claudia continued remorselessly. 'I have seen a letter dictated to you, Athanasius, in which Dionysius denounces his own beliefs and accepts the orthodox position, which, I believe,' Claudia closed her eyes, 'is that your Jesus Christ is of the same substance as the Father.'

The smoke made Claudia cough. She felt the phlegm at the back of her throat so she turned and spat, a gesture she knew would offend these men.

'You say I'm a spy, the Empress's messenger, so let me take a message to her from you.'

'Which is?'

'Where were you when Dionysius was killed?'

'We were gathered in council,' Athanasius blustered. 'Sharing ideas. You cannot place his death at our door.'

Claudia glared at these philosophers so passionately righteous about themselves. Athanasius returned her stare but looked away as Justin came over. He was acting the role of the professional mourner.

'Even in death,' he wailed, 'they will not leave us alone.'

Athanasius immediately asked what he meant by 'they' and an argument ensued. Claudia, bored, walked away. The flames were dying, the front wall had now buckled completely and all she could see were a few charred timbers. She crouched in the grass and plucked at a wild flower. She was sure the fire was arson, and certainly started by the same person who had killed Dionysius. The motive could have been to insult the dead man's corpse, though Claudia wasn't so sure about that. Arson took time to plan and posed risks for the perpetrator. She recalled the alarm being raised, hurrying across with Gaius. By the time they arrived, the fire had caught hold, so it must have started when they had been sitting near the fountain. The inside would have been soaked with oil and a fire brand thrown in, but why?

She rose to her feet and stared around. The spectators were now drifting away. She noticed Gaius talking with some of his soldiers near the entrance to the palace. She walked over and waited until she caught the Captain's eye. Gaius excused himself and strode across.

'Claudia, you should go to bed. There's been enough excitement for one day.' He waved a hand to waft away a gust of smoke. 'Undoubtedly arson.'

'Were any guards here?' Claudia asked.

'Outside the far wall, yes, but I didn't think two corpses needed to be protected. Apparently a servant smelt smoke and came running out. By then the flames were licking through the door, so the alarm was raised.'

'Why burn two corpses?' Claudia asked.

Gauis pulled a face.

'When you took Dionysius's corpse to the Death House,' Claudia continued, 'how exactly was it done?'

Gaius glanced back towards his men and ran a thumbnail around his lips.

'I found the corpse,' he began slowly. 'I was with a patrol. We were going for a pleasant walk rather than anything else. The Empress was called, and the villa physician, a garrulous old man with watery eyes.' Gaius smiled. 'I remember him because he made me laugh. He inspected the corpse very carefully and then pronounced, 'Yes, your Excellency, the man is dead.' Even Helena smiled. One of my men tried to cut the ropes, but there was very little slack between the dead man's wrist and the peg, so we pulled the pegs out. A stretcher was brought, and the corpse was loaded on.'

'With the ropes and pegs still around wrists and ankles?'

'Yes, yes, I'm sure! It was then taken to the House of Mourning. There are slabs around the walls, and the place stank from the old beggar who had been found earlier that morning. Anyway, we placed Dionysius on a slab and left him.'

'What would have happened then?'

'I'll make enquiries, but I suppose a slave was sent to strip the corpse and wash it.'

'So what would have happened to Dionysius's clothes, and the ropes and pegs?'

'They would probably have been left in the Death House,' Gaius replied, 'unless the slave took them to the rubbish heap. Why?' He peered at Claudia.

'If it was arson,' Claudia declared, 'the person who started it wanted to hide something. I wonder what? But you're right.' She stared at the sky. 'It must be near midnight.'

She thanked Gaius and walked back to the palace, pausing to admire a bust of the Emperor's father. Rufinus and Chrysis came out of a chamber, talking quietly to each other. They fell silent when they saw Claudia. Chrysis glared at her malevolently. He resented her presence and her influence with the Empress. Rufinus was about to smile but turned away, then clicked his fingers and came hurrying towards her.

'Claudia, I knew there was something I wanted to ask, Murranus, is he well?'

'A little embarrassed,' Claudia declared, 'but ready to fight again.'

'I know, I know.' The banker scratched his thinning silver hair, his lean face tense with concentration.

'I hope it doesn't happen again.' Chrysis spoke up. 'Rufinus is my witness, I placed a heavy bet on your boyfriend; we thought we'd at least get our money back.'

'You had such confidence in Murranus?'

'I know Spicerius,' Chrysis retorted, leaning closer like a conspirator. 'He drinks wine and spends too much time bouncing the divine Agrippina. They say he is slowing up. I actually laid two wagers: the first that Murranus would win and the second that there would be a kill within the hour. Didn't I, Rufinus?'

'He laid the wager with me,' the banker confirmed. 'All of Rome is talking about what we should do. Did Murranus win? Did Spicerius lose? Should the money be given back?'

'And what have you decided?' Claudia tried to keep her voice steady.

'Well, as you know,' Rufinus smiled sourly, 'in a week's time special games are to be held to celebrate the Emperor's birthday. All being well, Murranus and Spicerius will meet again. The bets will be carried forward.'

Rufinus bade Claudia goodnight, Chrysis waggled his fingers obscenely at her and they both went back along the corridor.

Claudia decided to wander the palace. She felt physically tired, but her mind teemed like a beehive. She found herself near the peristyle garden and asked the guard where the cellar was. He gave her directions. Claudia first went to the kitchens, where she borrowed a lantern horn from a sleepy-eyed cook, who lit the oil lamp inside, secured the small door and handed it to her.

'Don't walk too fast,' he warned. 'Let the wick burn fiercely for a while.'

Claudia sat outside on a bench and watched the flame in the lantern horn strengthen before picking it up and finding her way to the cellar. The door was now unguarded, off the latch. She went carefully down the steps. The door at the bottom was flung open and Claudia went inside. She walked slowly, tapping the ground with her sandalled foot. The floor was of hard baked brick; the lime-washed walls had some cracks and crevices, the occasional gap, but there was no opening or any sign of another entrance. The ceiling too looked firm and secure, ribbed by heavy beams, the plaster in between hard and even.

Satisfied, Claudia approached the great circle of sand and sat down on one of the stools, staring up at the chain. She noticed how the links were well moulded and the hook at the end long and sharply curved. She closed her eyes. How could the robbery have happened? Gaius had been sleeping in the garden. The door to the chamber was held secure by two different locks and guarded by the Empress's own mercenaries. Timothaeus and Burrus had unlocked it. The steward had explained to her how he checked the cellar three times a day to make sure that all was well, although, he confessed, he also wished to venerate such a holy relic. Claudia opened her eyes and glanced over her shoulder at the door.

'So you came in here, Timothaeus,' she murmured, 'reached

the edge of the circle, stared at the chain, and noticed the sword was gone?'

Claudia could understand Timothaeus's shock; no wonder he'd fainted! The disappearance of the sword, not to mention the Empress's wrath, would unnerve the strongest man. She stared down at the sand sprinkled with gold dust; now it had been disturbed by those who had come to search the cellar afterwards.

'Claudia! Claudia!'

She turned round and gaped in horror. A figure shrouded in a cloak stood in the doorway. Claudia, hand trembling, lifted up the lantern. 'Who is it?' she called. The figure remained still.

Claudia rose, carrying the lantern before her. She was halfway across the chamber when she realised that whoever it was had not only hidden their body under a heavy cloak but also their face under a hideous mask of a satyr. Claudia's mouth turned dry. She almost dropped the lantern as the figure moved quickly, coming into the chamber, slamming the door shut. Claudia moved back.

'Who are you?' she demanded. She tried to recall the voice, but it could have been anyone's. In the light of the lantern the satyr mask looked malevolent. She noticed the long stabbing dagger this grotesque now carried. She kept moving back, desperately trying to recall if she had seen anything in the cellar she could use to protect herself. Her leg hit one of the stools, and she picked this up and moved back into the circle of sand. She'd made a mistake! The sand was very soft and deep and her feet immediately sank, the sand coming up to her ankles, impeding her retreat. The figure walked slowly forward, carefully, measuring each step. Claudia lunged forward, trying to extricate herself from the sand. She flung the stool at her attacker. It narrowly missed. She picked up another stool. Retreating round the circle of sand, she began to scream and yell, throwing one stool after another, trying to discourage this nightmare figure, so silent, so menacing.

At last, desperate, Claudia threw the lantern. It crashed at the feet of her assailant, and the flame burst out and, by mere chance, caught the edge of the grotesque's cloak. Claudia, almost hysterical with fear, gabbled a prayer as the flame caught the dry cloth, and her opponent quickly retreated, taking off the cloak. The cellar door was flung open and the assailant fled. Claudia immediately ran after, through the half-open door, but there was no sign, nothing but a dirty cloak lying on the steps. She picked this up. The cloak was threadbare, soiled and smelt rank. The flames had died, leaving a charred, frayed edge lit by the occasional spark. Claudia stamped on these and returned to the cellar, picking her way carefully through the fallen stools. The lantern was smashed, the flame extinguished. Claudia cursed her own foolishness. She shouldn't have come here in the first place; perhaps it had been even more stupid to return. She ran to the door, slamming it behind her, and raced up the steps.

The small passageway beyond was empty, with no trace of her attacker. Claudia went into the peristyle garden and, for a while, sat on a bench, gulping in the fresh night air. She stared at the guard standing some distance away in the shadows, wondering if he had seen anything. She shrugged to herself. If he had, he would have come over.

Claudia washed her hands in the pool and made her way back to her chamber. Inside she found everything neat and tidy; a slave had lit the lamp on the table opposite her bed. She was too tired to wash and change, and she was about to blow out the lamp when she noticed the small purple chalice crudely painted on the wall above the lantern. She drew back. She didn't extinguish the lamp, but climbed into bed staring at the drawing. She let her mind drift on all that had happened today, faces, scenes and words, and all the time she glared at that crude drawing as if confronting an enemy, refusing to give way. She was still staring when her eyes grew heavy and she fell into a deep sleep.

Claudia woke early the next morning, roused by the sunlight and noise from the villa pouring through the unshuttered window above her narrow bed. She punched the flock-filled mattress and lay back, one hand beneath her cheek, recalling the terrors of the previous night and contemplating that hideous little picture above the oil lamp shelf. Eventually she got out of bed and examined it more carefully, tracing the outline with her fingernail. The paint was hard, a purple dye used by women to henna their nails, but when she pressed it, a crack appeared. Claudia was tempted to scrape it off but changed her mind. 'No,' she whispered, 'you can stay there, a reminder to me, a goad to spur me on. I shall find who you are and deal with you.'

She sat on the edge of the bed, reflecting how the mysterious painter, whoever he was, had intended to taunt and frighten her. She remembered that gruesome figure in the cellar, masked, armed and advancing so slowly towards her. 'That's it,' she whispered, 'you weren't trying to kill me, but terrify me!' She glared at the painting of the purple chalice. 'And you are trying to do the same now.' The confrontation in the cellar had been frightening but perhaps not deadly. She had watched gladiators train and fight; true killers came as swiftly as panthers or they struck from afar with arrow, slingshot, javelin or throwing knife. Last night's spectacle was intended to terrify

Helena's little mouse, to drive her off, make her scurry for safety.

Claudia stood up. Well, they would see. Nevertheless, although she summoned up her courage, she felt her stomach grumble with fear. 'This time was to frighten me,' she murmured, 'but next time . . . ?'

She grabbed her napkin and small leather toilet bag from the panniers slung on the peg on the door, then left her quarters and walked quickly to the luxuriantly furnished latrines, built near the kitchens so as to use the water flushed from there to keep them clean. She sat on a marble bench and stared at the mosaic on the floor, a beautiful scene depicting silver dolphins leaping about a golden sea. Timothaeus came in. He was much the worse for drink and squatted opposite looking dolefully into the middle distance.

'It's my stomach, you see,' he moaned. 'I drink too much wine and eat the rich food of the court.'

Claudia tried to engage him in conversation, but the steward shook his head and muttered about the anger of the Augusta. Claudia concluded he had been the recipient of her tart tongue.

After she had washed and left the latrines and bathhouse, Claudia returned to her own chamber, finished her dressing and decided to eat. She had to cross a small garden, nothing more than a lawn ringed with box hedges and shaded by laurel leaves. The Empress Helena, in an exquisite white linen robe, a purple mantle about her shoulders, was standing on a gold-fringed stool, gesturing with one hand, a cane in the other. Before her on the grass knelt Burrus and the entire German mercenary corps; they crouched heads down, hands to their faces, sobbing like children as Helena berated them.

'You are nothing but the scum of Germany,' she rasped, 'the filthy moss from your own dark forest, yet I have taken you and treated you like my children. I have clasped you to my heart and showered you with love and affection.' She paused to allow her words to sink in. She must have glimpsed Claudia, who stood fascinated beneath a tree, but she did not turn or acknowledge her presence. 'Have I not lavished upon you tasty food, comfortable quarters, as well as my protection and patronage? Have I not put up with your filthy ways and drunken singing?' She climbed down from the stool and walked amongst the warriors, giving each of them a rap on their shoulders with her cane. Now and again she'd pause to ruffle their hair or pat someone gently on the cheek.

Her diatribe had the desired effect. Burrus, thought Claudia, would make a fine actor. He threw his hands up in the air in a gesture any Greek dramatist would envy and began to tear the gold bracelets from his wrist and the thick silver chain from about his neck. Grasping these in his hands, he rose and walked towards Helena, tears streaming down his face, then threw himself at the Empress's feet.

'You've all been naughty boys,' Helena continued, digging her cane into Burrus's back, 'and yet, in my time, have I not praised you? Has not my son smiled on you and opened the hand of generosity to you? But what do you do? You repay my lavish kindness by becoming as drunk as sots and chasing every maid.' The rest of the German corps now had their noses pressed against the grass. Helena turned swiftly, and smiled and winked at Claudia before returning to the attack. 'You should have been more vigilant,' she declared. 'Dionysius should not have died, the House of Mourning should not have been burnt, but what cut my heart was the disappearance of the Holy Sword! I entrusted that to your care.' The wailing from her bodyguard grew. Helena returned to stand on the stool and Burrus tried to follow her, but she yelled at him to keep his head down. 'Nevertheless, you ungrateful scum,' she continued, 'I have decided to pardon you.' Burrus sat back on his heels and smiled dazzlingly at this woman whom he worshipped and adored. 'In my great kindness,' Helena rested on the cane, 'I have forgiven you.'

Claudia could no longer contain her own amusement. She hurried out of the garden and into the palace, where she stopped abruptly and glanced back. The Empress was an actress who kept that horde of ruffians in a grip of iron. The Germans worshipped the ground she trod on; they regarded it as the greatest honour to shed their blood for her. Helena knew that, so why berate them now?

Claudia sat down on a marble window seat and stared at a painting of Bacchus climbing a vine terrace to steal luscious grapes. Was Helena's confrontation with the Germans for some other purpose? The Germans were loyal, warriors born and bred; they were also drunkards, lechers and, above all, great thieves. Had they stolen the sword? The mercenaries had a deep awe of anything religious, and Burrus had refused to go into the Sacred Place, yet Claudia wasn't fooled by his slouching ways and uncouth appearance. Burrus was a highly intelligent man, sly and skilled. Had that been part of an act, a pretence to mislead people? Claudia recalled the cellar, the two guards outside, Burrus with the key. Timothaeus the steward was such a fusspot. Had the door been locked with two keys or only one? Had Timothaeus thought he had locked the door with his, but somehow been fooled by the Germans? If that was so, it would be easy for Burrus to unlock the door himself, take the sword, leave the cellar and relock the door. Timothaeus would come down ... Claudia paused. What would happen then? Had Burrus switched the keys, or had the lock been tampered with so Timothaeus thought his key was turning when really the door was already open?

Forgetting her terrors of the previous evening, Claudia borrowed a lantern and returned to the cellar, tripping quickly down the steps. She deliberately ignored what had happened previously and, crouching down, examined both locks, the first above the handle, the other beneath. Holding the lamp close, she examined the rim of the door and the lock but could detect no scraping, no sign of any tampering. Exasperated, she got to her feet. If her theory was correct, Burrus must have fooled Timothaeus into thinking that he had locked the door when he hadn't.

Claudia sighed, opened the door and went into the cellar. 'Let us say,' she spoke loudly, pretending to be in a school-room, 'that the thief enters.' She walked to the edge of the circle and stretched out to touch the chain, but couldn't reach. She climbed on to a stool but that too was fruitless. She recalled the long sword Burrus carried. 'He could have used that,' she whispered excitedly. Burrus could have drawn the chain towards him using his own weapon and taken the Holy Sword from its hook. Claudia climbed down from the stool and looked back towards the door. Four problems remained. First, Burrus would need the cooperation of the two guards outside. Secondly, there was the problem of the keys. Thirdly, what would Burrus do with the sword once he had stolen it? Finally, and most importantly, Burrus would have known he would face the Empress's fury.

Claudia sat down and considered this. Helena would be angry, but there again she would have no proof. The Empress was correct. Burrus often acted like a naughty schoolboy and accepted being lashed by her tongue as part of his military service. Was that why Helena had assembled them all this morning, to give them a tongue-lashing they would never forget? Did she suspect the mercenaries and hope she would frighten them into returning the Holy Sword?

Claudia cocked her head at the sound on the steps outside. She walked back through the door to see Timothaeus coming down, slowly, carefully, like an old man. He still looked anxious-eyed and troubled.

'I always come here.' He sniffed. 'I always think that perhaps I'll return here and discover the sword has been restored.' He sat down on the bottom step, where Claudia joined him. 'It's not there, is it?' he asked dolefully.

'No, it isn't.' Claudia grasped his arm. She rather liked this red-faced official on the verge of tears. 'Tell me,' she continued quickly, 'are you sure there's no trickery involved? I mean, when you locked the door, are you sure you locked it?'

'I know what you're thinking.' Timothaeus glanced at her out of the corner of his eye. 'I don't trust those Germans as far as I can spit. No, I was very careful, we always went through the same ceremony. I locked the door, then tried it. Only then did Burrus insert his key.'

'Ah.' Claudia realised her theory held no water. 'Could the keys be copied?'

'I wore mine on a chain round my neck,' Timothaeus declared, 'and, to be fair, so did Burrus. However, I can only speak for myself when I say that wherever I went, the key went too. We were never separated.'

Claudia thanked him, rose and went to her own quarters, where she changed, donning a dark green silver-edged tunic, a robe of a similar colour clasped round her shoulders, a leather belt about her waist. At the back of this hung a sheath for the sharp knife she intended to take everywhere for as long as she remained in the Villa Pulchra. She slipped her feet into boot sandals and took from her jewellery casket a small finger ring, one of the few heirlooms from her mother. She touched the painting of the purple chalice as if to remind herself, then hurried out to the servants' refectory, which adjoined the imperial kitchens.

She had to fight for her food, bullying the heavy-eyed cook for bread, cheese and honey, a goblet of watered beer and some rather dried grapes. Constantine loved his food, and the kitchens were once again busy, the cooks, scullions and maids preparing another repast for the Emperor and his court. Claudia sat at one end at the long communal table and hastily finished her food. The other servants avoided her. She knew the reason. They viewed her as a spy, but she took no offence because that was the truth. She, of course, was sure that the Emperor, not to mention the likes of Rufinus and Chrysis, also had their agents here listening to gossip and collecting information to pass to their masters.

When she had finished her meal, she wandered into the gorgeous atrium, with its marbled walls, exquisite paintings and eye-catching mosaics. She stopped before the shrine built into one of the walls where the Lares and Penates, the household gods, were venerated. She studied the tabernacle and the statues it contained. A bronze tripod stood before these, flames flickering up from a bed of charcoal laced with a fine covering of incense. The smoke rose, white and fragrant. Claudia watched it disappear. Did it go somewhere else, she wondered, or just vanish? Was that what happened to prayers? Did anyone listen? Or were they just gusts of incense, all show and no substance? She closed her eyes and prayed, she didn't know to whom, but she expressed her love for Felix, her dead brother, for her parents, for Polybius, Murranus, Poppaoe and all those bound up in her life.

'Are you ready?'

Claudia opened her eyes and turned round, so quickly she

felt rather giddy. She had thought she was alone, but Timothaeus, Burrus and Gaius stood behind her.

'Are you going?' Gaius smiled, his freshly shaved face gleaming with oil. He was dressed in a simple white tunic, a sword belt casually draped over one shoulder, a toga on the other, ready to dress more formally if the Emperor appeared.

'The debate,' Timothaeus explained. 'It's going to take place in the peristyle garden.'

Claudia smiled. In fact, she had forgotten. Now she remembered the steward breathlessly informing her the previous evening how the Empress was keen for the philosophers to meet and openly debate the issues between them.

'We have been discussing the Holy Sword.' Gaius grinned, nudging Burrus playfully. The German looked more composed. His icy blue eyes, no longer tear-filled, were studying Claudia carefully.

'Why have you been discussing it?' she enquired. 'Do you have a theory about its disappearance?'

'I wish to the gods we had,' Gaius replied. 'But the Empress has asked us to think, reflect and remember.'

The Captain talked like a schoolboy declining a verb, though his voice was rich with sarcasm and his eyes full of laughter.

'Well, we'll do that,' Gaius pulled a face, 'while we get the life bored out of us.'

Claudia joined them and the others drifting out into the peristyle garden. Purple-draped chairs had been set before the fountain and slaves were hurriedly putting up awnings to protect the imperial heads from the summer sun. Scribes in white robes, fingers stained with ink, were busy before the thrones, laying down cushions and preparing writing pallets. On either side of the long glistening pool were stools for the speakers, with a large podium directly facing the imperial presence. Everyone else had to find their own place, either in the garden or in the colonnaded walks. Porters carrying parasols moved amongst the flower beds or called in high-pitched voices for slaves to bring more refreshments.

Claudia moved back into the atrium. It would take some time for everyone to gather, and Constantine was notorious for his lateness, especially after an imperial banquet. As she wandered down a corridor, she started at a touch to her elbow, and spun round. Sylvester was standing at the doorway of a chamber, beckoning her in. She glanced quickly round and followed him into the furnished room. On the wall to her right was a portrait of two young girls looking out of a window, and on the other two were scenes from Etruscan history. The window was high and rather narrow. Sylvester led her over to a corner stool and perched on one end, indicating she should sit next to him.

'Do you know what this is?' he asked, gesturing around.

'An empty room,' Claudia laughed.

'No, a deaf room.' Sylvester's lined face broke into a smile. 'The Empress claims it is one of those few chambers with no secret panels or gaps.'

'In which case,' Claudia retorted, 'there must be at least a dozen.'

Sylvester smiled and patted her on the arm.

'You're going to the debate?'

'I'll stay as long as I can keep awake,' she replied.

'Oh, I think you'll stay awake,' Sylvester murmured. 'There's going to be fun this morning; allegations will be made.'

'About theology?'

'No.' Sylvester splayed his fingers as if examining his nails. 'Not theology, but treachery, betrayal and murder.'

Chapter 5

'*Furor Arma Ministrat.*'
('Fury supplies the weapons.')

Virgil, *Aeneid*, I

Murranus sat in the She-Asses tavern and lifted the goblet, a gift from Polybius and Poppaoe which was always kept in a special place. Polybius described it as the best Samian ware, and it boasted a Cretan motif depicting young men and women leaping over high-horned bulls. Murranus tapped the rim of the goblet and winked rather drunkenly at Polybius.

'That's very hard, you know. Years ago I fought in the Venatio. What do you think was the fiercest animal?'

'A bull,' Polybius slurred.

'Correct,' Murranus agreed. 'The big cats can be cowards, elephants are not fighters, but a bull is worse than a bear. They come at you so fast. People are actually surprised at their speed, you can never tell which way their heads are going to go. I have great admiration for these boys and girls who used to leap the bulls in Crete.'

'It's only a story,' Polybius mumbled.

'No it isn't. I've been to Crete.' Murranus leaned across the table. 'I've seen other drawings. More importantly, I've actually seen a boy leap a bull. That took courage and skill!'

Murranus sipped the wine; the best Falernian, Polybius had assured him. It certainly tasted delicious. He smiled at Polybius, who had just refilled his cup. The landlord tapped the side of his nose and put a finger to his lips, a sign that Murranus shouldn't relish the wine too loudly or the others would demand some. The tavern was full of the regulars. Simon the Stoic had recently purchased a pet mongoose; as Fortunatus the Fornicator had remarked, he had to have someone to talk to. Petronius the Pimp was trying to seduce Danuta the Dancer, whilst the Ladies of Lesbos, an acrobatic troupe, were now seated around the Syrian girls, a group of dark-eyed, flimsily dressed performers who had taken drinks from the Ladies but were making it very clear they were not for sale. Oceanus rested one elbow on the counter, staring dreamy-eyed at Januaria, who sat braiding her hair, leaning forward every so often so Oceanus could get a good view of her full ripe breasts.

Murranus studied the rest of the customers, then stared up at the charred timber ceiling. Was the roll of ham hanging there next to a bag of onions really moving, or had he drunk too much? The truth was that Murranus had become maudlin. He was missing Claudia and had openly wondered if he should visit the Villa Pulchra. Polybius had shaken his head.

'You know that's not possible. You will not be allowed in, and you must prepare for the fight. Spicerius is not only growing stronger, he is training hard and intends to be the victor . . .'

Polybius paused as the door was flung open and a group entered the tavern. They stood for a while with the light behind them, then moved into the eating room.

'Oh no,' Polybius groaned. 'The Dacians!'

Murranus looked up. The Dacians were, in the main, one of the ugliest street gangs from the slums, led by the most garishly dressed creature, who came tripping along the tavern floor in high-heeled pattens, hips swaying like a woman. At first it was hard to distinguish what sex he really was; he was dressed in a voluminous gown with a bright blond wig framing a large head, yet the face was masculine, hard and strong, though painted as vividly as any courtesan's: eyebrows plucked and darkened, cheeks both whitened and rouged, lips fully carmined. The Dacian leader moved in a jingle of bangles, whilst the sachets of perfume hanging around his neck gave off the most alluring fragrance. He paused and glared around the tavern, eyelids blinking.

'I want you to go.' The voice was high-pitched, like that of a eunuch. He clapped his hands. 'I want you to go now!'

The eating room soon emptied. The Dacians moved to stand round Polybius and Murranus.

'I'm Dacius.' The blond-wigged leader sat down opposite Murranus, fingers fluttering. 'But you know that,' he lisped as he examined his henna-painted nails.

The gladiator didn't move, but sat grasping his wine cup, staring at this grotesque. He had met Dacius before, in the slums and back streets as well as at the gladiator school, where the gang would come and watch the fighters so as to assess strengths and weaknesses. The Dacians were involved in a number of illicit pursuits: prostitution, abduction, murder and kidnap, but they were principally money-lenders who charged high interest and liked to finance their loans through judiciously placed bets. In fact, they controlled a great deal of the gambling in the slums around the Flavian Gate.

Dacius pointed a finger in Murranus's face.

'You are a very naughty boy! You were supposed to kill Spicerius.'

'Why?'

'Don't speak to me like that.' Dacius pouted. 'I had a great deal of money riding on you. It was obvious Spicerius was vulnerable; why didn't you strike?'

'I'm a gladiator, not a murderer. More importantly, I'm not a poisoner.' Murranus's anger was mounting; he didn't like either Dacius or his companions. 'Was it you who was responsible for the powders in Spicerius's drink?'

'Of course not!' Dacius lisped. 'That little bastard wouldn't let me anywhere near him.'

'Did you know he was going to be drugged?' Murranus pushed his face closer. 'You knew something was going to happen?'

'I couldn't believe my eyes.' Dacius waved his hands. 'There was the great Spicerius staggering around like a drunk; you should have put your sword straight through his throat!'

'I could see something was wrong,' Murranus replied, 'and, as I've said, I'm a fighter not a murderer.' He blew a kiss into Dacius's face. 'Next time you might win your bet, but it will be the result of a fair fight.'

'Fair fight?' Dacius raised his plucked eyebrows. 'Fair or not, you'd better win!'

'This is a lovely tavern.' One of Dacius's henchmen spoke up, a raw-faced man with a broken nose and slobbery lips. He patted Polybius on the arm. 'You always have to be careful against fire, don't you? You never know when one is going to

98

break out.' The oaf picked up Polybius's cup and sipped from it. 'And then, of course, there's your comely niece – what's her name, Claudia? She's at the Villa Pulchra, isn't she? We know she's there, and we've got friends there who can—'

Murranus's fist smashed on to the table. He grabbed the knife kept in a crack beneath the table-top, knocked two of the Dacians aside and launched a furious assault on the oaf, who now hastily tried to retreat under a rain of blows and kicks. Eventually Murranus cornered him and grabbed him by the hair. Pressing the tip of the knife into his opponent's fleshy throat, Murranus became aware of Poppaoe standing in the kitchen doorway, screaming. Other regulars now threw open the door and thronged in, overcoming their fear of this gang of roughnecks.

'That will be enough,' Dacius called out. 'That will be enough, Murranus! Dear boy, do turn round.'

The gladiator did so. Dacius still sat at the table, but two of his gang had dragged Polybius to his feet, whilst another forced the tip of his dagger under the taverner's chin.

'Fair exchange is no robbery,' Dacius lisped as he rose to his feet and came swaying across the room. He looked Murranus over from head to toe. 'I must say, dear boy, you are very fast. I do hope, however, you will be just as fast in the arena.'

Snapping his fingers, Dacius swaggered out of the tavern. Polybius was sent flying towards his wife, while Murranus lowered his dagger, grabbed the oaf by the hair and, giving him a good kick in the backside, sent him staggering after the rest. Polybius ran across, barred the door then slid down to the ground, face in his hands.

'Come on now.' Murranus went across and helped him to his feet. 'They're just bullies; they croak like bullfrogs.'

'They're nasty,' Polybius replied. 'Even the rats in the sewer would give them a wide berth.'

Murranus helped him back to the table, went to console Poppaoe and brought back two clean goblets. He filled both and thrust one into Polybius's hand, then sat down opposite.

'Why didn't you kill him? I mean Spicerius,' Polybius said, lowering his cup. 'Did you know anything about this before it started?'

'Before any great fight,' Murranus replied, 'you hear rumours, but it's mere chaff in the wind, nothing to worry about. Spicerius and I were both aware of large amounts of money changing hands. But why did Dacius bet on me, why were they so certain?'

'It could be one person,' Polybius replied. 'Someone, somewhere, has put a large amount of money on you to win; the bet's been frozen, so they send the Dacians in.'

'No, no it's more than that.' Murranus dipped a finger into his wine and ran it round his lips. 'Remember, Polybius, they are not only betting for me to win, but for Spicerius to lose. However, as little Claudia always tells me, life is never as simple as that . . .'

'I thought this meeting,' Claudia moved on the stool, 'was about theology, your Jesus Christ being truly God?'

'Claudia, Claudia,' Sylvester patted her on the arm, 'do you think we Christians are different from anyone else? There are two qualifications for joining our sect: the first is to acknowledge you are a sinner; the second is to realise that only the good Lord can change you. Our founder was, is,' he corrected himself, 'God, but our community is a collection of sinners.' He struck his breast. 'Myself included. We fight, we betray, we lust, we steal, we kill.'

'Does Helena know this?'

'Of course she does. However, Helena views the Christian Church as a means to invigorate the Empire and bind it closer together. Above all, she realises that the vast army of the poor regard our Church, with its promise of resurrection to Eternal Life, as their only comfort in this vale of tears. The Christian community,' Sylvester continued, 'has always been riven by dissent. Our Church is almost three hundred years old, but right from the start we have had betrayal and treachery. One of Christ's own followers, Judas, betrayed him to crucifixion. Peter, who later came to Rome, denied ever knowing him.'

Claudia listened carefully. She had never confessed this to anyone, but although she didn't accept the Christian religion, she was still fascinated by its teaching and, above all, its effect on the vast population of the poor of Rome.

'Our Church,' Sylvester held up his hands as if holding a bowl, 'has come out of the catacombs; it no longer hides underground. The shadows are gone, but now is also the time to settle grievances, to fight for power, to claim a place in the sun. Ten years ago, the old Emperor, Diocletian, launched the most savage persecution of the Christian Church. Our followers were roped in from as far away as Britain and the borders of Persia. You must have heard about the hideous spectacles in the Flavian amphitheatre. Men, women and children torn to pieces by wild animals or subjected to the most humiliating death.'

'I was a child,' Claudia whispered. 'I remember my father hiding Christian symbols. One morning, I think it was around the feast of Lupercalia, soldiers came to search our house.'

'Your parents were most fortunate,' Sylvester replied. 'Others were not. When a Christian was arrested, he was given the opportunity to purge himself, to sprinkle incense before a statue of the Emperor or the Standards of Rome. Naturally, many people succumbed; faced with the terror of death, they took the easy way out.'

'And what happened to those?'

'They were given a new name, a term of derision, the "Lapsi", the Fallen Ones. According to some members of our Church, these Lapsi should never be forgiven. Others, myself included, believe this is too harsh. The Lapsi should do penance, yes, but eventually be forgiven and re-admitted to the community.'

'How does this affect our philosophers?'

Sylvester grinned sourly.

'If you think the Lapsi are bad, they are not the worst. There is another group of sinners, nicknamed the Iscariots, after the man who betrayed Christ, Judas Iscariot. These are men and women who not only renounced their religion but offered, either for reward or to escape punishment, to lead the authorities to other Christian communities. Your father's house was searched, Claudia, probably because of an informant.' Sylvester drew a deep breath. 'Now, during Diocletian's persecution, the school of Capua was already marked down as a Christian community. Many of its teachers and scholars were known to be followers of Christ.' He shrugged. 'At least in theory. About six years ago, however, the authorities were given very precise information about where to search, who to look for, all the evidence they would need. At least forty people were arrested, thirty of whom were dispatched to Rome for execution.'

Claudia whistled under her breath.

'Now according to Athanasius, such traitors are amongst the Arian group. This morning he is going to divert the Empress's attention to this issue.'

'But why?' Claudia asked. 'Constantine doesn't care what happened six years ago. He is not a Christian and really couldn't give a damn about a mealy-mouthed traitor in your community!'

'Ah, yes,' Sylvester sighed, 'but Athanasius will argue that such traitors betrayed their own kind; they sent innocent men, women and children to their deaths. He might well argue that such people still lurk in the Christian community . . .'

'I see.' Claudia nodded. 'And people who betray once will betray again?'

'Precisely,' Sylvester agreed. 'Athanasius will hint that if such men and women are prepared to betray the Bishop of Rome, why not the Emperor of Rome?'

'But Athanasius is one of yours. Why not just tell him to keep his mouth shut?'

'We've already tried,' Sylvester retorted. 'You've met Athanasius, fiery-tempered and hot-eyed, but he's only half the problem. He claims that Justin, the leader of the Arian party, will level the same accusations of betrayal at the orthodox party. What I want you to do, Claudia, is have a word with the Empress. I do not want to show my hand in public.'

'But you've told me this for another reason, haven't you?'

'Yes, I have,' Sylvester conceded. 'Now you see, Claudia, how truly we Christians love each other! So much so,' he added wryly, 'that we are prepared to kill and maim. I only learned this morning about what is going to happen. I've heard rumours and it has to be stopped.'

'And that other reason?' Claudia asked.

Sylvester patted her on the shoulder and rose to his feet. 'Dionysius's murder may be connected to these allegations.

I don't know, but I have a feeling here,' he tapped his hand on his chest, 'that Dionysius may not be the last to die at the Villa Pulchra.'

When Sylvester had left, Claudia sat on the stool, staring down at her sandalled feet. Outside in the passageway she could hear talk and laughter as the court assembled in the peristyle garden. She got to her feet and left the chamber, forcing her way through the throng until she was out in the full blaze of sunlight. She sighed with relief; the Empress Helena now sat enthroned next to her son, but from the confusion amongst the scribes, Claudia gathered the debate had yet to begin. Pushing and shoving, excusing herself volubly, she made her way through the crowd. She reached the line of soldiers which protected any access to the imperial presence. A soldier brought up his shield. Claudia caught sight of Gaius and shouted his name. The officer came hurrying across, pulling forward the folds of his toga to shroud his head against the sun.

'Why, Claudia,' Gaius smiled down at her, 'the Empress was wondering where you were.'

'I need to speak to her urgently.'

Gaius beckoned her through and, grasping her by the shoulder, steered her between the imperial thrones. Claudia crouched down to the Empress's right.

'Why, little mouse.' Helena didn't even move her head in acknowledgement. 'I saw you coming. Have you been talking to Sylvester?' She turned and winked at Claudia. 'What did you think of my performance this morning? I just hope none of those lovely boys stole that holy relic, but that will have to wait. What do you want?'

Claudia told the Empress in short, sharp sentences how

Sylvester had warned that the debate might be used by both parties to level the most serious allegations against each other. Helena heard her out, now and again nodding in agreement, then dismissed her with a flick of her fingers and turned to talk to her son.

From behind the imperial thrones, Claudia watched how Chrysis imposed order as the orators took their stools either side of the peristyle pool. The chamberlain's introduction was short and slightly sardonic as he bowed mockingly to both sides. He was well aware of his audience. The Christians might be supported by the Emperor, but there were many in court who regarded the new sect with either amusement at best, or, in some cases, downright hostility. Chrysis was about to withdraw when the Emperor raised his hand and proclaimed in ringing tones that the meeting was to be about matters of theology and nothing else. He warned sharply that if any orator wandered from the agenda set before them, that speaker would face his most severe displeasure. The imperial proclamation caused consternation on both sides, a great deal of leaning and whispering.

'We are waiting,' Chrysis sang out, gesturing towards the podium. Athanasius rose to his feet, bowed to the Emperor and his mother, then climbed on to the podium, carefully arranging his sheets of vellum. He stared round at the various notables and sketched a dramatic cross in the air before pausing head down, as if in prayer. Claudia watched with interest. She herself often amused her uncle's guests with mime or playing out some role from one of the great classics. She recognised another actor in Athanasius. He began slowly, body tensed, voice rather low, but then relaxed, his voice echoing rich and mellow. Athanasius was also a scholar with a deep knowledge of the Greek tongue, not some bare-arsed philosopher or sophist playing with words or posing questions without giving answers. He immediately impressed his audience with quotations from the classics, before turning to his main theme, defining in very technical terms the Trinity and its three persons, Father, Son and Holy Ghost. He presented the dogma as radical and revolutionary, and cited one of the great Christian writers, John, quoting, he claimed, the first line of an account of a man who had lived and worked with Christ, seen him die and witnessed his Resurrection.

'John writes,' Athanasius paused, one finger jabbing the air, 'that our witness actually declares, "In the beginning was the Word and the Word was with God and the Word was God."' His mellow voice concentrated on the Greek for 'the Word', Ολογος, and he emphasised this before moving on to other texts which showed that the Word became Flesh. Justin was eager to intervene, but Athanasius was now in full flow, quoting further from the Gospels as well as from the writings of John, to demonstrate that Christ had claimed that he and the Father were one.

Claudia listened intently, drawn by the power of Athanasius's oratory as well as by his critical scholarship, which was making a deep impression on his audience. Even Constantine was listening carefully, whilst Helena was tapping her foot, a common gesture when she was pleased. Claudia studied the faces around her. She glimpsed Gaius Tullius, eyes closed in concentration, Timothaeus beaming with pride, whilst beside him Sylvester nodded in agreement. She wanted to stay and listen but decided this was the best time to visit the scene of Dionysius's murder. She slipped away from the crowd, along a warren of passageways and out through the garden into the orchard beyond. She entered the trees and noticed scuff marks on the ground, but she couldn't decide if these had anything to do with the murder or were the traces of those who found the corpse.

When she reached the place where the philosopher had died, the grass was dark-stained with blood, above which flies buzzed. In the branches overhead a bullfinch chirped noisily as if resentful of her presence. Claudia crouched down on her hands and knees, scrutinising the ground carefully. She found the small holes where the pegs had been driven in and could trace a faint outline of how the corpse had lain.

'So you died here,' she murmured to herself.

She retraced her steps, examining the ground carefully, until she reached an apple tree. The ground beneath it also bore marks of blood, and some distance away lay a moss-covered stone. She picked this up; it was heavy, yet she could carry it out into the pool of sunlight near a small bed of flowers. She placed the stone on the ground, running her fingers over it. The lichen had been disturbed, and she found traces of blood and a few hairs. Claudia squatted on the ground and stared at the apple tree.

'So, Dionysius,' she whispered. 'You were sitting there, meditating or sleeping. Your assassin comes creeping like a shadow. You are stunned with a blow to the head from this stone.' She rose to her feet. 'Then you're dragged deeper into the trees to be murdered.'

Claudia walked lightly forward. She made a slight noise, so she took off her sandals and found that she could move silently across the grass. Satisfied that she had learnt all she could, she moved into an adjoining garden and across the lawn to the burnt-out remains of the House of Mourning, now reduced to a pile of blackened rubble. Near by, a slave squatted on the ground, staring dolefully at the ruins.

'What are you doing here?' Claudia asked.

'The Captain of the Guard told me to stay here until he has examined the ruins more carefully, but there's nothing to examine.'

The man was narrow-faced, his cheeks and chin unshaven. He plucked at a loose thread on his dirty gown.

'I hope they don't blame me,' he moaned. 'That was my duty, you know, to watch the dead, to keep the House of Mourning clean and generally look after things.'

Claudia sat down next to him.

'What happened?' she asked. 'Tell me precisely, not about the old man's corpse but the one who was murdered in the orchard.'

'Oh, he was a proper mess,' the slave replied. 'The Captain of the Guard brought his corpse in and told me to wash it. There was a terrible wound,' he patted the left side of his head, 'while his body was sliced, arms, legs and chest, even the soles of his feet. He must have died in great pain. His eyes were still open, and that awful gag in his mouth, a piece of leather used to keep a door open.'

'And the bonds?' Claudia asked. 'The ropes,' she explained, 'used to bind the victim's hand and feet?'

'They were still attached to his wrists and ankles, tied very tightly they were. I had to slice them with a knife.'

'And what did you do with them?'

'I threw them on the floor. You see, mistress, I was getting hungry, and when you've washed one corpse, well, you can only take so much in one day. I didn't want to miss my ration so I thought I would finish him this morning.' The fellow rubbed his stomach. 'Of course, we were being fed scraps from the kitchen, so I ate well and went to sleep. The next thing I know the House of Mourning is burning.'

Claudia gave him a coin from her purse, then she rose and

walked across to the blackened remains of the mortuary. She was still carrying her sandals, so she put these on and stepped on to the smouldering stretch of ash. The building had been completely destroyed, timbers and stones mixed together, covered in a fine white dust and blackened ash. She had to step carefully among the rubble. Eventually she crouched down and, using her dagger, sifted through the debris. She caught the faint smell of oil and a strange sickly sweetness. The two corpses must have been consumed totally by the fire, along with everything else the House of Mourning contained.

She left the building, the slave watching her curiously as she walked its circumference. The fire had been quite self-contained, because the House of Mourning stood on a plinth of stone well away from the garden. The grass around was scorched, but Claudia could detect no sign that the fire had been started by a flickering brand or a pot of burning oil hastily thrown in. She entered the ruins again, and this time the slave came over to help her move charred bricks and pieces of timber, yet there was still nothing to be found.

Claudia thanked the man and went across to the gardens and into a small shaded portico, erected so imperial residents could shelter from the sun. On the breeze she heard the sound of voices, occasional clapping, and she realised the debate must still be going on. She lay down on the grass, staring up through the gaps in the portico's roof at the blue sky, scored by the occasional white wisp of cloud. She and Felix used to love doing this; when she was by herself, Claudia almost felt as if her brother had returned and was stretched out beside her, eyes watching her devotedly, wondering what his beloved elder sister would plan next. She blinked away the tears and concentrated on the mysteries at the Villa Pulchra. She had no explanation for the sword which had disappeared, whilst as for Dionysius's death, there were a number of theories for the motive in a villa packed with suspects. Beneath the polished façade of this elegant country estate swirled deep, dark passions as old memories and grudges surfaced. Yet what mystified Claudia most was the total destruction of the House of Mourning. She had, in the light of no other evidence, firmly concluded that the arson was not a further indignity against the hapless Dionysius; the assassin simply wished to destroy something which, if closely examined, might reveal his or her true identity. Claudia's eyes grew heavy. She thought of returning to the debate, but within minutes was fast asleep.

When she started awake, she realised from the lengthening shadow of a nearby tree that she had been asleep for some time.

'I've been watching you.' Claudia whirled round. A shadowy figure emerged, half concealed by a tree trunk.

'Who are you?' Claudia tried to rise but tripped on her robe.

'Here, let me help.'

She felt a hand grasp her arm and stared up at Athanasius, his eyes not so harsh now. She thanked him, a little embarrassed about her suspicions, as Athanasius brushed the blades of grass from her tunic.

'I'm sorry if I startled you.' Athanasius smiled. 'I can see the debate had, at least, one good effect: you were fast asleep. After I deliver a speech, I always like to soothe my mind, cool the blood, so I go for a walk.'

'Did you win?' Claudia sat down on the grass, and Athanasius joined her.

'Well, there wasn't a vote.' Athanasius chewed on his lip and stared at a point behind Claudia. He squinted. 'No, there wasn't a vote,' he repeated, 'but I think we made our point. Justin was unable to answer my authorities, the quotations from the scriptures. He became confused and rather garbled. I think we carried the day.'

'Why did Dionysius offer to come over to your party?'

Athanasius shrugged. 'Promotions, honours, wealth. He recognised the way the wind was blowing.'

'So he could have been murdered by one of his own party?'

'Or one of ours?' Athanasius sniffed. 'Religion is like politics, Claudia. We may all sing the same hymn but that doesn't mean we like to be part of the choir. Dionysius might have provided us with information about possible traitors in our own ranks.'

'Could he have been connected with the Lapsi?'

'Ah!' Athanasius smiled. 'So you know all about that – I saw you whispering with the Augusta. I wondered where the information came from. No surprise that the Emperor issued his decree.' He leaned forward, joining his hands as if in prayer. 'You see, Claudia, the oratory school in Capua is quite famous. Many Christian families fled there eager to escape the persecution in Rome. When Diocletian launched his attack, Capua was especially singled out. The authorities moved spies and informants into the town. We suddenly received a new influx of would-be scholars, some of them genuine, others looking for mischief. By the way, I'm not saying you're a spy.'

'Oh, but you're wrong, Magister.' Claudia smiled. 'I am a spy but not a traitor. There is a distinction.'

'I don't know what really happened,' Athanasius continued. 'We hid our sacred vessels away, and met at night in underground caverns or out in the countryside. We were safe, or thought we were, until all the demons of Hell were let loose. The raids grew more intense, more people were roped in. A troop of torturers arrived from Rome and the questioning began.'

'Were you arrested?'

'Yes, yes, I was. I was much younger then but I had powerful patrons and I had been taught my lesson well. If you are ever questioned, Claudia, do not remain silent but tell them a story, any story, as long as it holds together. I was released and fled before the real persecution began. Others were not so lucky. Some broke, some died under the torture, quite a number were dispatched to Rome to face a hideous death.'

'And Dionysius?' Claudia asked softly.

'Dionysius was barely out of his teens, a recent convert; something like you, Claudia, a messenger, a man who travelled between the various groups. He would know the places and times. He too was released around the same time I was.' Athanasius paused, clicking his tongue, and Claudia could see he was fighting back the tears. 'Shortly afterwards the Roman authorities became, how can I put it, more fortunate in their searches. And the prisons overflowed with their Christian prisoners.'

'Was Dionysius suspected of being an Iscariot, a traitor?'

'We were all suspected, myself included. The nightmare of the situation is that dozens of people died gruesome deaths.'

'So,' Claudia replied slowly, 'Dionysius could have been killed by his own party because they knew he was about to betray them. He could have been killed by one of your party because he was bringing information that might pose a threat. Or the killer could be someone else, settling scores for a relative or friend caught up in a savage persecution which began a decade ago.'

'And what do you think?'

Claudia studied Athanasius's clever, cynical face. Although she hadn't liked him at first, she felt she could trust this man, who had, in his own way, an integrity, a passion for what he believed in.

'Claudia?' Athanasius waved a hand in front of her eyes.

'I was thinking of passion.' She laughed apologetically. 'The person who killed Dionysius didn't creep up behind him with a dagger or an axe or beat his brains out with a club. Dionysius was first stunned, then dragged into the trees, gagged, bound and tortured.' She snapped her fingers. 'Tell me, Athanasius,' she continued hurriedly, 'isn't there a torture where the prisoner is hung in chains and death is inflicted by a thousand cuts?'

'I've heard of such cruelty,' Athanasius conceded. 'I see the path you are following. You've answered your own question: was Dionysius murdered to satisfy a grudge which the killer had nursed since the great persecution?'

'It's possible.' Claudia got to her feet and walked away. 'If you ever learn anything new . . .' she called out over her shoulder.

'You'll be the first to know,' Athanasius sang back.

Claudia felt refreshed after her sleep and decided to walk to the villa, hoping to meet the people she had secretly listed. She found Justin resting in a colonnaded walk, his disciple beside him. They were sharing a jug of wine, drowning their sorrows. They glanced up and welcomed her.

'I understand you did very well.' Claudia tried to put a smile on it.

'In which case,' Justin slurred, 'you are the only person here who thinks that. Athanasius confused me. I thought his speech would be about the Divine substance.'

'Yes, yes,' Claudia intervened, 'though I haven't come to discuss your opponent but Dionysius. Did you know he was going to betray you?'

Justin glanced quickly at his companion. He was going to lie, then his shoulders drooped and he nodded. Claudia thought he was upset, but when he lifted his tired face, it was hatred that blazed in his eyes. You've been trapped and humiliated, Claudia reflected. You are a very dangerous man.

'Dionysius,' Justin spat the word out, 'was a reed bending in the wind. We had our suspicions about him. He had become silent, withdrawn.'

'And?' Claudia asked.

'We'd received reports that he had been seen visiting Athanasius's house and frequenting his lectures. So he's not going to be missed, is he? I have nothing more to say about his death.' Justin turned away, picking up the wine jug to refill his goblet. The disciple sniffed and looked Claudia over from head to toe.

Claudia bit back her angry retort. As she turned away, Burrus and his cohort of mercenaries turned the corner and came swaggering along the colonnade. They always reminded her of a pack of shambling bears, with their thick beards and the furred cloaks they insisted on wearing whatever the heat. Despite the Empress's instructions, they had all been drinking. Claudia walked towards them and held her ground, blocking their path. Burrus stopped so suddenly his followers pushed and shoved into each other. They immediately ringed her. Claudia stared around; light blue eyes in scarred weathered faces gazed back. She could smell the grease and oil they rubbed on their bodies, as well as the perfume they sprinkled in a fruitless attempt to disguise it; they always reeked of the bear pit and the stable.

The Germans smiled benevolently down at her, either tapping the hilts of their swords or combing their beards and moustaches with their fingers, a common gesture whenever they were assessing the worth of a woman. Claudia smiled sweetly at them. They grunted and bowed back. They liked this little one, the Empress's mouse. They had seen the Augusta stroke her hair, and that was good enough for them. They also knew about Murranus, and concluded that such a man must have a shield-maiden with a warrior's heart. For her part, Claudia was not fooled by their bluster and comical ways; these men were killers, noted for their savagery and cunning. They had proved time and again how their coarse, rough appearance masked minds as sharp and keen as any sword. They also liked to help themselves to whatever was available, and this included women. They shuffled and moved around her. Claudia could see one or two trying to shelter behind the others; a rare event, because usually each warrior liked to be seen. She walked towards the two who were hiding, gesturing with her hand for the others to move aside. At first they stood their ground.

'Please.' Claudia smiled. They obeyed. She confronted the two she thought of as the Sulkers, who stood, hands hanging down, glancing fearfully at her from under their eyebrows. She noticed the slight bulge in both their tunics which they only drew attention to by trying to pull their cloaks over. 'Please,' Claudia demanded, stretching out a hand, 'let me see what you have.'

The Sulkers shuffled their feet; Claudia snapped her fingers. The Sulkers shrugged, threw back their cloaks, and pulled up tunics to reveal hairy stomachs. Each drew out a beautiful ivory statue of the goddess Juno, dressed in the Greek fashion, standing upon a small hillock with a rose

115

bush entwined around her ankles, in one hand a rod of light-ning, in the other a cluster of grapes. Claudia balanced both figurines in her hands and stared round the group. Burrus gazed at her open-mouthed. The rest were staring up at the sky as if they were seeing it for the first time. The two Sulkers sank to their knees and put their faces in their hands, a gesture of their tribe, a plea for mercy.

'What is this? What is this?' The mercenaries stood aside as Gaius Tullius and a group of household officers came walking along the colonnade. They were not dressed in uniform but wore plain tunics over rather baggy breeches, sandal boots on their feet. Gaius carried a sword belt over his shoulder. The mercenaries became alarmed. There was little love between the regular army and what they scornfully termed the 'auxil-iaries'. 'What is this?' Gaius repeated, forcing his way through the throng, his handsome face all tense, eyes watchful.

Claudia heard the scrape of steel as his companions drew their swords. One of the mercenaries, fearful of what was to happen, went for the dagger thrust in his belt, but Gaius smacked his hand away.

'You have no authority to draw your swords here. Claudia?' Gaius turned and stared down at the figurines she was holding. 'I see.' He took one of the statues out of her hands, turned and pushed it under Burrus's nose. 'Shall I tell you the penalty for theft from an imperial palace? Forty-nine lashes of the whip and possible crucifixion. I want the culprits!'

'Captain, Captain.'

Gaius turned.

'Yes, Claudia?'

'I think you've made a mistake.' Claudia deliberately spoke slowly so the Germans would understand her and not inter-vene. 'These gentlemen were on patrol in the grounds. They

116

found these figurines peeping out from beneath a bush, picked them up and brought them to me so I could find their rightful owner.'

'Could you show me this bush?'

'Captain,' Claudia fluttered her eyelids, 'you're not trying to say I'm a liar? After all, you have the proof. I was holding the figurines, not them. And I certainly haven't stolen them. I can prove my movements this morning. But if . . .'

'Of course,' Gaius replied hastily. He turned and slapped Burrus's shoulder. 'You are,' he said, 'the most fortunate of men.' The escorts sheathed their swords, and Gaius bowed and walked away.

Once they were out of sight, the Germans crowded in round Claudia. She was squeezed and hugged, lifted up and kissed on each cheek. She felt as if she had been taken over by a very friendly family of bears. The Germans grunted with pleasure. Some were laughing quietly, trying to hide their mirth, though the tears streamed down their cheeks. Burrus grabbed her by the shoulder and led her out of the colonnade and into the shadow of some very gnarled olive trees, part of an ancient grove included in the gardens when the villa was first built. Once they were away from the public gaze, he stood, hands on Claudia's shoulders, beaming down at her. Then he spoke rapidly in German over his shoulder. The two Sulkers came forward one at a time, and each knelt at Claudia's feet and, taking her hands, clasped them while they recited some oath, faces all solemn, eyes gleaming.

'They are now yours,' Burrus translated, 'in peace and war. Blood and fire will be no deterrent. You've just acquired two brothers, Claudia.'

She stared down at these new additions to her family, smiled and whispered her thanks. Once again the horde closed in for further communal squeezing. Claudia, breath-less and feeling rather bruised, thrust the figurines into Burrus's hands.

'For the love of life,' she swore an oath Burrus used, 'take these bloody things back to where you found them and never, never do that again.' She held his gaze. 'Now you can do me a favour. I want you to come to the cellar where the Holy Sword hung.'

They all followed her obediently along the colonnade, out across the gardens, through the peristyle court and down the steps leading to the cellar. At the bottom they would go no further but stood like children chattering amongst them-selves. Burrus explained they still regarded the cellar as a sacred precinct haunted by Christian spirits.

'Very well,' Claudia sighed. 'The rest of you brutes go back to the peristyle. Burrus, I want the two guards who were on duty the day the sword disappeared.' Burrus rapped out orders. For a while there was confusion. The Germans didn't really want to leave; they were quite fascinated by this wily little creature with the face of one of their wood elves who had managed to trick a powerful officer and so rescue two of their comrades. Nevertheless, after Burrus had shouted and slapped a few, they shuffled back up the steps. Claudia was not surprised that the two guards left were the Sulkers. They stood looking rather embarrassed, one staring at the wall as if fascinated by the brickwork, the other gazing at the floor as if he had lost something precious.

'Burrus,' Claudia tugged at the mercenary's cloak, 'did you take the sword?'

He replied in a flurry of oaths, which his companions repeated.

'Very well,' Claudia declared. 'Show me what happened that day.'

The two guards took up position either side of the door, squatting down on their haunches. Burrus showed how Timothaeus had inserted his key and so had he.

'And you're sure the door was locked?' Claudia asked.

Burrus grunted a yes.

'Now the door swings open.' Claudia noticed the two Sulkers didn't move, but Burrus jumped away as if someone was lurking in the darkness beyond. She went inside, and heard the door close behind her. She opened it and went back outside.

'Are you sure that happened? I mean, the door was closed?'

Burrus agreed.

'Did Timothaeus carry a lamp?'

'Oh yes,' the German retorted, using his hands to describe it. 'One of those lantern horns.'

'I see. Fetch me one.'

The mercenary Captain hurried off and came back with a large lantern horn, its frame made of bronze, the four sides hard sheets of polished vellum. Claudia opened the latch; inside, an oil lamp was fixed to the centre. One of the guards brought a tinder, the lamp was lit and Claudia returned to the cellar. She picked up one of the stools, sat by the edge of the circle of sand and stared up at the empty hook. She closed her eyes. Timothaeus came in here, she thought, he fainted. She opened her eyes and dug her hand deep in the sand. What had happened? How had that sword disappeared?

'Burrus,' she called. The German wouldn't answer, so Claudia went out. She asked if the cellar had been thoroughly searched after the theft. Burrus nodded.

'I think so, but it was obvious the sword had gone.'

'But had it?' Claudia asked. Whilst sitting in the cellar, the seed of a new idea had taken root.

Chapter 6

'*Probitas laudater et alget.*'
('Honesty is praised and left out in the cold.')

Juvenal, *Satires*, I

Claudia left the cellar and returned to the peristyle gardens. She watched servants pruning the luxuriant rose bushes which grew along a trellis dividing the lawn from the shady colonnade. A slave came and asked her if she wanted anything from the kitchen. Claudia smiled her thanks. A short while later another slave appeared bearing a tray with a well-stocked platter of smoked fish and vine leaves, savoury barley, eggs poached in wine, and a slice of cheese and pastry pie, as well as two goblets of white wine.

'Two?' Claudia lifted her head, shading her eyes against the sun. She recognised the slave as the same one she'd questioned near the ruined House of Mourning.

'You wish to drink with me?'

The man's tired face broke into a smile.

'I would dearly love so, mistress. I apologise for my impudence, but you have a kind face and a generous heart.'

'Who are you?'

'My name is Narcissus. I am, by nation, a Syrian.' Without being invited, he sat down next to Claudia. 'I was by profession an embalmer. I looked after the dead until I was swept up in a stupid revolt just outside Damascus.'

Claudia pushed the wine cup into his hands.

'You know how it is,' Narcissus continued woefully. 'Some idiot begins a fight. The innocent are drawn in, the legions arrive, the leaders are crucified and the rest are sold to slavery, end of story.' His face grew even more lugubrious. 'I used to be known as Narcissus the Neat, I was so skilled in my trade! I was especially proud of my precision in preparing a corpse. I always broke the nose bone with the greatest of ease and drew the brains out without creating too much mess.'

'Yes, yes,' Claudia interrupted, staring at the food. 'But how did you become involved in the revolt?'

Narcissus drained his goblet, and Claudia emptied hers into his. The slave relaxed sipping at the second goblet of wine, staring at Claudia like a hungry puppy.

'To answer your question, mistress, I lived five miles outside of Damascus. This madman appeared, calling himself Simon the Saviour, a great sombre-faced brute. He had been to Egypt and learnt a few tricks. He promised that those who believed in him would live for ever beyond the Far Horizon; they would die but, if they were followers of the god Osiris and were buried according to the sacred rite, they would not only live for ever but would be able to come back and assume different forms.'

'Surely you didn't believe that nonsense?'

'No, I didn't. But my wife did, though that was because she was sleeping with Simon, our so-called Saviour.'

Narcissus paused, watching a crowd of courtiers cluster in the colonnade. They had surrounded Athanasius, congratulating him in their high-pitched voices.

'I had no choice,' Narcissus continued. 'Some people answer to God; I answered to a higher authority, my wife. Anyway,' he blew his cheeks out, 'Simon said he needed me because I was an embalmer. The stupid fanatic seized a fort on the edge of the desert and proclaimed that the Day of the Far Horizon had arrived. We raised the standard of Osiris and defied the local governor. He sent troops, a tribune with a force of foot and cavalry. My wife was killed, Simon the Saviour impaled.' Narcissus sniffed. 'That gave me some satisfaction, even though I ended up on the slave block.' He looked at the platter of food and swallowed hard. Claudia heard his stomach grumble.

'Eat,' she ordered, handing it over, 'and I mean eat. You are my guest, Narcissus, I'll take responsibility.'

The slave needed no second bidding and attacked the food like a ravenous wolf. Claudia got to her feet, went over to a side table laid out in the shade and brought back another jug of wine. Narcissus was busy stuffing food into his mouth. Claudia felt a deep compassion for this middle-aged man, who was so hungry he had forgotten his status in order to fill his belly. Some of the courtiers were looking at her strangely; a pompous chamberlain, a eunuch, came waddling over. Claudia told him to stay well away.

'If you wanted food,' Claudia whispered, 'you should have asked, but there again,' she patted his shoulder, 'I should have noticed.'

'I wasn't just hungry,' he replied between mouthfuls. 'I wanted to tell you about the fires.'

'Yes, I know, the House of Mourning was burnt.'

'No, the fires,' he repeated. 'I have to tell someone what I saw. Last night, as I've said, I ate well and drank deep, on not very good ale. I became truly drunk and fell asleep just behind the latrines. I was roused by the clamour caused by the House of Mourning burning. I jumped up and ran round; the flames had caught hold. Gods, I thought, they'll blame me! I'll be for the stake or the cross, so I fled. I jumped the wall and ran to the top of the hill. This villa is built on the side where the ground has been levelled off. Anyways,' Narcissus wiped his mouth on the back of his hand, 'there I sat, staring at the stars above me, wondering what I should do. If I ran away they'd certainly blame me. Indeed, I had nothing to fear by staying. I had witnesses to say where I was, and the House of Mourning was left safe. There was no lamp there, no oil, nothing which could cause such a blaze. I'd done nothing wrong. I'd—'

'And?' Claudia interrupted.

'I calmed down. I stared up at the stars, the air was cool and sweet. I closed my eyes. I swear I could smell the jonquil which grew so rich and profuse in the valley where I played when I was a boy. Anyway,' Narcissus hurried on, 'I opened my eyes. From where I sat, I could still see the House of Mourning, but, staring out over the countryside, I glimpsed other fires.'

'What?' Claudia exclaimed.

'Other fires, mistress. They weren't blazing when I first arrived, I'm sure of that. But staring into the darkness, I could see one in the middle distance, then another a little further on. At the time I didn't think anything about it. I thought they were harvest fires, but there's been no harvest yet. Such blazes aren't lit for at least another two months. Then I thought about Simon the Saviour.'

'What about him?' Claudia tried to curb her exasperation.

'That was what he did when the revolt started. He lit beacon fires, piles of brushwood oiled and flamed. He called them the Lights of Heaven, much good it did him.'

Claudia stared around the exquisite, sophisticated garden. The peristyle was now filling up as more courtiers and officials wandered down to eat from the banqueting tables and take their rest in the coolness and fragrance of this lovely garden. She felt a shiver of fear. Something about Narcissus's account stirred her own memories of the previous evening. She recalled walking over to that sycamore tree where the imperial family were sitting. That was it! The night breeze had been blowing against her, in the direction of the burning House of Mourning, yet she still smelt wood smoke. What if Narcissus was correct? Was the House of Mourning a beacon light? A signal to someone outside which was then sent on? During her travels up and down Italy, as a member of the acting troupe, Claudia had seen the marching armies and heard the clash of battle. She recalled the dark hills further north, the beacon fires burning in the dead of night as the armies of Rome manoeuvred to face each other in bloody confrontation.

'Tell me,' she asked, 'did you look the other way?'

'What do you mean?'

'You were sitting on the hill staring down at the villa, yes? That lies to the south. Were there fires to the east and west, or behind you to the north? I'm giving rough calculations,' she added. 'Were the fires you saw in a direct line beneath you or all around you?'

'No, all before me, I could see nothing to the right or left. By the way, I've worked here for five years, I know my directions.'

Claudia's unease deepened. Narcissus was correct. Why were such fires blazing at the height of summer? According to him they were not brushwood or forest fires caused by the heat, but deliberately lit. If they were beacon fires, what was it all about? She racked her brains; there were no great feasts or celebrations. Should she tell the Augusta? Yet what if she was wrong? Claudia stood up.

'You're coming with me.'

'Where to? What for?'

'For a summer's day's ride. Go down to the stables and ask the grooms, on the authority of Claudia, messenger of the Augusta, to prepare my horse – it's a gentle cob – and a mount for you.'

'I prefer to walk,' Narcissus grumbled. 'That's how I was captured! Instead of running away, I stole a horse and fell off.' Muttering to himself, the slave hurried from the garden.

Claudia returned to her own chamber. All was in order. She filled her purse with some coins and collected her hat. A short while later, a water pannikin slung over the cob's saddle-horn, she and Narcissus left by a side gate. The villa was now falling silent as the imperial family and guests took their rest against the heat of the day. The same was true of the guards beyond the wall. Claudia noticed that these were few and far between and had retreated into the shade of the trees. She reined in and stared back. Narcissus, walking beside her, swinging a staff, stopped and gazed curiously up at her.

'Are you frightened?'

'No, just cautious. Tell me,' Claudia continued, 'did you know when the Emperor was about to arrive?'

'No, everyone was in quite a state. The kitchen master asked the Captain of the Guard, but he didn't know. The

Emperor comes and goes like the breeze. All the stewards and chamberlains had been told was that, once the games were over, the Emperor would leave Rome.' Narcissus shrugged. 'It was business as usual until that sword was stolen. By the Lord of Light,' he sighed, 'what a commotion! People running here and there. You know, I was ordered to help carry that fat steward Timothaeus from the cellar. White as snow he was, I thought he'd died. Oh well, I reflected, here's another whose nose I'll have to break—'

'Thank you,' Claudia intervened hastily.

When they reached the crossroads they turned on to a track towards where Narcissus had seen the first fire. The slave had become lost in his own thoughts, comforted by a full belly and the wine singing in his blood. He smiled contentedly, humming a tune under his breath. The countryside basked in the summer sun. They passed avenues of lime, plane and sycamore trees; occasionally they caught a glimpse of the red-brown earth, of green pastures turning yellow under the boiling sun. Fields of corn, barley and rye ripened in the summer's warmth. They passed small farmsteads where the air reeked with the stench of manure, milk and hay. The silence was broken by the bark of a dog or the strident call of a goose. Swallows, buzzards, starlings and sparrows swooped above them, darting in and out of the trees, and the constant chatter of the crickets was broken occasionally by the whine of some other insect or the monotonous buzzing of bees.

Claudia felt her eyes grow heavy. She wasn't the best of horse riders, yet the saddle was strong and the horse was gentle. For a while she dozed. She just hoped that Narcissus had a good memory as well as a sharp sense of direction.

'I'm sure it was here.' Narcissus shook her awake. They

had reached a stretch of arable land to the left of the track, lying fallow as the season passed.

Claudia dismounted, leapt across the narrow ditch and walked into the field. At the far end, a hedgerow divided it from the next strip of land. The ground was hard and crusty underfoot. An occasional bird pecked at the soil.

'I'm sure it was here,' Narcissus repeated. 'We've just passed a farmhouse. I remember staring at it. Shouldn't we hobble your horse?'

'Don't worry about her,' Claudia shouted over her shoulder. 'She's found some grass, so she's content.'

They walked across the field, Claudia slipping on uneven soil, broken by little ridges and the occasional gap. At first she thought Narcissus was mistaken until the ground dipped slightly and they reached a circle of ash and scraps of burnt wood. Crouching down, Claudia dug her hands into the earth and lifted a mixture of soil and ash. The stench of oil was pungent. She rose, brushing her hands, and stared round. The field, with its broad, silent expanse, appeared more threatening. Anyone could be watching them from the trees.

'It's best if we go,' she whispered, 'and walk fast, Narcissus.'

Claudia almost ran back to the track, the sun beating down, sweat breaking out, her mouth turning strangely dry. When she reached the line of trees, she rested in the shade.

'We came at a good time,' she observed. 'Everyone is sleeping.'

'Shouldn't we question the farmer?'

'We would only arouse suspicion.' Claudia pointed out across the field. 'There's no reason for that fire, none whatsoever. I expect the farmer had little to do with it. Imagine, at the dead of night, Narcissus! Someone piled brushwood and gorse along the edge of this field. Once darkness fell, they dragged it out, soaked it with oil and thrust in a torch. I wonder . . .' and before Narcissus could stop her, Claudia ran back across the field, head down, shoulders hunched, as if fearful of some bowman hiding amongst the trees.

Narcissus caught up with her as she reached the burnt patch of earth and turned round in the direction from which they had come. Her view was partially blocked by the trees and the heat haze of summer. She strained her eyes and, moving backwards and forwards, glimpsed the rooftops of the Villa Pulchra.

'At the dead of night,' she whispered, 'the blaze from the House of Mourning could be seen.'

'They could also see our villa from other places,' Narcissus agreed. 'They wouldn't have to stand just here.'

They hurried back, and Claudia mounted her horse, turning its head towards the Villa Pulchra.

'Shouldn't we see where the other fires were lit?' Narcissus was enjoying his summer's walk with this very kind but mysterious young woman.

'I've seen enough!' Claudia retorted. 'I know what I have to do.'

They hastened back to the villa, washed their hands and faces and immediately went to the Augusta's quarters. The entrances and doorways were protected by Burrus's guards, most of them asleep. Narcissus grew nervous and began to shake. Claudia could even hear his teeth chatter. The chamberlain informed her that the Empress was sleeping and must not be disturbed, but Claudia insisted, and a short while later she and Narcissus were ushered into the Empress's bedchamber. Helena had been lying on a couch on a dais beneath a window. She was dressed in a simple white tunic, her black hair falling loose around her shoulders. She now sat on an ornate padded stool, her feet bare, rubbing her cheeks and trying to stifle a yawn. Claudia noticed the scars on the Empress's bare left arm, as well as how strong her wrists and ankles appeared.

'When I was young, Claudia, I was an athlete,' Helena declared, following Claudia's gaze. 'I also went on campaign with my dear late husband. On one occasion our tent was attacked.' She rubbed the scars on her arm. 'Anyway, you've roused me from my sleep, little mouse, so you must have brought me some tidbits. Who's your companion?'

Claudia and Narcissus knelt on the floor. Narcissus was trembling so much the Empress gave him a goblet of wine and told him to drink it quickly, before gesturing at Claudia to sit down. At first Helena looked sleepy-eyed, but the more Claudia spoke the more alert she became. Now and again the Empress would glance at Narcissus, who would nod in agreement. Claudia related exactly what Narcissus had told her, and described their journey to that lonely field and the remains of the beacon fire.

'I agree,' the Augusta declared as soon as Claudia had finished. 'This is no coincidence.' She walked over and patted Narcissus's head as she would a dog. 'You have done very well. You shall be freed.'

Narcissus immediately fainted, toppling to the floor with a crash. Claudia knelt down beside the prostrate man, pressing the back of her hand against the blood pulse, listening to his breathing. Then, opening his mouth, she poked in a finger to detect any obstruction.

'He's all right.' Helena knelt smiling on his other side. 'Come, Claudia, let's make him comfortable.'

They turned Narcissus on his side, placing a blanket beneath his head and another over him.

'Poor man,' Helena declared. 'He has drunk too much wine, followed by a long hot walk in the sun, and now his life has just been changed. He'll sleep for a while, you look after him. I'll give you some money for him, but that'll have to wait. Come over here.'

Helena led her across to a table covered in scrolls. She searched amongst these and brought out a map of the Middle Sea depicting the main ports of Italy, Asia Minor and Greece.

'During the recent games,' the Empress explained, 'I received reports from a spy that Licinius, Emperor of the Eastern Empire, had sent a battle group of warships, triremes and support vessels into the Bay of Corinth. He is also strengthening the garrisons of Greece. Now, of course, according to the protocol signed between us, Licinius has to inform us of such manoeuvres. He claims to be mustering his forces against a powerful pirate fleet which attacked some merchantmen.'

'Are you fearing an invasion?' Claudia asked.

'No.' Helena shook her head. 'Licinius isn't capable of that, though he's steeped in treachery. I suspect he's planning a surprise.' She took out a local map, tracing the short distance between the Villa Pulchra and the Italian coast. 'If you are correct, Claudia, and I think you are, a whole series of fires were lit in a direct line starting at the Villa Pulchra and ending just above the cliffs on the seashore. I know what you are going to say, little one: we should alert the Emperor, have troops moved into the area. But what's wrong with that?'

'We don't know who the traitor is and we'll only alarm him – or her.'

'Precisely.' Helena smiled. 'I think it's best if you leave that to me and my noble contingent of German heroes. Now, let's get Narcissus removed.'

Helena summoned servants, who brought a stretcher. Claudia had the still prostrate corpse-embalmer taken back to her own chamber and placed on the bed. The chamberlain who escorted them there tapped her on the shoulder.

'Leave him for a while,' he whispered. 'I shall sit with him. The Augusta wants words with you.'

By the time Claudia had returned to Helena's bedchamber, the Empress had changed and was wrapping a purple shawl around her shoulders. Servants in the adjoining chamber were laying out robes, mirrors, combs and pots of perfume. Constantine had decreed that there would be another imperial banquet that night. Helena kicked the door closed with one sandalled foot and beckoned Claudia to sit next to her on a stool. The Empress pushed her face only a few inches from Claudia's, studying her carefully.

'I can be trusted,' Claudia whispered.

'I know you can, mouse. What worries me is who else can I trust? We have the business of the missing sword, the death of Dionysius, the destruction of the House of Mourning; now we have a traitor in our midst and it could be anyone. Narcissus has earned his freedom. What he saw were beacon lights, and I suspect they stretch down to the coast. Somewhere to the south, hiding from our searchers and lookouts, lurks a war trireme, its sail reefed, oars down, probably supported by supply ships and flying false colours. I suspect a cohort is to be landed and this villa attacked. If I alert the harbour masters and port commanders, this warship will simply vanish. If I tell my son, he'll go back to Rome or send out a fleet, and the traitor will simply bide his time and strike again.'

'But you are in danger.'

'No, no.' Helena's face became flushed with excitement. 'We are playing a game, Claudia, as dangerous as any your Murranus faces in the arena. At Nicomedia in the East, Licinius, our rival, sits and plots, or should I say, lounges and plots,' Helena added drily. 'He's received information that his great rival Constantine has gone to his summer residence not far from the coast, and has decided to strike. I shall frustrate that and, at the same time, show my beloved son that Licinius has to be destroyed.'

'You want war, don't you?' Claudia stared at this middle-aged woman. Once again the legions would march and the world echo with the clash of empires. 'You want war,' she repeated.

'No, Claudia, I want peace. I want those who write history to talk of the great Pax Augusta, a time when the world slept, when the harvest grew and was collected, when people lived in peace.' Helena leaned a little closer in a gust of fragrant perfume and sweet wine. 'A new Empire, Claudia, with a new line of Emperors, a new state religion which binds everyone together. We will never have that whilst Licinius and his gang strut the East and look for an opening. That's the way of the world,' Helena added wearily. 'Wars don't begin,' she stared round, 'in the council chambers of kings and princes, but often in boudoirs like this where a single decision is made and the die is cast. Now, little one,' she pressed a finger against Claudia's lips, 'keep these sealed. Tell no one, trust me, and make sure Narcissus enjoys his freedom.'

*   *   *

Claudia left the Empress's quarters and walked back to her own chamber. She stopped at a window embrasure and looked out at the flowers. Their scent was heavy, and even the bees and butterflies seemed to be overcome by such a fragrant opiate, a warm, lazy place ablaze with colour. She stared at a bust of some long-forgotten Emperor gazing sightlessly from its plinth. She walked over and read its inscription, short and terse, giving glory to the 'Divine Hadrian'. She studied the heavily bearded and moustached face, the sharp nose, the eyes carved as if the Emperor was looking upwards, a fashion sculptors had imitated from the many carvings and paintings of Alexander the Great.

'I wonder,' Claudia murmured, 'if in a hundred years someone will stare at a bust of the Augusta?'

She recalled the Empress's impassioned speech, and for a moment she was pricked by suspicion about the Augusta's intentions. Was Helena merely a spectator in all that was happening? Or was she, once again, controlling events? Claudia dismissed this as unworthy. She remembered Narcissus and hurried back to her own chamber. The chamberlain announced that the embalmer was still asleep, so Claudia sent for the court leech, who came shuffling along with a phial of pungent oil. He half dragged Narcissus up, pushed the oil beneath his nose and gently slapped his face. Narcissus wakened with a shake of his head, eyes fluttering. The leech examined him carefully, telling him to open his mouth, feeling the blood pulse in his neck and dragging down the folds of skin beneath his eyes, all the time keeping up a commentary to himself.

'Shall I bring some wine?' Claudia asked.

'Yes, yes, that'll be very nice,' the leech replied. When it arrived, the fellow promptly drank it, declared the patient was in better shape than he was and left. Narcissus pulled himself up.

'I don't believe it,' he gasped, sinking back on the bed. 'I truly don't believe it.'

'It's true.' Claudia smiled. 'Your observations were most valuable; you are a free man, Narcissus.'

He stared at her, then burst into tears.

'What shall I do? What shall I do?' he wailed. 'I cannot go back to Damascus. All my kith and kin are dead, those who survived will only think I'm a spy. I know nobody in Rome, I've got no money.'

'Oh, shut up!' Claudia was about to berate him when there was a knock on the door and an official entered, one of the Emperor's pretty boys, with black curly hair and smooth face. He was garbed in a skimpy tunic which showed his long legs off to their best effect.

'Claudia?' He looked her up and down, glanced at Narcissus sprawled on the bed, and sniggered behind splayed fingers, the nails of which were painted a bright scarlet. Around his wrist was fastened the leather strap displaying the seal of an official *nuntius*, or messenger, of the Imperial Chancery. He handed over a scroll and a small leather pouch, which clinked as it fell into Claudia's hand. 'I think,' he lisped, 'this is for your friend,' and he flounced out.

Claudia broke the seal, undid the scroll and read the opening words: 'Helena Augusta, Beloved Mother . . .' The usual phrases followed. Claudia handed it to Narcissus. 'Your freedom,' she declared, 'and some coins to help you on your way.'

She grasped Narcissus's hand; the man was still shaking, staring down at the scroll and bag of coins lying in his lap.

'You can lodge with my uncle,' she offered. 'He owns a tavern near the Flavian Gate.'

Narcissus's eyes welled up.

'Oh, no,' she protested, 'don't start crying again, you can do that later. Until we leave here you are to be my companion; there must be some small chamber nearby.' Her smile widened. 'You are already my friend and I want some help.'

Narcissus opened his mouth to wail, glimpsed Claudia's determined look and forced a smile.

'Whatever you say.'

Claudia brought him a fresh goblet of wine. The passageway outside was now busy with servants hurrying to and fro with platters of fruit and jugs of wine as the imperial guests roused themselves from their slumbers. She let Narcissus drain the cup.

'Narcissus, never mind your good fortune. I want you to remember Dionysius's corpse. You are an embalmer, you are skilled in scrutinising the dead; was there anything,' Claudia searched for the words, 'significant, exceptional about it?'

Narcissus scratched his nose and closed his eyes. 'Nothing,' he declared. 'All I can remember is a corpse slit, gashed and drenched in blood. I did wonder whether, as Dionysius was an Arian, there were special burial rites, I mean different from the orthodox. Ah.' Narcissus lifted a hand. 'No, no, there was something! There were more cuts on the right side of the corpse than the left. Does that mean the killer was right-handed? And the blow to the head was on the right side as well. Isn't it true, Claudia, that a killer will approach from the side he is used to; a left-handed man will attack me from the left . . . ?'

'I don't know,' Claudia interrupted. 'I never thought of that. I should ask Murranus, but there again, most people are right-handed. Anything else?' she added.

'Some of the wounds looked like crosses, you know, lines

scored across each other. The body was put on a slab and I remember loosening the cords, but by then I'd had enough and left soon afterwards. By the way, who is Murranus?'

'He's a gladiator, a friend of mine. Listen, Narcissus, you deal with the human body,' Claudia smiled, 'the dead rather than the living; do you know anything about poisons and their effect?'

'Oh yes.' Narcissus's tired face came to life. 'Some poisons are very easy to hide. You'd think the victim died of a seizure or some internal wound, but the organs of a corpse never lie. When you take out a heart that's black and shrivelled or a stomach which stinks like a sewer, you do wonder how that person truly died. Oh, indeed,' he continued, 'I've many a time embalmed a poor man whose organs had changed colour or reeked like a camel pen, then watched the grieving widow and wondered what the truth really was. Why do you ask?'

Claudia described what had happened in the arena: how Spicerius had drunk the poisoned wine; how he had collapsed and the finger of suspicion had been pointed at her friend Murranus. She also told Narcissus what the army physician had said. Narcissus nodded in agreement.

'Don't forget, my dear,' he waggled a finger in her face, 'many poisons, in very small quantities, can actually do you good. They can clean the blood and purify the humours, purge the stomach of excess waste, even remove blemishes such as warts. Spicerius must ask himself, did he take a powder or a food containing such a substance? Not enough to kill him, but, I would say, midway between the beneficial properties of that substance and its most noxious—'

Narcissus was about to continue when the door suddenly opened. Claudia turned round. At first she thought it was some court official coming to summon her back to the

Augusta. Taken by surprise, she could only watch, as in a dream, the oil lamp fall to the floor and smash, the oil spilling out, the flame from the wick racing across. For a few seconds she could merely gape in horror. Narcissus was no better, until the full enormity of what had happened hit him: that seeping oil, the flames growing hungrier as they caught hold of the linen drapes around the bed and licked greedily at the leg of a wooden stool.

Claudia jumped to her feet, and picking up her bag, cloak and hat, screamed at Narcissus to take the Empress's scroll and pouch, then pushed him towards the window . . .

Septimus, disciple of Athanasius, stalwart of the orthodox party, lay on his bed and stared up at the ceiling of cream-coloured plaster. He liked that colour, so soothing. Sometimes the vivid colours of this imperial villa, not to mention the guards standing around, brought back memories he would prefer to forget. Septimus had dined well. He had been watching Claudia chatter like a squirrel to that slave and idly wondered what she could find so interesting in him. After all, Septimus was sure that 'little Claudia', as Athanasius called her, had been brought to the villa to keep an eye on them, rather than the slaves.

Septimus was pleased at the way things were going. Athanasius had the upper hand. Justin was discomforted, and Dionysius was dead. He was glad about that and dismissed any guilty thoughts. Dionysius had known so much about him and his past. They had grown up together in Capua, attended the same school and converted to the new faith without any regret. They thought they would live in peace until the horrors of Hell were loosed. Dionysius thought they would be safe – after all, they were of good family – but he had miscalculated and they had been rounded up by Diocletian's agents. The doors to their houses had been broken open at the dead of night, armed men spilling into the atrium. The cellars and gardens had been searched and, of course, they had found enough evidence. Tight collars had been put about their necks, hands bound, and they had been dragged and pushed through the dark and bundled into carts.

Septimus would never forget that bone-jarring ride through the freezing night. They had been given no respite, their pleas and cries ignored, hoods pulled over their heads. He and Dionysius had only recognised each other by their voices; they did not know any of the other prisoners. They had been bundled out of the cart in a chilling dawn, the smoke and flame from the torches of their escort pluming about them, then pushed down yawning, hideous tunnels. Only then did Septimus realise, in his fear-crazed state, that they were within the bowels of the great Flavian amphitheatre, possible victims for the games.

Septimus knew all about heaven, the place of the Christ Lord, but the priest who had converted him had also described the torments of Hell. On that terrifying morning Septimus half believed he had died and was being exposed to the terrors of eternal darkness. They had been kept in a cavern which reeked of wild animals, the roars and snarls of which echoed threateningly through the darkness. The hours seemed to drag; they were given no food or drink. Septimus, overcome with exhaustion, had fallen asleep, only to be woken by the crowds roaring like the thunder of an angry sea. Black-masked guards had appeared, their hoods were removed and they were hurried along the filthy tunnels to the gaping Gate of Death, which stretched out to the great amphitheatre, ablaze with sunlight.

Septimus could only stand and watch as the horrors of the day unfolded. Men, women and children were pushed out to be hunted by wild beasts, brought down by panther, lion and tiger or gored and tossed by furiously stamping wide-horned bulls. He had watched other human beings being torn to pieces so that the golden sand of the arena became as bloody and messy as a butcher's stall. Yet this was only to whet the appetite of the mob. Septimus had been thrust aside as other victims, dressed in cloaks of tar and pitch and fastened to poles on moving platforms, had been pushed into the arena and lit by bowmen with flaming arrows, turning the victims into screaming, living torches.

Eventually Septimus fainted, only to be kicked awake, a coarse wine-skin bag pushed between his lips. He thought his turn had come and, looking around, glimpsed Dionysius, so overcome with fear he had lost all control over his bowels and bladder. Nevertheless, as the dreadful day continued, neither he nor his companion was thrust out with the rest. Instead, when the games were over, they had been taken back to a cell deep beneath the amphitheatre and visited by shadowy-faced men. They had made him an offer: life and freedom, protection against the macabre sights he had seen, on one condition. He must tell them everything he knew about the Christian community at Capua, then continue to give information, leaving it at certain specified places around the town when instructed. Septimus had agreed. He had fallen to his knees and begged for his life. His captors had dealt him a good beating, to convince the others back at Capua that he had not been treated tenderly. He had also been given a good meal, a purse of coins and released with letters of protection.

Once he had returned to Capua, Septimus explained how

he had withstood the torture, refused to break and was released for lack of evidence. He was regarded as a hero, fêted and honoured, being given a prominent place in the Christian assembly. A week later Dionysius returned with a similar story. The two men hardly ever spoke, avoided each other's company and never again referred to what had happened in those dark caves beneath the earth. The persecution had raged. Septimus had done his share of betrayal until the civil war had broken out. The authorities were no longer concerned about Christians but who was to rule in Rome. By then, Septimus had won a reputation as an orator and scholar, whilst Dionysius had espoused the teaching of Arius. Septimus liked that. It gave a name to their enmity, it separated them; until Dionysius had opened secret negotiations with the orthodox party and Septimus had begun to wonder how much he knew.

Septimus felt his belly grip with fear. He started in pain at the cramp in his left leg. He pulled himself up and became aware of the cries and shouts, the patter of running feet from outside. He hastily put on his sandals, grabbed a cloak, and ran out into the passageway. Servants were hurrying along. One was carrying a bucket of water. From deeper in the palace echoed the clash of cymbals and shouts of 'Fire!' Septimus decided to find out what was happening, but he and the rest were stopped by guards in the corridor leading to the imperial apartments. An officer brusquely informed him how a fire had broken out in one of the chambers but that no one had been hurt and the blaze had been quickly controlled.

Septimus walked away. He returned to his own room and found a scrawled note pushed under the door. He rubbed it between his fingers, screwed the piece of parchment up and thrust it into his wallet. He then left his chamber and, walking as nonchalantly as he could, went through the palace and out to the latrines. He opened the door and went in. They were empty.

'Are you here?' Septimus called.

A shadow moved from his right. Septimus didn't turn quickly enough to escape the stunning blow to his head, which sent him crashing to the ground in a heap. He was half unconscious, aware of being dragged across the tiled floor. He tried to move his hands but they were already bound. The terrors of what had happened before, his nightmares from years past returned to haunt him. A door opened and Septimus was dragged down into the darkness. He felt his belt and wallet removed. He was aware of a mustiness, a cloying warmth, the smell of stagnant water. He tried to groan and became conscious of the gag pushed into his mouth. Dionysius! Was the same thing happening to him?

Pains shot through his head, his body was sweat-soaked, the harsh breathing of his captor echoed ominously. Septimus was thrust against a pillar, ropes tied around him. He had lost his robe and now his tunic was ripped apart. Behind him he could hear shuffling feet, and someone gasping for breath, as if they had run fast over a long distance. A whip cracked, and Septimus screamed silently as the first lash cut across his exposed back.

Chapter 7

'Cui bono?'
('Who profits?')

Cicero, *Pro Milone*, XII

The galley which usually patrolled the Straits of Byzantium as the *Glory of Corinth* had been painted black. Its red-gold taff-rail had been covered over, as had the gold-embossed griffin's head on the stern, and the eagle with spread wings and the Horus Eye on the jutting prow. Its reefed sails were black, whilst its crew had been trained to row with muffled oars. The galley had slipped from the main battle fleet exploiting the late summer weather to leave the Aegean and enter the Middle Sea. It had stood off Sicily, then moved along the Italian shoreline, making careful use of deserted coves and inlets. If danger threatened, false flags and standards were raised. To the curious, it was just another war galley patrolling the coast against pirates. Well supplied with water and stores, the galley had taken up its agreed position on the appointed day and waited for the signal. At last it had come, a series of beacon lights clearly seen from the sea. The captain of the galley had moved his craft in, lean and low in the water like some sinister wolf slinking towards a sheep pen. The sea was calm and the pilot knew all about the currents and hidden dangers, so they successfully beached the galley at dusk.

The soldiers and marines, dressed in breeches and tunics under coats of mail, now prepared to move inland. They had all been selected for their loyalty and training. They were veterans, skilled in the ambushing and killing of bandits and outlaws in the Taurus Mountains near the Cilician Gates. They were armed with bows, arrows and long curved swords, with roundel shields slung over their backs, on their heads reinforced leather helmets with nose guards and earflaps. Some carried makeshift ladders, long poles with rods either side, as well as grappling irons, tubs of pitch and small pots of fire. They ate their meal of hard bread, dried fruits and salted meat and took a gulp from the small water bottle each man carried before moving forward.

Once they'd reached the sand hills they paused for a while to finish their preparations and sent their skirmishers forward into the trees. These scouts, Vandal mercenaries, silenced all life in the lonely farmsteads and cottages, cutting the throats of all they met, butchering the dogs and helping themselves to any plunder. The officers had studied their maps of the area most closely. The countryside around the Villa Pulchra was fairly deserted, the result of successive imperial decrees. This helped them, as did the information they'd received about the villa's security. It was under the command of Gaius Tullius, a veteran officer of Constantine who shared his command with Burrus, commander of the great bitch Helena's guard. The attackers had been given strict instructions. Constantine and his mother were to be assassinated, the likes of Burrus, Rufinus, Chrysis and Gaius Tullius taken prisoner, along with the priest Sylvester and the leader of the orthodox party, Athanasius. Everyone else was to be put to the sword.

The attacking force moved deeper into the woods. Climbing the slopes, they reached a glade, where they regrouped and rested, sharing out the paltry spoils of their plunder. They drank some more water and moved on. After a great deal of trekking they reached the approaches to the villa. Occasionally they would come across guards on picket duty, but these were few and sleepy-eyed, and soon disposed of. The undergrowth outside the villa was thick, so they were forced to use the only track. The captain in charge had no choice in the matter, yet he guessed something was wrong. He could feel it in the prickling of the sweat along his back. Was it the silence of the woods? The absence of any owl hoot or flurry amongst the undergrowth? Had the animals also sensed something threatening and fled? Now and again the captain would pause, listening for the sounds of the night. He looked back. All he could see in the faint moonlight was a bobbing line of men. Despite his suspicions, he was totally unaware of the dark, hulking shadows following his men either side of the path. These shapes, used to the pitch darkness of the German forests, slipped like hunting wolves through the bracken, grouping round the end of the column. As the line of attackers moved more quickly, stragglers began to appear, and the silent shadows took these, a hand about the mouth, a knife across the throat . . .

Claudia gazed round the opulent triclinium of the Villa Pulchra. The gold-edged couches were arranged in a horse-shoe fashion, and before each was a long, low table of polished

Lebanese cedar inlaid with strips of ebony and ivory. The tables were covered with small, fine gold dishes containing portions of beef casserole, hare in sweet sauce, ham in red wine and fennel, fried liver, baked plaice and spiced trout. On a piece of stiffened papyrus, its top and bottom embossed with imperial and Christian insignia, Constantine's personal chef had explained the menu with phrases such as: 'If they are young, hares are to be eaten in a sweetish sauce of pepper, a little cumin, and ginger . . .'

Claudia had eaten enough, and had drunk the blood-red Falernian wine, at least seventy years old or so the menu declared, mixed heavily with the slightly warm water served to each guest in little jugs. The chamber was lit by chandeliers, each holding six oil lamps in alabaster jars of various colours. The wheels on which these lamps stood had been lowered as far as possible to provide enough light, their fragrance mingling with the perfume from the pots of incense, vervins, maidenhair and frankincense as well as the countless baskets of flowers which ranged along the walls.

The guests had been entertained by various artists and musicians. Now the villa poet was quoting Ovid's sonnet: 'Since you are so beautiful, I cannot demand you to be faithful'. Very few of the guests were paying attention, busy with their own conversations or staring rather drunkenly into their cups. In the centre of the horseshoe Constantine was arguing fiercely with his mother. He looked agitated. Helena was holding a water jug, remonstrating with her son about how much he was drinking. Timothaeus was standing anxiously behind the imperial couches. Claudia would have liked to have caught his eye and summoned him over, but the steward appeared ill at ease. Chrysis sprawled, whispering to the pretty boy who shared his couch. Athanasius and

Justin, the respective party leaders, were deliberately separated, even though this cosy supper party was being held in their honour. Across from her, Gaius Tullius, his toga slipping on to the floor, yawned in the face of an elderly senator. The Captain glanced quickly across, winked, then turned back to the old fool, who was boring everyone with his denunciations about what was happening in the baths of Rome.

Claudia sat at one end of the horseshoe arrangement. From here she could see the musicians, who had tried their best but had now given up and were gorging themselves on wine and scraps taken from the tables. Directly across from her, at the other end of the horseshoe, was a tall, dark-haired man who had remained silent and tense. Claudia had seen Rufinus get up and go round to talk quietly to him. The stranger was sour-faced, with deep-set eyes, and moved restlessly on his couch. He was not a courtier despite the expensive robes; his face, arms and legs, burnt dark by the sun, glistened with oil. Claudia noticed the scars peeping out from beneath the sleeves and hem of his tunic and concluded he must either be a soldier or a gladiator, as he possessed that same restlessness Murranus did.

Claudia looked away. She was bored, tired, yet still anxious after that violent attack. She recalled the door being opened, the oil lamp tossed in, smashing on the floor to create a puddle of oil and flame. If she had been asleep on the bed, that bowl would have turned the sheets into her funeral pyre. Why had her attacker done this? She closed her eyes and recalled every detail. She had been sitting talking to Narcissus, and the door had opened quickly. That was it! Most of the villa's guests had retired to their beds during the heat of the day. The would-be assassin thought she would do the same. He had brought that oil lamp, waited until the passageway was empty and opened the door. He had not calculated on someone being with her. He – and Claudia, recalling the grotesque in the cellar, could only conclude it was a man – must have panicked at the sound of voices, and instead of taking more care and aiming the bowl directly at the bed, had simply tossed it in. The assassin had been frustrated, yet had caused enough confusion to send her and Narcissus fleeing through the window. The small chamber was of hard stone, with a few sticks of wooden furniture, so servants had soon brought the blaze under control with heavy cloaks and buckets of dry sand. Claudia and Narcissus had sheltered in the garden. She had told her companion to keep quiet while she informed a chamberlain that the fire was the result of an accident. In truth, however, her tormentor was hunting her, and Claudia wondered if the Augusta knew the facts of the matter. Every so often during the meal Helena would glance across at her, eyebrows drawn together as if curious or perplexed about something.

Claudia gazed around the chamber. Which one of these guests was responsible? Chrysis, who disliked her? The philosophers? Athanasius had approached her just before the meal, rather angry that he couldn't find his colleague Septimus. Claudia felt tempted to take another sip of wine to calm her nerves, but she didn't wish to become drunk. Rufinus, on the couch next to her, tried to converse with her, but his wife Fulvia Julia had sensed this and kept cooing like a wood pigeon, demanding her husband's attention.

Claudia decided to study a painting on the far wall of the triclinium. The dining room was grandly called the Chamber of Mars because its walls were decorated with war-like themes extolling the glory of Rome. The one opposite showed a prosperous country being laid waste. Enemy battalions were being massacred. Men were running away or being taken prisoner, the walls of a town lay smashed by siege engines, its ramparts stormed in a sea of blood, the defenders, unable to resist, lifting their hands in surrender. A cherry hit the table before her. Claudia glanced across. Sylvester was looking at her questioningly, as if he too was curious about the events which had taken place. Claudia gave him a quick smile. The Roman presbyter, like everyone else in this room, was to be regarded with suspicion. Aye, Claudia reflected, not to mention those outside, even woe-faced Narcissus. Claudia pinched her nostrils. There was something not quite right about Narcissus the Neat, something he had said, but she could not place what it was.

The murmur of the conversation died, the poet had withdrawn, having been tossed a silver piece by the Emperor. Chrysis, the chamberlain, took the floor; he was immediately greeted by a round of applause. Claudia suspected what was about to happen. Chrysis was a former actor, a propagandist, ever ready to proclaim fresh scandals about Licinius, Emperor of the East, and his corrupt court at Nicomedia. 'Fresh news from the East.' Chrysis spread his hands. 'Licinius is organising raffles. At his dinner parties he gives out lucky chances written on spoons. It can be ten camels, ten flies, a pound of steak or even dead dogs. I think he is running out of money.' He gestured with his hands for his audience not to laugh. 'The man's mad. He insists on eating fish in a blue sauce. He harnesses four huge dogs to his chariot, and listen, when he gets drunk, he locks his friends in their bedrooms then, at the dead of night, sends in lions, leopards and bears.'

'I might start that here,' Constantine shouted in a burst of laughter. 'What would you like, Chrysis, a bear or a panther?'

'Excellency,' Chrysis shook his head, 'Licinius is bankrupt. He is sending his hangers-on frogs, scorpions, snakes and other hideous reptiles, he is trapping flies in jars and calling them tamed bees.' Chrysis now had the attention of everyone in the chamber; this was not a game. The chamberlain was deliberately ridiculing Constantine's rival, raising the temperature of the court, another prick of encouragement for Constantine to try his chances in the East.

Claudia watched the Empress. Helena hadn't eaten or drunk anything. Claudia suddenly realised someone was missing: Helena's shadow, the man who had first recruited Claudia for the imperial service, the Christian priest and scribe Anastasius. Why had the Empress left him in Rome? What else was happening? Were there other dangers like those beacon lights? Claudia wondered why the Empress had quarrelled with her son. Moreover, since the poet had left, messengers had been coming in and out of the chamber as if informing Helena about something important happening elsewhere in the villa. Claudia stared round and suppressed a shiver. Helena had taken over the supper party. Before it had even begun she had insisted that everyone had to stay and be entertained. Was there a sinister reason behind that?

'Licinius is going to die soon.' Chrysis was now in full flow. 'It's been predicted by a Syrian priest that he will die violently. So he has prepared twisted ropes of purple silk so he can hang himself if necessary, and a golden sword on which he can fall when the day of judgement arrives.' Chrysis was now staring hard-eyed at his imperial master. 'Licinius expects death. They say he has poisons hidden away in amethysts and emeralds. He has built a very high tower with gold and jewelled slabs beneath on to which he can throw himself. Perhaps it is time, your Excellency,' he finished with a flourish, 'that Licinius was encouraged to play more mean-ingfully with these toys.'

His words were greeted by a thunderous roar of approval. Goblets were raised in toast. Constantine stared round, his heavy-jowled face flushed, nodding in agreement. The musi-cians struck up a tune, but they were so drunk Chrysis told them to shut up. Rufinus the banker used the occasion to turn back to Claudia.

'Are you still worried about Murranus?'

'I am,' she smiled, 'and intrigued by what Chrysis said. Did you really think Murranus would kill a man clearly in-capacitated?'

Rufinus shrugged. 'That's the law of the amphitheatre, Claudia. I've seen gladiators trip or fall ill; it's not saved them from death. But I'll tell you something,' he gave a lopsided grin, 'or I'll repeat myself. There's big money being moved around, a great deal going on Murranus to win.'

'But that's not the end of it,' Claudia interrupted. 'He will have to face Meleager the Magnificent, the Marvel of a Million Cities.'

'Would you like to meet him?' Rufinus asked. 'Meleager? He's been in the villa since you arrived. Meleager,' Rufinus called across to the dark-haired stranger Claudia had noticed earlier. 'You best come over here, I want to introduce someone to you.'

Meleager slid from the couch and came across. He was tall, and just the way he walked reminded Claudia of a panther in a cage. He was thick-set and heavily built but moved as gracefully as any dancer. He crouched down before Rufinus and stared at Claudia. He had deep, close-set eyes, high cheek bones, a slightly twisted nose, and thin lips above a firm chin. His black hair had been cut and dressed to cover a hideous scar close to his left ear. Claudia looked at his wrist; there was no purple tattoo.

'Meleager, can I introduce young Claudia, messenger and maid of the Augusta, dear friend of Murranus, whom you shall meet in the arena?'

'My lady.' Meleager took Claudia's hand and raised it to his lips. 'Your friend has won a great reputation. I hope to meet him at the games held in honour of the Emperor's birthday. My lady, are you well?'

Claudia's mouth had gone dry. She wanted Meleager to let go of her hand. She didn't want him to know how cold she had gone. He might not have had any tattoo on his wrist, but up close she recognised that voice, she recalled the smell, a mixture of perfume and sweat; even his touch was familiar. This was the man who had raped her, the killer of poor Felix.

'I . . .' Claudia's eyelids fluttered. She prayed she wouldn't faint. The room was moving. 'Do you know something,' she laughed, withdrawing her hand quickly, 'I've drunk far too much wine, I need to be sick.' And, scrambling off the couch, she fled the chamber.

She didn't know where she was going. She raced past guards and sentries, ignoring the challenge of an officer. She ran down a colonnaded walk, climbed a wall and fled into the darkness. She reached a tree and felt she could go no further. Her legs were growing heavy and a terrible pain pounded in the back of her head. She felt as if her breath had stopped and, falling to her knees, she was violently sick. As she retched she wiped the hand that Meleager had held, to brush away not just his touch but the very skin. She continued to be sick until her belly was empty; the acid bubbled at the back of her throat but she felt better. She moved away and lay face-down on the grass. It was wet and cool, just like that sand where she and Felix had been playing. He had been hunting for shells when the shadow had appeared. She began to cry, just letting the tears come.

'Claudia! Claudia!' She felt her hair being stroked, and tensed. A hand grasped her shoulder and pulled her gently over; she didn't resist but let herself flop, and stared up at an anxious-faced Sylvester. He took off his cloak, put it over her and sat beside her, plucking at the grass.

'I saw you leave. The others thought you were going to be sick. Claudia, you are never sick, you are never drunk! What happened there? Meleager thinks he frightened you.'

'He did,' Claudia replied, and struggled to sit up. She took Sylvester's cloak and wrapped it round her shoulders. 'He terrified me, Magister. He's the one!'

'The one?'

'The man who raped me and killed my brother.'

'Impossible! You saw the tattoo?'

'It's been washed off.' Claudia felt her strength returning. 'I know it's him, I'll never forget his smell, that voice . . .'

'Hush now.' Sylvester took her face in his hands. 'I'm a priest of Christ, Claudia, so what I'm going to say is hard. You must pretend, as you have done since that terrifying night. If justice is to be done, then let God take care of it. I swear by His Holy name that He will. Meleager is a gladiator. If he suspects, even for a few seconds, that you know who he truly is, then you are in very grave danger. No, no.' He pressed his fingers against Claudia's lips. 'Claudia, I beg you by all that is holy, hide your face and curb your heart! I swear that if God does not act, I will. I owe you that.' He took his fingers away. 'Think, Claudia,' he added, his words hissing through the darkness, 'think of yourself, and of Felix!'

Claudia stared into the night. The pain was going, her

stomach was empty and she felt hungry. So many thoughts milled about. Sylvester was stroking her hair just like her father used to. She leaned against his hand.

'Help me up,' she whispered, 'then I'll help myself.'

Claudia, unsteady on her feet, walked into the darkness and paused. She turned, cocking her head slightly.

'What was that?' she asked. 'Did you hear it, Magister?' She tried to sift the noises of the night. 'The clash of weapons, cries and yells?'

Sylvester listened intently. Claudia heard the sounds again. They were coming from somewhere to the south, beyond the villa walls.

'What is happening?' She was glad of the distraction. She listened again but the sounds had faded. She recalled those beacon fires, Helena poring over the maps. 'What is going on, Sylvester?'

'I don't know.' Sylvester shrugged. 'In the early evening Augusta was very busy. Have you noticed Anastasius is missing? She has left him to watch things in Rome. She has also sent an urgent message to the main German camp not far away. Did you observe her at the supper party? She was very distracted. She didn't want anyone to leave the triclinium. In fact,' Sylvester smiled through the darkness, 'it was she who told me to follow you.'

'Well, I'm safe and I will go and change.' Claudia lifted her hand. 'Sylvester, I thank you. I will act on your advice and,' she added, 'keep a still tongue in my head.'

Claudia reached the palace and went straight to her old chamber. Its door hung loose, and one side was badly scorched. She took a lamp and went inside. The floor was covered by a carpet of sand and ash and she had to probe with the half-burnt leg of a stool to ensure nothing was left. She was busy prodding when she recalled the sand in the cellar.

'Of course,' she whispered, 'it must be that!' She stood staring at the ash, then collected a few items still useable and went along to her new chamber.

Helena had been most generous – this room was more spacious. Scenes from a vineyard decorated the walls: dark green bushes with ochre-red trellises covered with snaking gold branches from which full purple grapes hung. Children collected them in heaped baskets. The painting on the next wall showed the workers in the wine press. Claudia again recalled wading through the sand in that cellar as she tried to flee from her attacker. The stuccoed ceiling was emblazoned with a brilliant picture of Phoebus in his chariot, whilst the mosaic on the floor depicted a young boy playing a flute. The bed was one of the couches taken from the triclinium. The rest of the furniture, stools and small tables, were gifts from the Empress's stores. New clothes and robes had also been provided. Claudia washed her face in a gleaming bowl, stripped and dressed again. She glanced in the copper-edged mirror, plucked at her cheeks, tidied her hair and sprinkled some of the perfume Murranus had brought her after he had won his last fight.

When she returned to the triclinium, she was relieved to discover her presence had hardly been missed. Athanasius was loudly demanding the whereabouts of Septimus. Chrysis the chamberlain was drunk; he had already been sick and listened bleary-eyed as he shared the couch of the strident orator. Constantine was talking to Rufinus, heads close together like fellow conspirators. Helena was missing. Claudia retook her own seat. She glanced quickly at Meleager, but he hardly spared her a glance; too busy playing the love dove with Rufinus's wife. Claudia controlled her anger. She felt like crossing the floor and confronting him. Her eye caught a sharp meat knife on the table, and she brushed it with her fingers. It would be so easy to grasp it, run across and plunge it into that bull-like neck! She was about to pick it up when a cherry hit her on the side of her face. She glanced up. Sylvester was staring across, shaking his head.

Claudia withdrew her hand. What could she do? She thought of Murranus moving like a dancer across the sand in the school of gladiators. She felt her empty stomach lurch and a slight flutter of her heart. She pulled across a platter of food, then started at the braying sound of a war horn. The noise and clatter in the triclinium died away. Gaius Tullius sprang to his feet. Constantine lurched from his couch, sitting on its edge, eyes popping, mouth open. The doors were flung open and Helena entered. She whispered to her son, who would have sprung to his feet, but the Empress, standing behind him, pressed firmly on his shoulder.

'My lords, ladies, fellow guests.' She smiled sweetly around. 'The alarm has been raised. This villa is under attack, but,' her voice rose to a shout, 'everything is under control. I ask you to return to your own chambers and stay there. My son and I, with others,' she glared at Claudia, 'will remain behind.'

She raised a hand, snapping her fingers. Burrus and a contingent of Germans entered the chamber. From the blood on Burrus's arms, the mud splattered on his face, the dirt and gorse which clung to his clothes, it was obvious that he had just returned from a savage affray. More of his guard entered. Gaius Tullius made to protest, but Helena barked at him to go about his duties, then clapped her hands. 'Come now,' she shouted. 'You all have your orders!'

The triclinium soon emptied, except for Constantine, Helena, Chrysis, who looked fit for nothing, the priest Sylvester, Rufinus and Claudia. More mercenaries entered, some of them newcomers from the camp which lay halfway between Rome and the Villa Pulchra. Constantine raised a hand, now intent on listening to the trumpets and horns, the sounds of running feet in the corridor outside.

'It is useless,' Helena snapped. 'Such preparations are now useless. I have everything under control.' She picked up her cloak, which was lying over the edge of her couch. 'I've given strict instructions, the gates are not to be opened.'

'Why not!' Constantine yelled like a little boy. 'My soldiers . . .'

'Son,' Helena lowered her voice, but the others in the room could still hear, 'the gates will remain closed until I say. At this moment in time, this hour of treachery, we do not know who we will be letting out, and if the gates remain closed, we will at least have some control over those who are let in. Now come, none of your bawling or shouting, it will do no good.'

Helena swept from the chamber, the rest following. Constantine kept pace with his mother, muttering obscenities under his breath. They were ringed by Burrus's men, who carried shields and drawn swords. The imperial staff officers standing in the corridors could only gaze helplessly on. They looked to the Emperor for a sign, but Constantine was no fool; drunk or not, he knew his mother was speaking sense. This was the hour of treachery and he trusted her implicitly.

They crossed the peristyle garden, through the atrium, where the oil lamps still glowed before the household gods, and started down the main path, past gardens and groves, to the gate. The area before this was now aglow with lighted braziers and small bonfires, and more of Burrus's men clustered around, guarding the gate with a ring of steel. Pitch torches spluttered on their stands along the parapet of the curtain wall. The steps to this were also guarded, the Germans swiftly standing aside as Helena swept up, her son stumbling behind her. At the top, the strong night breeze whipped their hair and fluttered their cloaks, Claudia had to protect her face against the sparks from the crackling torches. She glanced up. Storm clouds were gathering, moving fast together, blotting out the stars. Beneath her, guarding the external approaches to the gate, a contingent of Germans formed a horseshoe pattern, shields up, ready for any enemy. They looked ominous and sinister, their shadows long and shifting in the light from the roaring bonfire.

Helena called for silence. All chatter died, and Claudia heard it, a low, distant clamour coming from the darkness of the trees. At first she thought it was armed men massing for attack, until she heard the clash of weapons and faint cries, and glimpsed a glow of burning amongst the trees. A fierce bloody fight was taking place in the woods stretching down to the coast, warrior against warrior, in the pitch darkness of night.

'We have them!' Helena exulted. 'My boys have caught them in the dark amongst the trees. To them that's Germany and the enemy are the Legions of Varus.'

'It's bad luck,' Chrysis slurred, 'to talk of that.' He was immediately told to shut up.

'Mother, dearest,' Constantine rasped, 'I need an explanation, a drink, or both.'

The Emperor would have continued, but the clamour of battle grew more distinct. Claudia realised why the sounds of the fight had not been heard in the villa. Burrus's Germans must have trapped the enemy deep in the woods, driving them back to the coast. She also appreciated Helena's reluctance to share her knowledge of the attack or order the dispatch of imperial troops. The men dying in the woods had been brought here by a traitor; the real enemy was within. Constantine was Emperor because his troops had hailed him as such. He would not be the first to be overthrown by those close to him. On this issue Helena had instructed her son, pointing out that virtually every single Emperor who had been assassinated had been killed by those very close to him.

'I feel sick,' Chrysis moaned. 'It's like standing on the deck of a ship.'

Claudia watched the fat chamberlain hurry down the steps into the gardens, where the imperial garrison was beginning to muster under the direction of their officers. He headed into the bushes, and Claudia wondered if he had been plotting. She heard Helena exclaim and turned back. The Empress was pointing to where a tongue of flame was shooting against the blackness.

'Someone was carrying a pot of oil or a bucket of pitch,' Helena murmured.

The clamour and yells were now dying. Claudia was leaning against the wall, staring into the night, when the quiet was abruptly broken by a strange chanting. She recognised a favourite battle song of the mercenaries. Dark figures emerged from the trees, racing towards the gates; others carrying torches followed more slowly. A few of the figures danced like demons in the light, whirling round, leaping up and down, shaking the bundles in their hands. As they approached, Claudia realised these bundles were in fact severed heads. Other figures, a veritable flood, were emerging

159

from the wood. Burrus, who had been guarding the gate, now went out to greet his companions, who clustered beneath the curtain wall staring devotedly up at their mistress. They saluted her with a clash of swords, raucous shouts and frenetic dancing, all the time shaking their grisly trophies. Other figures came more slowly up behind this group, and Claudia saw they were guarding a few prisoners.

The Augusta, leaning against the wall, her face and shoulders illuminated by a gleaming torch held by her son, lifted her hands in greeting and shouted that they were a horde of ruffians but she loved them dearly.

'Let them in,' Helena sighed, pushing herself away from the wall. 'Let my lovely boys come in. Let them drink and eat to their hearts' content, then it'll be time for their beds.'

The gates were thrown open and the Germans swaggered in. Helena declared she could not stand any more of their salutations.

'Now's the time to think and talk,' she snapped. 'Claudia, tend to me. Son, praise the boys. Tell them that you kiss and hug them individually, promise them fresh meats and deep-bowled cups of wine. Order Burrus to bring the prisoners to the council chamber.'

A short while later, Helena, sitting on a stool next to her son, Claudia crouching beside her, waited for the arrival of Burrus and his prisoners. Rufinus, Chrysis and Sylvester had also been invited to this splendid chamber with scenes from the history of Rome decorating the walls under its domed ceiling, the star-painted plaster reflected in the sheen of the pure marble floor beneath. The windows were unshuttered and, because the hypocaust was sealed for the summer, the chamber was warmed by dishes of glowing charcoal and lit by countless lamps which a slave was tending. Gaius and his officers stood guard at the door. They stepped aside as Burrus and his captives swept into the chamber.

The barbarians looked ferocious and sinister, with their tangled hair and beards, faces, arms and weapons still splattered with blood. They dragged three prisoners with them, young men, cut and dirty, stripped to their loincloths, hands bound behind them. These were forced to kneel and give their names and ranks. One was a simple soldier, the other two were officers, decurions, from the garrison at Athens.

Helena snapped at Burrus to deliver his report, warning him not to brag. The German obeyed, describing how the attackers had made a mistake in following the path. He had killed their stragglers, rolling the line up like a piece of string until launching an all-out assault, surrounding them and carrying out bloody slaughter. Some of the attackers had fled back to the beach, where the galley had been protected by a line of archers. Burrus did not wish to expose his men and retreated, watching from the sand hills as the galley with its crew drifted back out to sea.

'But it was beached?' Constantine demanded.

'No, Excellency.' Burrus shook his head. 'They had already dragged it back into the water. It was too dangerous to attack.'

Helena turned to the prisoners, but they could tell her very little. They described how the galley had left the main battle fleet and lurked off the Italian coast until the captain had taken their ship in. They had been told what to attack and nothing more.

'Kill them!' Chrysis slurred. 'Take them outside and crucify them.'

Helena raised her hand. She got up from her stool and crouched in front of the prisoners.

'Are you Roman citizens?' she asked.

The two officers nodded, but the soldier was a mere hircling.

Helena unpinned a paper-thin silver brooch from her gown. She whispered to her son, who smiled and nodded in agreement, then handed the brooch to Burrus.

'Break it in two,' she ordered. 'Go on,' she urged, 'do as I say.'

The German took the brooch, snapped it and handed both pieces back to Helena. She crouched in front of one of the officers and placed half of the brooch on the ground before him.

'You're not going to die,' she said. 'You are all going to be washed and fed, given a fresh set of clothes, a hot meal and some soft straw for a bed. Tomorrow morning my mercenaries will take you down to the nearest port. You can take whatever ship you want back to Corinth or Piraeus, on one condition: you tell Licinius that the attack failed, and that I will root out the traitor. You will give him a gift, half of this silver brooch, and tell him, don't forget this, that one day soon my son will come to claim that half of the brooch back.'

Chapter 8

'*Quod Dei Omen avertant.*'
('May the Gods avert this Omen.')

Cicero: *Philippic*, III.35

Claudia rose early next morning and went immediately to the small chancery room between the atrium and the peristyle garden. The storm had broken during the night, the flower beds and paving stones were saturated and the sky still looked greyish dull. Claudia reckoned it must be at least an hour before sunrise. Slaves were slowly mustering, beginning the routine of the day, tidying the gardens and clearing food from the triclinium. The villa had turned into an armed camp: sentries had been doubled, soldiers patrolled the colonnades, archers had been posted on rooftops and the upper storeys of buildings. Helena's Germans had spent the hours of darkness roistering boisterously but were still able to patrol the gardens. They had set up camp around the gates and were now busy taunting the regular soldiers. Claudia could hear their shouts and guffaws of laughter even from the chancery room.

She slipped in, closed the door and hastily collected a writing pallet, styli, strips of ready parchment, ink pots, a pumice stone and a sand shaker. She put these carefully into her leather scribe's bag and went into the kitchen to beg a small jug of watered beer and a platter of yesterday's bread, some hard cheese and ripe plums. Once she'd eaten, she returned to her own chamber, secured the door, cleared a corner and squatted down cross-legged, the writing tray across her lap. She positioned the ink pot on the floor, sharpened a stylus, soaked the tip and began to write down the problems confronting her.

Gladius Sanctus – The Holy Sword

Primo:

The sword hung on a chain above a broad circle of sand. The chain could only be moved away from the centre by someone with a long pole, spear or sword. They might still have to stand on the sand, which would be disturbed. The door was guarded by two Germans, the keys held by Timothaeus and Burrus.

Secundo:

On the day in question, Timothaeus entered the chamber. The sword had gone. Timothaeus fainted and was carried out. No one else was there. The Germans were terrified at what they regarded as a holy place. The cellar was searched carefully by Gaius Tullius. Nothing was found. Nothing was out of place, although the sand had been disturbed due to Timothaeus fainting. Now the steward was lifted out on a stretcher; he could scarcely have hidden the

*sword on him – that would have been noticed. If he
had taken in a rod or hook, that too would have been
observed. The only thing he carried was a lantern
horn scarcely big enough to hide anything in. If the
sword or implement was hidden in the cellar, Gaius
Tullius would have found it in his search.*

Tertio:

*The door to the cellar had two locks, the keys held
separately. From everything I observed and heard
there was no evidence of any trickery here.*

Quarto:

*Narcissus was one of those who helped carry
Timothaeus's stretcher out of the cellar.*

Claudia drew a line and made a second heading:

Dionysius

Then she nibbled the end of the stylus and stared at the wall.
The philosopher's death was the key to so much mystery;
that and the burning of the House of Mourning. She dipped
her stylus and began to write.

Primo:

*Dionysius had gone to the orchard to think, to be
alone. Or had he been invited there? He was sitting
with his back to the tree when he was stunned by a
blow to the head, Once weakened, he was apparently
gagged and bound, dragged into the trees, pegged out
like a lion skin, cut countless times and allowed to
bleed to death.*

165

Secundo:

Dionysius's corpse was moved to the House of Mourning, joining that of an old beggar man. According to all the evidence, the cords and gag were removed but nothing remarkable was noticed.

Tertio:

Later that same day, after darkness, the House of Mourning was consumed by a ferocious fire. Did the killer burn the corpse to hide some mistake, some clue to his identity? Was it to start the beacon fire, or both? Such arson would have been easy to arrange. A cord leading to a cluster of oil skins which was lit whilst the perpetrator fled into the darkness. Yet would oil burn so fiercely as to create such an inferno?

Claudia remembered searching amongst the ruins. She had caught a certain sweetness but had put this down to some accident with the fire. Who was the arsonist? Gaius Tullius had been with her, but only the gods knew where everyone else was. Claudia paused. There was something about that fire she had missed, something she couldn't place. Recalling her suspicions about Narcissus, she sighed and returned to her task.

Quarto:

The motive behind Dionysius's death. Was it the result of bad blood between the orthodox and Arian parties, or did it have its origins in the betrayals which took place some ten years ago when Diocletian launched his savage persecution of the Christian faith and singled out Capua for special attention? The orators now live lives of apparent probity but what about their

*past? Are they hiding secret sins? Are they frightened
of old crimes catching them out? Or was Dionysius's
death the work of someone like Chrysis, a dyed-in-the
wool pagan? He would love to turn this public debate
into a bloody arena where the Christians could tear
each other to pieces in front of the Emperor and bring
their religion into public disrepute.*

Quinto:

*Why kill Dionysius in such a gruesome fashion? A
knife thrust, a garrotte string, a barbed arrow or a
cup of poison would have been just as effective. What
did the killer intend? Was the method chosen to
inflict as much pain as possible? What could prompt
such malice?*

Sexto:

*Finally, is there any connection between the theft of
the sword and Dionysius's death?*

Claudia picked up a new stylus, drew a line and made a
further entry:

The Traitor

Primo:

*The assault on the villa last night was launched from
a galley which came in from the sea to land a corps
of assassins. The galley was signalled to by a series
of beacon fires started here in the villa, which means
the attack was planned, Licinius was given precise
information about when and where the Emperor and
his mother were staying, but that was common*

knowledge. Constantine's love for the Villa Pulchra is well known. He published his intentions to come here. The galley must have stayed off the coast and waited for the signal that the Emperor had actually arrived.

Secundo:

Are Dionysius's killer and the traitor the same person? Was the sword stolen to hand over to Licinius, who could use it to ridicule the Emperor's mother? Had the arsonist always plotted to use the House of Mourning as a beacon light?

Claudia closed her eyes. Logic dictated a connection, she thought, but where was the evidence?

Tertio:

Was the attack the work of Licinius, Emperor in the East? Probably, yet as Chrysis illustrated at the supper party, there are those at court eager to seek a casus belli, *a reason to go to war and make Constantine Imperator Orbis, Emperor of the World.*

Claudia put the stylus down and leaned back, stretching out her legs to ease the cramp. She recalled the fierce discussion in the council chamber after the prisoners had been removed. Constantine had been furious that his mother had taken full responsibility for defending the villa. He had been supported by his officers, and even Rufinus had nodded in agreement. Helena, however, had remained calm and composed, arguing that the attack, by definition, was secret, composed of a modest force which, if surprised, could be defeated. The attackers would have had to move through woodland, during the dead of night. Such conditions were most favourable to her Germans. Finally, and on this point Helena would not concede, there was a traitor in the villa. If the attackers had been warned, they would have withdrawn and waited for another day. As it was, she had frustrated the attack and sent a powerful reply to Licinius. Sharp discussion had followed, but Helena had won the day.

Constantine then raised a question which had also concerned Claudia. If the House of Mourning had been fired by the traitor who had lit the other beacon lights, who was missing from the villa that night? Gaius Tullius went to check, returning sometime later, whilst Helena was still arguing with her son, to report that no one had left, although he could not be certain as most of the guards on picket duty had been massacred during the assault.

Claudia's stylus skimmed across the piece of parchment. She sanded it and moved to a new piece. Outside she could hear voices and realised the villa was stirring. She got up and stretched, then crouched back into the corner, making herself comfortable. She picked up the writing tray and wrote the final heading.

Spicerius, Murranus, Meleager

Primo:

People are intrigued as to why Murranus didn't close to kill his weakened opponent, but that is Murranus, the way he fights. Spicerius was poisoned, but the potion was not strong enough to kill him. Was the wine poisoned? Or was it some other method? Was Spicerius weakened so Murranus could kill him

*easily? Was the poisoning an act of personal
vengeance against Spicerius, or even against
Murranus? Or was it just the result of heavy betting?
Yet why were these wagers being laid unless
Murranus was going to win?*

Claudia chewed on her lip. In a few days' time Murranus
would fight Spicerius, and if victorious face Meleager. She
wrote down that fateful name and scored a line beneath it
time and time again. She could feel a surge of emotion, not
so much hot and angry, more cold and calculating. She felt
like a swordsman studying an opponent, watching for his
weakness, wondering where to strike. She threw the stylus
down to distract herself, and tried to review what she had
written, but she kept going back to that dreadful meeting.
Had Meleager recognised her? Rufinus said he had been in
the villa some time. Was it he who had attacked her? Drawn
that crude painting on the wall?

Claudia suddenly found it difficult to breathe, as if
someone was pressing on her chest. She got to her feet, rolled
the pieces of parchment into a scroll and squeezed them
into the square wallet on her belt. She left the chamber to
walk the corridor. She passed one of the guards and paused,
thinking about the oil lamp that had been thrown into her
room. Who was allowed into the imperial quarters? A slave
hurried by carrying two jugs of water; such individuals were
let through without a second glance. Was that what her
attacker had done? Pretended to be a servant or slave? She
continued walking and found herself in the peristyle garden.
The sun was beginning to rise, drying the paving stones,
flooding that beautiful garden with light which glimmered
in the pool and reflected on the marble pillars. The

flowerbeds seemed to come to life in a dazzle of colour, the birdsong was clear from the bushes and shrubs around the garden. Claudia found a dry seat and sat down facing the rising sun. She half closed her eyes, drinking in the beauty.

'Good morning, Claudia.' She started as Athanasius, his face heavy with sleep, sat down beside her. 'I'm sorry if I made you jump. I rose early. All this excitement from last night. What happened?'

Claudia told him about the attack, keeping the details as vague as possible. Athanasius, hitching his robe around his shoulders, listened with a half-smile as he realised she wouldn't tell him much.

'I'm searching for Septimus,' he said when she had finished. 'I haven't seen him at all. I'm a little worried. Where could he be?'

Claudia kept silent; she really wanted to be alone.

'Oh, sometimes he wanders off.' Athanasius nudged her playfully. 'He too likes to be alone. What a beautiful place. I remember the debate here and, afterwards, you talking to that slave.'

Claudia stiffened.

'You know the one.' Athanasius kept his voice level. 'He is responsible for the House of Mourning. Last night, at the supper party, I tried to make friends with Justin and, to be fair, he tried to do the same. He said something very curious about that slave . . .'

'Narcissus?'

'Ah, yes, Narcissus. Justin believed he'd seen him before, in Capua, a slave of a rather large Christian family. The head of the house was a funeral manager. Justin was sure Narcissus worked for him.'

Claudia tried to suppress her shiver.

'And there's something else. The afternoon Dionysius died—'

'Murdered,' Claudia retorted, 'Dionysius was murdered.'

'Ah yes, so he was. Well, I went down to the House of Mourning. The windows on either side were shuttered whilst the door was locked from the inside. In the Christian tradition, it is a just and holy thing to pray for the dead. I wanted to kneel by Dionysius's corpse and recite a few prayers. I was surprised the door was locked, so I knocked and knocked until my knuckles turned sore. Eventually the door opened, and Narcissus stood there looking very guilty. He claimed to have fallen asleep. I told him to stand aside and went in. I glanced around, but there was nothing amiss. The old man lay wrapped in his sacking, Dionysius was stretched out on his slab like a piece of meat. Now there was something about that chamber . . . I have been to Egypt, Claudia, I visited the Necropolis on the West Bank of the Nile. I've been to their embalmers' shops; that's what it smelled like.'

'Did you notice anything else?'

Athanasius closed his eyes. 'A large chest in the far corner, nothing else. After I'd finished my prayers, I went out.'

'Did you notice anything untoward? Please, Athanasius, think.'

'Just the corpses. Dionysius looked dreadful, mouth gaping, eyes half open. He looked as if he'd been soaked in blood. One thing I did notice, the ropes and gag the killer had used were piled on the floor just beneath the slab. When Justin was trying to be friendly last night, I told him how I'd been to the House of Mourning to pay my respects, and how the fire had had nothing to do with me. Justin didn't accept that; however, he did say that he too had gone down there to pray. This time the House of Mourning was locked from the outside and the slave Narcissus was sleeping under a sycamore tree, a beer jug next to him. Justin also demanded to see the corpse; Narcissus wasn't very pleasant about it.'

Athanasius got to his feet.

'Do you remember the poems of Juvenal?' He smiled down at Claudia. 'He once posed a question: who shall guard the guards?'

'And?' Claudia asked.

'In your case, little one,' Athanasius bent down, 'you must ask the question: who spies on the spies?'

The philosopher walked away.

'Claudia?'

She whirled round. Burrus and Gaius Tullius were standing at the entrance to the peristyle garden. The German was dressed in his shaggy fur cloak; Gaius had put on a leather breastplate, a sword belt wrapped round his waist, marching boots on his feet. He carried a helmet under his arm which displayed the imperial scarlet and black plume. He beckoned with his hand.

'Claudia, the Augusta has asked me to seek you out.'

She got to her feet and walked over.

'We are to walk the track down to the coast. The Augusta was quite specific. You are to accompany us. She says you have sharp eyes and perhaps will see things we would miss.'

'Not in a forest she won't,' Burrus grumbled.

'Do you want to collect your cloak?' The Captain ignored the German's interruption. 'Before we leave I want to show you something.' And, spinning on his heel, Gaius Tullius marched away, leaving Claudia and Burrus no choice but to hurry on behind. They skirted the palace going across to the ruined House of Mourning. Gaius didn't stop there but led them both into a clump of sycamore trees, a rather wild, untended part of the garden where the unruly brambles and gorse stretched up to the curtain wall. He pushed his way through these, Burrus behind opening a path for Claudia.

At onc point Claudia paused and squatted down to examine some bones, lamb and beef, with dried scraps of meat still clinging to them. Nearby, rolled up in a ball, was a soiled napkin and, under a thorn bush, an earthenware wine jug.

'Someone's been feasting.'

Gaius came back to stand over her. 'The servants are always stealing away to eat the food they've filched, but that's not important. Come on . . .'

They reached a small clearing just before the wall. Gaius pointed to the strong, reinforced Syrian bow lying on the ground, an empty quiver and, beside it, an earthenware pot blackened by fire.

'I found these this morning,' he explained, 'or rather, my men and I did. We decided to search the grounds for anything suspicious. There was always the possibility that one of the attackers had broken through and might be hiding here.'

Claudia went across and picked up the bow. The wood and cord were soaked, as were the quiver and the earthenware pot, which still reeked of pitch and fire.

'This must have been here some time,' she murmured. 'What do you think, Gaius?'

The Captain's smooth-shaven face showed the strain of the previous night, his eyes red-rimmed from lack of sleep.

'I wish the Augusta had trusted us,' he replied, as if talking to himself. 'I mean, no offence, Burrus.' He drew a deep breath. 'I suppose I'm trying to prove myself. I suspect the bow, the quiver and pot of fire were used by the traitor. The House of Mourning was not a beacon fire, but on the night it was destroyed, the traitor used the confusion to loose fire arrows into the air.'

Claudia, squatting down, stared at the bow and the wall, then back in the direction they had come. What Gaius said made sense, but it still left the question of who had started the beacon fires.

'Burrus!' She beckoned the mercenary forward. 'We will not be walking through the woods. No, no, Gaius,' she held up her hand, 'I will explain to the Augusta. I want you to send your best men into the woods, Burrus. I want them to stay away from where the battle took place. Tell them,' she gestured with her hand, 'to scour the area to the left of the path as you leave the villa.'

'What are they looking for?' Burrus asked.

'Signs of encampment, perhaps two or three men living in the woods. They must have left a camp fire, dug a small latrine pit. They were probably soldiers, or perhaps even travelling tinkers or pedlars. If they did set up camp it would be fairly recent. Search for fire pits, scraps of clothing or food.'

Burrus nodded and hurried off.

'And me?' Gaius grinned. 'Do you have orders for me?'

'Yes, Captain, in fact I do.'

She paused as Athanasius's voice drifted across the grass. 'Septimus? Septimus?'

'He's been searching for him,' Gaius groaned. 'Knowing these philosophers, Septimus is probably sleeping it off somewhere.'

'I want you to find Timothaeus,' Claudia declared. 'I want to talk with him about the wanderer in the woods.'

'The old man who was found dead on the track outside the villa?'

'The same,' Claudia replied.

As Gaius strode off, Claudia went back to re-examine the bow and quiver and the small pot used to carry fire. She was now genuinely puzzled and intrigued why Narcissus would lie. He had told her he had left the House of Mourning, filled his stomach, drunk too much and gone to sleep it off some distance away. She now believed he was lying and wondered why. But there again, she reflected grimly, she had a number of questions for her new-found friend.

A short while later Gaius came marching back, Timothaeus hastening beside him. The steward looked rather ill and unkempt, his face unshaven, his tunic stained.

'Sit down on the grass.'

'It's wet,' Timothaeus declared. 'Haven't you forgotten, Claudia, it rained last night?'

She shrugged and sat on a marble seat, inviting Gaius to join them.

'The wanderer in the woods,' she began. 'The old man found dead near the villa shortly before the Emperor arrived.'

'That's right,' the steward agreed, blinking wearily. 'Don't you remember, Gaius, I came and saw you about him. The old man was a nuisance.' Timothaeus turned back to Claudia. 'He wandered the woods and often came to the villa to beg for scraps. He was well known to the farmers around here, though there aren't many of these left now,' he added mournfully. 'I understand our attackers slaughtered everyone who couldn't flee. We should have crucified those prisoners.' His fingers flew to his lips. 'Crucified!' he muttered. 'I'm a Christian, I shouldn't have said that, should I?'

'Tell me about the wanderer in the woods,' Claudia insisted.

'One of the guards found the old man on the track.' Timothaeus tapped the left side of his face. 'He had bruises all along here. Sometimes he was drunk, I thought he'd had a fall or fit. Isn't that right, Gaius?'

The Captain agreed. 'At any other time,' he drawled, 'we would have tossed such a corpse into the undergrowth, but I felt sorry for him. The villa has a burial pit just beyond the eastern wall. I had the corpse taken to the House of Mourning and wrapped in a shroud. Timothaeus here,' he added sardonically, 'as a Christian, claimed it was a pious act to bury the dead, say a prayer and pour a libation over the grave.'

'Are you a Christian,' Claudia asked Gaius, 'or any of your family?'

'Go through the records, Claudia. I didn't take part in the persecution, but my family are no friends of the Christians. Nevertheless,' Gaius patted Timothaeus on the shoulder, 'some I like. Timothaeus is a good fellow. Anyway, my man declared what he had found, and Timothaeus asked for my help. I had the wanderer brought in; his body was dirty, the head all bloodied.'

'Could he have been murdered?' Claudia asked.

Gaius made a face. 'Possibly. But who would want to kill an old man? All I can remember is that he stank worse than a dog pit. The Emperor arrived in the early afternoon, just after we found the body.' Gaius moved his head from side to side. 'It was taken to the death house and then the fun began: Dionysius's murder.'

'Timothaeus, you said . . .' Claudia paused; she wanted to be precise as possible, 'you claimed the wanderer in the woods was a nuisance?'

'Well, he had been for the last few days before he died. Mistress, I don't know whether he had a fall or was attacked. I had his body taken up because I felt guilty. The old fellow kept knocking at the gate saying he wished to see the Emperor. I told him to bugger off.' Timothaeus looked wistfully at her. 'Perhaps I should have been kinder? We didn't really look at his corpse, did we, Gaius? The soldiers wrapped him in a shroud, no more than a piece of sacking, put it on a stretcher and brought it in.'

'Is there anything else?' Gaius asked.

Claudia stared at the ruined House of Mourning.

'What sort of people were taken there?'

'Now and again,' Timothaeus replied, 'the occasional guest dies. Anybody with family, well, we hold the corpse until kith and kin come and claim it. As for the rest,' he rubbed his eyes, 'usually servants, household slaves. They are put there and later buried or burnt.' He got to his feet. 'Now, mistress, I have duties, and so does Gaius.'

They both drifted away. Claudia got to her feet and walked over to the sycamore tree where the Emperor had sheltered on the night of the fire. She walked back to examine the remains of the meal strewn on the hard-packed earth. She also noticed how, here and there, the ground had been dug up, but now it was baked hard.

'Claudia!'

She got to her feet, brushing off the dust, and peeped around a bush. Narcissus was walking up and down, arms flailing. 'Claudia!'

'Just the person!' she whispered. She stepped from behind the bush and tiptoed quietly up to Narcissus, pushing him hard on the shoulder. He whirled round.

'I've been looking for you, Claudia.'

'And I've been looking for you!' She smiled back. 'Come, sit and talk with me!' She patted his arm. 'I thought I was a good actress but, Narcissus, your acting ability is equal to mine.'

'What do you mean?' he spluttered. 'Claudia, now is not the time for teasing. I want to know where I'm going to live. How long are you staying at the villa?'

'Never mind that.' Claudia gestured to the garden seat. 'I want to talk to you about the wanderer in the woods. No, Narcissus, don't start trembling or crying. You knew the old man?'

'Of course,' he muttered, avoiding her gaze. 'Everyone knew him. But I'm frightened. Claudia, what happened last night?'

'You know what happened, Narcissus: the villa was attacked. The beacon lights? You were the one who saw them, weren't you?' She noticed how flushed he'd become. 'The wanderer in the woods, do you think he was murdered?' She grabbed his wrist and dug her nails in. 'Don't lie, Narcissus. You examined his corpse, as you examine all the bodies taken into the House of Mourning. Some of those you don't dare to touch, but as for others, don't you practise your embalming skills on them?'

Narcissus refused to reply.

'Do you know something?' Claudia continued blithely. 'I think you've been telling me lies about a lot of things.'

'I . . .'

'Oh, don't start acting. You're an embalmer from Syria who became involved in a revolt and were sold into slavery. Yes?'

Narcissus nodded.

'You were dispatched to Italy and . . .'

'I came here.'

Claudia slapped his face. 'I'll slap you again if you lie. I liked you, Narcissus, but I don't really know who you are. You've been at this villa some time, haven't you? You know people like Timothaeus. You also know me, and you owe me a great deal, so let's have the truth.'

'I arrived in Italy,' Narcissus began slowly. 'I was put up for sale in Tarentum.'

'Capua,' Claudia interrupted. 'Don't forget Capua, Narcissus.'

'Well, yes,' he continued hastily. 'I was sold to a farmer who regarded me as next to useless, so I ended up on the slave block, where I was bought by a Christian family.'

'Ah,' Claudia smiled, 'and you're a Christian, aren't you, Narcissus? I'm sure you are a convert.' She patted his arm. 'You made a mistake. You actually wondered if there was a different funeral rite for the Arians as opposed to the orthodox. Strange, I thought, how come a pagan slave, a man immersed in the burial rites of Egypt, is so knowledgeable about orthodox Christians and Arians? Who knows,' she peered at him round-eyed, 'you may have made other slips.' Claudia was pleased; she wasn't ready to confront Narcissus on everything, but her remark had truly frightened him. 'You were saying?' she urged.

'My new master was a funeral manager. He was kindly, with a large family, boys and girls. They lived in a villa on the edge of the town, a lovely place, mistress, gardens and orchards, olive groves and a vineyard. He made his own wine; it tasted very good. I was so happy. What my master wanted, I wanted. I accepted the White Christ. I would believe anything my master did. I was often used by him as a messenger, as a trusted confidant. He admired my embalming skills. He used to laugh, slap me on the shoulder and claim I made the most grotesque corpse kissable. On the Sabbath day, just before the evening meal, his villa became the meeting place for Christians. Their priests, who received what they call the laying on of hands, would come to celebrate the Agape, the Eucharist, what they term the love feast: the breaking of bread and the drinking of wine. They believe it's the Body and Blood of Christ.

'Now, my master was very wealthy. He was patron of the oratory school in the town; he liked nothing better than to invite speakers to his villa for the Agape. After the ceremony was over we would have supper out under the stars, the night air sweet with the perfume of hyacinth. The speakers would entertain us debating some topic or other. On other occasions my master would take his entire household down to the school to watch the orators declaim.' Narcissus put his face in his hands. 'An idyllic time! Virgil would have sung about it in his poetry.'

'And?' Claudia asked.

'Oh, I met everyone there. The school of oratory at Capua was famous; even Chrysis came, to improve his speaking and public presentation. He considered himself a new Cicero. He loved to quote the *Pro Milone* or the *Contra Catilinam* and other speeches of the great orator. I'm not too sure,' Narcissus screwed his eyes up, 'I think Chrysis had to leave, some scandal about paying fees, or in his case, not paying them.'

'And Gaius Tullius?'

Narcissus shook his head. 'I've talked to him. He spent most of his time in Gaul or Britain. He is a pagan through and through and can't see what all the fuss is about. I never met him until I came here.'

'And the steward Timothaeus?'

'He never came, but I understand he had a brother there.'

'What happened to him?'

'He disappeared during the persecution. Timothaeus doesn't know whether he fled, was arrested or killed.' Narcissus shrugged. 'No one knows! The rest of the speakers were there, Athanasius, Dionysius and the rest. They were young then, learning the art of public speaking, being trained to deliver a speech with a pebble in their mouth or recite without notes. Looking back, they were all puffed up as barn-yard cocks. Justin regarded himself as the new Demosthenes.'

'You're an educated man, Narcissus, you know all the names.'

'My master was a great scholar. He educated me, he let me read his library.'

'Then it all ended?'

'Yes, it all ended,' Narcissus declared wearily. 'I loved that family, mistress. My master promised me my freedom, planned to have me as a business partner. We could have cornered the trade in that town. You should have seen his warehouses. He had the best funeral paraphernalia: masks, fans, caskets, even his own group of musicians. Diocletian ended all that. He issued his edict, Christianity was once again proscribed, its scriptures and symbols banned.' Narcissus began to cry, sobbing quietly. Claudia noticed his fists clenched in balls, the veins in his arms standing out like tight cords. This man, she reflected, could kill. And what about Timothaeus? He had had a brother in Capua who apparently disappeared. Chrysis? He was a different matter. He was always known for his sticky fingers, reluctant to pay his debts.

As Narcissus sobbed, he reminded Claudia of a child, his tears being those of anger rather than sorrow.

'My master's family,' he wiped his eyes on the back of his hand, 'were denounced. The soldiers came in the dead of night, they found a copy of the Christian scriptures, the *Chi* and *Rho* and the icthus sign, the fish, the letters of which, as you know, stand for "Jesus Christ, Son of God, Saviour of the World". I was there shivering in the dark when the soldiers pushed this symbol into my master's face asking him to renounce it. He refused, as did his family.

They were all taken up, bound and tied, pushed out of the door and into a cart. I was ignored; you see, I was a slave, I didn't exist. I was left like a ghost in that empty house. I stayed there for about four days. People came asking what had happened. I couldn't believe it! I saw it in their eyes: I was the traitor, I had betrayed my master. So I fled, and hid out in the countryside.'

'How did you survive?'

'I knew about the Christian community, names and places. Once I was in hiding, fleeing for my life, I was accepted as one of them, but I faced many dangers. I could be branded as a traitor by the Christians or a runaway slave by the author-ities. If I was captured I could expect the cross or end up facing some great bear in the arena. One of the farmers I sheltered with told me how the authorities had now made a tally of my master's possessions. I was on it but missing. They wanted me.' Narcissus held his hands up. 'Mistress, I swear I never betrayed them, but I knew if I was captured I would be tortured. I lurked out in the countryside,' he blew his cheeks out, 'oh, two or three years, then I was passed north and given shelter in the catacombs. I looked after the graves of the dead. The years passed quickly. I came to the attention of the presbyter Sylvester and confessed my whole story to him.'

'I'm sure you did.' Claudia smiled thinly. 'And Sylvester arranged for you to come here?'

'Yes, mistress, because of Constantine's Edict of Toleration. Our new Emperor made it very clear: runaway slaves had to recognise their status and surrender to the authorities. Sylvester explained he could do nothing for me but soften the blow. He would arrange a good post; sure enough, I was presented to Chrysis and dispatched here.'

'So you haven't been here five years?' Claudia smiled.

'Of course not.'

Claudia studied him closely. She believed Narcissus was telling the truth, or at least part of it. She could also understand the Augusta's generosity towards this Syrian embalmer. Helena knew everything and would have learned all about Narcissus's previous life.

'You're a spy, aren't you?' Claudia asked. 'Sylvester made that one of his conditions. Anything you learn you pass on to Timothaeus or someone like me; that's why you approached me in the garden in the first place. Sylvester does nothing without setting a price, which is always the same: the advancement of the Christian community. It's good to have a spy at the Villa Pulchra.'

'Just information,' Narcissus protested. 'I know what I saw that night, I mean the beacon fires. I swore an oath of loyalty to Sylvester and I kept it. At that time, sitting out under the stars, I didn't realise that what I had seen was so important.'

'Who did betray your master?'

Claudia had deliberately changed the questioning, and for a moment she caught the shift in Narcissus's eyes, a hard, calculating look. 'Come on,' she said, 'you must have made enquiries. People talk. Names,' she snapped, 'you must have overheard names?'

'Dionysius, Septimus.' Narcissus was now solemn.

'Did you dishonour Dionysius's corpse?'

'I spat in its face.'

'What else did you do, Narcissus? Did you examine that old man, the wanderer in the woods?'

'I . . .'

Claudia raised her hand threateningly. 'He was murdered, wasn't he?'

'I think so.' Narcissus looked away. 'Yes, I think so. He was covered in dirt and dust, some bleeding to the side of his head. He had thick shaggy hair. His skull was stoved in, but there again, it could have been an accident.'

'You practise your art, don't you?' Claudia asked. 'You're an embalmer skilled in the Osirian rites, drawing out the brains and entrails. You did that to the wanderer in the woods, as you've practised before on corpses of slaves.'

'No one knows,' Narcissus confessed. 'I felt I had to do it to help them on their journey, and to keep my art alive. What harm did I do? Who cares about some old slave?'

'You bury the waste in the woods, don't you? I've seen the places where you hide it. More importantly, you had a chest in the House of Mourning filled with resin oil and other combustibles. That was your little kingdom, which is why you never left it. You locked the door and slept underneath the nearby sycamore tree, where you were when the fire broke out. You thought you'd be blamed, so you fled in the night. You were terrified in case they found out what you kept there and what you did. Now, Narcissus, that's all in the past. On that particular night, did you see anything suspicious?'

'I was frightened,' he pleaded. 'Those orators coming to visit the corpse . . . I never expected that. I took a jug of beer and drank too deeply. When I woke up, the fire . . .' He sprang to his feet. 'I've got duties . . .'

'No you haven't, Narcissus. You are no longer a slave, but a free man.' She grasped him by the wrist. 'I have other questions for you, but for the time being, they will wait. Don't run off.'

Claudia basked in the sunshine reflecting on what Narcissus

had said. Slowly but surely she was collecting the pieces. She started up at the clash of weapons. Burrus and a group of his mercenaries came swaggering across, bringing with them a young man. His hair was tousled, and he was dressed in a dark tunic bound round the middle by a cord. Burrus was treating him gently, his great paw on his shoulder, but the young man was clearly terrified, and if the German had taken his hand away he would have bolted like a hare.

'We found it!' The Germans ringed Claudia, and the young man they'd escorted fell to his knees before her.

'Found what?' Claudia squinted up at them.

'Traces of camp fires, about two or three men camping out in the woods for some time. A water bottle, scraps of food and clothing.'

'And who's he?'

The young man knelt, teeth chattering, eyes all startled.

'Speak.' Burrus clapped him on the shoulder. 'Tell the mistress what you saw.'

The young man gabbled in a dialect Claudia found difficult to follow; she had to ask him to slow down and repeat what he had said. However, he was still distracted by fear, and only when Claudia offered a coin did he begin to talk more slowly. She established that he was a farm worker from a nearby estate who had fled when the attack had been launched on his master's house. He had come in from the field, glimpsed figures leave the tree-line and race towards the main door of the farm. He had stood terrified as he heard the clash of weapons, the muted screams.

Burrus punched him on the shoulder. 'No, not that. Tell the mistress what you saw!'

The young man declared how, on the night the House of Mourning had been burned, he had been out in the fields hoping to catch some game. He gave an accurate description of the field Claudia had visited: lonely, lying fallow under the moonlight and ringed by trees. He had been about to cross it when, through the dark, he glimpsed a fire burning. He'd sat and watched it flare, then decided to withdraw and tell his master, but all they found the next morning were burnt embers so they dismissed it as the work of poachers or people hiding out in the woods.

Claudia thanked the young man, gave him the coin and dismissed him. She expected Burrus to move away, but the German stood staring around.

'Where's he gone?' he asked abruptly. 'The one who walks so quietly?'

'What are you talking about?' Claudia replied testily.

'Gaius,' Burrus explained. 'I want to apologise.' He peered down at Claudia. 'Gaius is a good soldier, but he is deeply upset that the Empress didn't trust him. I've got to explain.' He snapped his fingers and left to continue his search.

Claudia stood up, stretched and decided to go back to the villa. She was approaching a side entrance when she heard her name called. Sylvester stood in a portico, beckoning her over.

'I was hoping I would meet you.'

Claudia leaned against a pillar, aware of its coolness.

'How do you feel?' Sylvester sounded solicitous. 'I mean, about Meleager. Don't be frightened of him, Claudia. God's justice is like a hound, it always finds its prey. You're amongst friends here. Anyway, Meleager has gone, he's left for Rome.'

Claudia felt herself relax, taking a deep breath. She was dreading meeting that gladiator again.

'So many unexpected things have happened.' Sylvester shook his head.

'Did you plan all this?' Claudia asked wearily.

'How could I plan such chaos?' Sylvester replied, staring over her shoulder. She turned and glimpsed Justin hurrying by.

'Well?' She turned back. 'We have all the people here: Timothaeus, Narcissus, Athanasius.'

'I never thought murder would join us,' Sylvester replied, 'or treason.'

'Why did you arrange this?' Claudia asked. 'Why ask orators from Capua, why not from some other city? There are similar schools in towns all over Italy.'

'Capua was chosen for two reasons. First, Athanasius is, perhaps, our greatest orator. Secondly . . .' Sylvester caught her by the arm and led her deep into the shadows, 'Militiades, the Bishop of Rome, had relatives, blood kin, who were caught up in the last persecution. They too came from Capua. He thought the debate might bring the matters to the fore, information might surface, some clarification of what happened so many years ago. So many people died in Capua, Claudia, but that's in the past.' Sylvester sighed. 'Militiades believes we will win the argument. I suppose,' he added, 'my Bishop hoped that this debate would show that the Arian party were the House of Traitors and Betrayers, but of course, life is not so simple. I did warn him about that. The persecution is over, but the blood feuds continue.'

'I know Narcissus is one of yours. The same is true of Timothaeus?'

'Of course. A good man, very devout. Timothaeus even questions whether he should serve in a pagan household.'

'You don't really care, do you?' Claudia retorted. 'You and Militiades, you brought people together whose lives are full of shadows and ghosts. You must have known that those shadows would surface. All the rivalry, all the grudges.'

'I do care,' Sylvester replied. 'A purging, a cleansing is very good. The Faith, our religion, must triumph. I said there were two reasons why this debate took place. In truth, there is a third, the cause and origin of it all.' He curled his fingers into a fist. 'We have Helena, the Augusta, and soon we shall have her son. Can't you see, Claudia, the real reason for this debate? We actually rejoice in the divisions, the acrimony, the rivalry. We want it like that. We want the Augusta to intervene, to become one of us, to support the Bishop of Rome. It's not just enough that Helena supports the Christian faith. Look, there are more divisions amongst Christians than there are fleas on a dog, but Rome holds everything together. One day we want people to see that an attack upon the Church is an attack upon the Empire, whilst an attack on the Empire is an attack upon us.'

Claudia stared at this clever priest who hid a cunning brain behind his gentle face and kind eyes.

'That's what it's all about,' she whispered. 'You want Helena to support the Bishop of Rome, right or wrong; you see yourselves as co-Caesars, the spiritual arm of the Empire. Helena will rule in favour of Militiades, and what the Empress says has the force of law. The Bishop of Rome and the Emperor will become indistinguishable. Christianity will be a state religion and Militiades its high priest. Some day you will anoint the Emperor, but you won't stop there, will you, Sylvester? Everything will come full circle; perhaps one day it will be the Bishop of Rome who decides who wears the purple, who dons the diadem.'

'Dreams,' Sylvester smiled, 'dreams of glory, Claudia, of God's kingdom being established on Earth. Helena has reached an understanding with us. We want a conclusion which will bind us together. We want her to rule in our favour so our teaching becomes an imperial edict. Now,' he continued briskly, 'one thing which certainly wasn't planned, or expected, was that attack. What have you learned?'

Claudia glanced up at a carving of a face at the top of a pillar, a cherub with pursed lips and full-blown cheeks, its head surrounded by vine leaves. Idly she wondered how many in the villa fully realised what Sylvester was plotting.

'Claudia?' Sylvester asked.

'The attack came from Licinius,' she replied. 'He dispatched a galley to the Italian coast but he already had agents in the countryside outside the villa. These lit the beacon fires once they had received the signal from here. The woods are thick and dense, and Licinius's agents could lurk safely whilst they were waiting for the agreed sign. However, what they didn't know, what they hadn't counted on, was the wanderer in the woods, an old man who travelled these parts. I expect he became aware of these strangers and came to the villa to report what he had seen. Unfortunately for him, our traitor or his accomplices learned what he was gabbling about and had him killed. The rest you know: the fires were lit, the galley came in and the troops were landed. Are you pleased, Sylvester?'

'At an attack on the Emperor? Of course not.'

'You know what I mean,' she taunted. 'Constantine now has a reason for war. Is that part of your dream, your clever design? For Constantine to march east, to issue edicts of toleration there. You'll be busy then, won't you, with your legion of agents, stirring up trouble in the eastern provinces, preparing the way for your Saviour?'

Sylvester just laughed, raised his hand in greeting and walked away.

Justin, leader of the Arian party, had seen Claudia and Sylvester close in conversation. He truly wondered what they were talking about but was desperate to reach the latrines. Once there, he was pleased to find they were empty, except for the villa cat, a sinewy black creature which fled through one of the half-open windows. Justin took a seat at the far end, staring mournfully across at the mosaics on the far wall. He did not feel well, his stomach was upset, and the rich food and wine of the previous night had not helped. He was also anxious. He should not have accepted the invitation to this debate. He was trapped. He had come here expecting discussion, but Athanasius was at his best, Sylvester had the ear of the Augusta, and now Justin was caught by ghosts from the past. Athanasius was not only a brilliant orator but also the only one amongst the philosophers who was blameless. After all, as Athanasius liked to point out, after Diocletian had launched his persecution, Athanasius had eventually fled north, well away from Capua, while the rest had been caught up in the net.

Absent-mindedly, still absorbed in the problems that beset him, Justin cleaned himself with a sponge on the end of a stick, and went into the small lavarium to wash his hands and face. He had left the latrines and was passing a low red-bricked building with stairs leading down to a cellar door when he heard a voice echoing up the steps.

'Justin, Justin.'

He stopped, recognising the building as something to do with the hypocaust; perhaps a place where fuel was stored.

'Justin.'

He heard a creak and, stepping to his right, peered down the steps. The door at the bottom was now open.

'Justin.'

The voice was eager, as if the person had found something. So absorbed was he with his problems that Justin forgot about Dionysius, or the fact that Septimus was missing. He went quickly down the steps and through the doorway; he was aware of a lamp glowing, of shadows flickering in the cavernous room. Someone was standing close to a pillar at the far end. He paused, and his assailant struck him on the back of the head.

Chapter 9

'*Nemo repente fuit turpissimus.*'
('No one ever becomes instantly depraved.')

Juvenal, *Satires*, II

'Come on.'

The principal chef of the imperial kitchens, Emperor Constantine's favourite cook, grasped the hand of the young kitchen maid and pulled her down the steps leading to the cellar where wood and charcoal were stored under a low roof supported by stout stone pillars. The chef always liked to bring his concubines, as he called his conquests, down here, especially in summer when it was so quiet. He wiped his greasy face, drying his hands on his tunic, and looked appreciatively at the girl. She was olive-skinned, with thick black hair and beautiful arms and legs. The chef in charge of the entrées had already lain with her and provided a graphic description of her skill and enthusiasm, her determination to please. The principal chef had immediately gone to work seducing the young woman with promises of preferment in the kitchens and, perhaps, even the prospect of promotion to serving maid with permission to enter the imperial dining room. He also made sure she was given the freshest delicacies left over after an imperial meal. Already this morning she had been given first choice of food from the previous night: cheese and honey, slices of walnut and fig cake, dried pear pudding, as well as various meats soaked in their sauces.

'Come on,' he repeated, stretching out his hand and grasping hers.

'Are you sure?' the maid whispered, acting like a frightened fawn. The chef's companion and friend had said she would protest like this, all coy and reluctant. She was certainly playing the part, gnawing her lip and standing so irresolute on the steps whilst he tugged gently on her hand.

'Just persist,' his friend had advised, 'and you'll enjoy a paradise of pleasures. Make sure it's somewhere lonely, where no one can hear.'

'Oh, don't be stupid!' The chef felt his stomach rumble with excitement. 'We'll kiss and cuddle, then go back to the kitchens for some honey water and pyramid cakes.'

The maid, still acting the reluctant lady, followed him down the steps. She was quite determined to give this important man the best of times and win his favour. She would love to be in charge of some of the others, to be given the best scraps and the driest and cleanest place to sleep.

The chef opened the door and fumbled on the ledge for the sulphur matches, which he used to fire the cresset torches as well as the twin earthenware oil lamps with the carving of Pegasus on each dish. As he did this, the girl walked away, staring down the musty chamber.

'There!' The chef stood back; the two lamps were burning

fiercely, and the cresset torches sputtered in a shower of sparks. Behind him the girl moaned.

'Oh, it'll soon be all right,' the chef murmured. He felt a hand on his arm and grinned round at her. 'What's wrong, girl?'

Even in the poor light her face had changed, all pale and drawn, her lower lip trembling. She pulled speechlessly at his arm and pointed down the cellar. As he followed her direction, his chin sagged and he gasped in amazement. He pulled the girl with him as he walked slowly forward.

'In Apollo's name,' he breathed, 'what is that?'

The girl broke free, gave a muffled scream and fled through the half-open door. The chef was made of sterner stuff. A veteran of the Ninth Hispania, he had seen his fair share of corpses, gibbeted, crucified, burned in oil, limbs severed, or lying bloated and stinking on some godforsaken battlefield. Nevertheless, there was something grotesque in the gruesome spectacle at the far end of the chamber, which the poor light only made more horrifying. Two corpses had been lashed to pillars next to each other. The chef walked closer, peering through the gloom. He recognised both the philosophers, visitors from the school of Capua; the elder one had his head tilted up, eyes staring blindly.,

'Justin,' the chef whispered, 'that's your name.' He spoke as if expecting the bloodied man to listen and reply, but Justin was dead. The old man had been stripped completely naked, his thin, bony body rendered all the more pathetic by his shrunken genitals, vein-streaked legs and dirty torso, which looked like the underside of a landed fish. The chef moved to one side. Justin had been gagged with a piece of leather, which still stuck out of his mouth. He had been shot to death at close range; the Syrian bow lay on the ground nearby, next to it a leather quiver empty of all its barbed, feathered arrows. Most of the shafts were embedded deep in Justin's flesh, the rest were scattered to the right of the pillar.

'Not a very good archer,' the chef whispered. At least four or five of the shafts had missed their mark. Justin had been bound tightly by a thick oily rope which dug deep in the flesh but left enough bare expanse of skin to receive the deadly shafts. The chef, curious, went and stared into the dead man's eyes, tilting the head forward. He recalled the old tale that the stare of a dead man often held what he had last gazed on. But Justin's eyes were mere black spots rolled back in his head to display the blood-flecked whites.

The chef moved to the second corpse; he couldn't remember his name, but recognised him as one of the orators. The younger man had also been stripped naked, then gagged and bound to the pillar. The chef pinched his nostrils. This man had apparently been dead for some time; the smell was offensive and the sight even more gruesome than the last. He had been stripped of all his garments, tied with his face to the pillar and flogged to death. An overseer's whip lay nearby with its bronze handle, the leather flails embellished with two or three razor-sharp slivers of bronze, copper or bone. The chef had seen such whips before; in fact, he owned one himself which he used to threaten the kitchen boys, but of course he would never actually use such a cruel weapon. The dead man's face was all bloodied where it had smashed into the pillar as his head rocked backwards and forwards during the flogging. The chef pressed the back of his hand to the neck of the corpse. It was cold, clammy, the muscles stone hard.

'Two men,' the chef murmured. He went back and touched Justin's corpse. He remembered his days in military service.

196

He had picked up enough corpses for the burial pit to conclude that the young man had been dead for at least twelve hours, but Justin's corpse was not so hard and cold; he had probably been killed just after dawn.

The chef suddenly recalled what he was doing, but he didn't want to run screaming like a chicken pursued by a flesher. He didn't want to become the butt of jokes and ridicule; he must act the veteran. He turned and walked slowly back to the door. He prided himself on being an old soldier, used to the sight of blood and gore, yet . . . He threw one last glance over his shoulder at those grisly remains. Those two corpses, the way they hung and the manner of their death, what sort of malice and feverish hatred had brought that about?

'Dead . . .' Narcissus stared at the two corpses sprawled out on the grass beneath the outstretched branches of a soaring holm-oak. 'Dead and rotting. Well,' he stretched out a hand, 'at least one of them is, mistress. You must tell the Augusta they should be consumed by fire.'

Claudia, holding a scented pomander to her nose, nodded vigorously in agreement. She stared at the corpses with the dappled shadows of the oak stretching over them. Such a beautiful day, such a lovely spot, with its fresh lawn sprinkled with wild flowers. A light breeze lessened the heat; out of the trees thrilled the song of a thrush, lucid and clear, ringing across the gardens. A green freshness surrounded these cadavers; it was like looking into a goblet which held a sickly brew. Two corpses, two beings, sharing the same substance in life as they did in death. She wondered what Athanasius would make of it. Were the Christians right? Did the substance known as Septimus and Justin survive their deaths? Did they beat upon the invisible yet eternal divide which separated them from the living, demanding justice from their God? Or had they disappeared like wisps of smoke from a spent fire? Or like the ghosts of Homer, fading spirits losing their strength as they sheltered in the darkness beyond life and the vital force ebbed from them?

'I wonder?' Claudia murmured.

'What?' Narcissus demanded.

'Nothing.' Claudia spread her hands. She didn't want to share her thoughts about the true reason she found it so difficult to accept the teachings of Christ. One man rising from the dead she could accept, an awesome event, a horrendous struggle between life and death. Christ was like Apollo or Hercules, a hero of the world! A crucified man condemned as a criminal, coming back as the Lord of Life and Light to whom all things were subject. She could understand that, but the likes of Dionysius and Justin, with all their petty faults and stupid thoughts, the very pathetic way they had died? How could they survive? And all the others, the teeming masses of Rome, or the surging hordes of barbarians who ringed the frontiers of Rome's Empire. Was each of them bound for immortality? Did they all carry the divine spark?

'Mistress?'

'I'm sorry.' Claudia broke from her thoughts. 'We have two corpses. You know all about corpses. Tell me what you've learnt.'

'Septimus died first,' Narcissus replied sonorously. 'He's been dead for at least twelve hours; the flesh is mortifying, the blood falling, he's ripe for embalmment but all my oils and instruments were burned in the blaze and that's the way he should go.'

'Never mind that,' Claudia retorted. 'What about his death?'

'He was first stunned like an ox for the slaughter by a blow to the head, then lashed to that pillar, gagged and flogged to death. The whiplash covered his entire body from neck to buttocks, though some blows fell as low as his knees and calves.' Narcissus knelt by Septimus's corpse. 'The lash curls around the back and the sharp pieces become embedded in the soft flesh of the belly and groin.'

Claudia stared at the blue and red welts and sniffed once again at the pomander.

'The assassin is ambidextrous,' Narcissus continued blithely. 'He became tired and changed hands. I say he, but it could be a woman. Now the whip is a fearsome weapon. I know,' he added grimly, 'I've had a taste of it myself. The leather strips and metal hooks tear at the flesh and injure all within, but the real effect is the shock and pain.'

'And?'

'Septimus probably did not feel the lash long; his heart gave way, I can tell that from his face. The skin is puffy and mottle-hued. I doubt if he lasted longer than a few minutes.'

'And Justin?'

'Again a savage knock to the back of the head. He was probably murdered some time after dawn. Well,' Narcissus shrugged, 'you saw him. He was stripped and lashed to that pillar, the archer stood close, the arrows are embedded deep. I would say the assassin stood no more than a yard away from his prisoner.'

Claudia looked at the corpse. Narcissus had first broken the arrow shafts, before digging out the fish-hook barbed points with a special knife borrowed from the kitchens.

'He didn't survive long,' Narcissus added mournfully.

'And the archer?' Claudia asked.

'Not a very good one! The assassin had to stand up close.

He favoured the left hand; some of the arrows, as you know, were found to the right of the corpse.'

Claudia nodded absent-mindedly. She had talked to the chef, listening carefully to his graphic description, before examining the cellar. It was a dark, musty place with a store of charcoal and timber. It had been empty through the summer months, clean and tidied, and would not be filled until late autumn. She had found nothing to identify the killer, but realised why the store room had been chosen as the execution yard. It was some distance from the villa, but close to the latrines. The assassin must have been waiting for his two victims. In fact, the more Claudia reflected, the more certain she became that these two men had been chosen indiscriminately. The orators of Capua were, by nature, lonely men. They were also frightened, with a great deal to hide. Such men would brood, would want to be alone, and so were ideal victims. What she couldn't understand was why. She had no real evidence for the motive, but, studying the malice the killer had shown, she strongly suspected that these two deaths, like that of Dionysius, were connected with what had happened in Capua during Diocletian's savage persecution. The rest of the philosophers had accepted that, and were already making preparations to leave, frightened out of their wits at what had occurred.

The villa had been roused by the kitchen maid, who'd run through the gardens screaming her head off and, when stopped by the guards, was unable to give a coherent explanation of what she had seen. The chef, however, had been coolly nonchalant and had searched out Gaius Tullius to raise the alarm. Helena herself had come down to the cellar, stared at the corpses and given vent to her fury, snapping at

Athanasius and Sylvester that the debate was now over. She had also turned on Claudia, hissing her disapproval.

'The Holy Sword has gone.' Helena wiped a white fleck of spittle from the corner of her mouth. 'Three of the orators are dead, my son is attacked. Little mouse, you know nothing. You've discovered nothing.'

Claudia knew better than to argue back; she had simply stood, head down, whilst Helena raged and fumed before stalking away.

Now Claudia walked back to the buildings and stared up at a cornice embellished with the face of a laughing Bacchus. Some distance away, Burrus and his guard were watching her intently. She heard a sound and whirled round. Sylvester, with Timothaeus trailing behind him, had appeared as if out of nowhere. The presbyter stood in the shadow of the oak, staring sadly down at the two corpses.

'The devil is an assassin,' he declared, not raising his head. 'I wonder why Dionysius died in such a macabre way. And now these two. The killer certainly hated them.'

'I agree,' Claudia replied.

'But the killer is also mocking our faith.'

'What do you mean?' Claudia asked.

'Study your history, Claudia. Dionysius, Septimus and Justin all died deaths similar to those of our martyrs in the arena: cut and sliced, left to bleed to death; flogged senseless and exposed—'

'And shot to death like Sebastian.' Claudia finished the sentence.

'Wouldn't you agree, Timothaeus?' Sylvester called over his shoulder. The sad-faced steward nodded in agreement.

'Presbyter?'

'Yes, Claudia.'

'May I have a word in private?'

Sylvester walked over. Claudia plucked him by the sleeve and took him out of earshot of both Timothaeus and Narcissus.

'Do you have anything to do with this?' she asked. Sylvester glanced at her in shocked amazement.

'With murder? Torture? Claudia, I intrigue, I plot, but I don't kill.'

Claudia held his gaze. 'Do you have any suspicions?'

'Yes, I do.' Sylvester bit his lower lip. 'And the list is long. Every man or woman in this villa can be suspected.' He glanced away. 'It could be anyone,' he whispered hoarsely. 'Is the Emperor involved? A possibility. Athanasius? Some of his friends in Capua were killed during the persecution. Burrus? He's a paid killer, he could be carrying out someone's order. The same goes for Gaius Tullius. Chrysis? He went to Capua.'

'Oh yes, what happened there?' Claudia asked.

'Chrysis didn't pay his fees; there was also the question of items going missing. Rufinus?' Sylvester shrugged. 'Timothaeus? Narcissus?' The names came tumbling out of the priest's mouth. 'But you want me to state more than the obvious, don't you?'

'Yes, I do,' Claudia replied. 'Tell me, the Christian martyr Paul, the great preacher, how did he die? Where is he buried?'

'Paul was both a Jew and a Roman citizen,' Sylvester replied. 'He was brought to Rome to face charges late in Nero's reign. Blessed Paul's opponents had the ear of Nero's mistress and the death sentence was passed against him. Unlike the saintly Peter, who was crucified upside down, Paul claimed the rights of a Roman citizen, and was sentenced to decapitation. He was taken from his prison to beyond the city walls, near a small fountain close to a cemetery on the road to Ostia. He was executed there, and his disciples later came and buried his body close by.' Sylvester smiled wryly. 'There's already a monument in the making for him, a shrine. Why do you ask?'

'Oh, nothing.' Claudia walked away.

'We'll be leaving soon,' Sylvester called after her. 'The Emperor will be returning to Rome to celebrate his birthday and attend the games. I understand your Murranus will be fighting. If he vanquishes Spicerius, he will meet Meleager in the arena.'

'He's not my Murranus,' Claudia retorted, coming back. 'You're telling me what I already know. What else do you want to tell me, priest?'

'Meleager.' Sylvester played with the ring on his little finger. 'I made a few enquiries on your behalf. You're correct. Meleager acts the reserved warrior but he's a vicious fighter. A man who likes killing, not a professional like Burrus or Gaius. According to Rufinus, Meleager sometimes plays with his victims in the arena like a cat does with his prey. I just thought I would let you know. No, no,' Sylvester slipped the ring on and off his finger, 'not to frighten you. I wouldn't do that. One interesting fact I've learnt, there may be a school of orators at Capua—'

'But there's also a school of gladiators, isn't there?' Claudia added quickly. 'I've just remembered that. It's a very famous school. Wasn't that the place where Spartacus started his rebellion?'

Sylvester was watching her strangely. 'Meleager was there,' he replied, 'when the persecution broke out. According to reports, and this is just chitter-chatter, he helped in the rounding up of Christians. He not only guarded them but was often present at their interrogation.'

'In other words, he was a torturer?'

'Yes, Claudia, you could say that.' The presbyter walked away.

'What should I do?' Narcissus called out, gesturing at the corpses. 'You can't leave them here, they'll begin to stink.'

Sylvester strolled over and whispered to him. Narcissus nodded and shouted for Burrus and his mercenaries to come and help him.

Claudia walked across the lawns, down the steps back into the store room. She picked up a stool and sat down, staring at the two pillars still flecked with blood. Flies buzzed over the cut, stained ropes and other splashes of blood on the floor. There were vents in the far wall which allowed in some light but, for the rest, there was nothing more than the glow thrown by the torches, which were now sputtering weakly, sending black tendrils of smoke into the air. She reflected on what Sylvester had told her. The murderer, who could be anyone, had enticed those two men away from the rest, stunned them, and dragged them here. She was certain their deaths had nothing to do with the theological debates taking place; it must be the past, but whose past?

Claudia rose and walked across to pick up a piece of rope. She studied the knot. It was nothing more extraordinary than a simple knot double tied. She wondered if the ropes left behind at Dionysius's corpse had been the same. She heard a sound behind her, the slither of a footstep, and her hand went to the dagger sheath sewn against her belt. She turned quickly, plucking up the stool as if it was a shield, dagger out, turning sideways as Murranus had taught her. The murky light hid her visitor until he clicked his tongue.

'Chrysis,' she whispered, 'what are you doing here?'

The chamberlain came forward. 'Claudia, Claudia, what is this?'

'Don't creep up on me,' Claudia warned. 'Imperial chamberlain or not, Chrysis, you don't like me and I don't like sitting with my back to you.'

'You're far too suspicious,' Chrysis whispered. 'You're a little bitch, Claudia, with a tart tongue and a hard heart.'

'I always like being lectured by moralists.' Claudia put the stool down.

'I only came to talk.'

'What about?'

'Capua.'

'You were there?'

'You know I was. You, with your darting eyes and twitching nose! I went there to learn how to speak, to get rid of my stammer and lisp. I ran out of money, so I helped myself to other people's. In the end I couldn't pay my bills, so I fled.'

'Were you an informant, Chrysis? Did you give information against the Christians?'

'Bitch!'

'Well, did you?' Claudia sat down on the stool.

'None of your business.'

'So why are you here?'

'Because I believe that anyone who was at Capua faces the risk of murder.'

'Or could be a possible suspect.'

'Claudia,' Chrysis shuffled closer; she didn't like his bulky body, or the way he was pretending to smile, 'I want to be your friend. I came to give you information.'

'What about?'

'Meleager is from Capua.'

'I know that,' Claudia snapped.

'Ah, but did you know that although the betting is very heavy on Murranus to beat Spicerius, it's nothing compared to the money being wagered on Meleager to beat and kill Murranus.'

'What do you mean?' Claudia was about to re-sheathe the knife, but instead pointed it at the fat chamberlain.

'Betting,' Chrysis explained, drawing even closer, 'is a strange world, Claudia. It's like life at court; things are never what they appear to be. You can bet on doubles, or spread your wager in a variety of ways. Now, according to Rufinus and Meleager, who preens himself and cannot keep his mouth shut . . .' Chrysis picked at his nose. 'Oh, by the way, have you ever met him before? I had breakfast with Meleager this morning before he left, he's sure he knows you, but couldn't place from where and when.'

'He's mistaken.'

'Anyway,' Chrysis chattered on, 'the news is that the money, bag after bag of sestercii, is being laid on Meleager. Now, such wagers can be simple: Murranus to win, Murranus to die, or Murranus to win against Spicerius but lose against Meleager. To cut through the tangle, Murranus is the favourite against Spicerius on one condition: that he loses to Meleager.'

Claudia's stomach lurched, and her throat seemed so full she was unable to swallow.

'So?' she stuttered.

'So,' Chrysis explained, 'let's go back to Spicerius's little accident, the day he felt faint in the arena. The money was on Murranus to kill him, leaving Murranus free to face Meleager. If that had happened . . . listen now, Claudia,' Chrysis wagged his finger in her face, 'Murranus would have been all upset, poor boy, accused of cheating, and perhaps when he stepped on to the sand to face Meleager, he might not have been, how do I put it, at his best.'

Claudia wished she could have some water, clean and fresh, to take the acid from her throat. Chrysis was a dangerous but knowledgeable man. He was frightened by the murders and probably trying to placate her. Claudia wetted her lips. Chrysis was merely voicing hints and possibilities that Claudia had already received from the likes of Helena. Spicerius was meant to die – Murranus could have killed him but would have entered the next bout a vilified, disgraced gladiator. A fighter in the arena needed to be confident.

'Why didn't Rufinus tell me all this?'

'He would have done,' Chrysis hunched his shoulders, 'but all this clamour and upset has disturbed everyone. No wonder the Emperor wants to go back to Rome. He said it's more peaceful there.'

'And what do you think will happen to Murranus?' Claudia asked.

The chamberlain pinched his nostrils, a common gesture whenever he was thinking deeply.

'Two things occur to me, Claudia. First, something might still happen to Spicerius. Secondly, is Murranus still being put under threat, his peace of mind shattered? You know how it is? Professional men like Murranus train their minds as well as their bodies. They regard themselves as the victor; to do anything different is to court disaster.'

'True.' Claudia folded her arms against her chest. Murranus had told her how fighters taunted each other, trying to break their opponent's will, to stir the heart and agitate the mind.

'What you also have to worry about,' Chrysis added, a hint of malice in his voice, 'is that when they, whoever they are, are finished with Spicerius, will they move against Murranus? Rufinus thinks the same.'

Claudia stared at this fat chamberlain, with his bland face and a mind teeming like a box of worms.

'So what you are implying,' she spoke slowly, 'is that something could still happen to Spicerius, and once he is out of the way, it will be Murranus's turn. I wonder who they are?'

'Someone who's wagered a fortune,' Chrysis muttered. 'Lots and lots of money.'

Something in his voice alerted Claudia, the way he said 'lots', like a man who sees a good meal and whose mouth starts to water. She laughed.

'You think it's funny?'

'No, you're funny, Chrysis. You've come to tell me this because Rufinus told you to. More significantly, you're a gambler. You've wagered heavily, haven't you? You've taken every coin your little fat fingers could collect. Who are you backing, Chrysis?' She got up. 'Don't come here pretending to be my friend. You are more concerned about your previous life in Capua being exposed. More importantly, you're anxious about my Murranus.'

Up close, Claudia could see the chamberlian was sweating. She prodded him in the stomach with the hilt of her dagger.

'You fat liar!' she whispered.

Chrysis blinked and swallowed hard, like a schoolboy being reproved.

'You've put all your money on Murranus, haven't you?'

Chrysis nodded. 'I'm frightened,' he bleated. 'I'm frightened of Murranus losing. I could lose at least ten thousand sestercii.'

'By the light! What on earth made you do that?'

'I didn't know about Meleager. No, no, that's not true. I've watched Murranus. You see, Claudia, he loves you, I know that. And a man who has someone to love wants to live, and so fights better. You've got to go back to Rome Claudia, you've got to warn your man. If he goes down, so will I.'

Chrysis walked away. Claudia turned and stared at the rope heaped on the floor.

'Mistress?' Narcissus appeared in the doorway. 'Mistress, what are you thinking about?'

'About having a bath!' Claudia snapped. 'What do you think I'm thinking about, one problem after another.'

'And what will you do?'

'Go back to Rome, see Uncle Polybius. I think it's time I had words with Sallust the Searcher . . .'

Murranus ducked and swiftly drew away, feet stamping the hot sand of the Ludus Magnus, the great gladiatorial school not far from the Flavian amphitheatre. The net man he was practising against danced after him, sandalled feet kicking up the sand, hoping the breeze would take it into Murranus's face whilst he trailed his net, moving the wooden trident ready to smack Murranus in the throat or make a swift thrust to his exposed belly. Murranus felt the cloying heat. The helmet he was wearing had grown stifling, sand was seeping through the gaps for the eyes, ears and mouth, whilst the leather padding stuck to his face. The greaves on his legs seemed to have grown heavier; the shield straps were wet with sweat. He had deliberately asked for the bout to be in the full heat of the day and had chosen the school's fastest net man, a Gaul from Narbonne, a true dancer who could shift like a shadow.

Through the slits of his helmet, Murranus watched his opponent move swiftly from side to side. He was trying to disconcert Murranus, striving to manoeuvre him so that he had his back to the sun. The net man had a piece of metal protecting his left arm which he deliberately used as a mirror to dazzle his opponent. Murranus recognised all these tricks; the net man would be watching carefully. If he could clog up the gaps in Murranus's helmet, cake his mouth and nose with dust, dazzle his eyes, already blinking because of the sweat, he might have a chance to trap him with his net and bring him to the ground. Murranus moved away, cleaning his mouth with his tongue. He held the long shield up and gripped the wooden sword even tighter. He moved his helmet, caught the breeze and felt a little better. He was aware of the tiers of seats in the amphitheatre quickly filling up as the various collegia arrived to watch him fight. Spicerius was there, Meleager had just arrived; so had the Dacians, gathering like a swarm of flies to study his every move. Well, he would educate them.

The net man was moving in, his net ready to sail out like a spider's web. Murranus darted forward but hastily retreated. Again he went in. Now he was concentrating hard; he no longer heard the moan of the crowd, he'd forgotten about the clammy helmet, the sweat soaking his face, the ache of his leg muscles or the pain in his right arm where he had received a vicious rap from the wooden trident. Indeed, Murranus was beginning to hum a song he had learned as a child. He was enjoying himself, this was his being, his very existence. All of life had come down to staring through that gap at a man who, under different circumstances, would try to kill him.

Murranus now had the measure of the moment. He settled to the fight, aware of the sheer music of this macabre dance. It thrilled his body, and his mind and heart were now set on victory. He'd made his decision. He knew which choice to follow; the die was cast. In the shuffling dance beforehand he had scrutinised the net man carefully, looking for his opponent's mistakes. A little too quick for his own good, Murranus thought, too impetuous.

Murranus darted in, moving his shield to the left, sword flickering forward like a snake's tongue. The net man shifted to close with him. Murranus retreated. The gladiator repeated the same manoeuvre until he was ready, then he lunged again, but this time he did not retreat, instead moving swiftly to the right. His opponent, surprised, let his net sail out, missing its target. Murranus darted in, using his shield like a battering ram, sending the trident spinning from the net man's hand. The net man rolled in the sand, ready to spring up, but it was too late. Murranus was over him, knocking him on the back of the head, sending him face down on to the sand and thrusting the tip of his sword into the nape of his opponent's neck. The net man lay silent as Murranus lifted his shield to acknowledge the cries and applause from the crowd, then stepped back, dropping shield and sword, and took off the plumed helmet. A slave ran across to remove the heavy leg greaves. Another brought a jar of water. Murranus sipped from this and poured some over his face, then pulled his opponent up and thrust the water jar into his hands.

'You were too fast,' the net man gasped, his face grimed with sweat and sand. 'I never thought you would do that.'

'You should have expected it.' Murranus grinned. 'You can bet a coin to a coin that if your opponent is moving backwards and forwards, especially one with armed with a sword and a heavy shield, sooner or later he'll attack you in the flank. I used my shield, but there's variations. I could have entangled your net with my shield and dragged you in on my sword.' He gently patted his opponent's face. 'Remember this,' he added quietly, 'and you might live. In the arena the shield is more dangerous than the sword; it can catch your net, blunt your trident, but above all, it can deliver a hammer blow. Now let's celebrate with some wine.'

They moved across to join their comrades. Murranus was congratulated by Spicerius, who pushed a goblet of wine into his hand, patting him on the back, praising his moves but offering his own criticism. Murranus caught Meleager's gaze and nodded a greeting.

'He's full of himself,' Spicerius whispered. 'One of us will have to meet him and teach him a lesson, eh?'

A crowd had formed around Meleager, questioning him. The Dacian leader glared across. Agrippina was also flirting with the newcomer.

'Oh let her be!' Spicerius whispered. 'As long as she visits me at the She-Asses tavern, I don't really mind. I'll teach her to moon-gaze at an opponent.'

Murranus collected his weapons and entered the bath house, plunging into the warm water before moving on to the cold. He kept thinking about the recent fight. He hoped his opponents were stupid enough to believe he'd repeat the same tricks in the arena. Spicerius joined him, keeping up a running commentary on Meleager's skill, what to look for, what to avoid. Murranus crossed to the ointment room and lay on a slab, while the masseur of the school coaxed and smoothed his muscles with his expert touch and soothing oils. Murranus sniffed their fragrance and felt himself relax. Spicerius was now chatting about the party Agrippina had planned. They would spend the early afternoon in the coolness of the garden, and when darkness fell, the real revelry would begin.

Murranus fell lightly asleep and was woken by the masseur slapping his back, pointing to his clothes laid out across a chest near the door. He put on a loincloth and his long white linen tunic, then went across to the Keeper of Valuables to retrieve his collar, bracelet and rings. He put on his sandals and joined Spicerius outside in the cool colonnade.

'Do you know something?' Spicerius put his wine cup down and pointed across to the other colonnaded walk, where Meleager was deep in conversation with the Dacians. Agrippina seemed to have disappeared. 'We gladiators,' Spicerius continued, 'are great boasters, but Meleager seems so certain of victory.' He turned and clutched Murranus's arm. 'May Hercules bless me,' he whispered.

'What's the matter?' Murranus was concerned by Spicerius's haunted gaze.

'You know how it is,' Spicerius continued, tightening his grip. 'You've been there, Murranus, waiting in the cavern to go out into the arena. The music is playing, the crowd are baying for your blood. Now and again I've seen gladiators, brave men, suddenly look shocked, frightened, and if you ask them why, they'll tell you they feel as if they've been brushed by the feathers of the Wings of Death.'

'And?' Murranus asked, releasing Spicerius's grip.

'I feel that now, Murranus.'

Chapter 10

'Dux Femina Facti.'
('The Leader of the Enterprise is a Woman.')

Virgil, *Aeneid*, I

As they left the Ludus Magnus, Murranus stifled his own disquiet as he tried to reassure Spicerius. Once they'd turned off the main via, going down the many side streets and alleyways, conversation proved impossible. Murranus thought of Claudia and wondered when she would return. He'd heard the chatter, the gossip, the tittle-tattle of messengers and servants that all was not well at the Villa Pulchra, though he could make little sense of it. Rumours swirled about killings and fires whilst news had seeped through of some attack upon the villa. Such gossip was now being discussed in the forum, whilst, from acquaintances and friends in the city garrisons, Murranus had learnt that coastal defences were being strengthened and war galleys had put to sea, even though this was during the height of summer and a time of peace.

Murranus reflected on all this as he led Spicerius through the noisy trading areas. Business had begun shortly before dawn, and the lucky wine merchants had taken over the porticoes in the colonnades, tying their flagons and flasks to pillars so as to advertise their stock. The butchers and fish sellers were also busy. Barbers had set up stalls under the trees, waving their cushioned stools and touting for business. The itinerant cooks, with their mobile stoves in one barrow and slabs of bloody meat in another, moved about looking for a suitable place to stand and sell well away from the watchful eye of the Vigiles. The successful ones had already taken over the prime places and were doing a vigorous trade, offering grilled meats sprinkled in spice, 'hot to the taste', and wrapped in fig leaves. Water sellers shouted for custom claiming their buckets were full of the purest water drawn from a newly found spring in the countryside outside Rome. Traders, festooned in their cheap blue trinkets to advertise their products, offered to barter two or three items with a packet of sulphur matches thrown in for free.

Murranus edged round these and down a side street where he had once taken lodgings. The place hadn't changed. The stench of the latrine, cesspit and midden heap mingled with the smell of herbal oil, sizzling sausages, coarse bread and stewed vegetables. They crossed a dusty square, where a ragged schoolmaster declaimed a poem; a host of children grouped round him under a tree echoed back, shouting above the hammering and the clattering from their fathers' workshops around the square. The beggars, genuine and false, swarmed like flies over a turd. Drunkards and roisterers from the previous night, holding aching heads and queasy stomachs, lurked about looking for shade and some water. A few recognised the gladiators. Murranus was happy to ignore them by standing aside to let an expensive funeral cortège go by, with its flute players, horn blowers, actors in their masks, professional mourners and a gaggle of shaven-haired priests who chanted so fast no one knew what they were saying. Two funeral processions of the poorer sort hurried along behind, the corpses resting on tawdry wheelbarrows, the mourners eager to share the free pomp of the wealthier procession.

Murranus and Spicerius were now in the slums, where the streets and alleyways spread out like tunnels in a rabbit warren. Shadows lurked in doorways, prostitutes whispered for custom; pimps, fingering their knives, gestured them over. Fights and squabbles were commonplace; men and women armed with skillets, ladles, hammers and clubs brawled in doorways or rolled across the street pummelling each other. The hubbub fell silent as an execution group, led by an officer with medals gleaming on his chest, escorted four prisoners, murderers and housebreakers, to the Place of Slaughter beyond the gates. The prisoners, stripped naked except for a breech-clout, carried their own crossbeam against which they would be crucified, to hang and die under the sun.

Once this grim procession had passed, the tumult recommenced, with tanners and fullers offering free drinks of water to those who would piss in their pots so the urine could be used in the treatment of leather. Many of these petty tradesmen were keen supporters of the games and were quick to recognise Murranus and Spicerius, although their cheers were muted by shouts of 'Fix!' and 'Coward!'. Thankfully the insults were shouted in a number of tongues and dialects; the slums held every type of inhabitant of the Empire, from Britain in the far west to the Caspian Sea in the east. Now and again Murranus glanced at Spicerius, who still looked troubled and anxious. Murranus too felt uneasy. Spicerius was usually arrogant and distant, full of himself, boasting of his own powers; and yet since the notorious incident, he had become quiet and withdrawn. He would actively seek Murranus out, and was obviously grateful that Murranus had not exploited his weakness in the arena. Protection, Murranus thought; that was what Spicerius seemed to want, as if he had been secretly threatened and menaced and believed Murranus could shelter him. Spicerius was now a frequent visitor to the She-Asses, and the only people from his own entourage whom he seemed pleased to see were the old military doctor Valens and the boisterous, ever-colourful Agrippina.

As they reached the end of a narrow street, a flash of colour caught Murranus's eye, and he glanced at a shadowy doorway to his right. A warlock and his witch stood there, faces painted, necklaces and bones around their necks. Squatting between them was an ugly Egyptian baboon on a silver chain, while a trained crow, with gleaming eye and sharp beak, rested on the warlock's shoulder. They looked like macabre statues, with yellow rings round their eyes and blue paint on their cheeks. The man lifted a small black *flabellum*, a fan made out of raven wing, beckoning them across. Murranus spat in their direction and moved on.

He was relieved to reach the She-Asses tavern, with its cheery-faced Hermes and its small votive statue to the god Priapus just inside the doorway. Polybius, followed by Poppaoe, bustled out of the kitchen to welcome them. The rest of the customers greeted them with shouts and cheery toasts. They had all gathered from their various trades to quench their thirst and feed their hunger. Simon the Stoic sat perched on a stool chattering to a dusty-garbed wandering scholar. Simon had, apparently, bought him a drink, and was now busy boring him to death. Petronius the Pimp was informing the rest of the customers, to hoots of laughter, that if they had hairy arses he could sell them a powder which would get rid of the excess hair, as well as a polish to wax their bottoms. Of course no one believed him, so Petronius explained to his disbelieving audience that he had found the cure whilst serving in the ranks, where he had won the Hasta Pura for distinguished service. This second revelation was greeted with 'Prove it!' and 'Where is the little silver spear?' Draco, a grizzled veteran from an apartment three storeys above, led the attack. The old man always carried a *draconarius*, an imitation feather-tailed standard, maintaining that he had carried such an insignia across the Danube and could list all the tribes on its southern bank, if anyone cared to listen – which very few did.

Murranus, chatting to Polybius and shouting out greetings, deliberately delayed in the eating hall. He wanted Spicerius to feel at home, to be cheered and comforted by this motley collection of rogues and eccentrics. Januaria came sidling up, hips swaying, forcing her way through, glancing moon-eyed at Spicerius. Murranus asked Polybius if he had heard from Claudia. The landlord shook his head and replied that he had heard rumours, some sort of trouble, but didn't know any details, and would Murranus like to come through to the garden? Polybius kept this privilege for what he called his 'treasured guests', as well as those individuals, such as the local police, whom he wanted to talk to well away from keen eyes and sharp ears.

He led them through the eating hall and out past the kitchens. Murranus's mouth watered at the smell of savoury meat and onion sizzling in a spiced sauce. They were taken across the grass, past the small dovecote, to what Polybius grandly called his orchard, a shady nook with stone benches and a small carp pond. For the umpteenth time, and Murranus hadn't the heart to stop him, Polybius described his vegetable garden and herb plots, rich with lettuce and onions, chervil, coriander, fennel and parsley, and talked expansively of deepening the orchard so that he could produce quinces and damsons. He offered to show them around his small vineyard, but Murranus laughed, slapped him on the shoulder and said they would be satisfied with a platter of meat and a jug of wine. The two gladiators sat in the shade whilst Polybius served them, still chattering about his wine, swearing by his penis that it was the best in Rome. Once he had gone, Murranus lifted his goblet in toast.

'Peace,' he whispered. 'At least until we meet.'

Spicerius drank deep. 'I saw them,' he murmured. 'You know what I'm talking about, the warlock and his witch.' He suppressed a shiver. 'I made a hex against them.'

'Stop thinking such black thoughts,' Murranus teased. 'Save yourself for the fight.'

'One of us will die there.'

'Not necessarily,' Murranus answered cheerfully.

Spicerius glanced away. 'I want to tell you something, Murranus.' He put down his wine goblet and stretched out his right arm. 'You see this tattoo, the purple chalice? I told you it was worn by members of a drinking club.'

'And I believed you.'

'And so you should. I'm going to have this washed off – I will not wear it again. You see, Murranus, beneath the chalice some men wear a circle that denotes something else: these men attend special brothels where they can be violent with children.'

Murranus stared in disbelief.

'You know, the world we live in, Murranus, the deeper you go, the filthier it gets. I like my women, especially the rich, plump ones, but some things, well, they're like streets you just don't go down. The man who attacked your Claudia, I expect he was one of those. After we met last time I could see she was deeply upset, so I made a few enquiries. It's the sort of thing that is well hidden, the type of house frequented by quite wealthy men, be they gladiators or senators.' He shook his head. 'This is all I know.'

'And the incident?' Murranus asked. 'The poisoning?'

'I am not sure,' Spicerius replied. 'That wine wasn't poisoned, even though it was later found tainted. I'm sure I was poisoned before I drank it. Anyway, you've heard the rumours, Murranus? They're betting this time for you to win against me but not against Meleager.'

Murranus could see his friend was on the verge of sinking into another black mood. He asked him again about the purple chalice tattoo, but Spicerius declared he had told him everything he could, so Murranus changed the subject. Spicerius ate well but drank sparingly, and when Murranus questioned him, he laughed and explained he was saving himself for the evening, when Agrippina had promised to join him for their own special celebrations. Polybius, who had come to collect the platters and overheard this, now acted like a conspirator, tipping his nose, winking at Spicerius and declaring that the room was ready when he was.

The afternoon wore on. Spicerius began to doze, so he took his wine and went up to what Polybius dramatically described as the 'Venus Chamber'. Intrigued, Murranus decided to follow him. The room was on the second floor, overlooking the garden, and boasted a large bed with stout ends, a thick

221

mattress and a bolster all covered in pink and gold. A rather blotched mirror stood on a decorated square chest. The floor was of polished wood, a rare form of timber. Polybius explained that he had discovered it when he first bought the place and decided to polish it up. The walls were lime-washed, and Murranus had to stifle a laugh as he stared at the crude paintings which Polybius was so proud of. A fat, bloated Venus cavorted in a garden surrounded by even plumper cherubs, who looked so heavy they would find it impossible to fly.

Spicerius went and sat on the bed, and Murranus returned to the garden and sat in the shade. He soon felt the effects of the wine and the lazy summer heat, and drifted off to sleep, his eyes growing heavy as he watched a resplendent butterfly flutter amongst the flowers. He started awake some-time later. He realised it must be late afternoon, for the breeze had strengthened and the shadows grown longer. Yes, he had felt something else: his hair had been tugged! He whirled around.

'Claudia!' He jumped to his feet, left the stone chair and grabbed her up. 'When did you . . .'

'Let me breathe!' she gasped.

He released her, and she sat down on the grass, plucking at the blades, quickly describing what had happened at the Villa Pulchra and how she had asked the Empress's permission to leave.

'They are all coming back anyway.' She smiled back. 'In four days' time you meet Spicerius. Oh, by the way, where is he?'

'Fast asleep, I think. Anyway, tell me again what happened.'

Claudia repeated everything about the murders, the fire

and the assault. She vaguely referred to meeting Meleager, but made no mention of who he really was and the hideous damage he had wrought in her life. She decided that would wait. She wanted to be careful; after all, there were other problems to address. For a while they discussed the doings at the Villa Pulchra and the events at Capua. Murranus explained how he knew the town boasted a large Christian community, many of whom had suffered under Diocletian. The people she described he had also met, but they were merely passing acquaintances, though he was intrigued when Claudia made her final revelation about the pattern of the betting, and how Chrysis had wagered thousands of sestercii on him.

'It's all a mystery.' Murranus rubbed his face. 'It always happens with the games. This gladiator is a favourite, this one isn't, and interference, to help the money on its way, is common enough. But listen to my news.' He described the visit of the Dacians, Spicerius's forebodings and his own anxieties.

'Will it be a fight to the death?' Claudia asked.

'I doubt it,' Murranus replied. 'On a good day Spicerius and I are equally matched. We'll put up a good show. If either of us goes down, the crowd will not demand our deaths; the same goes for Meleager. We are not in this for blood but for the Crown of Victory.' He caressed Claudia's face. 'And don't worry about the betting. You tell your uncle, not to mention Chrysis, to put everything they have on me; they won't be disappointed. Now,' he cupped her face in his hands, 'why have you really come back?'

'Well, the court was returning.'

'No, the real reason.'

'To see you.' She grinned. 'I also want to talk to Sallust

223

the Searcher. It's time I had a little help. Oh, by the way,' she pointed back to the tavern, 'Uncle has a new helper. He's called Narcissus the Neat. He's the man I described to you. There's nothing for him at the Villa Pulchra and he knows no one in Rome, so I—'

'Murranus!'

The woman's voice carried across the garden. The gladiator groaned as Agrippina came tripping over in a beautiful white linen gown, a multi-coloured stole across her shoulders. Once again every item of jewellery, be it bracelet or earring, glowed a deep red.

'Murranus!' She flounced her long dressed hair, gingerly touching her exquisitely painted face, her perfume drowning every other smell. 'Murranus.' She held her hands on her hips, totally ignoring Claudia. 'Tell that oaf Polybius I want to see Spicerius.'

'He's in his chamber, fast asleep,' Murranus replied. 'I left him there, he's expecting you.'

'Well, I'm rather late. I've been up there, but the door's locked, there's no answer. That oaf is too busy laughing with his customers about waxing people's bottoms.'

'That oaf,' Claudia replied, springing to her feet, 'is my uncle. We are very particular who visits our tavern, so you'd better follow me.'

They went into the eating hall, where Polybius, leaning against one of the wooden pillars, was offering Petronius the opportunity to wax his arse. Claudia grabbed her uncle by the arm and whispered in his ear; he sighed, mopped his brow and led her up the stairs. They stood outside the Venus Chamber, knocking and hammering. Claudia glanced along the passageway. Narcissus was standing at the top of the landing, looking rather frightened. Claudia realised how unused he must be to the noise of a tavern. Oceanus came up, pushing people aside. Claudia felt a tingle of excitement in her stomach. Something was wrong, she could tell that from Murranus's face, whilst Oceanus shook his head in disbelief, claiming he was sure Spicerius hadn't left.

The door was tried again, and eventually Polybius ordered Oceanus and Murranus to break it down. They first used their shoulders, until Polybius intervened, warning Murranus not to injure himself, so a log was brought up from the cellar. The door was hammered until it sprang back on its leather hinges. Claudia made sure she was first into the room. Spicerius lay sprawled on the bed, the wine goblet beside him. He was half sitting up against the bolsters, face to one side, mouth gaping, eyes staring.

'By the balls of a pig,' Polybius groaned. 'Oh no, not here.'

Claudia climbed on to the bed. Spicerius had lost all his warrior's elegance and grandeur; he had the grey, lined face of an old man, and a white dribble of dried saliva stained the corner of his mouth. She felt his arm. The flesh was cold. Agrippina was screaming. Other customers were coming up. Claudia got off the bed wiping her hands, then picked up the goblet and sniffed the bittersweet tang. Taking advantage of the upset and chaos, she quickly searched the bed and the floor around but could detect nothing except a square piece of parchment with love symbols on it. It was yellowing and wrinkled, caught amongst the folds of the mattress.

'We'll have to call the bloody police,' Polybius groaned. 'There'll be questions and more questions.'

Claudia told her uncle to take the shrieking Agrippina downstairs, and asked Murranus to send in Narcissus then guard the passageway and let no one through. She could feel the anger boiling within her. She felt like screaming, not only at the danger which threatened her beloved, but at the way this horrid death had upset all her plans. As soon as she had arrived at the She-Asses, she had asked Polybius to send one of the kitchen boys to fetch Sallust the Searcher. She realised that, in the case of the Holy Sword, she only had a little time to prove her suspicions and get the relic back. She stared at the corpse, felt guilty at her angry thoughts, slumped down on the edge of the bed and clasped Spicerius's hand, brushing his cold, hard fingers with her thumb.

'It's not your fault,' she whispered, 'and if your shade lingers nearby, I wish you well in whatever journey you take.'

She tried to forget her own troubles, experiencing a deep sadness at the brutal death of this young man, once so full of pride, vigour and courage.

'You deserved a better death,' Claudia gripped the fingers, 'than dying alone in a tavern chamber with no glory or praise ringing in your ears.'

She became aware of Narcissus standing in the doorway, so she moved to hide her face. She must remember the deep comradeship which existed between gladiators. Murranus had regarded this man as his friend. She must do everything to help.

Claudia scrutinised the corpse carefully. Spicerius's face was full of the ugliness of a violent, sudden death: the muscles of his cheeks and chin were hardening, his eyes rolled back, his mouth was gaping, the lips forward as if Spicerius still wished to retch and vomit. The gladiator was dressed in a simple tunic; his belt and sandals lay on the floor. She pulled these close, picked up the cup and once again sniffed that bittersweet smell. What was it? She stuck her nose in again and offered it to Narcissus, gesturing at him to keep it.

Outside, Murranus was pacing up and down like a sentry on duty. In the eating hall below, Agrippina was still shrieking and wailing. Claudia cocked her head and listened intently. The tenor of that spoilt, rich hussy was beginning to change. Was grief giving way to anger? Was she shouting curses? Making allegations? Would Murranus or Polybius be accused?

Claudia stared round the tawdry chamber, so different from the Villa Pulchra. It now seemed an age since she and Narcissus had left. Claudia had obtained permission from the Augusta, pointing out that she could do more good in Rome, where the court was about to return, than by staying at the villa. She had also begged Helena to keep the rest of the philosophers close and not allow them to return home until this mystery had been resolved. The Augusta's reply had been ugly, ungracious and hard. She'd dismissed Claudia with a flick of her fingers, telling her to get back to her slum and, as she withdrew, followed her to the chamber door bellowing how it was a pity that some of her servants did not serve her as well as she served them. Once she was out of sight, Claudia had made a rude gesture in the direction of the imperial apartments before scurrying off to her own chamber to hastily pack her belongings. Narcissus had followed her like a shadow, only too eager to flee the villa and reach Rome, but now, he was not so sure, uncertain and frightened of the future. Claudia closed her eyes. It was important to keep Narcissus near to her.

'Almonds!'

Claudia let go of the dead man's hand.

'Almonds!' Narcissus repeated. He thrust the cup at her. 'Bittersweet,' he explained. 'The juice from certain seeds can be the deadliest poison; it has an almond taste.'

'How do you know that?'

'Because I've cut more corpses than you have pieces of meat, mistress.' Narcissus gabbled on. 'But where will I stay, what will I do, how will I—'

'Almonds,' Claudia retorted, lifting her hand. 'Forget about the rest, Narcissus. You're going to sleep here and get a good meal, so don't worry, just tell me about almonds.'

'Milk of almonds.' Narcissus pulled a face. 'That's what we call it in Syria. It's not really milk, more a juice; they gather it from certain seeds, I mean the poison, and distil it. It's got many strengths.' He leaned down, face all solemn. 'I can't tell you, mistress, how many times I've cut open the corpses of men and women and smelt that bittersweet odour! Oh, I don't say much, but I know! Go down to the slums, ask the locust men, the warlocks, the poison boys, they'll tell you all about it. You take a sip of that, a really good sip, and all your troubles are over. Do you know, mistress, there are poisons which will stop your heart in the blink of an eye.' Narcissus went round the bed. 'But you don't need me to tell you that; just look at the poor bastard's face. The skin's all mottled, with a slightly blueish tinge, the throat muscles are constricted, the skin's hard to the touch as if he's been dead for hours. But you just wait,' he warned, 'in a few hours the blotches will appear.' Narcissus felt the back of the gladiator's head. 'Ah, I thought as much. Slightly bruised; it's where he banged his head in his death throes.'

'Would death have been swift?'

'Like an arrow to the heart, mistress. Some jerking, some convulsions, the pain would have been hideous, but don't let's leave him like this.'

Claudia helped pull the corpse down by its feet so it lay straight. She started as a gasp of air escaped from the dead man's lungs.

'He's not been dead long.' Narcissus pointed to the cup. 'A nice goblet of sweet wine, fruity and tangy. I heard Polybius say he had served the stuff. Now, mistress, before you ask, that's just the drink to hide the taste. But never mind the dead, what about the living? Your Murranus, he's the one you told me about on the way here? Well, gladiator or not, champion or not, he's in deep trouble. Wasn't he supposed to face—'

Claudia got to her feet and, snapping at Narcissus to keep quiet, began a thorough search of the chamber. She scrutinised the corpse and Spicerius's purse and clothing, but apart from some coins, a dagger, personal jewellery and a good-luck amulet she could find nothing. She knew there were no secrets to this chamber, whilst it was ridiculous to imagine anyone climbing through the window. So what had really happened? Suicide or murder? The only thing she had found was that love charm written on a piece of parchment. She picked this up and looked at it again. It displayed a crudely drawn heart with, above and beneath it, the words '*Amor vincit Agrippinam*' and '*Amor vincit Spicerium*'. 'Love conquers Agrippina', 'Love conquers Spicerius'. She felt the parchment with her thumb, sniffed it, but the only smell was Agrippina's heavy perfume. Exasperated, Claudia sat down on a stool.

'Nothing!' she snapped. 'Narcissus, go and get Polybius and Murranus. Tell Oceanus – you've met him, the big fat one – to guard the stairs. Just ask my uncle and Murranus to join me here.'

A short while later both men entered the room. Claudia tried to close the door but it was useless. She noticed the bolts at top and bottom were heavy and stout.

'Tell me what happened,' she urged, going back to sit on the bed.

Polybius and Murranus explained how they had entertained Spicerius in the orchard. They had eaten and drunk. Spicerius had seemed a little withdrawn but was looking forward to seeing Agrippina. He had taken his wine and come up to the Venus Chamber to have a little sleep before his girlfriend arrived.

'And no one came up,' Polybius warned. 'Before you start, Claudia, no servant, no member of this tavern climbed those stairs. If Spicerius wanted something, he could send for it. I did get concerned he had gone so quiet, but there again, it is not for me to disturb someone.'

'Nothing suspicious happened?'

'Nothing,' Polybius retorted. 'No one can enter that garden without me knowing, and we had no suspicious characters. I mean,' he grinned, 'apart from our usual clientele this afternoon.'

'Murranus?' Claudia turned. The gladiator was leaning against the wall, staring up at the ceiling. 'Could Spicerius have committed suicide?'

'No, he was a warrior, Claudia, he would take his chances in the arena. All he was frightened about was another accident, poor bastard.'

'So he was murdered,' Claudia concluded. 'Somehow someone got into this room and poured poison into his goblet. Yet that's impossible; as you say, Spicerius was a warrior, he would have challenged anyone who came in.'

'More importantly, I would have known about it.' Polybius groaned. 'You know what they're going to say, Claudia, don't you?' He glanced from under his shaggy eyebrows. 'They are going to allege that I, or Murranus, or both, put that poison in his cup before he left the orchard. That silly bitch downstairs is already beginning to sing that song.'

'Ignore her.'

'I'd love to,' Polybius moaned, 'but there's an ugly crowd gathering, both inside and outside.'

'I liked Spicerius,' Murranus shouted. 'I didn't kill him, he didn't commit suicide, but they say his blood is on my hands.' He stood breathing deeply. 'Now I'm up against Meleager, and all the money will be on him. Oh, by the way, there was a man at the foot of the stairs listening intently. Every so often he would go and bellow at the servants in the kitchen, telling them the news.'

'Oh, him!' Polybius's eyes rolled heavenwards. 'Mercury the messenger, the teller of tales, the herald of the people.' He clapped Murranus on the shoulder. 'If Mercury's got hold of this tale, then by nightfall half of Rome will know it. Anyway, let's go down and face the bastards.'

There was a knock at the door; Valens, the old military physician, stepped through. He bowed at Claudia and, holding his threadbare cloak about him, crossed to stand by the bed, staring down at the corpse. Claudia watched him intently and realised from the shaking of his shoulders and the way he wiped his cheeks that Valens was crying. She was also certain that he was making Christian signs with his fingers. He glanced quickly at her over his shoulder, then moved so his back was completely to her. He leaned over, whispered something into Spicerius's ear and touched him on his brow, eyes and mouth. Afterwards, he stood rocking backwards and forwards, chanting a prayer Claudia couldn't understand, then he gave a great sigh and assumed the role of a doctor, examining both the corpse and the goblet. When he had finished, he picked up a stool and sat opposite Claudia.

'What happened?' he murmured.

There was no pretence or imitation with this man; he had a

blunt honesty which appealed to Claudia, so she told him everything she'd learned. When she had finished, Valens nodded in agreement.

'Your diagnosis is correct, mistress. I just wish I knew why Spicerius was so anxious, and yet,' he cleared his throat, 'at the same time I do. I know it sounds a contradiction, but have you noticed anything different about him?'

Claudia stared at the corpse.

'His face,' Valens explained. 'He stopped wearing make-up; that was one small change. I agree with you, he would never take his own life. What happened in the arena that day truly frightened him; one of Rome's best gladiators lost his power, his strength, so suddenly, so dangerously, without any warning or explanation. You see, Claudia, people like your Murranus expect death in a certain way. I once had a patient who truly believed he would die of the flux, and when his heart gave way he was truly shocked. Spicerius was the same. He thought he'd die after some heroic struggle, not retching on the sand like some pathetic drunk.' Valens got up, kicking back the stool. 'He was so looking forward to today; he regarded Murranus as a brother and liked to be with him. He wanted to see Agrippina and spend the night roistering.'

'Did he love Agrippina?'

'She's a shameless hussy, but yes,' Valens patted Claudia on the head, 'in his own way I think he did, but his anxieties . . .' Valens's voice trailed off and his hand fell to his groin. 'Spicerius's fears troubled him. He'd lost his virility; he said if he won against Murranus he might well retire.'

'His virility?' Claudia asked.

'Yes, for a while.' Valens grinned. 'It often happens to men, nothing serious. Ah well, I shall wait for the Vigiles, then collect his corpse. I'll take it back to Sisium; it's a small village near Capua, have you ever visited it?'

'No.'

Valens walked to the door. 'Ah, here they come.' He turned back.

The Vigiles had arrived. Claudia heard their heavy boots on the stairs, and a short while later the local police commander, Saturninus, accompanied by his leather-clad acolytes, marched into the room, together with Polybius, who indicated with his head that she should leave. Claudia realised what would happen. The Vigiles would group round the corpse, demand goblets of the tavern's best wine, take a bribe from Polybius so they would declare that the death had had nothing to do with him, then march off to their next piece of mischief.

Claudia slipped down the stairs into the hubbub of the eating room. The usual customers were grouped round Murranus, but Claudia noticed a gang of strangers at the far end sitting close to Agrippina and comforting her. Oceanus had also come down and was standing guard at the door, shouting that the tavern was overflowing so other customers would have to wait. From the noise outside Claudia realised the local alleyway mob had been roused and people were gathering to see what had happened as well as sniff out any profit for themselves. Murranus beckoned her over, but Claudia ignored him and walked straight to Agrippina, pushing her way through the group.

'Mistress.' She tapped Agrippina on the shoulder. 'I need a word with you.'

'I don't talk to kitchen wenches or tavern maids.'

Claudia bent down and whispered in her ear. Agrippina shot to her feet, face all troubled.

'I . . . er . . . I . . .' she stammered.

'In the garden,' Claudia offered, and turned away, not waiting for a reply.

The light was fading, dusk creeping in like a mist. Claudia walked across the lawn, sat on a turf seat and patted the place next to her.

'I never realised you actually knew the Augusta.' Agrippina sat down in a gust of perfume, fastidiously hitching up her robe so that the grass wouldn't brush it.

'More importantly,' Claudia retorted, 'the Augusta knows me. Now, as regards Spicerius, I'm truly sorry he's died. I liked him and so did Murranus. If you start screaming allegations or making foul accusations you can't prove, I will appeal to the Augusta for justice.'

'I'm upset,' Agrippina whined.

'Shut up! Did you ever find out what happened to Spicerius in the arena – I mean, the cause?' The other woman shook her head. 'Or this afternoon?'

'You know as much as I do.' Agrippina pushed her night-black hair away from her face. 'I saw Spicerius last night, I agreed to meet him here. I was sorry I was delayed. When I came, he was dead.' Her voice broke. 'Murdered.'

'What makes you so sure of that?'

'Well, look, a healthy man, a gladiator . . . I came to this tavern to meet a lover, not a corpse. I've answered your questions, I cannot say any more.'

Agrippina got to her feet. Claudia waved her hand and let her go. What was the use, she thought, the hussy would only tell her what she wanted. Claudia sat half listening to the noise of the tavern, allowing herself to be lulled by the green coolness of the garden. A sudden roar from the tavern made her realise things had gone from bad to worse, and she hastened back inside. The eating hall was now set to become an arena.

At the kitchen door stood Murranus and Polybius, whilst at the far end, and still spilling through the main entrance, were a group led by a man dressed garishly like a whore, wafting his face with a pink fan. The new arrivals had apparently entered the tavern immediately after the Vigiles had left, and their leader now stood languidly, one hand resting on Agrippina's shoulder. Round him ranged his gang of bullyboys and their hangers-on, pimps and gaudily garbed prostitutes of every nationality. Polybius was roaring at him to leave.

'Get out of here!' he shouted. 'Do you understand me, Dacius? You and your gang of degenerates.'

'Or else what?' Dacius tripped forward in his high-heeled sandals. He looked grotesque; not comical, but very dangerous, a man of shifting shadows with his masculine face and his very feminine wig; his swagger saucy yet his body hard and muscular; his voice lisping but the tone ugly and threatening. Claudia had met him and his like before, scum from the sewers, swirling through the slums like some poison, polluting everything they touched. She was fearful about their presence. Their arrival appeared a little too swift. Was it that they were expecting news? Or were they here to provoke Murranus, whose hot temper was well known? The gladiator had now picked up a cleaver and a pan lid. Anyone else would have looked comical, but Murranus was highly dangerous. Claudia didn't like the way Dacius kept swaying from side to side, taunting Murranus and every so often glancing at Agrippina, who simpered back. The more she watched, the more convinced Claudia became that Agrippina had had a hand in the poisoning of Spicerius both this time and before; yet what proof did she have? More importantly, what cruel trap had they set for Murranus? Would they accuse him of murder and unsettle his wits, disturb his concentration?

Dacius raised his hand, shutting and opening that ridiculous fan, and his gang fell silent.

'You see, my dear,' he drawled, jabbing the fan in Murranus's direction, 'whatever you do, dear boy, no matter how you glare, people are going to say . . .' he dropped the fan back to his chin and stared up at the ceiling, 'yes, that's what they'll say, that you were frightened of Spicerius.'

'That's a lie, you're camel shit!'

Dacius laughed like a mare neighing in its stable. 'Dear boy, they'll say you were the last man to drink with him, you invited him here. What I want to know is how you will deal with Meleager.' He stepped forward, folding back the right sleeve of his gown. Claudia glimpsed the purple chalice tattoo and the ring beneath it. She would have leapt to her feet but Murranus distracted her by lunging at Dacius, only to be blocked and pulled back by Polybius and Oceanus. The mood in the tavern grew tense, hands fell to knives; those who wished to avoid the fight were already crawling away.

'Prove me wrong,' taunted Dacius. 'Perform some feat, strangle a lion with your bare hands.'

'I'll strangle you!'

'Prove your innocence,' Dacius taunted, and the refrain was taken up by his henchmen: 'Prove it! Prove it! Prove it!'

'I'll prove it,' Murranus retorted, pushing Polybius away. 'On the day of the fight, the very day I meet Meleager, I'll take part in a Venatio; I'll confront and kill any animal you choose to release against me. I'll offer it as a gift to Spicerius's shade and a vindication of my innocence.'

Murranus's words were greeted with a loud roar. Claudia put her face in her hands. The trap had been baited, Murranus had stepped in, and now it had snapped shut.

*   *   *

In the Martyrs' Gallery, one of the largest passageways in the catacombs beneath the cemetery where St Sebastian the soldier had been shot to death, Presbyter Sylvester stood gazing in puzzlement at the desecrated grave. This was a most sacred place, the repository for the remains of those savagely executed during Diocletian's recent persecution. The walls on either side of the gallery were a honeycomb of broad shelves, about a yard wide, the same deep. The remains of those slain in the Flavian amphitheatre were brought here, identified where possible, blessed with a sprinkling of holy water, incensed, and placed in a tomb. The grave was then crudely plastered over and, where possible, signs were scratched into the plaster identifying the occupant, their status, and the year they died, with some pious inscription carved beneath. These holy men and women were to be venerated, their remains honoured until Christ brought them back to life on the Last Day, when he would appear in glory for the Great Judgement.

Sylvester stared up and down the passageway, now lit by lamps and torches: an eerie, sombre place, full of strange echoes, as if the ghosts of the dead were calling to each other; a place of mystery, yet one of peace, a sharp contrast to the last few hours in the lives of the occupants who lay there. The catacombs were now unused, deserted, many people reluctant to return to a place which still rang with memories of the days of terror. Who would break in and remove dusty bones and skulls?

'Why? When? Who?' Sylvester turned in exasperation to the Guardian of the Tombs, a pinched-faced elderly scribe with ink-stained skin, yet a man who took his responsibilities very seriously. The scribe had apologised profusely for bringing the presbyter here, but what else could he do? Why had a simple tomb been broken into? It contained no treasure. He had already expressed his fears that although the cemetery was a holy place where martyrs were buried, it was also a place of black magic, where witches and warlocks gathered to perform bloody sacrifice under a brooding moon.

'How long ago?' Sylvester asked.

'Days, even weeks. I have so much to supervise, so little help.'

'Yes, yes.' Sylvester looked down at the slabs of plaster lying on the floor. 'Look,' he ordered, 'examine these. See if they have a name, any indication of who they were.'

Sylvester walked away while the scribe and an assistant, grumbling under their breath, knelt down and began to assemble the pieces of plaster as if they were arranging a mosaic on the floor. Sylvester walked further down the gallery, reciting a short prayer under his breath, but he was already distracted. He was pleased at the events at the Villa Pulchra; he regretted the murders and the disappearance of the Holy Sword, but that was Claudia's responsibility. Athanasius had done well. He had won the favour of the Empress, who had agreed to meet Militiades, Bishop of Rome. When the weather cooled and the autumn winds brought a little peace to the feverishly hot city, Sylvester would be ready to persuade the Empress to grant more concessions; above all to make sure the Church of Rome had a seat at the council of war when Constantine marched east.

'Magister!'

Sylvester walked back. He took an oil lamp from a niche and crouched down to examine the cracked plaster. Pieces were missing and some of it had crumbled, but the scribe had done a good job. Sylvester traced the inscriptions with his finger.

'Lucius et Octavia ex Capua, Christiani,' he read. 'Christians from Capua.' He traced the date on the plaster and realised it must have been the last year of Diocletian's reign, some four years ago. 'Do you know who they were?'

The scribe wearily got to his feet. 'In my office,' he explained, 'I have, as you know, Magister, a list of Christians in each town, while Lord Chrysis has handed over the names of the *proscripti*, those who were condemned by the state. I will have to check these.'

Sylvester nodded. They walked back along the gallery to a small cavern which the scribe grandly described as his 'writing office'. When the catacombs had been handed over to the care of the Bishop of Rome, Sylvester had immediately set up guardians and scribes to look after this sacred place and collect every document which might identify those buried here. During the persecution, people had been dragged from their homes in the dead of night, condemned without trial, killed immediately or dispatched to the arena. He had begged for imperial documents, and although some of these had been destroyed, deliberately so, the rest had been handed over, and the chief scribe took particular pride in the way he had organised these. They were now filed in reed baskets, long boxes and chests.

Lamps were lit, and the scribe organised his helpers to search for the necessary documents. Sylvester sat within the doorway, staring across at a crude drawing on the wall of Christ in triumph. This cavern had once been a holy place where the bread and wine had been changed into the Body and Blood of Christ. Once again Sylvester marvelled at how quickly things had changed. He closed his eyes and tried to recite the psalm for the evening, but instead he dozed off, and was shaken awake by the scribe.

'Magister, we have found something very strange. We have no evidence for any Christians, man and wife, brother and sister, from Capua bearing those names. However, we do have a list of prisoners here. It is four years old and contains the names of Lucius and Octavia, farmers. More importantly, the documents say they had no heirs or family.'

'So their holding was forfeit to the state?'

'Precisely, Magister. Consequently, when the Edict of Toleration was issued, two years ago, all such property was granted back to the Church as compensation.'

Sylvester tapped a sandalled foot. 'What is this?' he whispered. 'A man and woman, probably husband and wife, of whom we have no knowledge, yet they were obviously killed as Christians and their property confiscated. They were brought here to be buried and now their bones have been removed. Look,' he got to his feet, 'you have a messenger? I want this information sent to the woman known as Claudia, staying at the She-Asses tavern near the Flavian Gate . . .'

CHAPTER 11

'*Dux atque Imperator Vitae Mortalium Animus est.*'
('The Soul is the Leader and Ruler of Men's Lives.')

Sallust, *Jugurtha*, I

Claudia sat in the garden. The morning mist still hung like a veil, and birds darted about, foraging amongst the long grass for crumbs and seeds. Caligula, the tavern cat, a true killer, came slinking out, but the birds recognised the danger and Caligula had to satisfy himself with glaring up at a tree, where a thrush sang its warning. Claudia watched the cat and wondered if death was like that, creeping out of the dark to seek its prey. Death had visited this tavern last night and taken Spicerius; had it sat in the corner gibbering while poor Murranus blundered into that trap? Dacius had clearly been delighted, taunting Murranus to repeat his promise, which of course he had. The die was now cast, the news would be all over Rome; there would be no turning back. In the end Polybius had forced Dacius and his gang back out into the streets, and only then did the enormity of what he had done dawn on Murranus.

'You've offered to fight twice on the same day,' Oceanus slurred as they drowned their sorrows in wine.

Polybius had urged Murranus to withdraw, but the gladiator was too stubborn. Poppaoe, all tearful, had asked what it meant, and Oceanus had explained. The games would start with criminals being executed, then in the afternoon there would be the Venatio, when a gladiator would face wild animals. Murranus had agreed to pit himself against some ferocious beast, and Dacius had chosen a bull, a ferocious, deadly animal which combined speed, cunning, strength and a determination to kill whatever confronted it.

Claudia had sat, face in hands, trying to control her trembling. She had seen these fighting bulls from Spain and North Africa, muscles rippling under sleek skins, powerful legs which could launch them into a ferocious charge, and, above all, those wide-spaced, cruelly tipped sharpened horns. A wild bull could move like the wind yet turn as fast as any coin spinning on the floor. Oceanus, full of wine and his own importance, had not spared them the details, describing how the bull could charge, feint, and use its horns like an expert swordsman would a pair of blades. Yet this was only half the danger. Murranus had to fight, escape unscathed and, an hour later, enter the arena to confront Meleager. That was the trap! Claudia recognised how crude but effective it was. Polybius had declared it was like weighing a runner down with weights: Spicerius's death, its effect on Murranus, the baiting and accusations, the simpering Agrippina, and now the prospect of a ferocious battle before Murranus even met his opponent.

Claudia straightened up and took a deep breath. She felt sick with fear and anger, yet there was something else which she was reluctant to face. She had glimpsed the tattoo on Dacius's wrist and recalled what Spicerius had told Murranus. If that was true, then Meleager and that degenerate from the slums were allies, even close friends. They meant to kill Murranus and had arranged the baiting so as to gamble on the future. Murranus would die so the likes of Dacius, Meleager and Agrippina could eat more delicacies, swill more wine and decorate their bodies with finer clothes and trinkets. It had all been planned from the beginning. Spicerius had been marked down for death and Murranus was the second ox for slaughter. And yet? Claudia ground the heel of her sandal into the grass. She had to face it, her own hate and desire for revenge throbbed loudly. She wanted Murranus to fight Meleager; she couldn't ask for a better champion for herself and poor Felix. No greater vindicator or righter of wrongs. Over the last few days Claudia had made her decision. Meleager had to die. Murranus must kill him. There was no alternative, and if he didn't, she would. So what could she do to help? She thought of Agrippina sitting like a pampered cat fed on cream, acting the victim with her wailing and lamentation, her pitiful glances as she tried to provoke sympathy and win support.

'Bitch!' Claudia breathed. 'You painted bitch! You murderous whore! I'll begin with you.'

Caligula came over, brushing itself against her legs. Claudia scratched the cat between the ears as she reflected on the other mysteries. The Holy Sword? Well, she smiled grimly, that would be a matter of catching the culprit red-handed. And as for the murders? Claudia narrowed her eyes and watched a blackbird, bolder than the rest, go hopping across the grass. The murders were, perhaps, not such a mystery; small items were beginning to prick her suspicions. She knew where Timothaeus was, and she also quietly vowed to keep an eye on Narcissus.

The tavern door opened behind her and Caligula streaked for the gap.

'Claudia?' Polybius, red-eyed and much the worse for drink, stood under the porch. 'They've arrived, your visitors have come.'

She followed her uncle back into the tavern to where a man sat hunched near the door. On the other side of the door were a group all huddled, clustered together like mourners.

'Sallust? Sallust the Searcher?'

The man pushed back his hood and undid the cord of his robe. Claudia was always fascinated by the old man's face. It looked so commonplace: unshaven, watery-eyed, runny-nosed. The shock of white hair was unruly, the tunic he wore that of a peasant, the sandals bought second-hand from some army quartermaster. A pallid face with a snub nose, the eyes dark brown like those of a puppy, trusting and eager; not the face of a searcher of things, and as such it was his best disguise.

'Why, Claudia!' Sallust's voice was just above a whisper. She grasped his hand. 'It's so good to see you. How long is it now?'

'A few months. Would you like something to eat?'

'Polybius is going to give me and my boys a jug of beer and a slice of pear tart. We eat very little, you know.'

Claudia sat down next to this searcher for things. Despite his appearance, or perhaps because of it, Sallust was the most expert of the men and women who watched and reported. During the recent civil war he had backed the wrong party. He'd been used by Maxentius and, when Constantine marched into Rome, had had to go into hiding. It was a long story, but Sallust, who knew Polybius from their military days, had appealed for help and Claudia had approached the presbyter Sylvester. A pardon and amnesty had been issued, confiscated property was returned and Sallust had become Claudia's firm friend and ally. He had immediately returned to his searchings, aided and abetted by his extended family of sons, sons-in-law, kith and kin of many varieties.

Sallust didn't work for the state but for private individuals. If a debt wasn't paid or a wager withdrawn, a slave escaped, a child went missing or valuables disappeared, Sallust and his searchers would soon put that right. He had lost some of his wealth during the confusion following the civil war and was eager to make up his losses. He already owned a palatial town house within walking distance of the Palatine, as well as a restful villa out in the Campania. Sallust, however, liked to act the poor man, the nondescript, the person who could sit in a tavern and never be noticed or missed.

For a while Claudia just chattered about the She-Asses and Polybius's garden, but Sallust gave her a grim reminder of what had happened the previous night, whispering that he and his family already knew about Spicerius's death and Murranus's boast.

'Well, mistress?' He drained his beer and gazed across at his huddle of relatives, busy filling their bellies with pear tart.

'They're so quiet!' Claudia murmured.

'Always like that,' Sallust declared. 'That's how we do our business. Now, mistress, you asked to see me.'

'Ah.' Claudia edged a little closer. 'I want to discuss three things with you: love tokens, a holy sword, and the town of Capua. Now . . .' She paused at the knocking on the door. She got up, opened it and stared at the tinker with a tray slung round his neck. She would have immediately closed the door, but he lifted his hand, displaying the crude icthus ring on his middle finger.

'I'm looking for the woman Claudia.'

'I'm she.'

'Are you?' He peered closer. 'You know the turnings?'

'Across the cemetery to the tomb dedicated to Servilius.' Claudia gave the agreed answer.

'He sent you this.' The tinker handed across a scroll, waggled his fingers and disappeared.

Claudia made her excuse to Sallust and went out to the garden, where she undid the scroll and read Sylvester's message. She was so surprised she read it again.

'What is this?' she exclaimed, staring down at the carefully formed letters.

Sylvester had described a mystery involving a violated tomb and the remains of a man and a woman known as Lucius and Claudia, not listed as Christians but still martyred for that faith. Apparently they were a childless couple whose holdings had been forfeit to the State but which now, under the Edict of Toleration, had been restored to the Church. Claudia reflected on her own suspicions and returned to Sallust.

'As I said,' she smiled, sitting down, 'love tokens, a holy sword and the town of Capua.'

Sallust listened carefully to the problems facing Claudia, asking a few questions as she spoke. An hour later, he and his entourage left, promising to do what they could. The tavern was now stirring, and Claudia broke her own fast. Narcissus came down and sat in a corner, eating a bowl of yesterday's meat and onions. Januaria sat next to him, all smiling and simpering. A short while later Murranus clattered down the stairs, complaining of a dry mouth and sore head. He wanted to be alone, to reflect on what had happened the previous day. He grunted greetings but said he had to hurry, wolfed down some bread soaked in milk, took a mouthful of beer, kissed Claudia on the brow and almost fled through the tavern door. Narcissus, tired of Januaria, came edging over.

'Mistress,' he asked plaintively, 'what are we going to do?'

'We are going to sit and moan,' Claudia replied, mimicking

his voice, 'about having a soft bed, freedom, a purse of money, good food and a pretty girl to smile at you.'

'I'm sorry.'

'Don't be sorry,' Claudia snapped. 'Go down to the stables and saddle my cob. If you want, saddle a mount for yourself. We are going back to the Villa Pulchra.'

'Then I'll walk, I don't like horses.'

'Please yourself,' Claudia retorted. She was eager to do something rather than sit and let the terrors seize hold of her.

Claudia collected her cloak, belt and purse, pushed some bread and dried meat into a napkin, borrowed a leather bag from the kitchen and made her farewells. Narcissus didn't object to her proposal; he walked beside her describing how horses made him seasick before asking her why she wanted to return to the villa, pointing out that no one would be there; Timothaeus and the rest would now be in the imperial palace on the Palatine. Claudia murmured, 'Good, I hope they stay there,' before returning to her own thoughts and the list of suspicions she'd drawn up last night as she had lain in bed waiting for sleep.

Their journey through the streets was quick; only a trickle of early-morning travellers were taking advantage of the good weather and the half-empty streets. For most of their journey down to the Flavian Gate they followed a cohort of lightly armed legionnaires tramping out to one of the small forts on the approaches to Rome. Narcissus commented on how there seemed to be more troops on the move, whilst Claudia privately wondered if Constantine had decided to retaliate against his rival in the East. She was glad to be free of the She-Asses. Murranus had placed himself in great danger, but she did not want to worsen matters with sharp advice and a tart tongue. She made herself as comfortable as possible in the saddle, half dozing as they left the busy streets with their noise and smell, on to the main via which ran through the Flavian Gate. They passed the place of the dead and Claudia wondered about Sylvester's enigmatic message. She was sure Sallust would help with that. Beside her Narcissus hummed a love song Januaria had taught him, whilst swiping with his stick at the brambles and weeds on the side of the path.

They made good progress, only standing aside for imperial messengers who came thundering along the via with their military escort. Soon they left the main road and followed the winding country paths, past the pickets guarding the approach to the villa, now reduced to only two or three men squatting before a fire, more interested in their oatmeal than a traveller who carried an imperial pass. When they reached the villa, a yawning guard opened the gate and ushered them into the cobbled yard. An under-steward came down to greet them, all blustering and protesting, but the protests died on his lips when he recognised Claudia and the pass she carried. He listened with astonishment as Claudia demanded that he summon all the servants and what guards were left down to the yard as soon as possible. He made to protest, but smiled at the prospect of a silver coin and hastened away. Claudia knew that once the court had left the villa, the servants would enjoy themselves doing as little as possible, hiding away and finding whatever mischief they could to while away the boredom. They soon flocked down to the yard, full of curiosity at this visitor and what she proposed: kitchen maids, page boys, gardeners, cleaners and washerwomen. Claudia asked them to gather round. She opened her purse and took out five silver pieces, promising them that anyone who found a weapon of war, as she described it, in the countryside to the south of the villa would receive a lavish reward.

'What do you mean,' the under-steward shouted, 'a weapon of war?'

'You'll know it when you see it,' Claudia retorted. She was standing on an upturned barrel; she felt it sway beneath her, so she snapped her fingers and told Narcissus to steady it. 'You've all heard about the attack on the villa and the direction it came from. There's a path leading down through the woods. I want you to go along that, oh, no more than two hundred paces from the walls, and search for any weapon of war, a dagger, a spear, an arrow, a sword or a shield. Anything which looks suspicious. Now, you know what I mean.' She indicated with her hand. 'On the right of the path leading from the main gate are woods, trees, shrubbery. Just ignore these. I want you to form a line and search the ground to the left of the path. As I've said, go no further than two hundred paces deep.'

'And what happens if we don't find anything?' a gardener shouted.

'Then you'll still be rewarded.' Claudia smiled. 'I'll leave some money so you can have a feast, Oh, and by the way,' she added sharply, 'I won't tolerate any nonsense.' She glared at the guards lounging about. 'I don't want some weapon taken from the armoury and placed under a bush. I'm not as stupid as I look.' She hardened her voice. 'I'm here on the Empress's orders. Those who do her will shall be rewarded.' She let the threat hang in the air.

The under-steward soon had them all organised, aided and abetted by some of the guards. The day was a fine one, they had little to do and all were eager to earn the reward. Once they'd left, Claudia went to the cellar and the House of Mourning, studying them carefully before going back to the kitchen, with Narcissus trailing behind like a ghost. They sat outside in the small courtyard and divided the food between them. Claudia ate and listened as Narcissus described how he would work at the She-Asses in preparation for his return to the embalming trade.

'There'll be plenty of custom for you,' Claudia remarked drily, 'amongst those who live near the Flavian Gate, though I'm not too sure how you'll get paid.'

Narcissus, however, would not be deflected, but gave a dramatic account of how Polybius might lend him the money and even be his business partner. He chattered so quickly that Claudia wondered if he was nervous about what she might know. She swilled the wine round her cup. She had begged it from the cask man in the kitchens, who was too busy, as he'd put it, 'to go out with the rest and get involved in childish games'. Claudia noticed a fly floating on the top of the wine. She plucked this out and wiped other specks from the not-so-clean goblet. She stirred the wine with her finger but didn't wipe it dry, so it became sticky. She rubbed it, looking at the hardened whitish grains, and recalled sitting beside Spicerius's corpse the previous evening.

'That's it!' she exclaimed.

'What is?'

'Never mind,' Claudia replied and leaning back against the wall, she stared at the white doves on the red tower roof across the courtyard.

The heat grew intense, so they moved into the gardens to enjoy the coolness of their shade near a bubbling water fountain. The under-steward found them there; he was hot, rather dusty and none too pleased with what had been found.

'There wasn't much,' he grumbled. 'You'd best see for yourself.'

The rest of the servants were gathered in the stable

courtyard and had laid their finds on a sheet stretched across the cobbles. There were pieces of strapping, a buckle, a weatherworn sheath, a javelin head, and even the rather battered handle of a sword, as well as scraps of leather and armoury. Claudia sifted through them. Some of the items must have been there for years, but others were clearly remains from the recent attack. She made sure that they had searched the area she had described. The servants, red-faced and perspiring, all loudly agreed that they had pushed their way through bracken and gorse but found very little. Claudia thanked them, and handed over the five silver pieces and one more. She also authorised the under-steward to draw wine and food from the stores and feast at the villa's expense all those who had searched.

It was well past noon, but despite Narcissus's grumbles, Claudia decided it was cool enough to return to the city. They had an uneventful journey back, joining a convoy of wine merchants who'd heard about the games and were hastening to Rome in the hope of greater profit. The She-Asses was almost deserted. Claudia went up to her own chamber, took out a small writing casket and, as if she was listing items to buy, wrote down everything she'd discovered. Then she slept for a while, going down to join a taciturn Polybius for the evening meal. Her uncle announced mournfully that Murranus had decided to stay at the gladiator school, determined to train for the coming conflict.

The mood of the tavern had changed. The wine had worn off, the excitement had soured. Many of the customers secretly suspected Murranus had been trapped, his chances of victory greatly reduced. Claudia knew she would have to wait. She had gambled on Sallust the Searcher making a quick discovery, but it wasn't until the following evening that he slipped into the tavern. Despite the warm weather, he still wore his cloak, and insisted on speaking to Claudia out in the garden, where no one could see or hear them. Only then did he undo the cloak and hand across the bundle.

'I think that's what you're looking for?' He smiled, winked at her and got to his feet. 'I don't want to stay; after all, my boys and I could be accused of robbing a tomb.' His smile widened. 'Your suspicions were correct.'

'And the other business?' Claudia asked.

'I'm afraid that'll take more time. Everyone is excited about the coming games. It's hard to sift the wheat from the chaff and so discover the truth.'

Claudia thanked him, and the searcher left, pausing in the tavern for a jug of beer. Claudia made sure Narcissus wasn't about and went to her chamber. She opened the bundle to check its contents, then hid it under her bed and hurried down to the kitchen, where Narcissus was helping Poppaoe. Claudia asked him to go to the Palatine with one of the tavern boys to inform Timothaeus the steward that she must see him urgently on a matter concerning the Empress. Polybius came in as Narcissus made to object.

'I think you should go,' Polybius declared. 'It's the least you can do for someone you owe so much.'

Grumbling under his breath, Narcissus took his staff, put on his sandals and left with a little tavern boy whom everyone called 'Sorry' because that was all the lad would say as he pushed himself through the throng to serve a customer.

'You're excited.' Polybius put his hand under Claudia's chin. 'Your face is slightly flushed, eyes bright as polished buttons.'

'Uncle, I would like you to do me a favour. What's on the menu today?'

'Same as yesterday,' Polybius pulled a face, 'and last week. Fish, sausage and vegetables, though we are serving some fruit.'

252

'I want you to serve me and my guests something tasty out in the garden. Narcissus and Timothaeus the steward will appreciate your cooking. I also want a bucket of sand and a kitchen knife.'

Polybius, intrigued, replied with a stream of questions, but Claudia only laughed, shook her head and walked away.

Noon had come and gone by the time Narcissus brought a red-faced, perspiring Timothaeus into the She-Asses. Claudia greeted the steward warmly, introduced him to everybody and then, winking at her uncle, took her guests out to the orchard. Polybius had put out a small blanket on the ground; the bucket of sand and kitchen knife were half hidden behind the stone seat. Timothaeus was full of bluster and questioning, and protested at being pulled away from his busy duties, but a goblet of Polybius's finest white wine and a platter of freshly caught fish took the edge off his temper. Narcissus, however, was much more watchful. Claudia wondered if someone in the tavern had warned him of her preparations. For a while they discussed the coming games. Timothaeus explained how Murranus's boast was known all over the palace. 'The bets are being laid,' he exclaimed, 'and people are already buying up the best seats. The master of the school of gladiators has been to see Rufinus to organise the events. They say everyone in Rome who matters will be there; they are talking of a fight to the death, and whoever goes down,' he added darkly, 'is staying down. Oh, by the way, the Augusta sends her warmest greetings, as does Chrysis. Burrus said he hasn't forgotten what you did for him, though the Empress,' he added shrewdly, 'is still full of questions about what you should do for her.'

'I'm glad you've finished your food.' Claudia sat cross-legged and smiled dazzlingly at Timothaeus. 'You see, gentlemen, I have found the Holy Sword!'

She needed all the training of her acting career to keep her face straight. Narcissus almost choked on a plum and had to spit it out, while the goblet slipped from Timothaeus's hand. Claudia caught it deftly and put it on the grass beside her. Narcissus began to shake as if at the onset of a sudden fever; all colour drained from Timothaeus's face.

'You're not going to faint, are you?' Claudia teased. 'That's something both of you are very good at, fainting. Oh, and don't start jumping to your feet, please; the less that people know, the better.'

Claudia rose, walked into the orchard and brought back the parcel the searcher had given her. She undid the cloth and they all stared at the old legionary sword, its polished hilt shimmering blueish in the sunlight, the ruby in the ivory handle glowing with its hidden fire. She picked the sword up, balancing it in both hands.

'I think this could be the sword,' she declared evenly. 'It feels like a legionary sword, I mean the balance. The blade is polished and is rather old, though the handle's new, which makes it a little top heavy, I mean with the ivory and the ruby.'

'Where . . . where?' Timothaeus's voice faltered.

'Where? Where?' Claudia teased. 'There, there! I realised you had stolen the sword, Timothaeus, but you're a good man, a devout Christian.' She ticked the points off on her fingers. 'You wouldn't sell it; that would be sacrilege and highly dangerous. You wouldn't keep it for yourself; that would be selfish and very dangerous. Thirdly, you couldn't give it over to the Church; they would immediately hand it back to the Empress.'

'So?' Narcissus spoke as if he was choking.

'I came to the logical conclusion.' Claudia smiled. 'If this was the sword responsible for the martyrdom of the Blessed Paul, then what better place for it than the shrine, the monument which now covers his tomb on the road to Ostia, the very place where the Apostle Paul was executed? Now, I was back in Rome before you so that I could get everything prepared. I met an old gentleman, a friend of mine, Sallust the Searcher. He literally has a legion of relatives, and it was simply a matter of him organising these to watch the most famous Christian holy spots around the city, with a particularly close guard over the tomb of the Blessed Paul. Sallust himself watched that! This was the first time you had been back in Rome since the sword was stolen. You smuggled it from the Villa Pulchra and I realised you would try and get rid of it as soon as possible.'

'I thought I was being—'

'Watched?' Claudia asked. 'Of course you were, just as you ordered Narcissus to watch me.'

Timothaeus swallowed hard.

'Do you know something?' Claudia put the sword down beside her, covered it with the cloth, leaned across and patted both Timothaeus and Narcissus on the face. 'If I ever go back to acting and organise my own troupe, I will ask you two to join. What a performance! Surely you are going to ask me how I discovered this? How I found out? Oh, don't be frightened, Timothaeus. I'm not going to have you arrested.'

Both men smiled in relief. Claudia got to her feet and brought out the bucket of sand and the sharp kitchen knife.

'Once upon a time,' she smiled, 'there was a very devout Christian steward called Timothaeus, who truly believed in the teaching of Christ. Being a non-Jew, a former pagan, he had a special devotion to the Apostle Paul, who, I understand, first brought Christ's teaching to the Gentiles. Didn't Paul preach in Antioch; that's the first place your sect were called Christians, wasn't it? Anyway, Timothaeus is also a loyal servant of the Empress; he adores her. Thanks to her and her son, the Christians have been allowed out of the catacombs. The Empress Helena flirts with Christianity: will she, won't she convert? She also has a deep interest in all things Christian. The Empire is being ransacked as the Augusta searches for the True Cross, the Crown of Thorns, the spear which pierced Christ's side, the nails driven into his wrists. Helena's one great prize is the Holy Sword which cut the Blessed Paul's neck and was splashed with his holy blood. She organises a great debate at the Villa Pulchra and decides to put the sword on show.

'Of course, in any royal palace things go missing, so she chooses that cellar, where the sword will hang from a hook and chain above a pit of sand. If anyone tries to touch it, they'll mark the sand where their feet will sink deep. The chain is suspended so you would have to stretch out with a rod to pull it close and unhook the sword. The cellar has no windows and is guarded by the Augusta's German ruffians, whilst the heavy door is kept locked by two different keys. One held by you, and the other by Burrus.'

Claudia picked up Timothaeus's goblet and pressed it into his hands. 'Go on,' she urged, 'drink. And you too, Narcissus.' She paused, staring up through the branches of a tree. 'As I said, Timothaeus, you are a devout Christian; you also have scruples.'

'What are they?' Narcissus intervened.

'You know full well: doubts, uncertainties. You were rather repelled, weren't you, Timothaeus, by such a sacred Christian relic being owned by pagans and put on display to be visited by the likes of Chrysis, or, worse still, the followers of Arianism, Justin and his gang. You saw it as blasphemy, a form of violation. So you decided not to steal it, but to take it from the gaze of the vulgar and return it to a more sacred spot. You'd do it in such a way that no one could be blamed or punished, but you needed help. Now I know, you know, that Narcissus is a Christian. He secured his post at the Villa Pulchra because of the influence of the powerful Sylvester. Narcissus is your drinking partner, isn't he, Timothaeus, someone you confide in? And because you are the steward at the palace, you also exert a lot of influence.'

'Are you saying we both stole it?' Narcissus asked.

'Of course I am. Timothaeus, as I said, is full of scruples. He prayed for divine guidance. How could he take such a sword so cleverly guarded? I suppose the gods answer our prayers in peculiar ways; in this case, the answer was Burrus.'

'He had nothing to do with it,' Timothaeus blurted out.

'Precisely,' Claudia replied, 'but he was the answer to your prayer. Burrus and his guards are highly superstitious. They wouldn't go into the cellar or anywhere near the Holy Sword. So, Timothaeus, you laid your plans. You pretended to have a bad leg and, the day before, walked into the cellar with a stick, which you left there hidden in some crevice or by the wall. I remember one of the guards asking about your leg but you quickly dismissed it. Anyway, the following day you returned. By now, Burrus and his guards were used to your routine; they were quite happy to let you in and out. You moved quickly. You took one of the stools, placed it near the sandpit, grasped your walking cane, climbed on the stool and dragged the chain closer. You unhooked the sword, climbed down, hid the walking stick away and moved the stool back.'

'And the sword?' Timothaeus asked.

Claudia picked up the kitchen knife and drove it deep into the sand in the bucket.

'You buried it in the sand.'

'But they would have noticed.'

'Oh, don't say that the sand would have been disturbed.

You'd already prepared for that eventuality. Notice how the blade of the kitchen knife sinks deep.' Claudia pressed on it until the hilt almost disappeared. 'I remember standing on that sand,' she continued. 'It was finely grained. My feet sank deep, well over my ankles. You could either have driven the sword in hilt first, or hidden it and covered it with sand. You may even have practised that in the days beforehand. You then pretended to faint. Your hand and arm brushed the sand, so if anyone did notice anything untoward, they would see it as the effect of your faint. Poor Timothaeus, overcome by fright! Of course, Burrus and his guards become curious and look in. They see what's happened and raise the alarm. Now, the person who should be dealing with the crisis is lying in a dead faint in the cellar, and the Augusta hasn't arrived yet. There's a great deal of chaos and consternation, people running about, and lo and behold, by mere chance,' Claudia leaned over and patted Narcissus's hand, 'there's a slave from the House of Mourning who happens to be a Christian and a close friend of the now prostrate steward. I mean, what were you doing there, Narcissus?'

He opened his mouth to answer, only to sigh and glance away.

'You told me yourself,' Claudia continued, 'how your duties were in the House of Mourning. What were you doing near that cellar? You were waiting, weren't you? You helped take the stretcher in. You made sure that you stood on the sand, that the sword was hidden. Moreover, who would notice as poor Timothaeus was taken from the cellar that you picked up his walking stick and took it out for him? People were not looking for a walking stick, they were looking for a sword.'

'And?' Timothaeus asked, wiping the sweat from his brow.

'Well, Burrus and his boys are quivering like saplings in a

storm; they think the sword is sacred and your God has come to claim it. Gaius Tullius is a pagan and a cynic. He searches the cellar but finds nothing. He's not really interested, is he? It's not his responsibility – what is a Christian relic to him? A short while later Timothaeus, now much recovered, returns to the now unguarded cellar, takes the sword out and hides it away.' Claudia paused, as if listening to the birds singing in the branches above her. 'You were very clever,' she added. 'But it was Narcissus being so close to the cellar when it happened which made me curious; that and logic. I mean, the sword disappeared but no one saw it leave, so it must have been left in the cellar. The question was where.'

'You suspected me?' Narcissus asked.

'Oh yes, you're very suspect, Narcissus. Remember the night of the fire, when the House of Mourning was burned to the ground? You were actually asleep close by, under the shade of a sycamore tree. You said you had been drinking heavily. Now you are a free man, but then you were a slave. Every other servant in the Villa Pulchra, not to mention the slaves, only eats and drinks *after* the banquet. But you, by your own admission, were probably as drunk as any of Constantine's guests. I made enquiries in the kitchens, but no one remembered serving you a drink.'

'It was me,' Timothaeus confessed.

'Yes, it certainly was.' Claudia smiled. 'A small reward for Narcissus's help. What did you give him? I found the bones – a nice fat piece of capon, a juicy slice of beef and a jug of the best Falernian. A suitable reward for a slave who'd helped you so much, who had to be bribed silent and, knowing you, Narcissus, who was grumbling about how nervous he felt. Timothaeus went down to the villa kitchen and brought you out certain delicacies and a nice deep-bowled goblet of wine.

You've got a good appetite, Narcissus, I've seen you eat. You were nervous, agitated, and you ate quickly and drank just as swiftly. You fell asleep. When you woke up you must have thought you were in a nightmare. The House of Mourning was burning, enquiries might be made and questions asked – what was a slave in charge of the House of Mourning doing filling his belly and drinking the best wine?'

'What will you do?' Timothaeus took his hands away from his face.

'What will I do?' Claudia shrugged. 'Look, Timothaeus, the best and safest place for this sword is with the Empress. You will make some excuse and go straight back to the Villa Pulchra, where you will hang the sword back on its hook. No, no, that's too stupid!' Claudia scratched her chin. 'You'll take it back to the villa and organise a search of the gardens. You will find it, hand it back to the Empress, and receive her thanks, as well as a lavish reward. This idle bugger,' Claudia pointed a finger at Narcissus, 'will help you. You'll be the heroes of the hour.'

Both men sighed in relief. Timothaeus stood up, stretched to ease the cramp and crouched before Claudia. He took her face into his hands and kissed her gently on the brow.

'I wondered,' he pulled a face, 'I really did wonder about you, Claudia. I could tell just by the way you were looking at me that you knew something was wrong. It is as you say. I used to see the sword hanging there. Sometimes I thought I could see the holy blood of Blessed Paul glistening on its blade. I realised how easy it would be to stand on one of those stools and take it. I used the stick to measure the sand. It's very soft and very deep. Burrus and his Germans would never come in. So I persuaded Narcissus to help. I told him what I wanted, that I could make his life ever so comfortable, so he agreed. I didn't plan,' he added, glaring at his companion in crime, 'to make him drunk, or imagine that the House of Mourning would be burned.'

'What else can we do?' Narcissus intoned mournfully.

'Oh, I think you can help me with a number of things.' Claudia smiled. 'But first take this blessed sword back to the Villa Pulchra, and when you have found it, hasten back to the Palatine and show the Augusta what you have achieved. Tell her your sleep was racked by dreams.'

Both men got to their feet.

'Oh, Narcissus, do something else for me. On your journey to and from the Villa Pulchra, ask yourself what you saw that night.'

'Which night?'

'The night the House of Mourning burned to the ground. Every single thing you saw! You must go to the villa with Timothaeus, but when I send Sorry for you, you are both to come here immediately.'

Claudia watched the two men leave. Timothaeus had wrapped up the sword carefully.

'Ask Polybius for a bag,' she called, 'a leather sack. It's up to you whether you walk or ride.'

Timothaeus raised his hand and disappeared into the tavern. Claudia lay down on the grass and stared up through the branches. Timothaeus would do what she asked, and as for Narcissus . . .

'I haven't finished with you yet,' Claudia whispered. She felt her eyes grow heavy and drifted into sleep, and when she woke she was aware of a figure, dark against the sunlight. She immediately lunged for her dagger.

'Mistress, it's only me!'

Sallust the Searcher crouched down on the grass. Claudia apologised, rubbing her face with her hands.

261

'You've been asleep for at least two hours,' Polybius shouted from the porch. 'I didn't want to disturb you, but if you slept too long . . .'

Claudia raised her hand. She asked Sallust to make himself comfortable whilst she went across to the latrines and into the small wash house nearby. She bathed her hands and face, wiping the sleep from her eyes, and idly wondered how Timothaeus and Narcissus were faring at the Villa Pulchra. She went out and rejoined Sallust.

'I've left the boys in the tavern.' The searcher mopped a platter with a piece of bread, popped it into his mouth and started on the fruit which Timotheus and Narcissus had left. 'So you got the Holy Sword back?' He smiled. 'It was so easy, you know. I kept the palace under watch! I have some friends there, so I could drift in and out. Timothaeus was acting like a scalded cat, he was highly nervous. He came sneaking out at the dead of night when he thought no one was watching, through a side gate, and by the time he had reached his sacred place, the tomb of that Christian – what's his name? Ah yes, Paul – there were more people watching him than spectators do an actor in some play. The tomb stands off the road. Timothaeus went as close as he could, dug a hole and buried it.'

'I didn't ask him for the details,' Claudia confessed. 'He was just so relieved, he couldn't get away fast enough. You'll keep it quiet?'

Sallust raised his right hand.

'Claudia, Claudia. If I told the police everything I knew, half of Rome would be arrested! Now, I've got news for you. You were correct. Spicerius was murdered. I don't know how, but the bitch who poisoned him was certainly no friend.'

262

Chapter 12

'*Crimine ab uno, disce omnia.*'
('From one crime, learn about them all.')

Virgil, *Aeneid*, II

You're not Rome's most skilled assassin, Claudia reflected, as she sat in the shade of the orchard trees and squinted across at Agrippina on the stone bench opposite. The morning was still cool; a breeze had sprung up the night before and brought in refreshing showers. Once Sallust had left, Claudia had spent the previous day feverishly preparing for this confrontation. Narcissus returned full of the news about how their supposed discovery of the Holy Sword had won him and Timothaeus the favour and generosity of the Empress. Each had been rewarded with a leather purse of coins and invited to join the Emperor in the imperial box for the coming games. Narcissus was so overjoyed Claudia had to secretly remind him that they had not really found the sword, and if the truth were known, the Empress's mood would change violently. Claudia did not intend to be nasty; she needed

263

Narcissus's attention and cooperation. Due to her warning, the former slave recollected himself abruptly and became all serious and wary.

'Do you think the Empress suspects anything? You don't think she'll challenge us later?'

'She'll never hear of it from me,' Claudia whispered. 'It's best if you accept her reward, bask in her favour and keep your mouth firmly shut. I know Timothaeus will. Now look, Narcissus, one thing I've learned about you is that you have a natural talent for acting, and I have a job for you.'

Narcissus's mood soon lightened as Claudia told him what she had planned at her meeting with Agrippina. He proved to be an able pupil and had soon perfected the look he was to adopt and what he was to say. Valens was also drawn into the conspiracy. The old army doctor needed no prompting. He deeply mourned his friend and was only too eager to seek justice for Spicerius's untimely death. They had all met here in the garden, and Valens had helped Narcissus, teaching him certain names and terms, how he was to act and sit. Claudia insisted on both of them becoming word perfect; her only worry was that Agrippina might recognise Narcissus and challenge the trap which would close around her. She had also brought Polybius into the plot. Her uncle was sworn to silence.

'I don't want you drinking,' Claudia warned, 'because once you open your mouth in the eating hall, half of Rome will know within the hour.'

Polybius had promised, swearing by his cock that not a word would pass his lips.

Claudia had worked long and hard trying to distract herself and not think of Murranus or his preparations for the combat which would take place the following day. Accordingly, she found it very difficult when Murranus, lithe and fit, his face shaved, looking positively boyish, had visited the tavern just after nightfall the previous evening. Claudia thought her heart would break at the sad look in his eyes, his quiet courage and confidence, which carefully masked his own fearful anticipation. He only stayed an hour, coming out here into the garden and embracing her fiercely and kissing her gently before slipping away.

Claudia had sat and wept until Narcissus and Valens came out to comfort her, but the pain of Murranus's farewell still made her heart ache, so she had no compassion, not a shred of kindness for the treacherous, murderous, spoilt bitch who'd wandered like a fly into her web. Agrippina had arrived mid-morning, black hair flouncing, mouth pouting, her blood-red jewellery clattering and clinking. She showed no guilt or fear, but rather smugness at being escorted by two oafs, followers of Dacius by the looks of them. Oceanus had kept this precious pair in the tavern whilst Claudia, chattering like a sparrow, had taken Agrippina out into the garden. Claudia's visitor was now beginning to lose some of her calm poise, staring anxiously across to the porch where Polybius stood on guard against any intrusion.

'Your messenger said,' Agrippina turned on Claudia, 'you had some very valuable property belonging to Spicerius.'

'Yes, that's what the messenger said.' Claudia scratched her head and leaned closer. 'Now, Agrippina, listen to me. I want you to keep that big mouth of yours shut. I don't want to frighten you, but if you go across to the tavern my uncle will remind you that I have powerful friends at court. I work for the Agentes in Rebus – you know who they are, don't you? The Doers of Things. Men and women who can bring the likes of you, a nasty pampered bitch, crashing down; their loyalty is to the Empress and no other.'

Agrippina sat swallowing hard, her lips moving soundlessly. Claudia sensed she was cursing her own arrogance at coming here.

'I could leave,' Agrippina blustered, tapping her mullet-red sandals.

'You can try.' Claudia lifted her goblet and toasted her. 'Do you know what I've been thinking, Agrippina? That you are not Rome's most skilful assassin. You are, in fact, a blundering murderess who thought no one would see through her deceitful, nasty tricks.'

Agrippina jumped to her feet, gathering up her robe.

'Oh, sit down!' Claudia drew her dagger, slicing the air so Agrippina stepped back hastily and sat down with a bump. She was trembling, glancing fearfully across at the tavern.

'You're an assassin.' Claudia smiled sweetly. 'You're also a fool. You tried to kill Spicerius once and bungled it, hoping Murranus would finish the job. So you tried again, thinking you were ever so clever.'

'I don't know what you're talking about,' Agrippina gasped. 'You have no proof.'

'Oh, I've got plenty of that.' Claudia turned. 'Uncle, you should ask our visitors to join us.'

Polybius stepped aside as Valens, accompanied by Narcissus, left the tavern and strolled across the grass towards them. Claudia vowed to keep her face straight. She and Valens had done an excellent job. Narcissus had been transformed. His hair was clipped, his face oiled; his tunic and robe were the best, and no one could fail to admire the jewelled rings displaying the insignia of Aesculapius, as well as the polished walking stick embellished with the hawk wings and all-seeing eye of the Egyptian god Horus. Narcissus even walked like the learned physician he was pretending to be, his head slightly to one side as if weighed down by knowledge, his face twisted in a look of cynical superiority, his mouth pursed as if he was sucking on a plum and had discovered it was a prune.

'I think you know Valens.' Claudia waved her hand. 'This is Narcissus, a specialist physician from the House of Life at the Temple of Isis in Alexandria. He's an expert on the ailments men suffer from.'

Valens nodded at Agrippina and squatted down next to Claudia. Narcissus, who seemed more interested in his fingernails than anything else, looked Agrippina up and down as if she was some unpleasant symptom, then flicked his fingers fastidiously for her to move up so that he could share the garden seat. He rested his cane between his knees and smiled at Claudia.

'Darling.' His drawl was so pronounced, Claudia had to tighten her mouth to hide the smile. 'Darling, I'm so glad you're not wearing face paint.' He turned and wagged a finger at Agrippina's nose. 'And you, my darling, should be more careful. You have more paint on your face than I've seen on a villa wall. You never know what those creams and oils contain. I used to say the same to dear Spicerius; surely you noticed the golden boy had stopped wearing his face paint? But there again, darling, you know so little about medicine. I mean, that's obvious.' He fluttered his eyelids. 'What on earth made you think that the juice of almonds would be a love potion, a cure for impotence, when in fact,' Narcissus threw his head back and neighed with laughter, 'well, to be honest, it is a cure, isn't it? I mean, everything disappears.' His face became serious. 'Including life itself.'

Agrippina stared at him in horror.

'What are you talking about? she shrieked. 'You, you . . .'

267

'Physician.' Narcissus smiled. 'I'm a physician; didn't Spicerius ever tell you about me?' Narcissus patted his groin. 'Poor thing, he had problems down here; it's a common enough complaint. Many soldiers, fighters and wrestlers complain how their manhood is drained. I mean, usually there's nothing wrong with them.' He tapped the side of his head. 'More a problem with the mind and heart than anything else. A disturbance of the humours.' He sighed. 'Dear Spicerius was so agitated! He lusted after you, darling, but he had dark thoughts.'

'What is this?' Agrippina made to rise, but Narcissus, edging closer, gripped her wrist.

'I wouldn't leave, darling. You see, I'm your friend. You may need my help because these good people here think you poisoned Spicerius. You should really sit and listen to them, as I will before I make up my mind.'

'I've had you followed,' Claudia declared. 'You often visit Dacius's house. You've also been seen with his men. I suspect you've already opened your legs for Meleager. You're a heartless whore, Agrippina, who likes the company of gladiators so as to get rid of your boredom. You have a nose for mischief; that's how Dacius drew you into his plot. Dacius thinks he controls most of the gambling in Rome, the money lending, the high rates of interest, and every so often he likes to make a killing, doesn't he, whether it's a cock fight, a wrestling bout or two men fighting to the death in the arena. Dacius and Meleager . . .' Claudia paused. 'Dacius and Meleager,' she repeated, 'are friends. Dacius plotted that Meleager should be the champion, the Victor Ludorum. Meleager is a good fighter, perhaps one of the best. Dacius and his friends arranged . . . what would you call it? A double wager? Spicerius to lose, Murranus to win; Murranus to lose,

Meleager to win. Can you imagine the profit, Agrippina? The money being moved, accumulating rapidly as it shifts from one bet to the other? I understand you could make millions, a veritable fortune. Am I expressing myself clearly? Anyway, that's what Sallust the Searcher says.'

'Who?' Agrippina's lips hardly moved.

'Oh, you don't know Sallust?' Claudia moved her dagger from hand to hand. 'You don't know him but he knows you. He's been watching you very carefully.'

'I'm a free citizen, I can go where I wish. I'm not a slave or a tavern slut.'

'I don't deny that.' Claudia smiled. 'And you can sit and insult me to your heart's content. When people see you, they just say, "That's Agrippina." What they would find more interesting is your knowledge of love potions.' She dug into the wallet on her belt and drew out a piece of parchment. 'You do recognise this?' She held it up. 'It's in your hand. "Love conquers Agrippina. Love conquers Spicerius"?'

'I gave it to him, there's no crime in that!'

'No, but there is in poisoning. You first tried it at the amphitheatre and you failed. You mixed the potion with Spicerius's face paints and, only later, when no one was looking, poured some into the cup he had been drinking from in order to cast suspicion on Murranus or even Polybius. Murranus was meant to kill Spicerius but didn't. The poison you used, or so physician Valens will tell you, wasn't strong enough. It was meant to be absorbed through the skin; I don't know how it works.' Claudia waved a hand at Valens. 'Perhaps you can explain to our friend.'

'It's true.' Valens needed little prompting; his intense dislike of Agrippina was vibrant and passionate. 'A physician,' he kept his voice low, 'removes all possible causes for a disease or infection. What he cannot remove is usually the true cause. I questioned Spicerius very closely about that day in the amphitheatre. He had eaten the night before and drank some water before he left for the arena. However, he insisted he felt hale and hearty until shortly before the fight.'

'He drank the wine,' Agrippina intervened.

Valens shook his head. 'What Spicerius told me, and no one else, was that he felt the first, early symptoms *before* he drank the wine.'

'You're lying!' Agrippina shouted.

Valens was, but he held her gaze. 'What you did, you murdering bitch, is what Claudia has described. There are women in Rome who've actually poisoned themselves with their creams, powders and oils. Some of the paint they use to decorate their eyes contains belladonna, whilst their powders hold a deadly form of lead, even arsenic, which can eat away at their faces. You must have seen it yourself. Such noxious potions enter the body's humours, rot the innards and pollute the blood. On the morning Spicerius was to fight Murranus, you visited him, bringing your face paints mixed with poison. Spicerius always liked to look his best. He claimed that if he painted himself liked a woman it often disconcerted his opponent. Do you remember that morning, Agrippina? His face was heavily painted. He felt the first symptoms when he arrived at the amphitheatre, but dismissed them as tension. He drank the wine and walked into the arena. Any physician will tell you that a mixture of wine, intense excitement, fear or pleasure, combined with physical activity, will send the blood racing. It was then the poison took effect. However, because it had not been absorbed totally through the skin,' Valens leaned over his finger, only a few inches from Agrippina's face, 'and because of his splendid physique and fitness, Spicerius survived. He retched and he vomited, and that saved his life. Meanwhile, in the cavern beyond the Gate of Life, while everybody was distracted by the uproar caused by his condition, you went across and poured the same poison into Spicerius's cup.

'I don't really think,' Valens smiled grimly, 'that you intended to kill him, just weaken him and allow Murranus to do the rest.'

Agrippina's face was ashen and sweat-soaked.

'You have no proof of this, you're making it up.'

'Spicerius didn't.' Valens smiled grimly. 'He maintained he was in fine condition until he painted his face. He began to wonder, but he was so infatuated with you, he couldn't believe his darling Agrippina wanted him dead. I advised him, as I had before, not to wear face paint; even the most innocent creams and oils can contain a noxious potion.' Valens stamped his foot. 'At first I thought it could have been an accident, but . . .' His voice trailed off. 'I began to wonder . . . Anyway,' Valens clicked his tongue, 'Spicerius became agitated, withdrawn, deeply troubled. He swore he never suspected Murranus and looked forward to a second fight. He also complained he was suffering from impotence. He was, wasn't he? He told me how you had given him love potions; he truly believed they worked. There are drugs in Rome which can cure a man of such a malady, at least for a while. Isn't that true, Narcissus?'

'What you didn't know, darling,' Narcissus now took up the story, gripping Agrippina's arm tightly, 'was that my good friend Valens had sent his patient to me. I examined Spicerius most carefully, his groin, his anus. I could feel no growth or source of malignancy. I believe that on the day he died he went down to the gladiator school to meet Murranus. Before he arrived there he visited you, but he also visited me. He showed me that love potion: the piece of parchment and the two dried tablets it contained, baked hard like biscuits, though they'll crumble when mixed with water or wine. I, of course, dismissed them as nonsense, but Spicerius was adamant. He said you had given him love potions before, mixed with wine, and he had suffered no ill effects. I took a little of that potion, sliced it off with my knife and placed it on a weighing scale. I meant to examine it, but,' Narcissus shrugged elegantly, 'you know how it is, darling, such a busy life! I didn't think of it again until Valens told me how Spicerius died.'

'Agrippina,' Claudia tapped the woman on the knee, 'Agrippina, look at me.' The murderess did so, her lower lip trembling, her right hand shaking so much the bangles and bracelets rattled.

'You told your love to come here,' Claudia exclaimed. 'Not to eat too much or drink too much but to be waiting for you in the Venus Chamber; that he should rest and relax and, of course, mix the potion in his wine. He did so. When physician Valens examined Spicerius's corpse, he found the index finger of Spicerius's right hand very sticky, where he had mixed the powders with Uncle Polybius's sweet white wine. Moreover,' Claudia continued her deception, 'because Narcissus had sliced a little bit off, one of the tablets had begun to crumble. We found traces of it on the sheet. Poor old Spicerius,' Claudia sighed, 'he sat there, full of sweet thoughts about Agrippina, her love note in one hand and his poisoned wine in the other.'

'The juice of the almond is a deadly potion,' Valens declared. 'Death would have been swift, like an arrow to the heart.'

'I didn't do it!'

Claudia's heart sank as she looked at Agrippina's face. 'Oh but you did,' she replied quickly. 'Narcissus still has part of that powder, Valens knows what he saw; there's enough to put you on trial. Have you ever seen a woman burn to death? Just think, Agrippina, of Narcissus talking to the prosecutor, of Valens corroborating the evidence, of my uncle and others declaring that Spicerius truly believed Murranus was his friend. Then we'll begin to search Rome. That's why I hired Sallust. He'll find out where you bought the poison.'

'I didn't buy it.' Agrippina caught herself. She put her face in her hands and sobbed loudly. 'I didn't do it!' she shrieked, so loudly that Polybius came out from the porch. Claudia waved him away.

'I didn't do it!' Agrippina repeated. The tears rolled down her cheeks and mixed with the paint, turning her skin garish.

'Of course you didn't,' Claudia soothed. 'It was Dacius, wasn't it? He bought the powder and claimed it was an aphrodisiac; he told you what to do. You didn't really know, did you?'

Agrippina stepped into the trap.

'No, I didn't.' She lifted her face. 'I never knew anything about this. I came here expecting Spicerius to be waiting for me, as rampant as a stag. I wished him well.'

Claudia rose to her feet and re-sheathed her dagger. 'But you did bring him the face paint?'

'Yes, yes.' Agrippina became deeper enmeshed in her own lies. 'Yes, that's it! I wanted something to make him fight better. Dacius gave me a powder. I mixed it with my face paints, but when I saw Spicerius collapse, I panicked and poured it into his cup. I didn't intend Murranus to take the blame.'

'And the same with the two tablets?' Claudia asked. 'Dacius's cure for impotence?'

'It's as you said.'

Claudia hid her disgust at this treacherous woman lying to save her own life. Agrippina sprang to her feet. Narcissus went to restrain her, but Claudia nodded her head.

'If you want to go, you had best go.'

Claudia stepped aside. Agrippina brushed by her, almost running across the grass and back into the tavern.

'Are you going to let her go?' Narcissus asked.

Claudia ran her finger round her mouth. 'I don't think we have to do anything. Inside that tavern are two Dacians. Agrippina has convicted not only herself, but the man who controls her. What do you think, Valens? She'll go back and tell him we know everything. I don't think Dacius will like what he hears.'

Claudia stared up at the sky. 'I think Agrippina is about to spend her last day on earth.'

'I agree.' Valens clambered to his feet, brushing the grass from his robe. 'But with your permission,' he sighed, 'I would like to help matters along. I know a friendly police commander. I think I'll go and tell him what I've learnt.'

'They won't have enough evidence to arrest Dacius.'

'Oh,' Valens's old face creased into a smile, 'I think Dacius will be dealt with in a different way. Spicerius had many friends. They will take care of him as he will take care of Agrippina. I shall simply help things along. Your uncle's talked about Mercury the messenger.' Claudia grinned as she followed Valens's line of thought. 'I'm going to tell Polybius everything that's happened out here. By the time Murranus steps into the arena tomorrow, most of Rome will know.'

*   *   *

The sun blazed in the noonday sky. The heat was so oppressive the imperial engineers had fully stretched the great awning which protected the crowds in the amphitheatre; others worked hard on the pumps which sprayed the crowds with cool scented water. Claudia sat at the back of the imperial box and gazed through half-open eyes at Constantine and his family. They were all there – the Emperor, the Augusta Helena, Rufinus, Chrysis, whilst Gaius Tullius stood behind the imperial throne resplendent in his dress armour. Wives, friends, clients and hangers-on milled around. Servants hurried about with jugs and goblets of cold drinks and silver platters piled high with iced fruits. Rufinus's wife was laughing; more akin to neighing, Claudia thought, like a mare on heat. The woman was leaning over the Empress's throne, eager to share some titbit of gossip. Scribes and clerks were busy with rolls of parchment as they brought documents to the Emperor and his mother to read, study and seal. The imperial box on its central podium in the Flavian amphitheatre was rich with the smell of ink, parchment, perfume, melting wax and, of course, the ever-pervasive stench of blood from the gore-drenched sand below.

The specially imported soft sand, which glowed like gold dust, was now being turned, raked and sifted, the blood cleaned away, the fragments of human flesh piled into buckets of brine to be taken to the animal dens in the caverns deep below the amphitheatre. The roars and cries of these savage, hungry penned beasts could be heard echoing along the grim tunnels. There were not so many of them now. Most of the tigers, panthers, lions and bears had been killed in the morning slaughter. The tens of thousands of spectators seated in the steep tiers of the amphitheatre were now using the break in this ritual of blood to buy spiced meats, crushed fruit and iced melon water from the traders and hucksters who, sweating over their produce, went up and down the steps shouting the prices. Claudia had always resolved never to buy from them; Polybius had told her dreadful tales of how the meat, bread and fruit were heavily spiced and crushed to remove all sign of mould and decay.

People moved around the various sections, though they never wandered far from their seat. The sections were divided by high walls to denote the different classes of the city. At the bottom, on either side of the imperial box, the spectators were garbed in white togas and expensive tunics which marked them out as senators, knights, high-ranking officials, merchants and bankers. Above this border of white, like a dark, dirty, seething wave, ranged the greens, blues, yellows and browns of the lesser sort. The wealthy were not harassed by the traders. They had brought their own parasols, awnings and gold-fringed shades, as well as hampers and baskets of rich meats, soft bread and delicious wine. The spectators ignored the bloody mess of the arena, gaping instead at the imperial box, decorated with its gorgeous drapes. They strained to catch sight of the Emperor and his mother, distant figures garbed in purple-edged clothes and crowned with silver-tinted laurel wreaths, surrounded by the majesty and pomp of empire. They stared at the guards in their dress armour and ornately plumed helmets, breast plates gleaming in the sun, and, either side of the box, the standard bearers carrying the eagles and feather-tailed insignia of the legions, their holders dressed in the skins of panther, bear, lion and wolf. Above all, they watched for the imperial trumpeters with their gold-edged horns; these would be lifted to bray for silence when the Emperor decided the games should recommence.

The crowds shifted and surged, their excitement palpable. Their blood lust had been whetted, but now they were impatient for the crowing glory of the games: Murranus fighting for his life and honour. Claudia sucked on a piece of pomegranate as she gazed at the aristocracy of Rome. She quietly congratulated herself on what she had achieved the previous day. Valens had been correct. Agrippina had disappeared, whilst Dacius seemed to be very busy with his affairs. Rumour had it that he had slipped out of Rome that same evening, eager to take a ship to Syracuse to visit certain business partners.

Claudia had waited at the She-Asses tavern, hoping that Murranus would come, but her uncle whispered to her that Murranus was training secretly, preparing himself. Polybius sent Sorry to the gladiator school with a message, but all the boy brought back with him were the two words, 'Remember me.' Claudia had tried not to weep as she sat in the eating hall listening to Mercury the messenger regaling them all with the news that Spicerius had been murdered by his degenerate girlfriend, whilst Dacius might also have had a hand in it. Word had spread like fire amongst dry stubble. Polybius had used all his acquaintances along the stinking alleyways and streets of the slums to whisper the news. Sallust the Searcher had also helped, whilst Valens had visited old friends in the various garrisons around the city.

Claudia had cried herself to sleep, and long before dawn had been aroused by an imperial messenger with an invitation she couldn't refuse: the Augusta required her presence in the imperial box at the beginning of the games staged to mark her glorious son's birthday. Claudia had washed, dressed and hurried along the streets, one hand grasping her walking stick, the other the dagger in her belt. Even at this early hour, she noticed the placards and makeshift posters which announced not only the games and the odds on the various fighters but the scandalous news about Spicerius's poisoning. Despite her own sorrows, Claudia realised that this news was not just an indication of the city's infatuation with tittle-tattle and gossip; it also reflected the serious nature of the business of bets and wagers, of fortunes being gambled, of gold and silver exchanging hands.

The imperial party had scarcely arrived in the amphitheatre, taking their seats to the bray of trumpets, the clash of cymbals and the animal-like roar of the crowd, when Helena had snapped her fingers, beckoning Claudia forward. The Empress was in fine fettle, overjoyed at the return of her precious sword. She gave Claudia a strange look as she described Timothaeus's great find, and Claudia wondered whether she suspected the real truth.

'But never mind that,' Helena chattered on. 'What is this news about Spicerius? Is it true? Does Murranus know? How does he feel? Does he sense victory?'

Claudia tried to answer as directly as possible. Helena excitedly beckoned Rufinus over, whispering quickly to him, making signs with her fingers. Claudia suspected the Empress was changing her bets. Rufinus summoned a scribe with a tally book, and only when the banker moved away was Claudia ordered back for a fresh set of questions about the murders at the Villa Pulchra. Did she have any news? Had she made any progress? Helena's eyes flashed angrily as Claudia shrugged and mumbled a reply, but the Empress also called her a very good mouse and handed over a small purse for her trouble, before dismissing her to her stool at the back of the box. Rufinus had drifted across to learn a bit more, and was followed by Chrysis. The plump, sweaty-faced chamberlain had been all a-flutter, and Claudia considered him to be a finer actor than Narcissus, whom she had just dispatched to the Gate of Life below with a message for Murranus.

Chrysis had waved his hand in front of her eyes to attract her attention.

'Why,' the chamberlain hissed in her face, 'does Murranus still insist on the fight with the bull? He can repudiate the allegations. I've heard what happened . . .'

'I don't know,' Claudia whispered back through clenched teeth. 'I've sent messages to Murranus but he's hidden himself away. He wants to vindicate himself. I'm not responsible for your wagers and bets.'

Now Claudia took a deep breath and stretched out her legs, forcing herself to relax. She stared around the box. Sylvester, Athanasius and the other orators were present, although they had turned their backs on the arena, showing their public disapproval of such bloody games. Claudia sympathised with them. She had hidden herself away from the morning spectacle when condemned criminals had been killed, bodies blooming blood, flesh stripped away as they were mauled by tigers or panthers. The sand in the arena had blossomed like some gruesome flower, the blood spurting and spluttering, the air riven by the roars of beasts and the shouts and cries of their victims. Claudia couldn't decide which was more terrifying, the hideous scenes in the arena, or the complete lack of interest shown by those in the imperial box. Constantine gossiped with his friends; Helena dictated to her clerks and scribes, or loudly demanded that a scroll be brought to her.

Claudia felt she was a lunatic in a house of fools. The blood flowed, criminals were slaughtered, eaten or burned but no one cared; yet was she any different? The problems which vexed her were like the men and women who died in the arena, something to be dealt with. She concluded that the human heart could only take so much fear, feel only a certain amount of compassion before it turned to its own problems. She was only concerned with one thing: would Murranus live or die? What happened in the next few hours would decide her life, perhaps change it for ever. The past and present were coming together like curtains being closed around a bed. What was she now? No longer Helena's agent, her spy, the niece of Polybius, the friend of this person or that. Her mind was now dominated by images of Felix, Murranus and Meleager. She wanted justice for murder and rape, she wanted to be purged of such thoughts, she wanted the ghosts to let go. Only then would she be free. She felt as if she was in one of her plays. People were talking and moving around but they were no longer part of her.

Claudia steadied herself. The trumpeters were moving, Constantine had raised his hand. Narcissus slipped into the box, shaking his head sadly.

'Are you well?' Gaius Tullius stood over her, a look of concern on his face. 'Are you well, Claudia? You look pale. Do you want some wine or fruit?'

He didn't wait for an answer, but moved to a side table, filled a goblet, came back and thrust it into her hands.

'Don't think,' he whispered, 'just watch! The fates will decide.'

His words were drowned by the shrill blasts of the trumpets. Claudia heard a hideous creaking, took a sip of wine, stood on tiptoe and peered over. The cochlea, a huge swinging door on a movable stand, was being dragged and pushed into the centre of the arena. At least it had been drenched and washed after the previous massacre. She put her wine down. They were giving Murranus a chance; those who engaged in fighting a wild animal could use the door as a place to distract their opponent, gain a respite, rest for a while.

At last the cochlea was in place. Again the trumpets brayed, and the crowds surged to their feet, a great roar of greeting echoing to the skies as Murranus walked out through the Gate of Life. Claudia felt herself sway even as she heard the gasps and cries from those around her. The gladiator wore no sandals or body armour, no helmet or breast plate, no leg greaves; nothing except a white loincloth tied tightly. In one hand he carried a short stabbing sword and in the other the long oblong shield of a legionnaire.

'What is he doing?' Gaius Tullius whispered.

Murranus, moving slowly, walked to stand beneath the imperial box and lifted both shield and sword in salute. Constantine raised his hand in reply. Claudia was crying, her body shaking with sobs. Murranus, head shaved, face oiled, was smiling lovingly up at her as if preparing to go for a swim, or a walk across Polybius's garden to sit beneath the shade. She would have called out, but the trumpets were shrilling again, the great iron trap door on the far side of the arena was being opened and the fighting bull emerged. It was a magnificent animal, black as night, slim and lean, long-legged with powerful haunches and shoulders. Its glossy hair gleamed in the sun, and it tossed its head, snorting and bellowing, those sharp scythed horns shimmering in the light, their tips razor sharp. For a while the bull was disconcerted, pawing the ground, moving its head against the bright light. The crowds were now chanting at it. The bull pawed the ground, head going down, swinging from side to side as it looked for its prey.

Murranus sauntered across, and stood in front of the cochlea, using the red shield to attract the bull's attention, moving it from side to side. The bull, however, trotted backwards and forwards, shaking its head, snorting, almost as if planning what to do. Claudia noticed how swiftly it moved, gracefully, like a dancing horse, its sharp hoofs barely touching the ground. She ground her teeth in anger. She knew nothing about animals, but someone, probably Dacius, had chosen well. The bull was a superb specimen, probably the victor of many fights.

Murranus danced forward, trying to entice the bull. The animal moved backwards. The crowd gasped as if in one voice, for, without waiting or the usual pawing of the ground and tossing of the head, the bull burst into a charge, a powerfully fast canter, aiming straight for Murranus. The crowd roared as the gladiator dropped his shield and retreated hastily behind the cochlea. The bull turned slightly and came in, thrusting with its horns at the fallen shield, butting it with his head and trampling it under its feet. It then backed off, pawing and snorting, as if studying the cochlea and wondering what it was.

The mood in the amphitheatre changed. Claudia felt the muscles in her legs and thighs tense. Some of the crowd were jeering, deriding Murranus's efforts. The bull had now caught sight of him and moved round the cochlea for another confrontation. The game continued, the bull charging in swiftly, Murranus running away, using his shield, which he had now picked up, as well as the cochlea to protect himself. The visitors in the imperial box were discussing tactics heatedly. Some whispered cowardice, others pointed out that Murranus might be tiring the bull.

Claudia couldn't understand what was happening. It looked

as if Murranus was weakening, his body coated in a sheen of sweat, while the bull was as impetuous and aggressive as ever. The only thing she did notice was that the bull no longer withdrew, but circled the cochlea before breaking into a thundering charge, almost crashing into the barrier, or turning to gore the battered shield which Murranus dropped now and again. On occasions Murranus didn't move swiftly enough; once he stumbled, rolling in the sand to avoid the hoofs and slashing horns.

The fight wore on. People were jeering but also mystified. The bull began to show signs of exhaustion and baffled fury. Its charges became shorter but were still as vigorous. Then it happened. Murranus, once again armed with shield and sword, stood in front of the cochlea, baiting the animal to charge him again. Hoofs pawing the ground, the bull tossed its great black head and broke into a charge as fast as an arrow leaving a bow. This time Murranus did not retreat. In fact he dropped his shield and ran to face the bull. The crowd gasped and shrieked. The bull tried to slow. Murranus, like a dancer, like an athlete clearing a gate, leapt in the air, a graceful somersault which took him over the bull. The animal, disconcerted, could not stop, but crashed into the wooden platform supporting the cochlea. The blow seemed to stun it; it staggered, attempted to turn. Murranus moved in fast, at a half-crouch. He brought back his sword back and sliced at the animal's left leg, cutting muscle and sinew. Moving swiftly away, he inflicted a second cut on the other leg, though not as deep or dangerous. The bull, roaring in pain, turned, but now it was slowed, dangerously impaired. It appeared unaware of the injury until it tried to break into a charge, and bellowed as its rear legs buckled. Again Murranus moved in, stabbing and cutting, this time slicing at one of the front legs just above the hoof. The bull, seriously injured, staggered and swayed. The crowd was roaring, praising Murranus's skill and bravery. The gladiator brought his sword up, pressing the flat of the blade against his face as if saluting his opponent. The bull staggered forward and sank to its knees. Murranus slipped to one side and drove the sword deep into the back of the bull's neck. Blood sprayed out of the wound. The bull coughed, roared and slumped, even as the crowd rose and gave vent to its approval.

Chapter 13

'Quod erat demonstratum.'
('What has to be proved?')

Euclid, *The Elements*

'I didn't know you were a bull leaper!' Claudia hoped she could disguise her trembling as she sat on the bench in the small cell-like tavern off the main tunnel beneath the amphitheatre.

'Neither did I.' Murranus grinned and, at Polybius's request, stretched out his arms so both the tavern keeper and Oceanus could dry his sweat and oil his body. They took off his loincloth. Claudia, embarrassed, glanced towards the entrance, where two burly mercenaries kept away sightseers and well-wishers.

The tunnel was dimly lit; a place of flickering shadow and dancing flame, echoing ghostly with the sound of distant voices, the roars from the animal pens, and the shouting of the crowd now waiting for the high point of the day. The clamour from the tunnel grew abruptly louder. Claudia walked to the doorway. The arena was being cleaned, the bull's corpse dragged out to the slaughter yard.

Claudia returned to her seat. She felt weak with relief, yet fearful at the imminent confrontation with Meleager, now arming in a chamber further down the tunnel. The crowd had been ecstatic over Murranus's performance, truly astonished by his cunning tactics and the skill of that leap. Of course, others had seen the bull dancers of Crete, but very rarely had such prowess been shown in the arenas of Rome. Even the Emperor had risen in acclamation. Claudia had jumped up and down and it took some time for Uncle Polybius to calm her and whisper the message that Murranus wanted to see her.

'There.' Claudia looked round. Murranus patted the new loincloth. 'As neat and tidy,' he winked at Claudia, 'as a bridegroom on his wedding day.'

Polybius and Oceanus now began to arrange the armour piled on the floor, the silver filigreed breastplate, the leather kilt, the oblong shield, the embroidered sword belt, leg greaves, and a shimmering arm guard.

'Wasn't that Spicerius's?' Claudia asked.

'It was,' Murranus murmured. 'Today I'll wear it in his honour.'

He picked the arm guard up. Oceanus hurried to tie the straps.

'You seem little interested in the gossip.' Polybius lifted up the ornate Thracian helmet, with its broad brim and heavy face guard. He used his fingers to brush the gorgeous scarlet horsehair plume. 'I mean, don't you want to know,' Polybius thrust the helmet into Oceanus's hand, 'what they're saying about Meleager?'

'I'm not interested.' Murranus was staring at Claudia. 'I

don't give a damn about tittle-tattle. What does it matter, if I'm killed in the next hour?'

'Don't say that,' Polybius urged.

'I said if.' Murranus patted him on the shoulder. 'I have sacrificed the bull. Now I'll go out and defeat Meleager, but, gentlemen, I thank you for your care and attention.' He gestured at the entrance. 'In ancient Greece the heroes of Homer always armed for battle with the help of a beautiful maiden.'

Polybius and Oceanus took the hint, clasped his hand, embraced him, wished him good luck and left. Outside, the tunnel echoed with the sound of voices. The herald shouted that Meleager was ready. Murranus walked over to Claudia, embraced her gently and kissed her on the forehead.

'Bull leaper,' she whispered as she leaned against him.

'I didn't want to tell you.' Murranus kissed her again. 'I was practising. I didn't know whether such a trick would work. I couldn't see you beforehand, I didn't want to alarm you.'

'You must not die,' she whispered.

'Pray to whatever god you desire, Claudia. I'll call on the ghost of Spicerius and all the dead to be with me. At a time like this you can feel your dead thronging about you.'

'There are other ghosts.' Claudia had made a decision. She pushed herself away and walked back to the bench, patting it for Murranus to sit next to her.

'What is it, Claudia?'

'There are ghosts here,' Claudia declared. 'My father and my mother and, above all, little Felix. Murranus, I'm going to tell you something about which I'm certain I have not made a mistake.'

She grasped his callused hand. At first she spoke haltingly, but eventually the words came hot and fast. She described her meeting with Meleager, his friendship with Dacius and her unshakeable belief that he was the man who had raped her and killed her brother.

Murranus listened intently. Only a muscle twitching high in his cheek and the cold, dead look in his eyes betrayed the anger seething within him. When Claudia had finished he gathered her in his arms, pushing her head against his chest whilst stroking her hair. She wished she could stay there but she had spoken enough.

'Murranus, are you ready?'

The herald, dressed like the god Mercury, stood in the doorway, his white wand beating the air.

'Murranus,' the messenger's voice sounded hollow behind the grotesque mask, 'the Emperor awaits, the people of Rome are waiting.'

Murranus gently pushed Claudia away and stood up. She helped him arm, fastening the straps. Once finished, he stretched and flexed his muscles, then he kissed her once more, put on the helmet, picked up the sword and shield and walked out into the passageway. Meleager, similarly armed, his breastplate gleaming, was already waiting, helmet crooked under his arm. As Murranus approached, Meleager put his helmet on. Claudia noticed how the great horsehair plume seemed like a spray of blood above his head. Meleager went to grasp Murranus's hand, but the other gladiator just brushed by him, sending officials and servants scattering out of his way as he walked into the glare of the arena. Meleager had no choice but to follow, as the trumpeters, caught off cue, brayed their salutation. The crowd sprang to its feet and roared in acknowledgement that the height of the games was about to begin.

Claudia did not return to the imperial box. She stood at
the Gate of Life. Murranus and Meleager were now striding
across the sand to stand in front of the box. They took off
their helmets, raising sword and shield in salutation, and
gave the usual cry: 'We who are about to die salute thee.'

Constantine raised his hand in acknowledgement. The
gladiators separated. Murranus put his shield and sword on
the sand and took off his helmet, the agreed signal that he
wished to talk. He wasn't aware of how silent the arena had
become; he just wanted to see Meleager's face, to tell him
directly that he was about to die.

'What is it?' Meleager took off his helmet and shook the
sweat drops from his face. 'Are you willing to concede? The
crowd will understand that, especially after your luck with
the bull.'

Murranus smiled lazily back. He wanted to study this face,
remember how Meleager looked. The crowd was now
shouting, but Murranus didn't care. He picked up his helmet
and brushed the sand from its plume.

'Your friend Dacius.' He could tell by Meleager's expres-
sion that his opponent knew only too well what had
happened. 'He's fled Rome.' Murranus winked. 'He won't be
here to see you die.'

The fixed smile faded from Meleager's face.

'And you *are* going to die,' Murranus continued. 'In a
tunnel behind you stands a young woman, Claudia, the love
of my life. Eighteen months ago she and her brother were
down at a lonely spot on the banks of the Tiber. A stranger
attacked them. He killed the boy and raped that young
woman. Her assailant was strong and muscular, and on his
wrist he had the tattoo of a purple chalice, the same insignia
Dacius wears. You've had yours washed off.' Murranus

noticed how his opponent was breathing more quickly, blinking in astonishment. 'You've had it washed off,' Murranus repeated, 'but you can't wash away the crime, and you'll pay for that now.'

Murranus put his helmet on, fastening the buckle, only now becoming aware of the shouts and catcalls interspersed with a few boos from the increasingly restless crowd. He had chosen his time well. Meleager was disconcerted. Murranus was the first to re-arm, and walked away so that he stood with his back to the imperial podium. The crowd's curiosity was now whetted. They wondered what had happened and were taken aback by the fury of Murranus's attack. Usually professional gladiators danced and skirmished, testing their opponent's agility, assessing his strength. Murranus would have none of this. Shield up, he rushed straight at Meleager, sword flickering like a serpent's tongue, seeking the soft lower neck. Meleager, taken by surprise, retreated quickly, turning slightly so that the death-bearing cut merely sliced a piece of leather off his shoulder guard. Again Murranus charged, using both shield and sword like a battering ram, kicking the sand, forcing his opponent back. Meleager fell, rolling in the sand, losing his sword. Murranus drew back and kicked the weapon towards his opponent; a casual gesture, full of contempt, as if he had already decided he was the victor and it was only a matter of time. The crowd was now roaring its approval.

Murranus turned, eyes searching for that lithe, small figure standing just within the Gate of Life. He lifted his sword in salute, then continued his onslaught, fighting like a man possessed. He no longer thought of tactics. He was only aware of his opponent: his grunts, his smell, the face behind that visor, his body protected by armour, sword and shield. He was not conscious of any ache or any fear; he was determined to destroy his opponent, take away both life and honour.

The end came swiftly. Meleager, taken completely by surprise by the swift ferocity of Murranus's attack, tried to curb his opponent's onslaught by making a cut at his leg. For a few seconds he left his shoulder exposed, and Murranus brought down his sword. Meleager moved, avoiding the full force of the blow, yet the sharp edge of Murranus's sword dug deep. Meleager dropped his own weapon and staggered away, Murranus following in pursuit, using the boss of his shield to knock his opponent over. Meleager tried to roll away, but Murranus followed, finally putting his foot on his fallen opponent's chest. Then he leaned down, took off Meleager's helmet and tossed it across the arena. The entire amphitheatre was now standing, cloths being waved, hands extended to indicate Meleager's fate. There were shouts of 'Kill him!' and 'Let him have it!'

Meleager lay still, staring up at Murranus through half-closed eyes. He didn't ask for mercy, whilst Murranus didn't even look at his face, but turned to the imperial box, sword raised, waiting for the Emperor's wish. Constantine was now leaning over the purple balustrade, right hand extended, thumb out. If he turned his thumb upwards, Meleager would die; down and Murranus, must show mercy. The gladiator waited. Someone was talking to Constantine; the hand fell away, then came back, a swift thrusting movement, thumb downwards. Meleager was to live. Murranus leaned over, pressing the tip of his sword against his opponent's neck.

'You fight like an ape,' he hissed, 'and you will die like an old dog.'

He stepped away, kicking his opponent's sword towards him.

'Use it,' he taunted, 'to get up and hobble back to your degenerate friends.'

Murranus walked away. Claudia, standing in the entrance of the Gate of Life, watched as if it was a scene from a play. Murranus had now dropped his shield, but was still holding his sword, striding towards her, his booted sandals kicking away the sand. People were standing in the imperial box; the crowd still shouted their approval, saluting the hero of the games. Claudia saw Meleager move. He grasped his fallen sword and got to his feet, scrambling towards Murranus at a half-crouch, sword out. She opened her mouth to scream but she couldn't. Murranus turned abruptly, his sword coming up. He knocked his opponent's arm away before thrusting his own sword deep into Meleager's belly, turning it to the left and right, dragging Meleager close so he could watch the life light die in his eyes. Only then, using his foot, did he free his sword and allow the corpse to collapse on to the sand, a pool of blood gushing out from the jagged cut which had sliced his stomach.

The crowd was stamping and screaming, coins and flowers were thrown, trumpets blared. Murranus took off his helmet, threw it on the sand and turned, sword raised, Meleager's blood coursing down it, to receive the applause of the Emperor and people of Rome.

Claudia could only stand, body taut, thrilled with excitement, watching this man turn round and round, screaming back his own song of victory. The Emperor had allowed Meleager to live and the fallen gladiator had breached both imperial wishes and the only rule of the arena: a man could live for his courage but had to die for cowardice. Meleager's attack had been treacherous. If Murranus hadn't killed him, Constantine would have sent troops to finish the task. Very few spectators realised how

Murranus had provoked his opponent before walking slowly away. Claudia had seen him turn his left hand, using Spicerius's arm guard to watch what was happening behind him. Meleager had been a dead man as soon as he grasped his sword and decided on that last cowardly attack.

Any hopes Claudia had that she and Murranus would be left alone were quickly dashed. As soon as Murranus entered the Gate of Life, court officials came hurrying down with the Emperor's demands that he appear in the imperial box to receive the victor's laurels. Constantine was apparently delighted, eager to be associated with this new champion of Rome, even though the mob's memory was fickle and Murranus's exploits would soon take second place to anything which occurred during the games over the next few days. Murranus hugged and kissed Claudia. The officials collected his weapons and he was escorted back up through the tunnels, along the passageways, to where Constantine was waiting for him. Claudia watched him go. She couldn't stop her trembling, and she felt the little food she'd eaten curdle in her stomach. She sighed with relief as she walked back to the tunnel and Narcissus stepped out of the gloom.

'Just the person I want! You have my walking cane and cloak?'

Narcissus gestured to a shelf behind him.

'Good,' Claudia breathed. 'I'm going home, Narcissus, and you're coming with me. I'm going to forget Meleager and fall asleep beneath the orchard trees whilst you stand guard over me.'

The sun was beginning to set and the breeze had turned refreshingly cool when Claudia was woken by the sounds of Polybius and Poppaoe preparing the tavern garden for what her uncle proudly termed a 'midnight feast'. She struggled awake, rubbing her face.

'I'm too busy to talk to you.' Polybius wagged a finger. 'I've got Oceanus with some of the local lads guarding the door, otherwise we'll have half of Rome here. What we're going to do is feast Murranus, toast his victory, and get as drunk as sots.'

'Have there been any visitors for me?' Claudia asked.

'Visitors?' Poppaoe came running across the grass, her arms full of crockery. 'Where's that bloody table?' she shouted.

'Visitors?' Claudia repeated.

'I don't know,' Poppaoe sighed. 'We have half of Rome here and you're talking about visitors?'

Claudia soon realised which way the tide was turning. Poppaoe and Polybius were not only celebrating, but giving vent to their own relief. Polybius adored Murranus, saw him as the son he had always wanted, and during the preparations he kept up a constant commentary about what he had seen in the arena that day. Claudia helped her uncle, bringing out cushions and stools, oil lamps and candles, before going into the kitchen to lend a hand with what Polybius termed 'a feast for an Emperor'. Oceanus guarded the door and only a few chosen clients were allowed in. Once they were inside, Simon the Stoic and Petronius the Pimp included, Poppaoe immediately grabbed them to help with the preparations.

Dusk had fallen when the shouts and cries from outside signalled that Murranus had returned. He staggered into the eating hall, the victor laurels all crooked on his head, in one hand a silver wine cup and in the other a gold-embossed jug.

'The Emperor himself gave them to me,' he slurred. 'I'm going to marry his mother!' Then he looked up at the ceiling, rolled his eyes and fell to the floor, sending jug and goblet dancing across the room. Claudia helped take him out to the garden, where he was made comfortable on a makeshift bed of cushions, with Sorry kneeling beside him to waft away the flies.

'He'll be all right,' Polybius shouted. 'A couple of hours' sleep and he will be in fine fettle.'

Claudia stayed chatting to Sorry until Poppaoe ushered Sallust the Searcher into the garden.

'I have news for you.' He glanced down at the prostrate Murranus. 'I'd have got it to you sooner, but your man's to blame, very much the hero of the day.'

Claudia took Sallust down to the vine trellis and listened intently as he reported what his man had found in the town of Capua. When he had finished, she offered to pay him, but the searcher shook his head, gesturing back at the preparations.

'If Polybius invites me to that, I will consider it a job well done.'

Claudia arranged this with her uncle, and while Poppaoe dragged Sallust off into the kitchen to dice some meat, she went up to her own chamber, took out her writing tray and squatted with her back to the door, listing everything she had learned. She felt certain about her conclusions but wondered what to do next. In the garden below, someone began to sing a soft, lilting song about unrequited love.

'That's the cause of it,' Claudia murmured. 'Love all twisted turns to hate.'

She made a decision and brought Sorry up to her chamber. She thrust a coin and a small piece of parchment into his hand.

'You are to go to the palace on the Palatine,' she insisted. 'You are to seek out the Captain of the Guard; his name is Gaius Tullius.' Claudia tapped the piece of parchment.

'Sorry?' the boy said.

'Gaius Tullius. Tell him he is to seek the help of . . . Oh, never mind,' she snapped, 'you can keep the coin.'

'Sorry,' the boy wailed.

'No, no,' Claudia replied, 'it's a complicated message. I'll get Sallust to do it. Come on, Sorry, who's looking after Murranus? We have to get him ready for the feast.'

Murranus woke an hour later to find the banquet prepared and himself the guest of honour. He struggled to his feet, stretching and yawning, and begged for a mug of clear water and would the musicians please not play so loud? In the end the banquet was a great success. Time and again Murranus was questioned, particularly about the agile leap, and only Oceanus could restrain him when he offered to repeat it. Sallust the Searcher came back from the Palatine, whispering to Claudia that tomorrow morning Gaius Tullius would bring Burrus and Timothaeus to the She-Asses tavern.

'I told him it was important. Urgent business!'

'Yes, yes, so it is,' Claudia replied. 'Come, Sallust,' she thrust a goblet into his hands, 'this is a time for celebration.'

The party lasted long into the night. Many of the guests fell asleep on their cushions. Claudia was careful what she ate and drank. She just sat and watched as Murranus was toasted and hailed as a champion. One question which did strike a chord with her was why the Emperor had shown mercy to Meleager. She had reflected on this time and again after she had left the arena, but of course, there was no one here close to the imperial family who could tell her; well, at least not until tomorrow. Eventually she kissed Murranus good night and went to her own chamber, where she lay on her bed half listening to the revelry from the garden, going over everything she had learned about those hideous murders at the Villa Pulchra. She had trapped Agrippina; now she wondered if she could do the same with the assassin. Time and again she had listed the evidence.

'First Sisium, secondly fire in the sky, thirdly ropes, fourthly Capua, fifthly the silent walker, sixthly silence and stealth.' She kept murmuring these words until she fell fast asleep.

She woke just after dawn, and peering through the shutters she could tell the day would be beautiful. She stripped, washed and dressed and raced down the stairs to the kitchen, where she had some bread and olives and a jug of rather weak ale. Oceanus was already up, beginning to clear the rubbish from the garden as well as rouse the various customers who had fallen asleep in the most surprising places. Simon the Stoic was found in the small vineyard, lying on the pebble path, as comfortable and relaxed as if it was a feather mattress. Petronius the Pimp and two of his girls were deep in the orchard, fast asleep, backs to a tree. Oceanus woke them all up with a dash of water to their faces and a vigorous shake on the shoulder.

'Where's Murranus?' Claudia asked.

Oceanus pointed with his thumb. 'Fast asleep in the Venus Chamber. Why?'

'I'm expecting visitors,' she confided.

'Oh, no!' the ex-gladiator groaned. 'Polybius is already grumbling about you using his garden as a council chamber.'

'Well, this is the last time. When my visitors arrive I want you to bring out jugs of wine, water, some fresh bread and sliced fruit. You'll find them in the kitchen. Afterwards, go and rouse Uncle and Murranus; they must arm themselves.'

Oceanus grabbed her by the shoulders.

'No, Oceanus, you listen. I want these visitors to come in

297

unsuspecting. However, once you have served the food, you must fetch Polybius and Murranus. Polybius has a bow and a quiver of arrows somewhere. He must find these and be prepared to use them. Finally, nobody, and I mean nobody, comes out to this garden without my permission.'

Oceanus, surprised, faithfully promised that he would do what Claudia asked. She went round the garden just to make sure no other customers were sleeping off last night's wine, before bringing out cushions so that her visitors could sit in the shade of the trees. The sun was now high, and noises echoed from the streets beyond. Poppaoe came out all a-bustle, asking Claudia what the matter was. Her niece kissed her on the cheeks, politely asked her to mind her own business and repeated what she had said to Oceanus. Then she returned to her own chamber and fetched a dagger and a walking stick, which she brought to the garden and hid under a pile of cushions. She sat there, legs crossed, a linen cloth over her knees as she collected daisies and began to tie them into a chain.

She was halfway through when her guests arrived. Burrus marched across the garden, cloaked and furred, armour clinking as if he was striding through some snowy forest in Germany. He roared a greeting to everyone, and was about to pick Claudia up to hug her when he saw the daisy chain, so he satisfied himself with a quick kiss to the brow. He wanted to discuss the fight with Murranus, but Claudia ordered him to sit down next to her. Timothaeus looked rather sheepish, biting his lip and scratching his unshaven cheek. Gaius Tullius was, however, calm and collected. He was dressed in a red-edged snow-white tunic, marching boots on his feet and a sword belt slung over one shoulder. He greeted Claudia with a friendly clasp of hands and stared round the garden, openly admiring it, before sitting down opposite her.

Oceanus came out with a jug and a tray of goblets. He looked enquiringly at Claudia, who thanked him and asked that Narcissus join them, to be dragged out of bed if necessary. She poured the wine. Narcissus came out yawning and scratching, gently burping and loudly apologising that he had eaten and drunk too much the night before. He made himself as comfortable as possible. Claudia caught the warning glance Timothaeus sent him.

'Why are we here?' Burrus slapped his thigh. 'It's good to see you, Claudia, but why are we here? Where's Murranus? Everyone is talking about his heroic feat. What he achieved would be hard enough even for a German, a chieftain like myself.'

Claudia put down her daisy chain. 'Gaius,' she leaned across, 'I need your sword belt.'

He pulled a face, but handed it across. Claudia immediately passed it to Burrus; Gaius made to object, but Claudia held out her hand.

'Gaius, I want you to listen to what I have to say, because I've brought you here away from the court, be it the Palatine or the Villa Pulchra, to accuse you of murder. You are responsible for the deaths of Dionysius, Justin and Septimus.'

'This is nonsense,' Gaius breathed, eyes drifting to Burrus, who was now clutching his sword belt.

Narcissus and Timothaeus gasped; Burrus looked puzzled, though the cunning German knew enough about Claudia to sense that she would not make allegations unless she was certain. Claudia pointed across to the tavern.

'My uncle and others are in there armed. Polybius,' she lied, 'is a very good archer, whilst Burrus, of course, will do his very best to prevent you escaping from this garden. You are a killer, Gaius, a pagan with a particular hatred for

Christians, especially the Christian community of Capua. When I first met you I brought good wishes from Spicerius. You and he were boyhood friends; you chased each other through the fields near Sisium, a small village outside Capua. At the time you changed the subject very abruptly and never mentioned it again.

'At the Villa Pulchra I'm certain you once said you knew nothing about Capua, its Christians or the persecution there. Of course, you were lying, I can prove that. My friend Sallust the Searcher made careful enquiries, not in Capua but amongst the farming community around that town. He came across evidence concerning Lucius and Octavia Quatis. They were a childless couple who took in an orphan boy, the only son of people who had worked for them. I believe the father was an overseer on their farm. The parents died of a fever; their son, little Gaius, was raised by this kind-hearted couple and treated as their own. People always remembered Gaius and, indeed, Spicerius, playing soldiers out in the fields and woods. Scarcely in his teens, the young boy joined the army, and that was the last the local community ever saw or heard of him. They believed he had been posted abroad. By the time he'd reached any senior rank, Diocletian had launched his ferocious persecution against the Christians and Capua was brought under the scrutiny of the Emperor's agents. Capua was dangerous because its Christians were not only slaves or minor servants but important people who were beginning to control the schools and other institutions in the town. It was a time of terror, wasn't it, Gaius?'

She paused. Timothaeus and Narcissus were now sitting closer together, as if for protection. Burrus had thrown Gaius's sword belt well away, and one hand rested on the hilt of his own stabbing dagger. Gaius had paled; only a bead of sweat running down his cheek betrayed his agitation.

'I *was* an orphan,' he stammered, 'but I never knew Capua, I . . .'

'Don't lie,' Claudia replied softly. 'You may have added to your name, but one thing about the Roman army, it does keep scrupulous records. Somewhere amongst those records I will find your real name, your age and where you come from.'

She paused again and sipped her wine. She looked Gaius up and down but could not detect any concealed weapon.

'A time of terror,' she repeated. 'Christians from Capua and elsewhere were rounded up; it was a time for settling grudges and grievances. Dionysius and Septimus were Christian scholars who were terrorised into betraying other names. Lucius and Octavia were not Christians but somehow they got caught up in the persecution. They were only poor farmers with no one to help them, whilst their adopted son was possibly hundreds of miles away. We don't know who betrayed them, or why; it may have been Dionysius or Septimus. I'm sure you've been through the records yourself, though men like Chrysis are only too willing to destroy anything about those days, when Christians were hunted like rats in a sewer.'

Claudia picked up the daisy chain, balancing it in her hand. 'An old man and an old woman,' she continued, 'innocent of any crime, dragged into Rome. And of course, the more they denied their crime, the worse it become. They were kindly people, weren't they, Gaius? Had they allowed Christians to meet on their farm, or had they sheltered a Christian? Whatever, these poor people were murdered and their farm was confiscated by the State. It would take months for you to learn the news; you were, by then, an ambitious army officer, a trusted member of the staff corps in Constantine's Army of the West. Diocletian abdicated and the civil war broke out, but you had not forgotten.' Claudia broke the daisy chain. 'You returned to Rome with the conquering army and you conducted a thorough search. You are a good soldier, you know how to plan an ambush. You don't go riding into Sisium or Capua; rather, you search the records and listen to rumour and gossip. You're not a Christian, are you, Gaius?'

'I hate them, I always have,' came the quiet reply. 'It's a sect of slaves and anarchists. Like many officers, I believe Constantine has made the wrong choice.'

'Do you feel he's betrayed you?' Claudia asked. 'Is that why you are also the traitor in the Emperor's camp? Have you already sold your soul, sword and loyalty to Licinius's agents? Are you so furious at the death of your foster parents, so incensed at the Christian faith that you have lost all trust in Constantine and his mother?'

Gaius gazed solemnly back.

'You watched and you seethed,' Claudia continued. 'You learned as much as you could about the horrifying details of your foster parents' cruel capture and death. What rubbed salt in the wound was what happened to the home where you played as a child, their farm. It had been confiscated by the State but Constantine restored it to the Christian sect. Insult upon insult, injury upon injury. You discovered that Lucius and Octavia had even been buried in the Christian catacombs, only their first names carved on the tomb. The catacombs are now deserted; it would not be difficult for a soldier like yourself to creep down, break open the tomb and remove their remains for what you'd call an honourable burial.'

'I didn't know this.' Timothaeus spoke up. 'Gaius, you always seemed so tolerant.'

'Contemptuous is a more accurate description,' Claudia interrupted. 'You hated the Emperor and men like Sylvester; you were ready to support Licinius.'

'But he's a bodyguard,' Burrus broke in. 'He could have killed the Emperor whenever he so wished.'

'Could he? With other soldiers standing about? What if Constantine is murdered but his family still survive, above all the Augusta? More importantly, Gaius Tullius wanted to live. He wanted to witness the return of a new pagan Emperor who would set his face, and raise his hand, against the Christian Church. Oh, I'm sure if a new persecution broke out, Gaius Tullius would prove to be the most zealous hunter of Christians.' Claudia spoke evenly.

'Do continue,' Gaius snapped. 'I'll listen to you, little woman, then I'll decide.'

'You have no choice,' Claudia replied. 'This may not be a court of law, but can you imagine if it was? After all, you are a soldier; you will be tried in front of a military tribunal where the rule of law is not so scrupulously observed.'

Claudia stared across at the tavern. A shutter opened and closed, and she briefly glimpsed Murranus standing there. She turned back to Gaius Tallius, spreading her hands out.

'Astrologers claim that sometimes the stars and planets move into a favourable conjunction. This is what happened with events at the Villa Pulchra. You knew the Emperor would be going there, not the precise day, but you could make an accurate guess about when he would arrive; after all, you are one of his staff officers. You gave that information to Licinius's agents and the war galley was dispatched. All the enemy had to do was wait for the agreed signal. You would give that from the villa, and Licinius's agents, hiding in the woods, would pass it on. You overlooked one thing: the wanderer in the woods, that inquisitive old man who knew the lie of the land like the back of his hand. He must have realised something was wrong and came to the villa to pester Timothaeus. You decided he was too dangerous, so you killed him!'

'That's not true!' Gaius Tullius broke in.

'Yes it is.' Timothaeus spoke up again. 'On the day that old man was found, you left the villa early; you said you were going for a ride.'

'You were busy plotting,' Claudia continued, shifting on the grass, staring back at the tavern window. 'You were planning not only to betray your Emperor, but to seize a splendid opportunity for revenge. The Christians were coming to the Villa Pulchra, the orators from Capua, at least two of whom you suspected of being turncoats. Those orators are lonely men, much given to brooding; they like to be by themselves. You didn't really care who died as long as you inflicted revenge and depicted these Christians to their Emperor as being as murderous, quarrelsome and vindictive as the rest of his subjects.'

'You walk softly,' Burrus interrupted. 'That is how you killed Dionysius . . .'

Gaius Tullius dismissed him with a contemptuous flick of his hand.

'You killed them,' Claudia accused him. 'You caught them on their own, like rabbits in a snare. Dionysius you stunned, then cut to death. Next came Septimus, and finally Justin. You must have been pleased to use Dionysius's corpse, and that of the wanderer, as part of your beacon light.'

'I was with you when the House of Mourning caught fire . . .'

'Of course you were.' Claudia smiled. 'But you also knew Narcissus was fast asleep. It is easy to take a length of old rope, grease it with oil, strike a tinder and watch the flame burn fiercely but slowly away, giving you sufficient time to be with a witness when the conflagration broke out. The House of Mourning was neglected, Narcissus had drunk deep; it posed little problem.'

'Why did you burn it?' Narcissus asked crossly.

'As I've said, it was the beacon light,' Claudia accused. 'The agreed signal for the assault on the villa to be launched. You also wanted to conceal your own handiwork, just in case you'd made a mistake: the way you tied those ropes around Dionysius, perhaps, or that I might examine the corpse of that old man and wonder if he were a murder victim too. You really didn't care. If the attack had been successful, Licinius's men would have taken you away, ostensibly as a captive, though one who would later change sides.'

Gaius Tullius made to rise, but Burrus's hand went to his war belt and the soldier slumped back down. Some colour had returned to his face, but his darting glances and the way he kept wetting his lips betrayed his agitation.

'You enjoyed killing them,' Claudia continued. 'You did your best to confuse me by pretending that Justin had been murdered by someone not used to drawing a bow, just as you tried to frighten me with that painting on the wall, or by coming into the cellar, your face hidden behind a mask, an old cloak about you. When I wouldn't be cowed, you threw that lamp into my chamber. Gaius Tullius had every right to be in the imperial quarters; it was easy enough to conceal a lamp under your cloak and, when the passageway was empty, open a door and throw it in. The rest of the villa was sleeping; you thought I'd be doing the same.' Claudia leaned over and touched Narcissus's hand. 'But, the gods be thanked, I was talking to my new-found friend!'

'When the Holy Sword disappeared,' Timothaeus pointed his finger, 'you enjoyed the confusion.'

'That helped his plan,' Claudia agreed. 'The Emperor was tired, the Augusta worried about the coming debate, the orators from Capua were at each other's throats, the Holy Sword had disappeared; such confusion helps to distract people. When I found out about the beacon lights, you decided to deepen the confusion further by supposedly discovering that bow, and the fire arrows.' Claudia leaned closer. 'You did find them, don't you remember, near the wall?'

The accused stared sullenly back.

'You hoped the burning of the House of Mourning would be seen as an accident or as caused by someone loosing fire arrows into the air. However, on that night,' Claudia nodded at Narcissus, 'our sharp-eyed former slave here was sitting on top of a hill brooding about his future. He saw no fire arrows. More importantly, once the court left the Villa Pulchra, I returned and organised a search of the woods.'

'Yes, yes, I heard about that,' Timothaeus broke in.

'I told the servants to search for any weapon of war.' Claudia smiled. 'Now, Gaius, if you loose an arrow up into the sky, the flame eventually dies, but part of the feathered shaft remains. Yet nobody found anything. The quiver you supposedly discovered was fairly empty; it would take at least four or five arrows to attract the attention of Licinius's agents.' She pointed her finger at him. 'That's when I began to suspect you.'

'You have no real proof.' Gaius Tullius wiped sweaty hands on his tunic.

'Don't I?' Claudia retorted. 'There is a logic to what I've

said. We can search the army records. We can establish a strong link between you and Capua. We can prove that, as an officer, you could go anywhere in that villa, and you did: you kindly brought me that scroll you found in Dionysius's chamber, anything to deepen the confusion and sharpen the rivalry between your enemies. Above all, we can keep you prisoner here while your own chamber and possessions are ransacked . . .'

Gaius Tullius closed his eyes and turned away, a sign that he was conceding defeat.

'We'll find something,' Claudia insisted, 'which connects you with Licinius, which will prove you to be the traitor.'

'I am no traitor.' Gaius stared up to the sky. 'At least not to Rome, but to the fools who wear the purple.' He took a deep breath. 'It is as you say, a coming together of events.' He made himself comfortable on the grass, talking softly as if to himself. 'I couldn't believe my good fortune. The attack on the villa was planned. Constantine and his bitch of a mother did not deserve my loyalty, or to wear the purple which men like me had won in the heat of battle. I later learnt about the orators coming. Oh yes, I had been through Chrysis's records. They were all weaklings who couldn't even support their own faith; men like Septimus had betrayed the only two people I really loved. I felt like a fox in a barnyard. It was just a matter of seeking every opportunity, creating chaos, and if the attack had been successful, don't worry, little mouse, I would have ensured they all died.' He gestured back at the tavern. 'Is Murranus watching me? Shall I tell you something? When he brought Meleager down, I advised the Emperor to spare him. Do you know why?'

'Yes, yes, I think I do.' Claudia half smiled. 'The Holy Sword had been found, the attack on the villa beaten off; you are sharp-eyed, Gaius, and calm. You saw how I fled from the triclinium the night I met Meleager. You claimed you knew all about me. I suspect you were one of the few people in that room who realised I'd met the man who raped me and killed my brother. Meleager was also a gladiator; what did he call himself? The Marvel of a Million Cities.' Claudia used her fingers to emphasise her points. 'Meleager fought in cities in the East. He could be cast as a supporter of Licinius. Secondly, he had good reason to fear me, hence your attack on me at the villa; Meleager could be blamed. Thirdly, Meleager was linked to Capua; he may well have been a torturer when the Christians were persecuted, so he could be viewed as a man who had a motive for silencing the likes of Dionysius and Septimus. Finally, he was at the villa when all the murders took place and the attack was launched. Were you going to use him as your cat's paw, a scapegoat for the murders? You are a powerful officer, Gaius, it could be so easily done.'

Gaius lowered his head and laughed softly. 'One favour.' He raised his head. 'Not on the cross! I don't want to die nailed to a piece of wood.' He gestured at Burrus. 'You have your men outside; not far away lies a stretch of wasteland.' He glanced at Claudia, begging her with his eyes. 'I'm a soldier, I deserve a better death.'

Claudia glanced at Timothaeus, who nodded imperceptibly.

'Let him fall on his sword.' Burrus rose to his feet, gesturing at Gaius Tullius to stand. 'I'll take your Murranus with me; he can be the official witness.'

Gaius Tullius was now brushing the grass from his tunic, slowly, as if preparing to go for a stroll. 'Well, mistress?' He glanced at Claudia.

'Go!' Claudia nodded at the tavern. 'Take Murranus with you, let it be done quickly.'

Gaius's hands went to the small purse on his belt. He undid the cord and threw the pouch at Narcissus. 'Take care of my body.' Then, spinning on his heel, he allowed Burrus to guide him by the arm across to the tavern.

Claudia sat and listened. She heard Polybius exclaim. Murranus came out and lifted his hand; Claudia nodded back.

'I didn't think . . .' Narcissus began.

'Hush now,' Claudia whispered. She rose to her feet and walked down to the vine trellis to stare at the ripening grapes. She plucked one, squeezing it between her fingers, watching the purple juice drip. She closed her eyes. Somewhere close by, on a piece of wasteland, Gaius Tullius would be kneeling, grasping the hilt of his sword, ready to thrust it deep between his own ribs. She recalled his handsome, boyish face. 'So much blood,' she whispered. She opened her eyes and stared at the trellis again. Yet she also felt relieved. Meleager was dead. She'd experienced justice for herself and Felix. Now she could reflect on that, open her heart to Murranus and close that door against the horde of ghosts from her past.

'Mistress?' Claudia turned round. Narcissus stood staring sorrowfully at her. 'Will our lives change?'

'Of course they will.' Claudia smiled. 'Haven't you learned that yet? Our lives are always changing! Now come.' She grasped him by the arm. 'I think it's time we both had words with Uncle!'